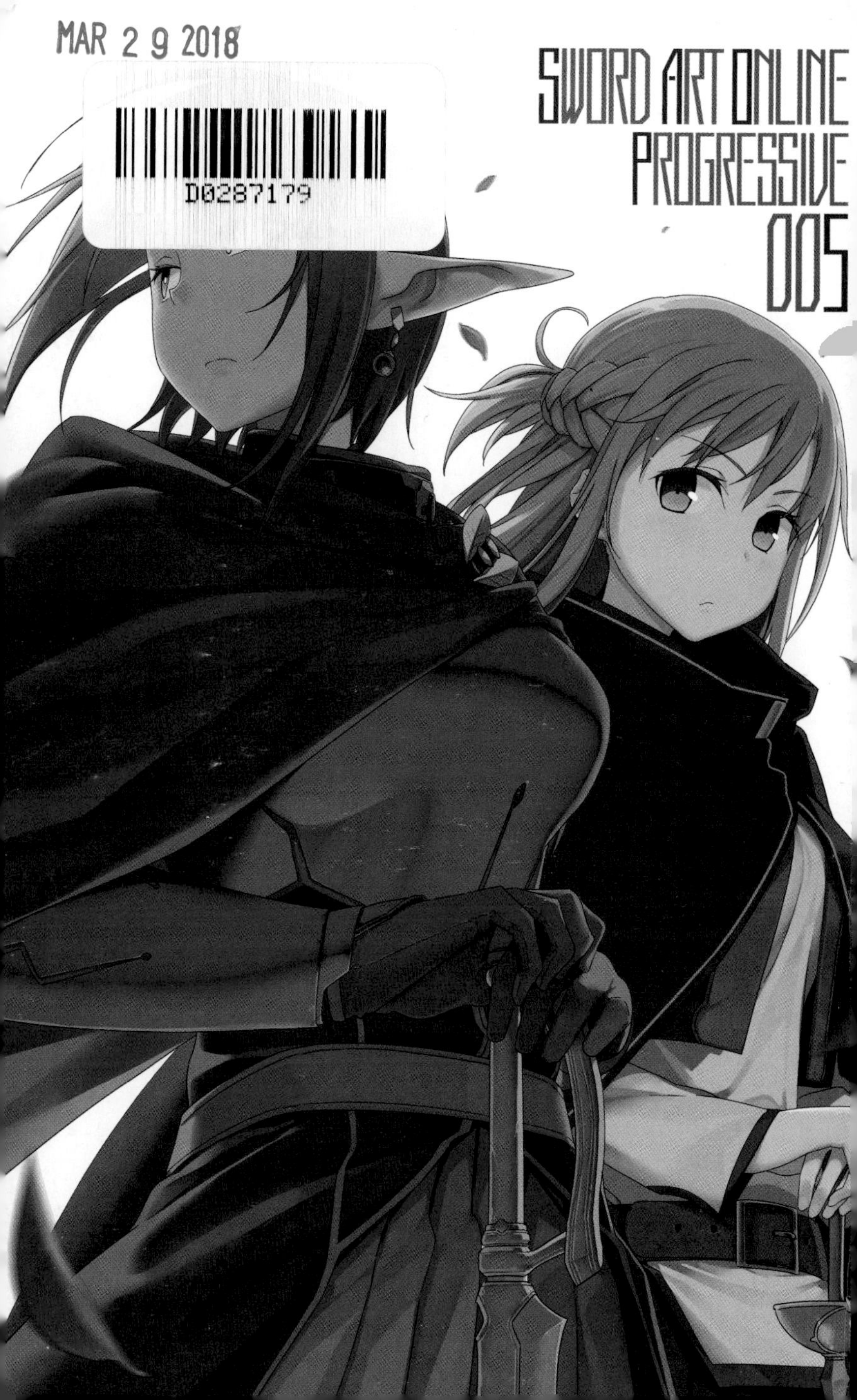
SWORD ART ONLINE
PROGRESSIVE
005

SWORD ART ONLINE PROGRESSIVE 005

CONTENTS

»022 Encounter ——————— 003

»023 Aid ——————————— 023

»024 Vengeance ——————— 043

»025 Loss ——————————— 061

»026 Wolfhandler —————— 091

»027 Loss II —————————— 115

»028 The Protector ————— 145

»029 Story ————————————— 173

ART: KISEKI HIMURA
ORIGINAL STORY: REKI KAWAHARA
CHARACTER DESIGN: abec

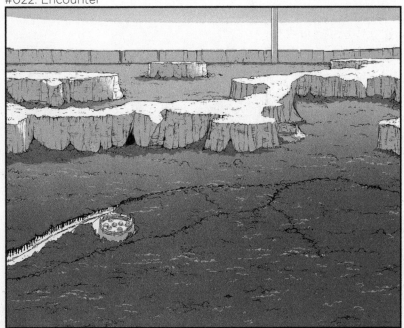

LET'S GO FOR A PINCER ATTACK!

MORORORORO (MOLOLOLOLO)

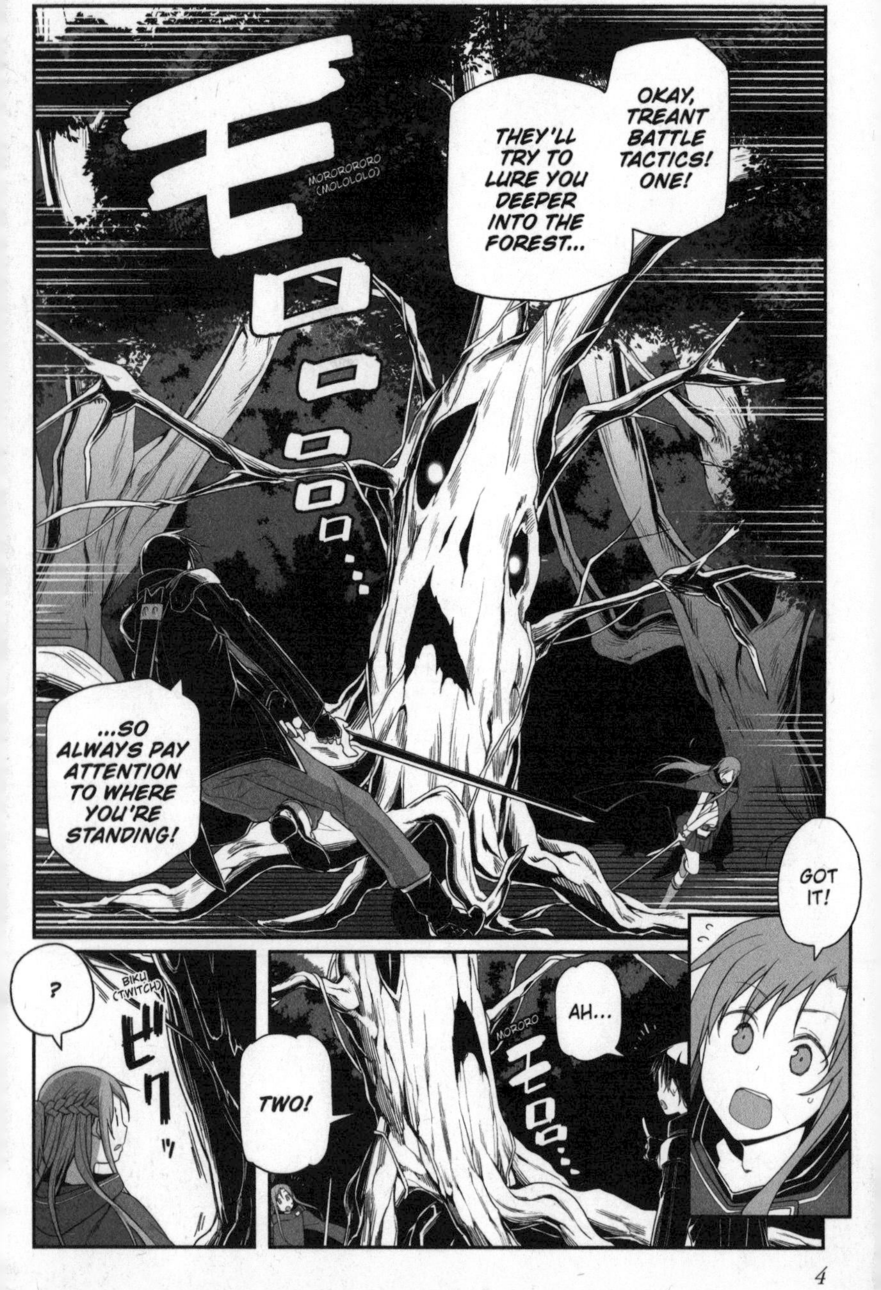
OKAY, TREANT BATTLE TACTICS! ONE!
THEY'LL TRY TO LURE YOU DEEPER INTO THE FOREST...
MORORORORO (MOLOLOLO)
...SO ALWAYS PAY ATTENTION TO WHERE YOU'RE STANDING!
GOT IT!
AH...
MORORO
TWO!
BIKU (TWITCH)
?

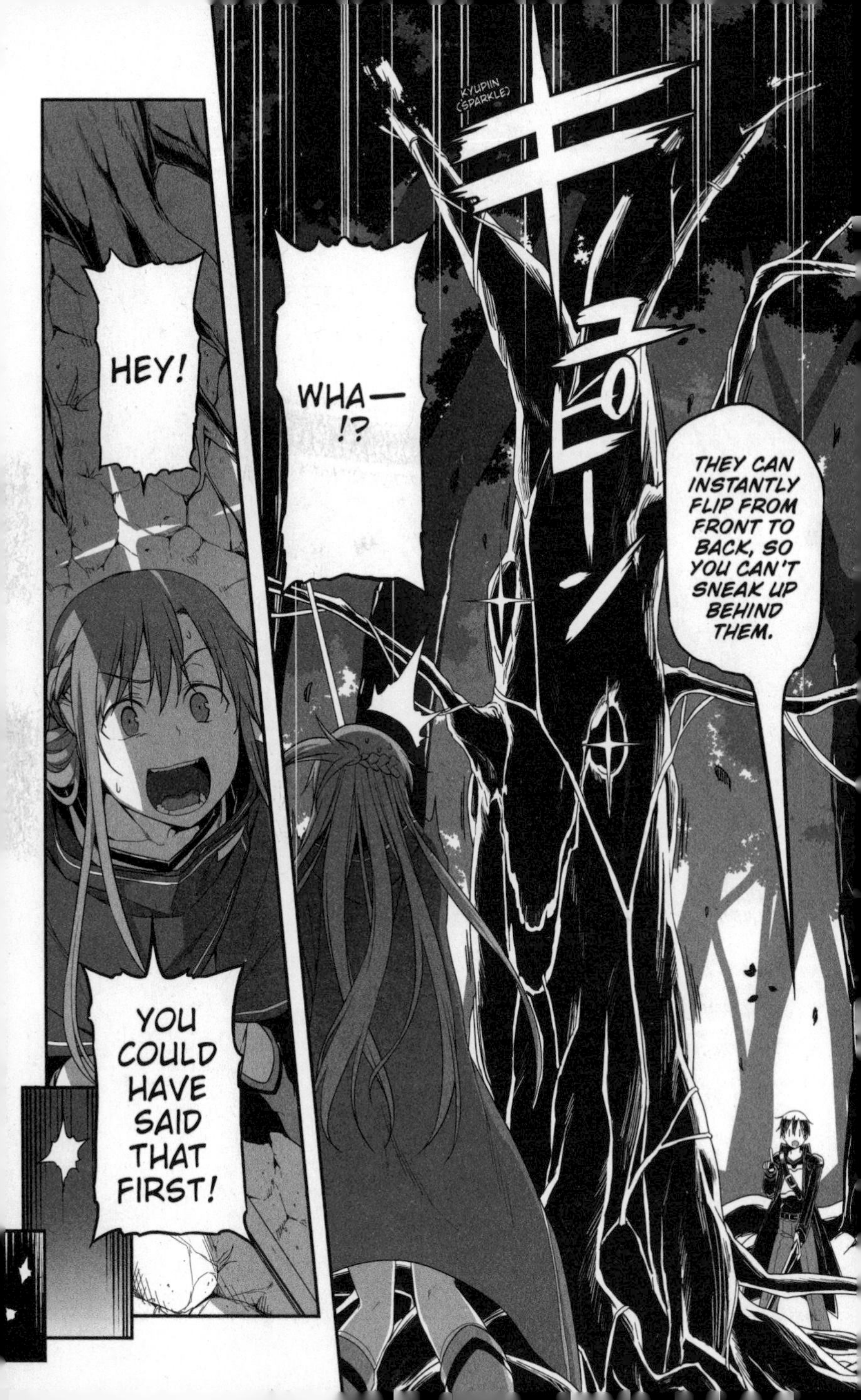
KYUPIIN (SPARKLE)
THEY CAN INSTANTLY FLIP FROM FRONT TO BACK, SO YOU CAN'T SNEAK UP BEHIND THEM.
WHA—!?
HEY!
YOU COULD HAVE SAID THAT FIRST!

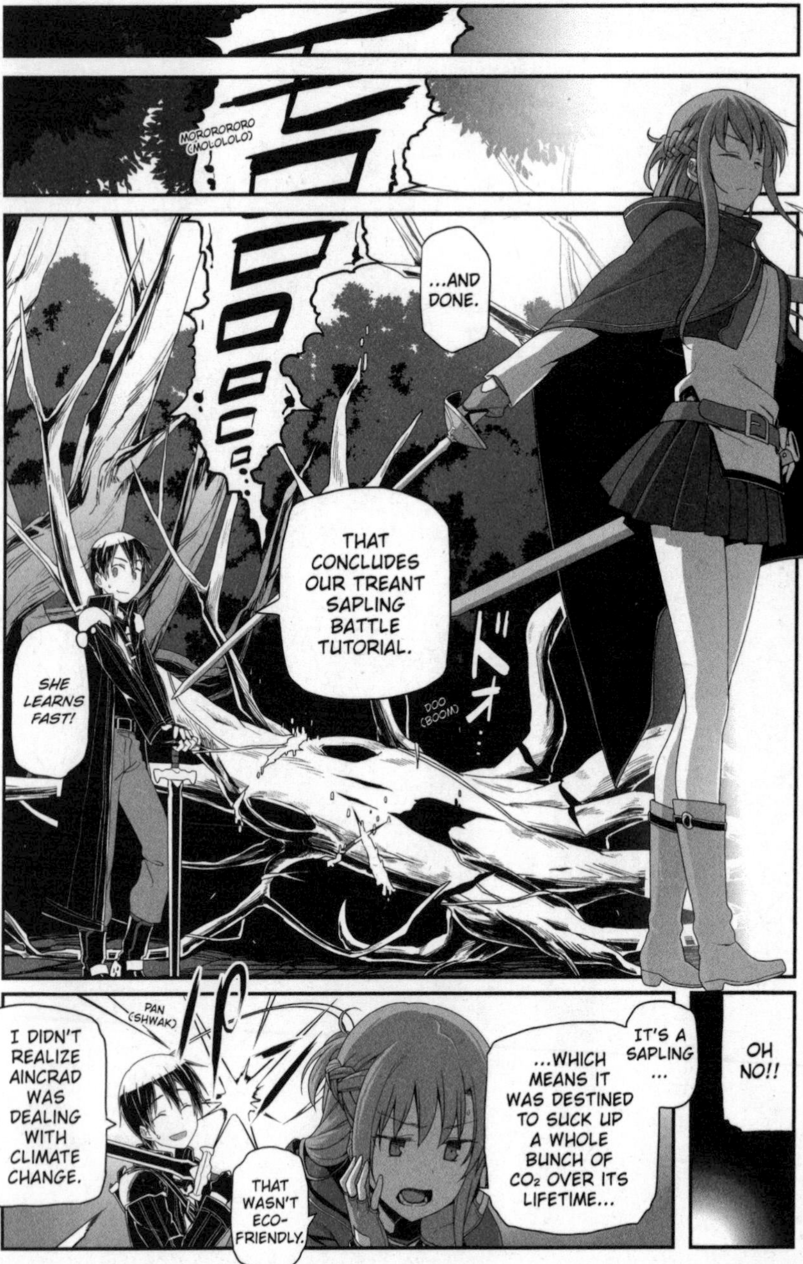
MORORORORO (MOLOLOLO)
...AND DONE.
THAT CONCLUDES OUR TREANT SAPLING BATTLE TUTORIAL.
DOO (BOOM)
SHE LEARNS FAST!
OH NO!!
IT'S A SAPLING...
...WHICH MEANS IT WAS DESTINED TO SUCK UP A WHOLE BUNCH OF CO_2 OVER ITS LIFETIME...
THAT WASN'T ECO-FRIENDLY.
PAN (SHWAK)
I DIDN'T REALIZE AINCRAD WAS DEALING WITH CLIMATE CHANGE.

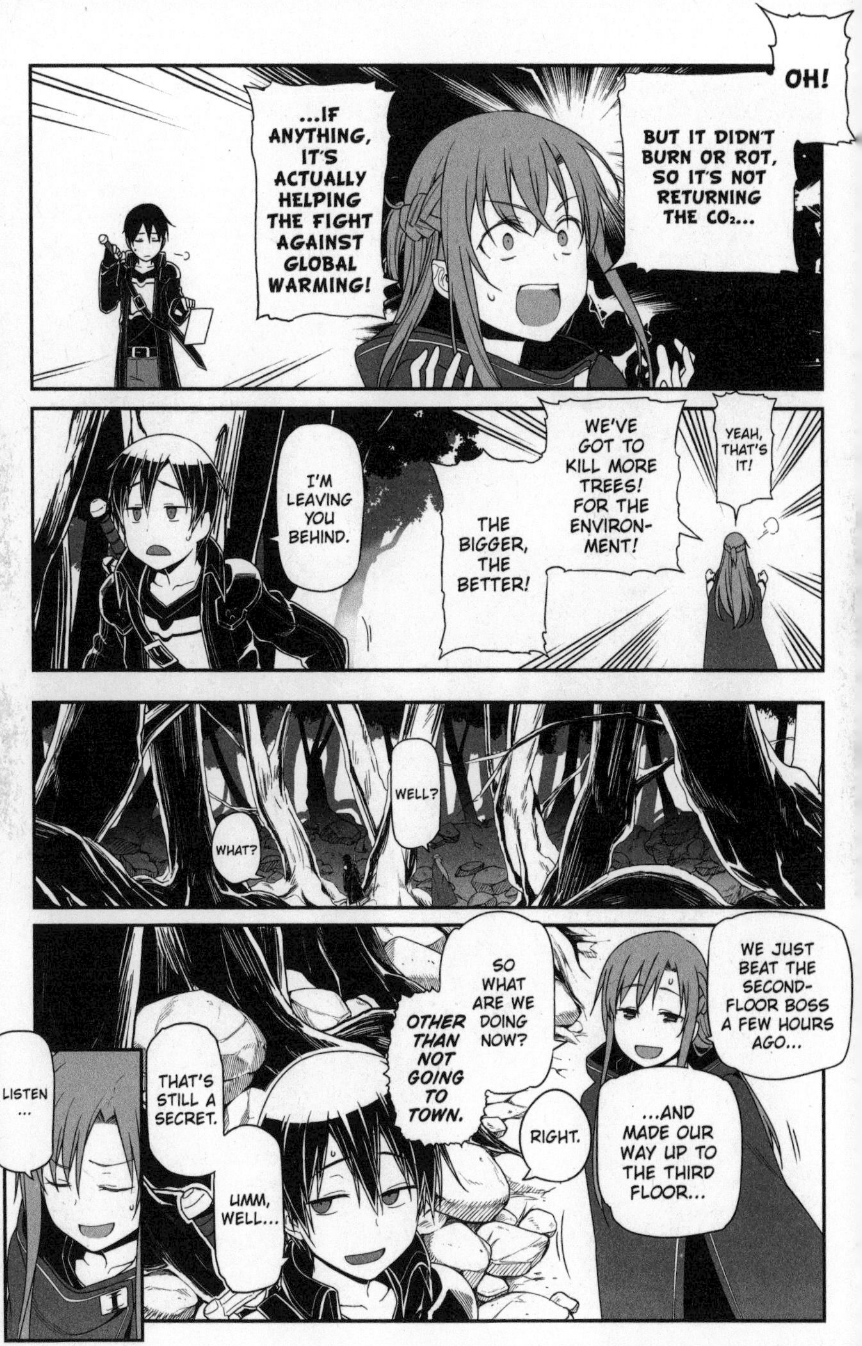
OH!
BUT IT DIDN'T BURN OR ROT, SO IT'S NOT RETURNING THE CO_2...
...IF ANYTHING, IT'S ACTUALLY HELPING THE FIGHT AGAINST GLOBAL WARMING!
YEAH, THAT'S IT!
WE'VE GOT TO KILL MORE TREES! FOR THE ENVIRONMENT!
THE BIGGER, THE BETTER!
I'M LEAVING YOU BEHIND.
WELL?
WHAT?
WE JUST BEAT THE SECOND-FLOOR BOSS A FEW HOURS AGO...
...AND MADE OUR WAY UP TO THE THIRD FLOOR...
RIGHT.
SO WHAT ARE WE DOING NOW?
OTHER THAN NOT GOING TO TOWN.
THAT'S STILL A SECRET.
UMM, WELL...
LISTEN...

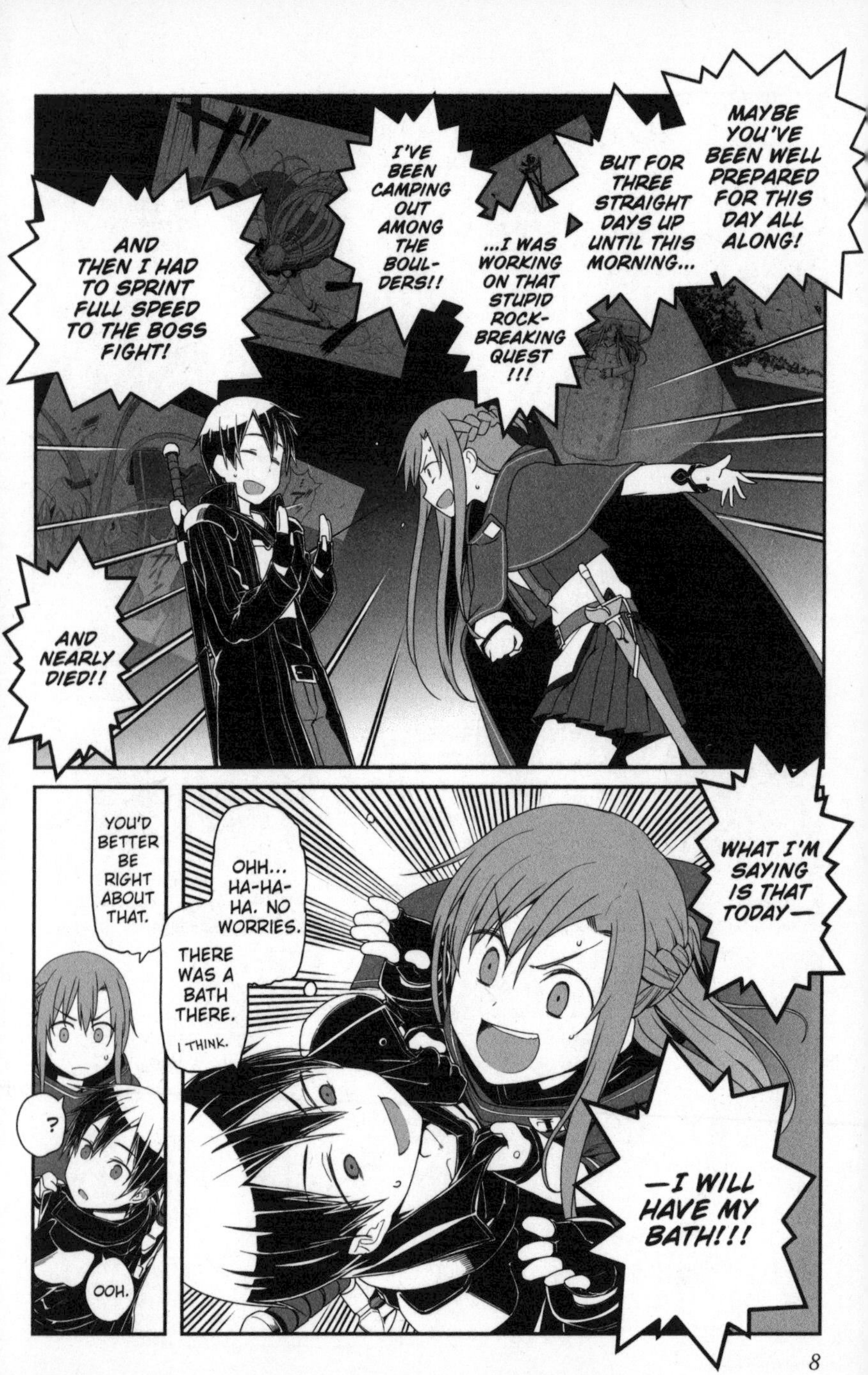
MAYBE YOU'VE BEEN WELL PREPARED FOR THIS DAY ALL ALONG!
BUT FOR THREE STRAIGHT DAYS UP UNTIL THIS MORNING...
...I WAS WORKING ON THAT STUPID ROCK-BREAKING QUEST!!!
I'VE BEEN CAMPING OUT AMONG THE BOUL-DERS!!
AND THEN I HAD TO SPRINT FULL SPEED TO THE BOSS FIGHT!
AND NEARLY DIED!!
WHAT I'M SAYING IS THAT TODAY—
—I WILL HAVE MY BATH!!!
OHH... HA-HA-HA. NO WORRIES.
THERE WAS A BATH THERE.
I THINK.
YOU'D BETTER BE RIGHT ABOUT THAT.
?
OOH.

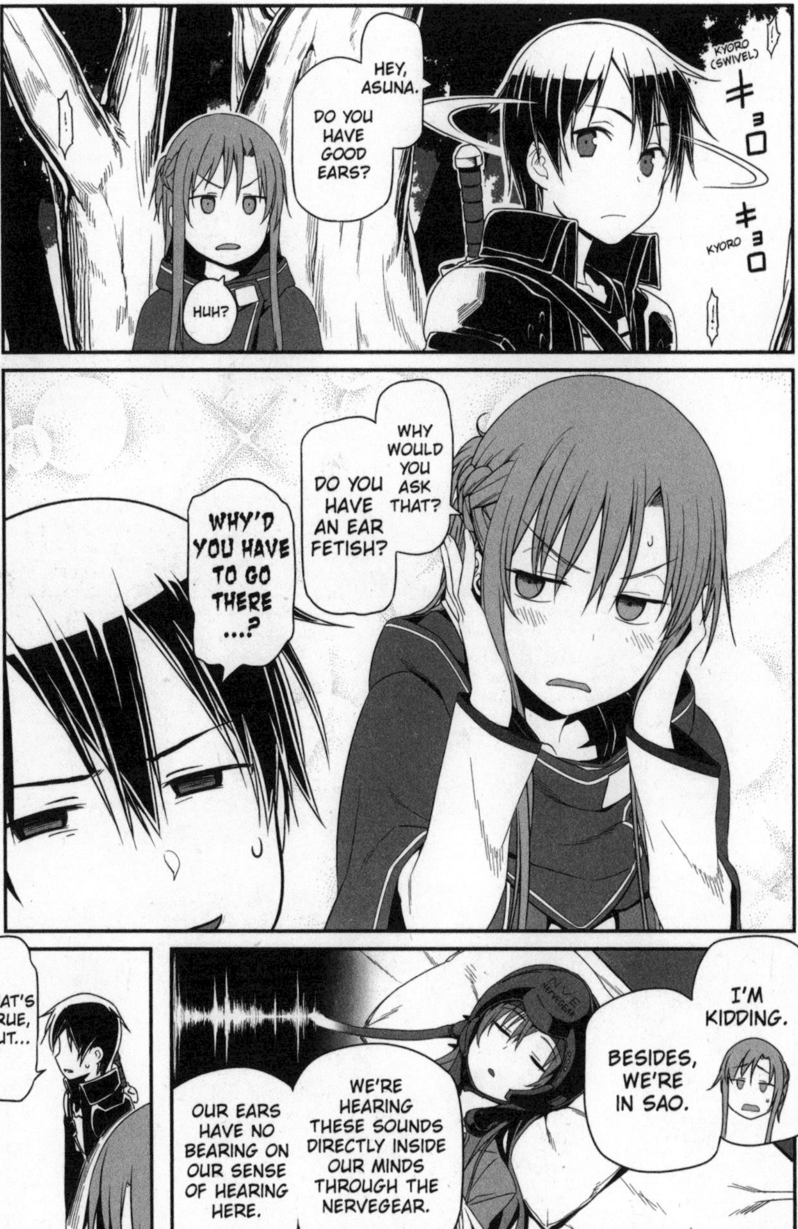

KYORO (SWIVEL)
キョロ
KYORO
キョロ
HEY, ASUNA.
DO YOU HAVE GOOD EARS?
HUH?
WHY WOULD YOU ASK THAT?
DO YOU HAVE AN EAR FETISH?
WHY'D YOU HAVE TO GO THERE ...?
I'M KIDDING.
BESIDES, WE'RE IN SAO.
WE'RE HEARING THESE SOUNDS DIRECTLY INSIDE OUR MINDS THROUGH THE NERVEGEAR.
OUR EARS HAVE NO BEARING ON OUR SENSE OF HEARING HERE.
NERVEGEAR
THAT'S TRUE, BUT...

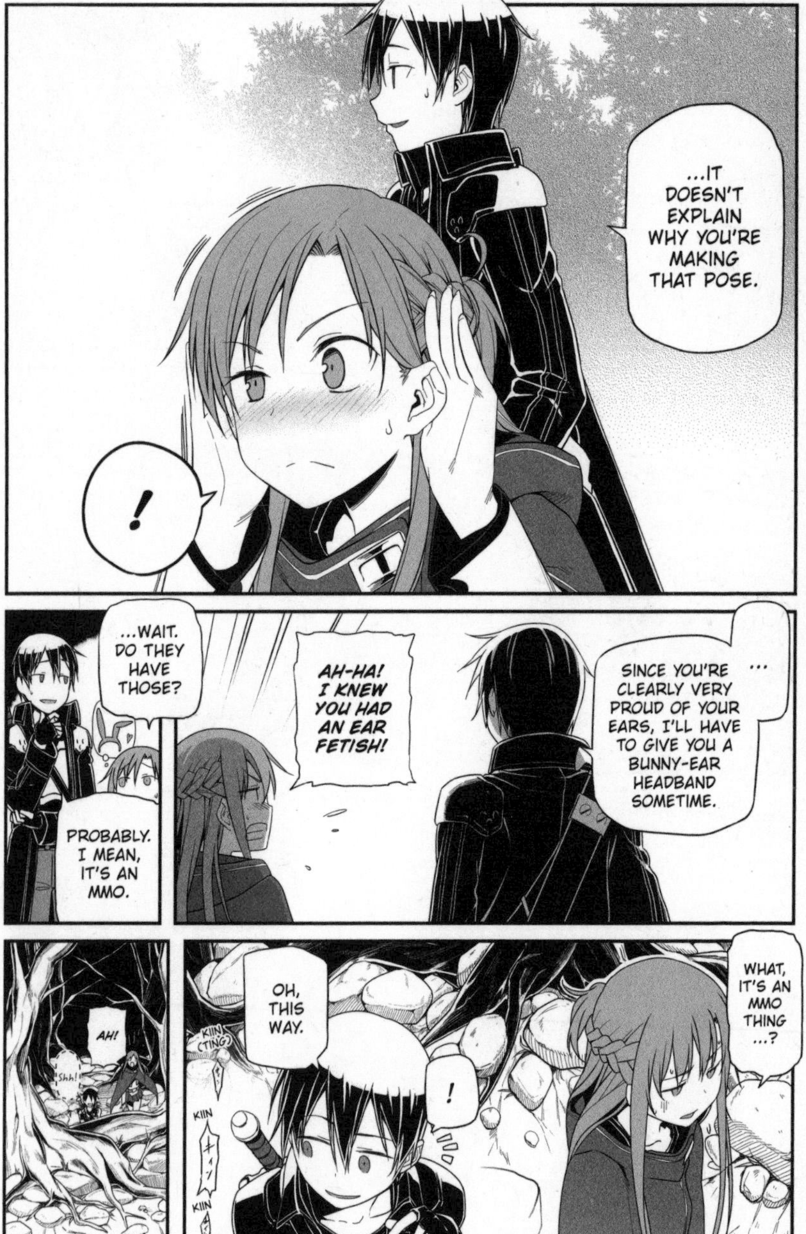
...IT DOESN'T EXPLAIN WHY YOU'RE MAKING THAT POSE.
!
...
SINCE YOU'RE CLEARLY VERY PROUD OF YOUR EARS, I'LL HAVE TO GIVE YOU A BUNNY-EAR HEADBAND SOMETIME.
AH-HA! I KNEW YOU HAD AN EAR FETISH!
...WAIT. DO THEY HAVE THOSE?
PROBABLY. I MEAN, IT'S AN MMO.
WHAT, IT'S AN MMO THING...?
OH, THIS WAY.
KIIN (TING)
!
KIIN
KIIN
AH!
Shh!

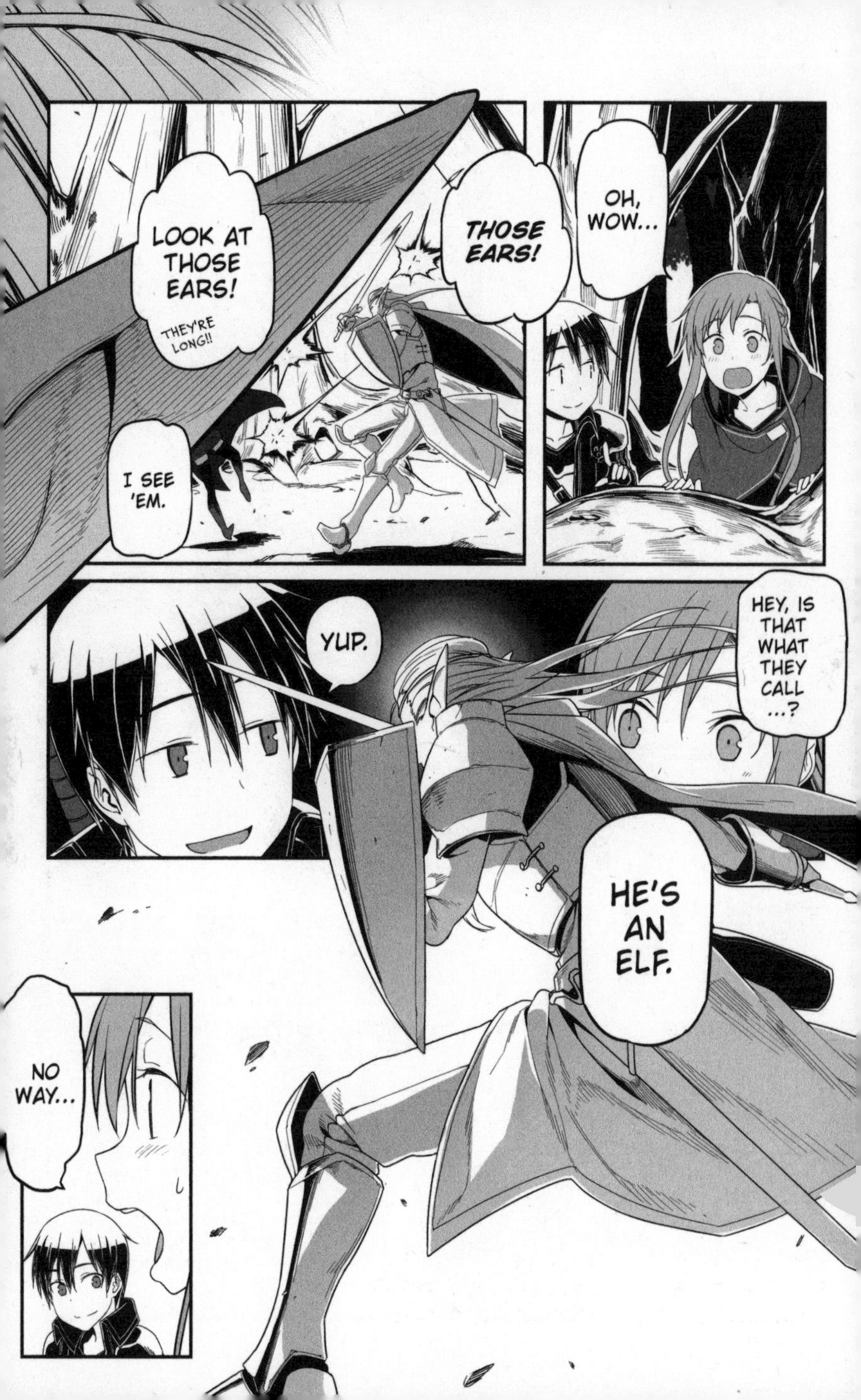
OH, WOW...
THOSE EARS!
LOOK AT THOSE EARS!
THEY'RE LONG!!
I SEE 'EM.
HEY, IS THAT WHAT THEY CALL ...?
YUP.
HE'S AN ELF.
NO WAY...

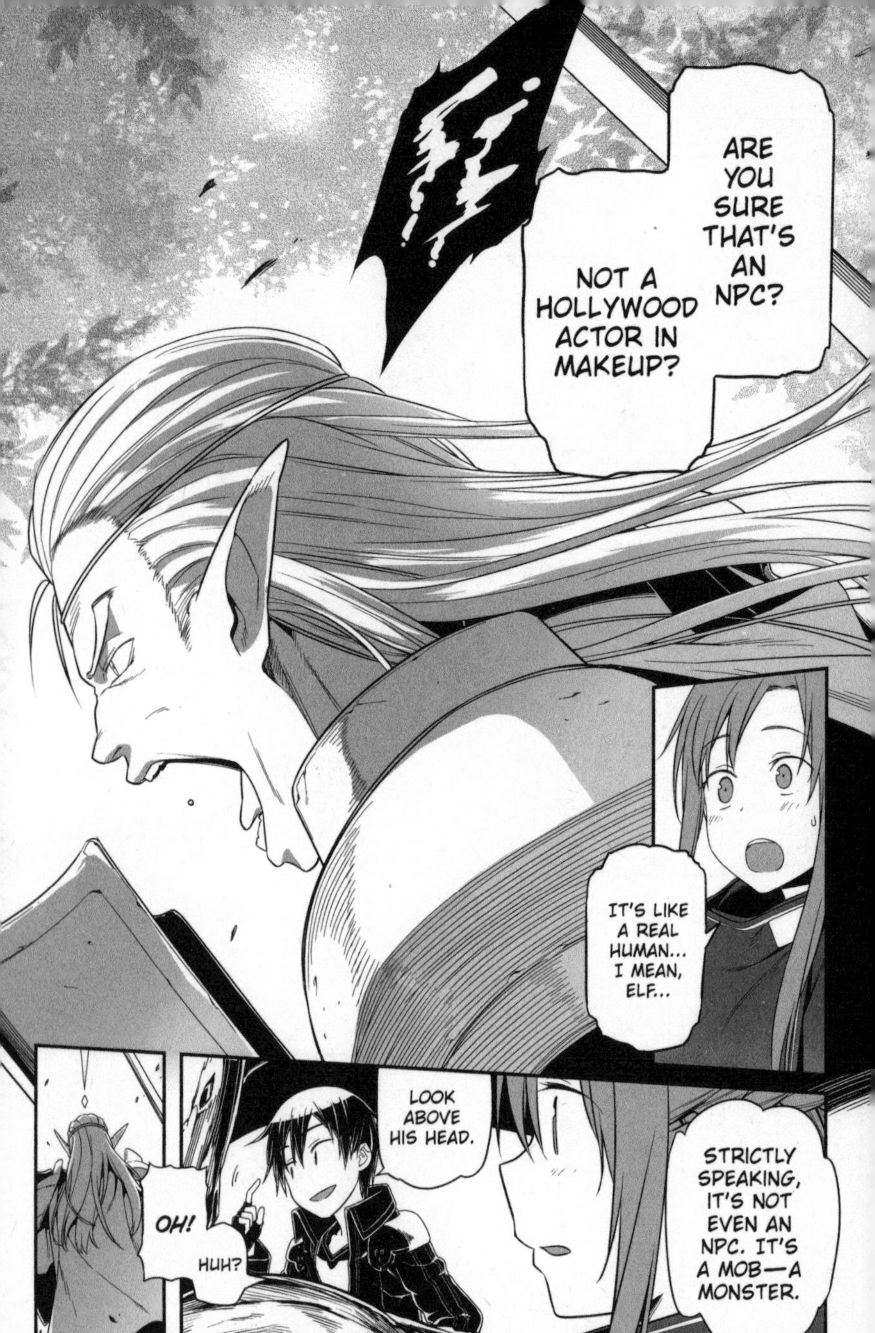
ARE YOU SURE THAT'S AN NPC?
NOT A HOLLYWOOD ACTOR IN MAKEUP?
IT'S LIKE A REAL HUMAN... I MEAN, ELF...
STRICTLY SPEAKING, IT'S NOT EVEN AN NPC. IT'S A MOB—A MONSTER.
LOOK ABOVE HIS HEAD.
HUH?
OH!

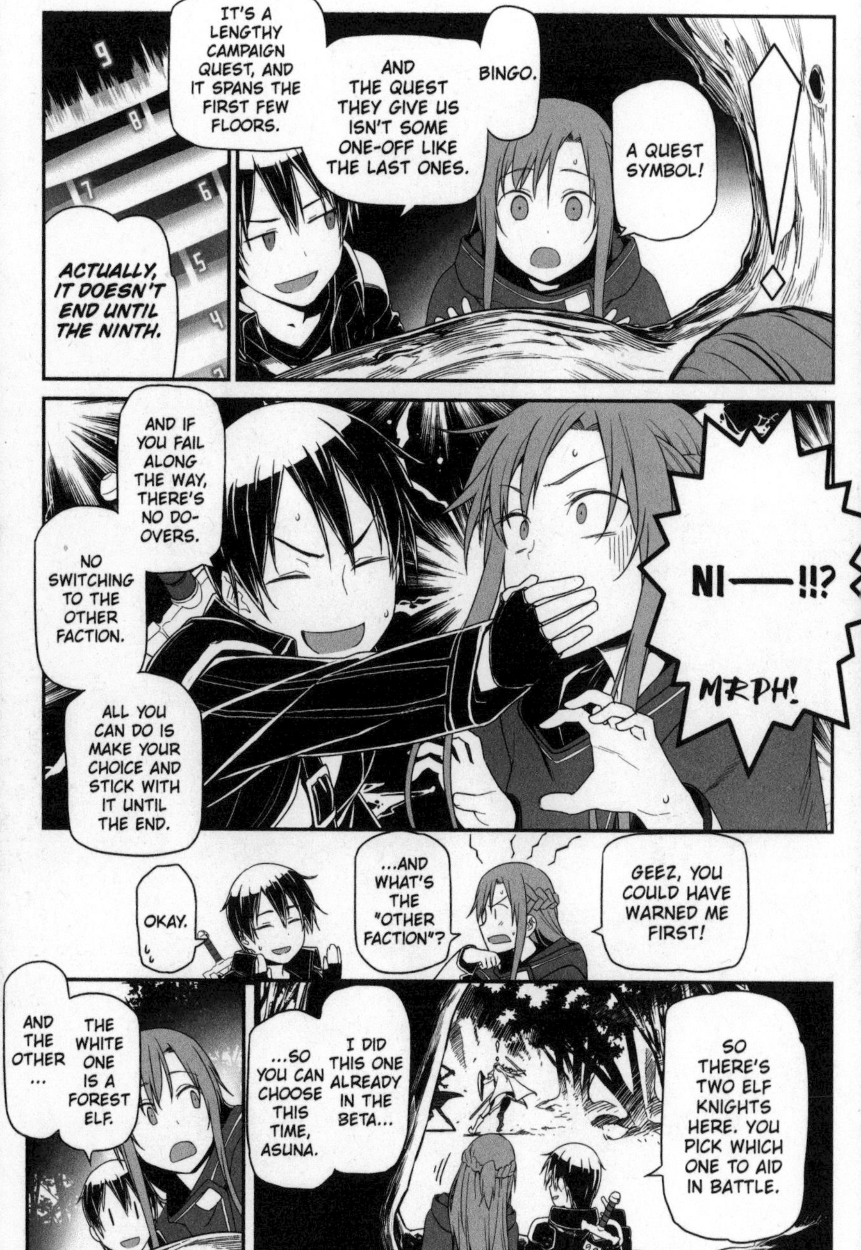
A QUEST SYMBOL!
BINGO.
AND THE QUEST THEY GIVE US ISN'T SOME ONE-OFF LIKE THE LAST ONES.
IT'S A LENGTHY CAMPAIGN QUEST, AND IT SPANS THE FIRST FEW FLOORS.
ACTUALLY, IT DOESN'T END UNTIL THE NINTH.
NI——!!?
MRPH!
AND IF YOU FAIL ALONG THE WAY, THERE'S NO DO-OVERS.
NO SWITCHING TO THE OTHER FACTION.
ALL YOU CAN DO IS MAKE YOUR CHOICE AND STICK WITH IT UNTIL THE END.
GEEZ, YOU COULD HAVE WARNED ME FIRST!
...AND WHAT'S THE "OTHER FACTION"?
OKAY.
SO THERE'S TWO ELF KNIGHTS HERE. YOU PICK WHICH ONE TO AID IN BATTLE.
I DID THIS ONE ALREADY IN THE BETA...
...SO YOU CAN CHOOSE THIS TIME, ASUNA.
THE WHITE ONE IS A FOREST ELF.
AND THE OTHER ...

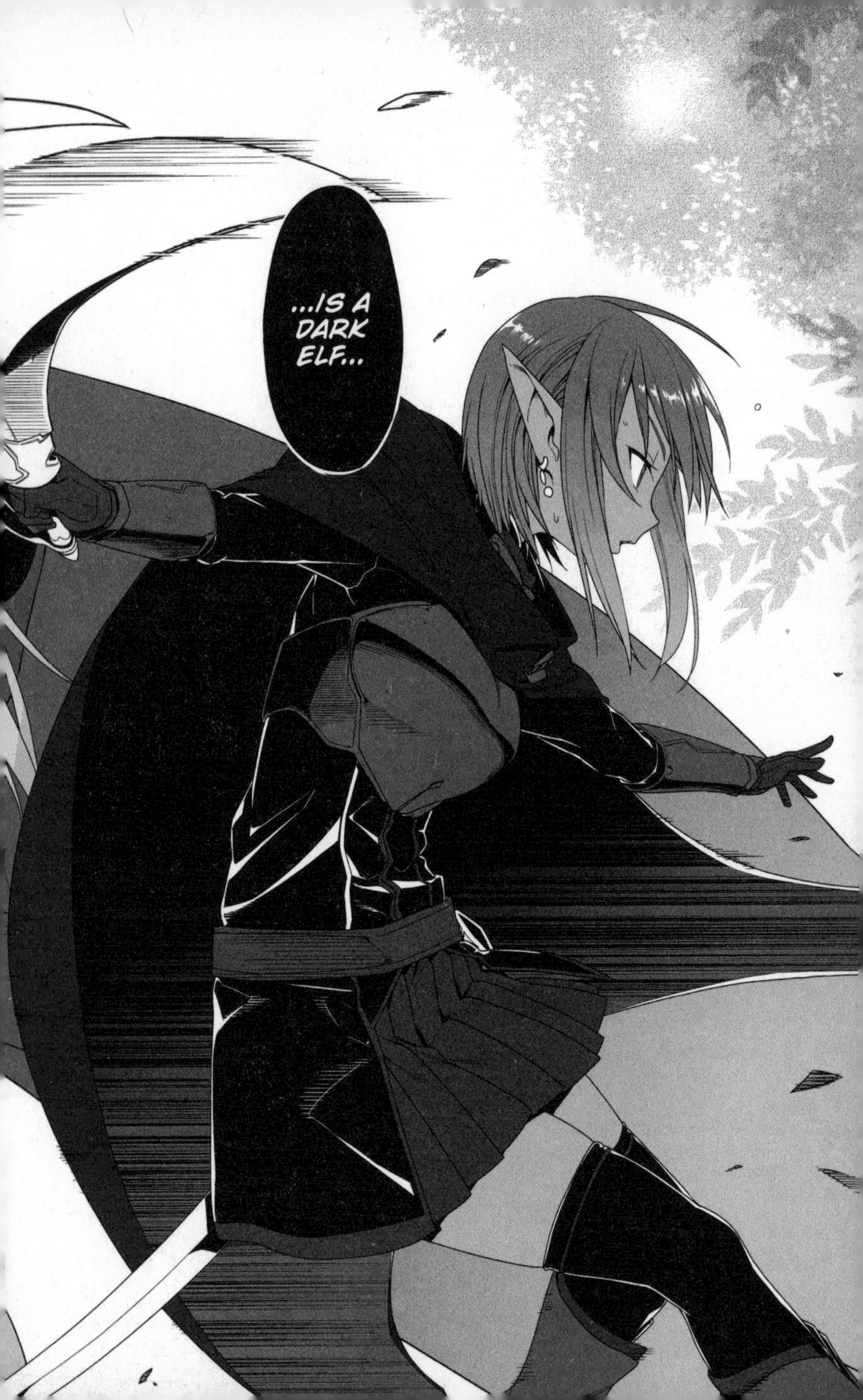
...IS A DARK ELF...

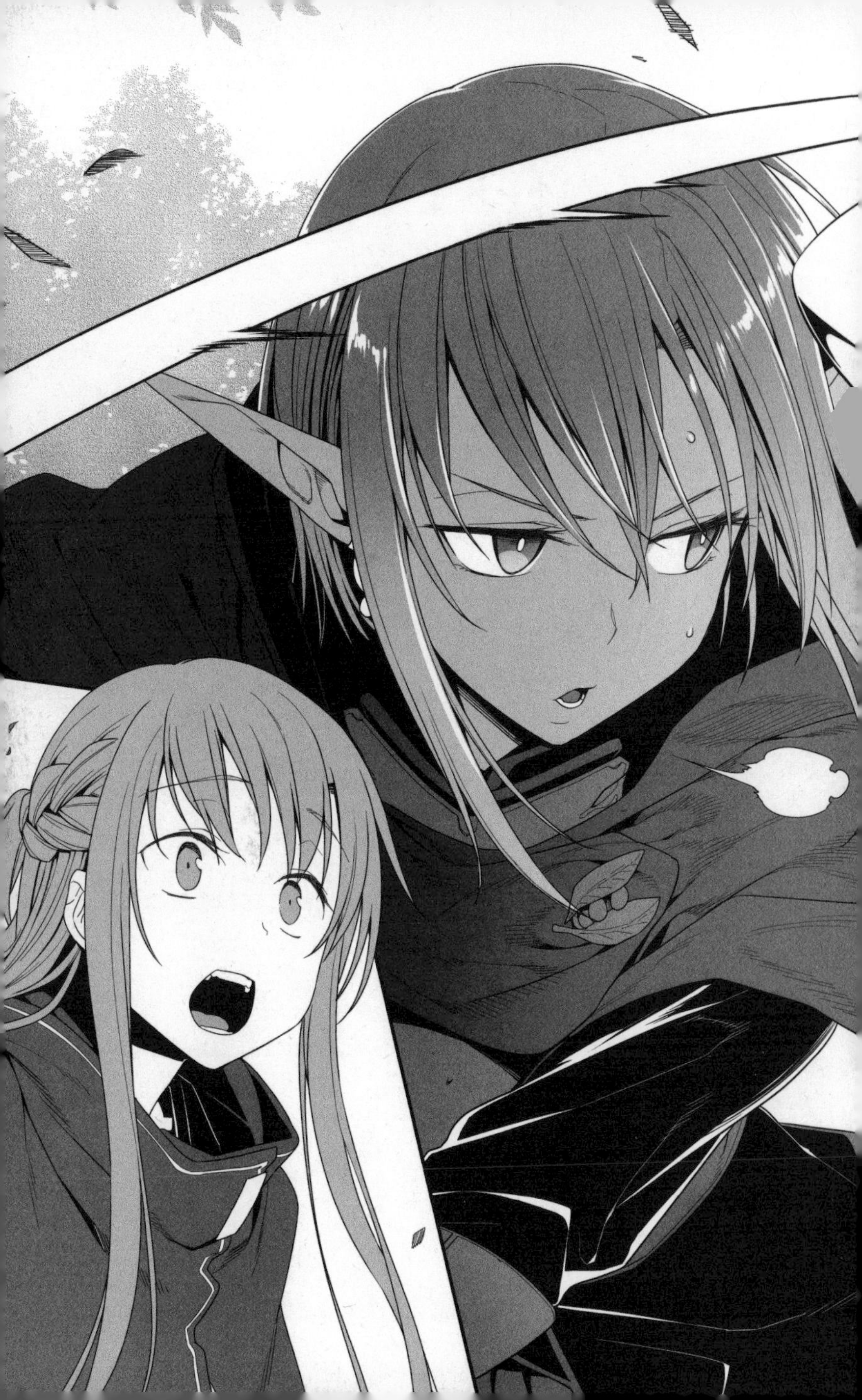

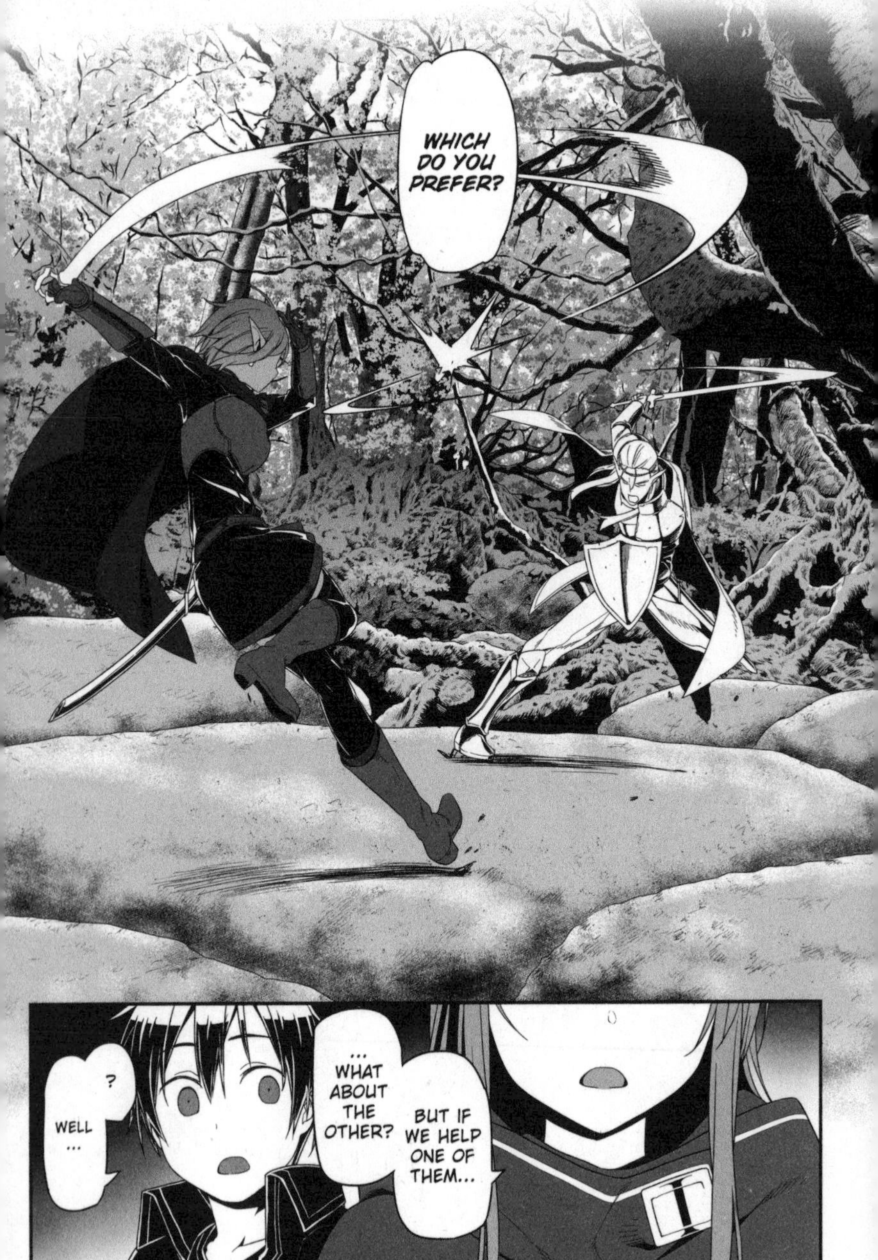
WHICH DO YOU PREFER?
BUT IF WE HELP ONE OF THEM...
... WHAT ABOUT THE OTHER?
? WELL ...

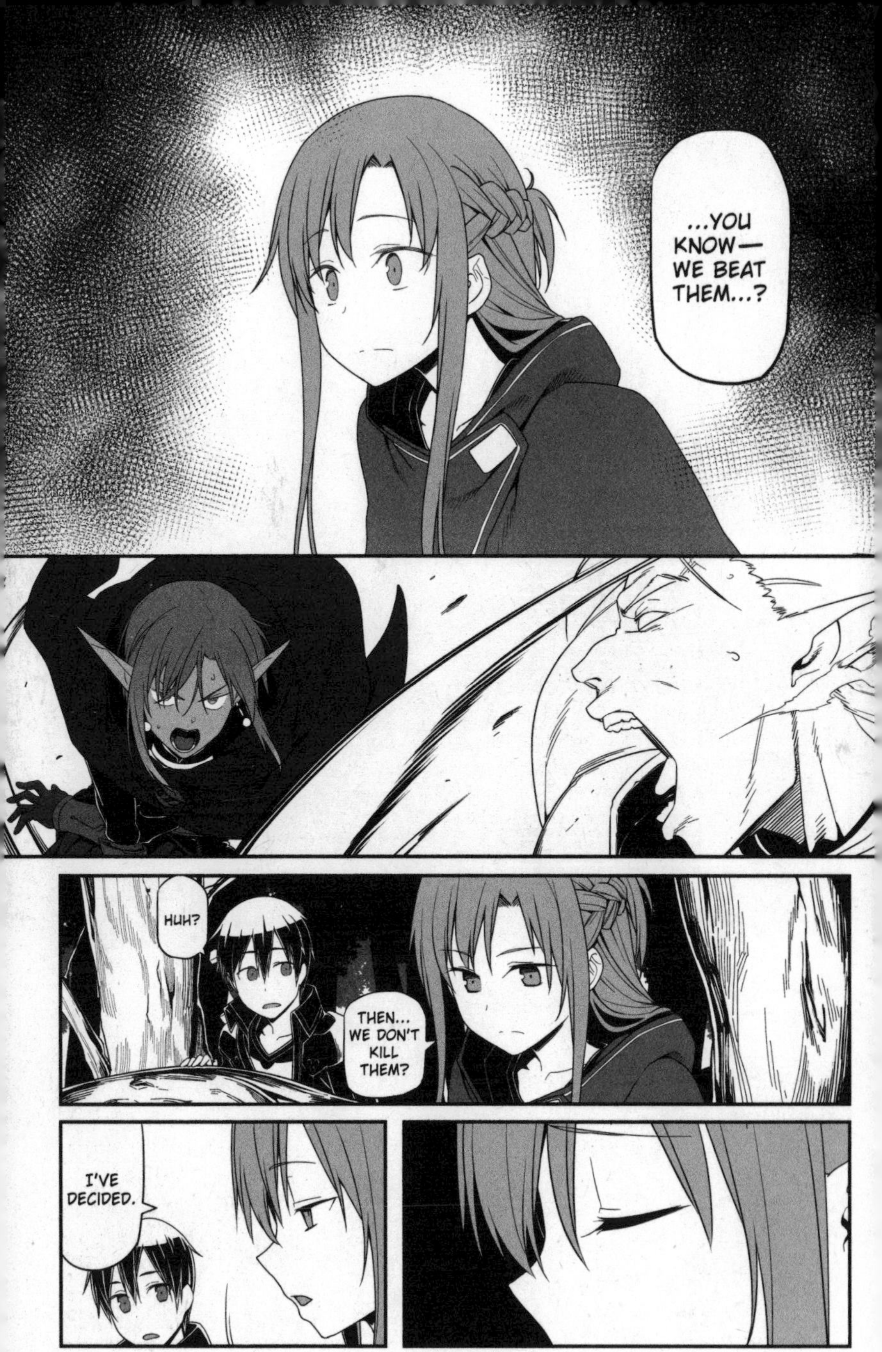
...YOU KNOW—WE BEAT THEM...?
HUH?
THEN... WE DON'T KILL THEM?
I'VE DECIDED.

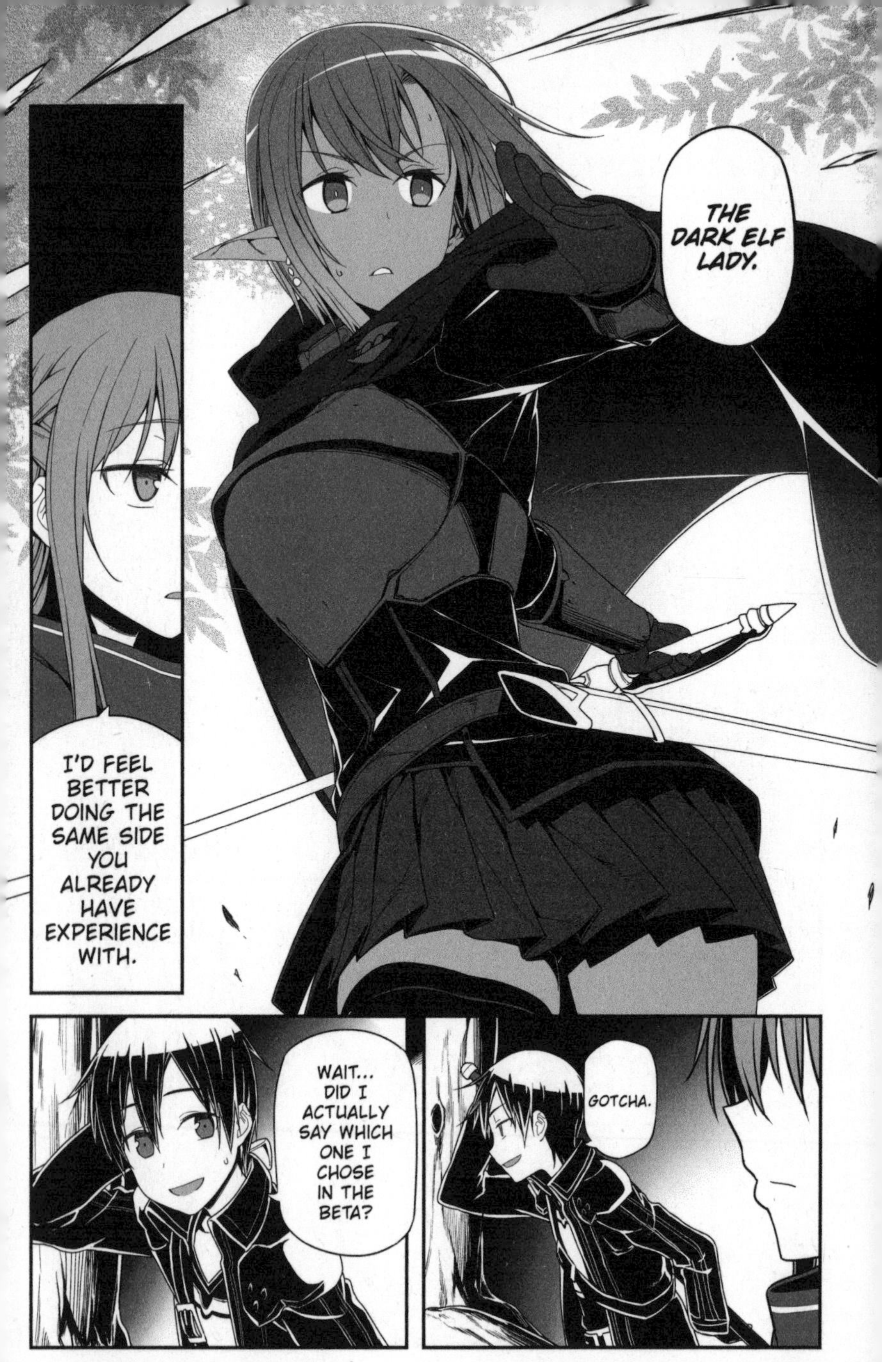
THE DARK ELF LADY.
I'D FEEL BETTER DOING THE SAME SIDE YOU ALREADY HAVE EXPERIENCE WITH.
GOTCHA.
WAIT... DID I ACTUALLY SAY WHICH ONE I CHOSE IN THE BETA?

HEH!
YOU THINK I CAN'T TELL?
URK!
OH!
HANG ON!
WHAT?
IT'S ALL WELL AND GOOD TO SIDE WITH THE DARK ELF...
...BUT KEEP IN MIND, THOSE TWO ARE ELITE MOBS, SIMILAR TO THOSE YOU'D FIND ON THE SEVENTH FLOOR.
SO THE THING IS...
...WE CAN'T ACTUALLY DEFEAT THE FOREST ELF.
SO DON'T ATTACK HIM. JUST FOCUS ON GUARDING.
GOT IT?
WE...

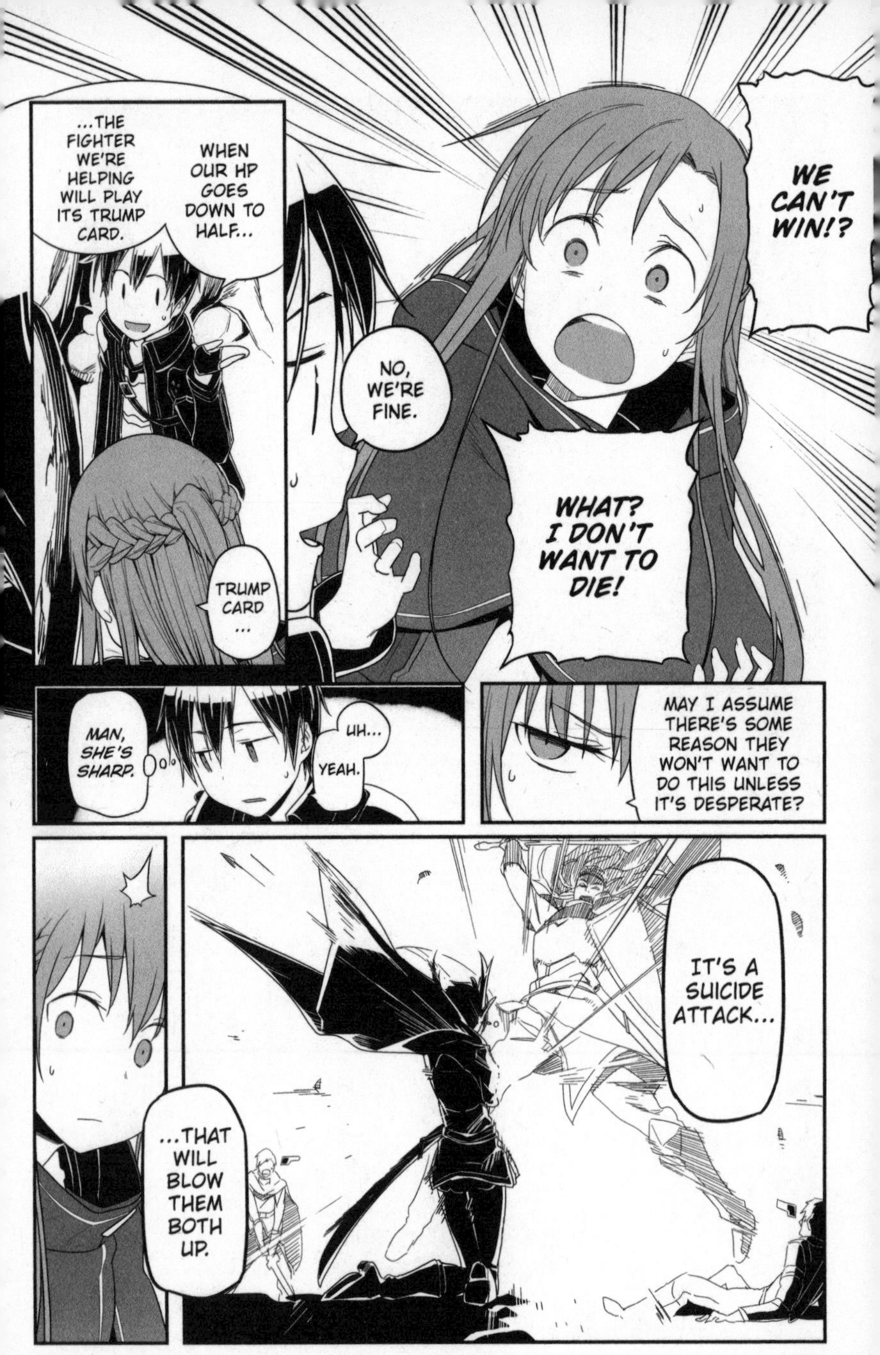
WE CAN'T WIN!?
WHAT? I DON'T WANT TO DIE!
NO, WE'RE FINE.
WHEN OUR HP GOES DOWN TO HALF...
...THE FIGHTER WE'RE HELPING WILL PLAY ITS TRUMP CARD.
TRUMP CARD...
MAY I ASSUME THERE'S SOME REASON THEY WON'T WANT TO DO THIS UNLESS IT'S DESPERATE?
UH... YEAH.
MAN, SHE'S SHARP.
IT'S A SUICIDE ATTACK...
...THAT WILL BLOW THEM BOTH UP.

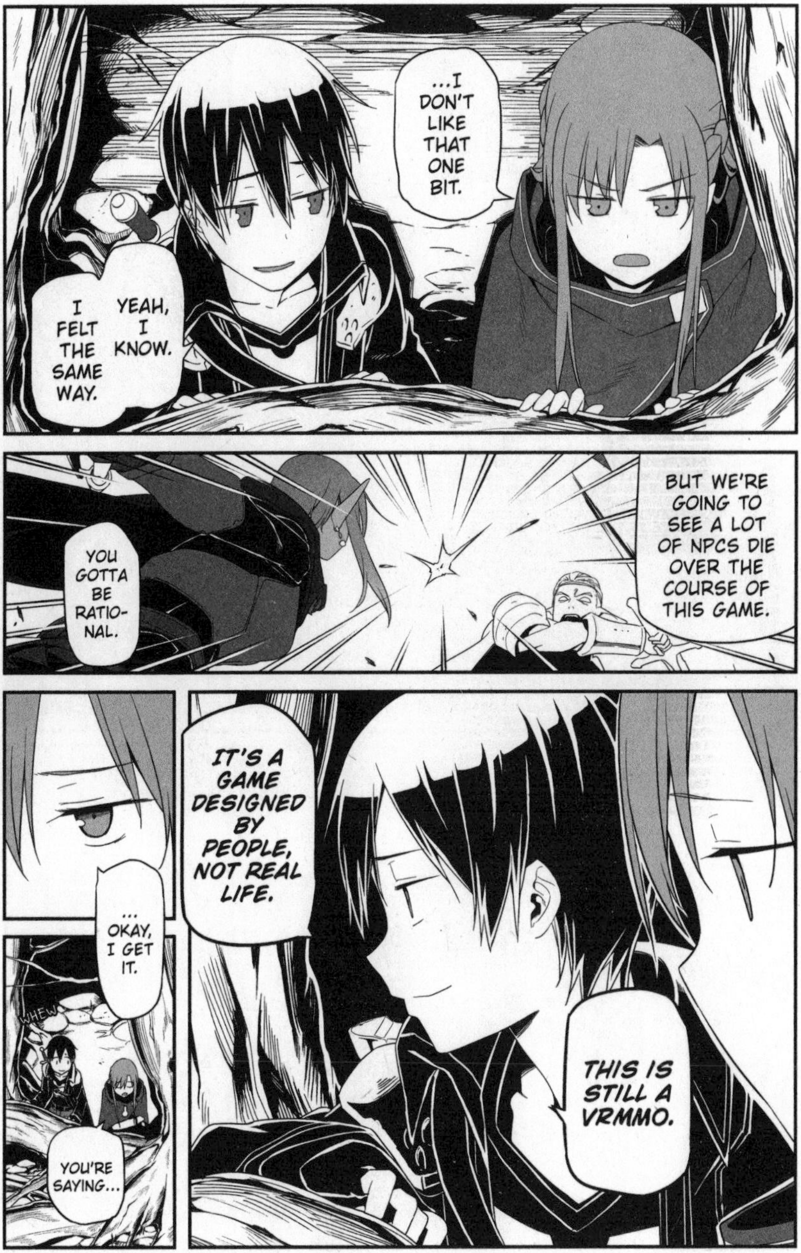
...I DON'T LIKE THAT ONE BIT.
YEAH, I KNOW.
I FELT THE SAME WAY.
BUT WE'RE GOING TO SEE A LOT OF NPCS DIE OVER THE COURSE OF THIS GAME.
YOU GOTTA BE RATIONAL.
IT'S A GAME DESIGNED BY PEOPLE, NOT REAL LIFE.
THIS IS STILL A VRMMO.
... OKAY, I GET IT.
WHEW
YOU'RE SAYING...

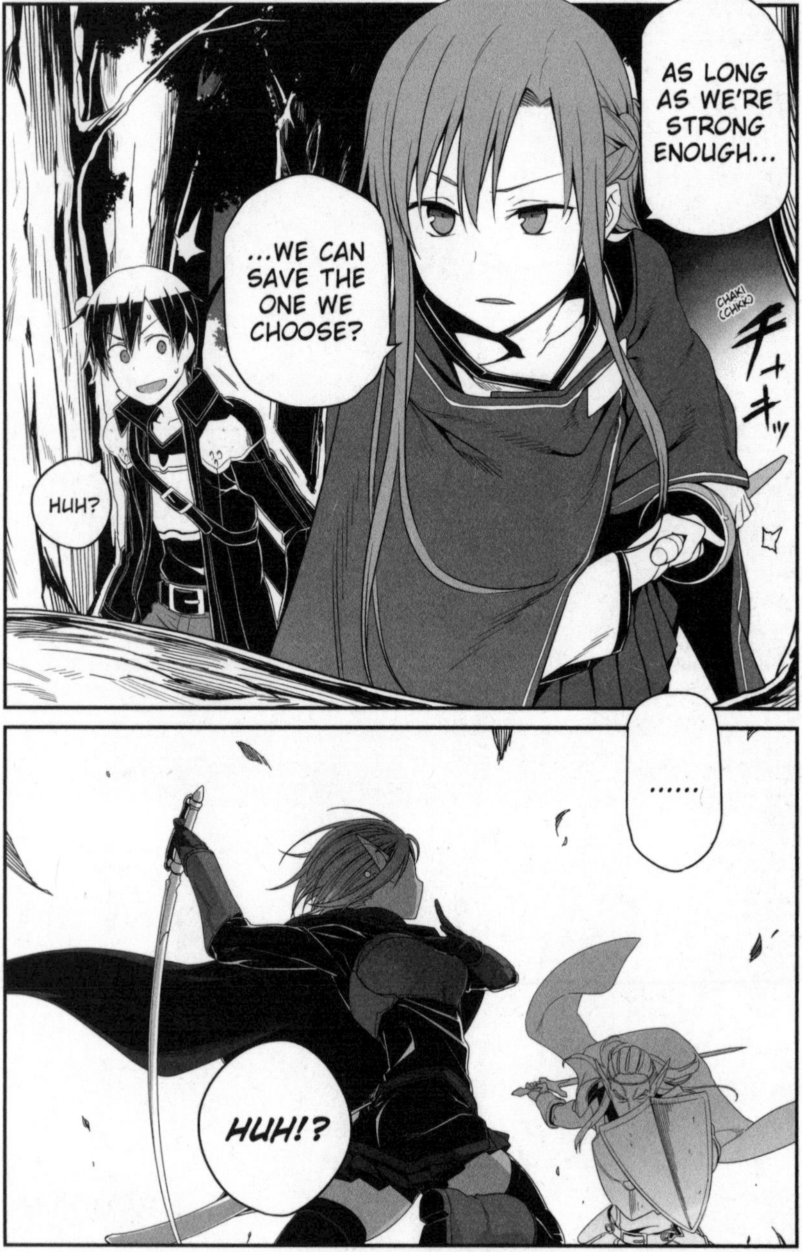
AS LONG AS WE'RE STRONG ENOUGH...
CHAKI (CHKK)
チャキッ
...WE CAN SAVE THE ONE WE CHOOSE?
HUH?
......
HUH!?

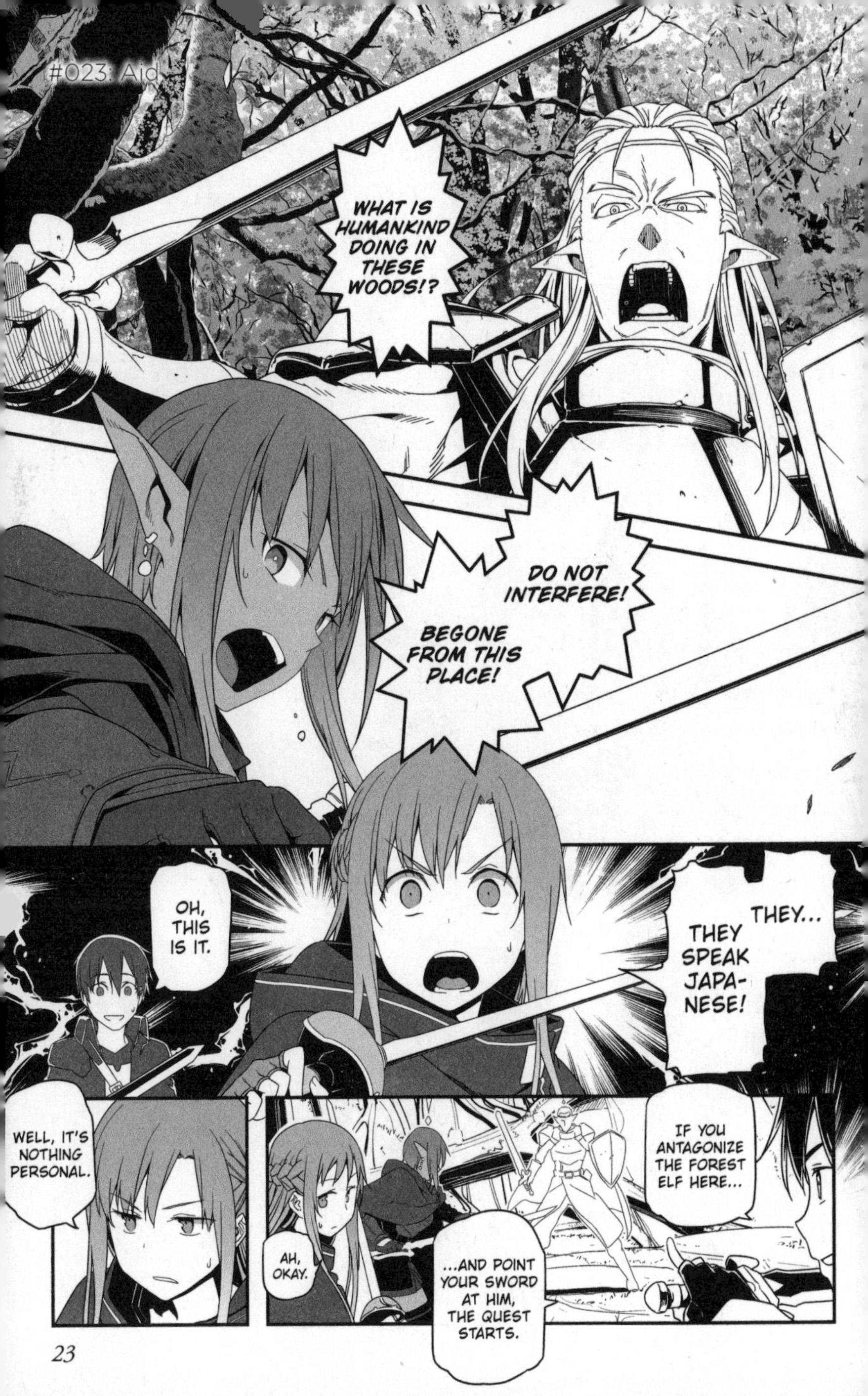
#023: Aid
WHAT IS HUMANKIND DOING IN THESE WOODS!?
DO NOT INTERFERE!
BEGONE FROM THIS PLACE!
THEY... THEY SPEAK JAPANESE!
OH, THIS IS IT.
IF YOU ANTAGONIZE THE FOREST ELF HERE...
...AND POINT YOUR SWORD AT HIM, THE QUEST STARTS.
AH, OKAY.
WELL, IT'S NOTHING PERSONAL.

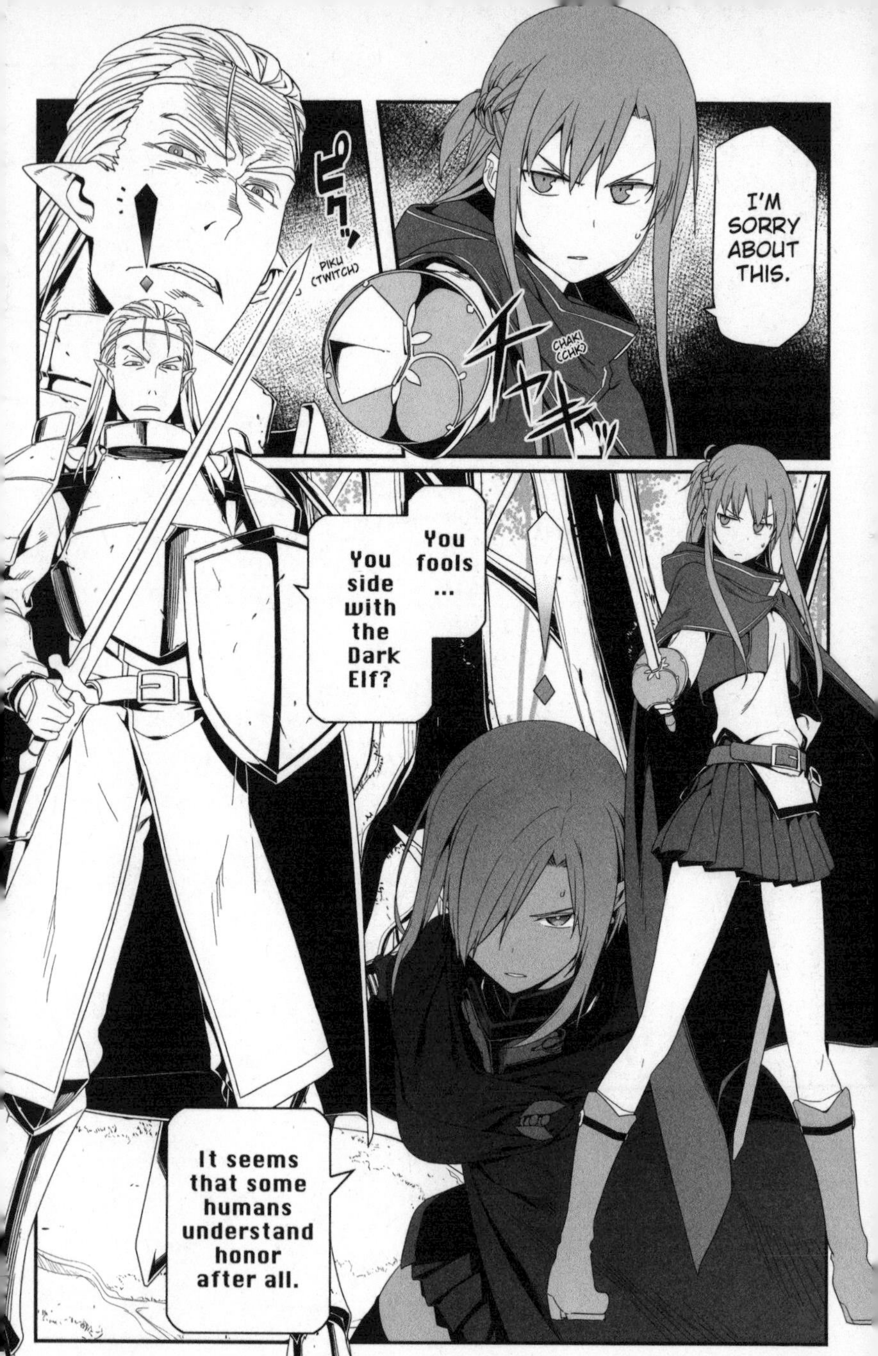
I'M SORRY ABOUT THIS.
CHAKI (CHK)
PIKU (TWITCH)
You fools ...
You side with the Dark Elf?
It seems that some humans understand honor after all.

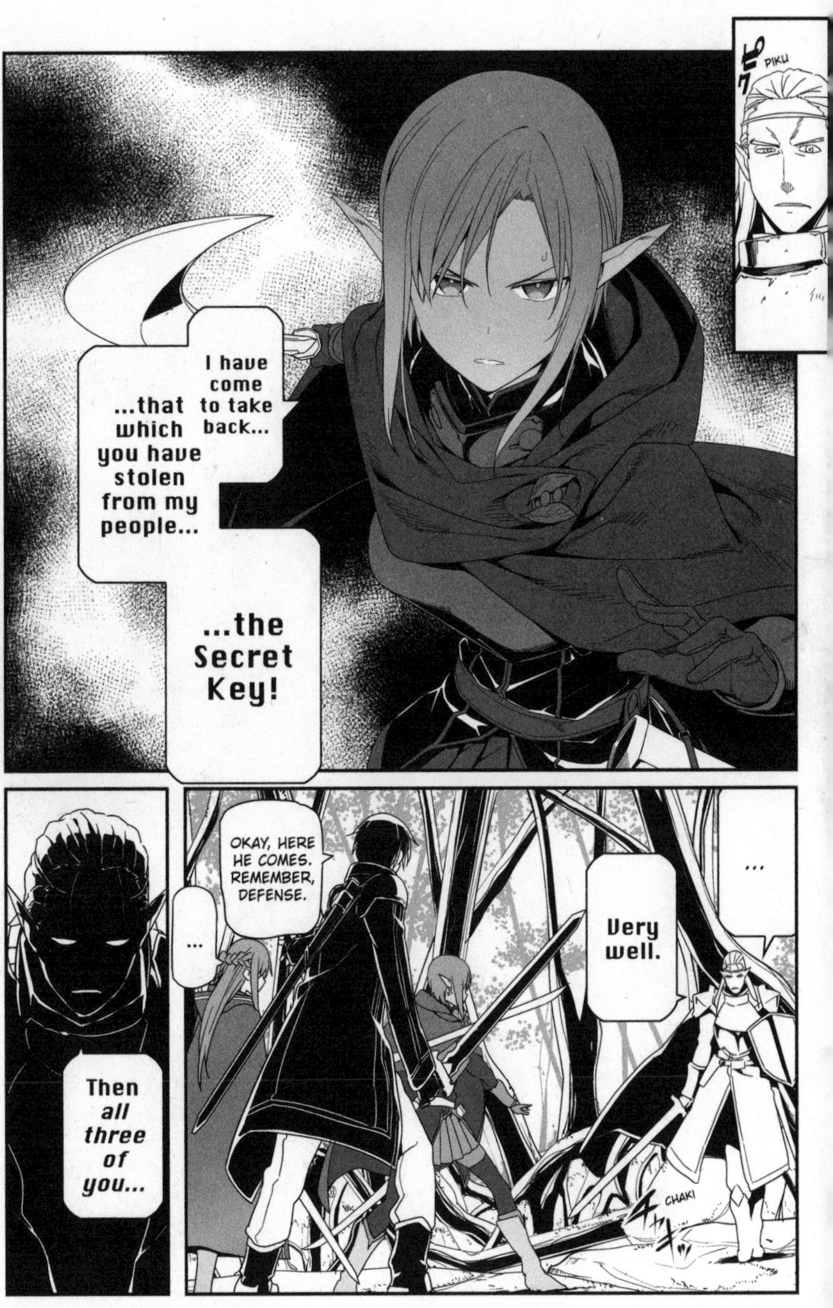

PIKU
I have come to take back...
...that which you have stolen from my people...
...the Secret Key!
...
Very well.
OKAY, HERE HE COMES. REMEMBER, DEFENSE.
...
CHAKI
Then *all three* of you...

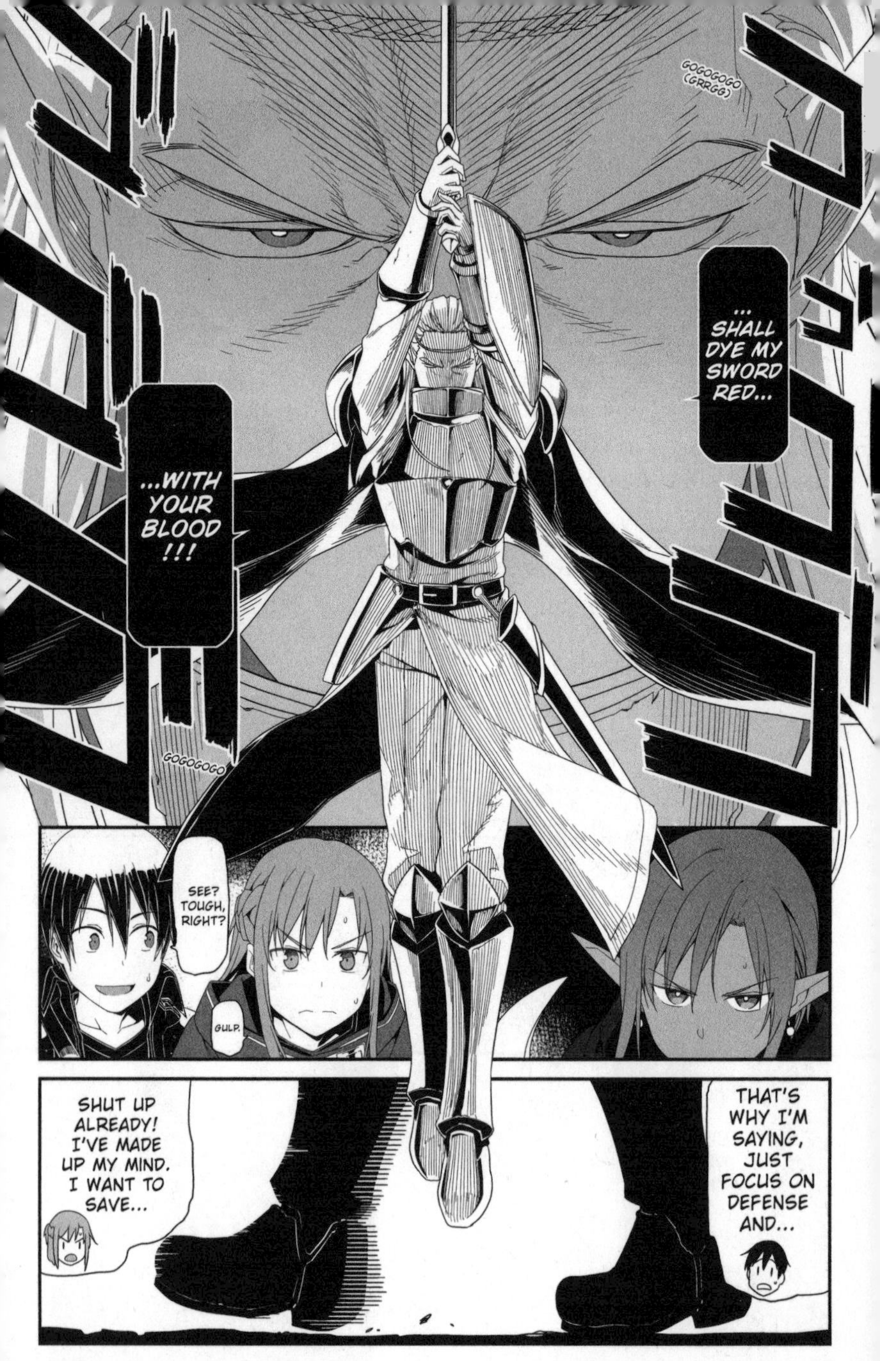
GOGOGOGO (GRRGG)
...SHALL DYE MY SWORD RED...
...WITH YOUR BLOOD!!!
GOGOGOGO
SEE? TOUGH, RIGHT?
GULP.
THAT'S WHY I'M SAYING, JUST FOCUS ON DEFENSE AND...
SHUT UP ALREADY! I'VE MADE UP MY MIND. I WANT TO SAVE...

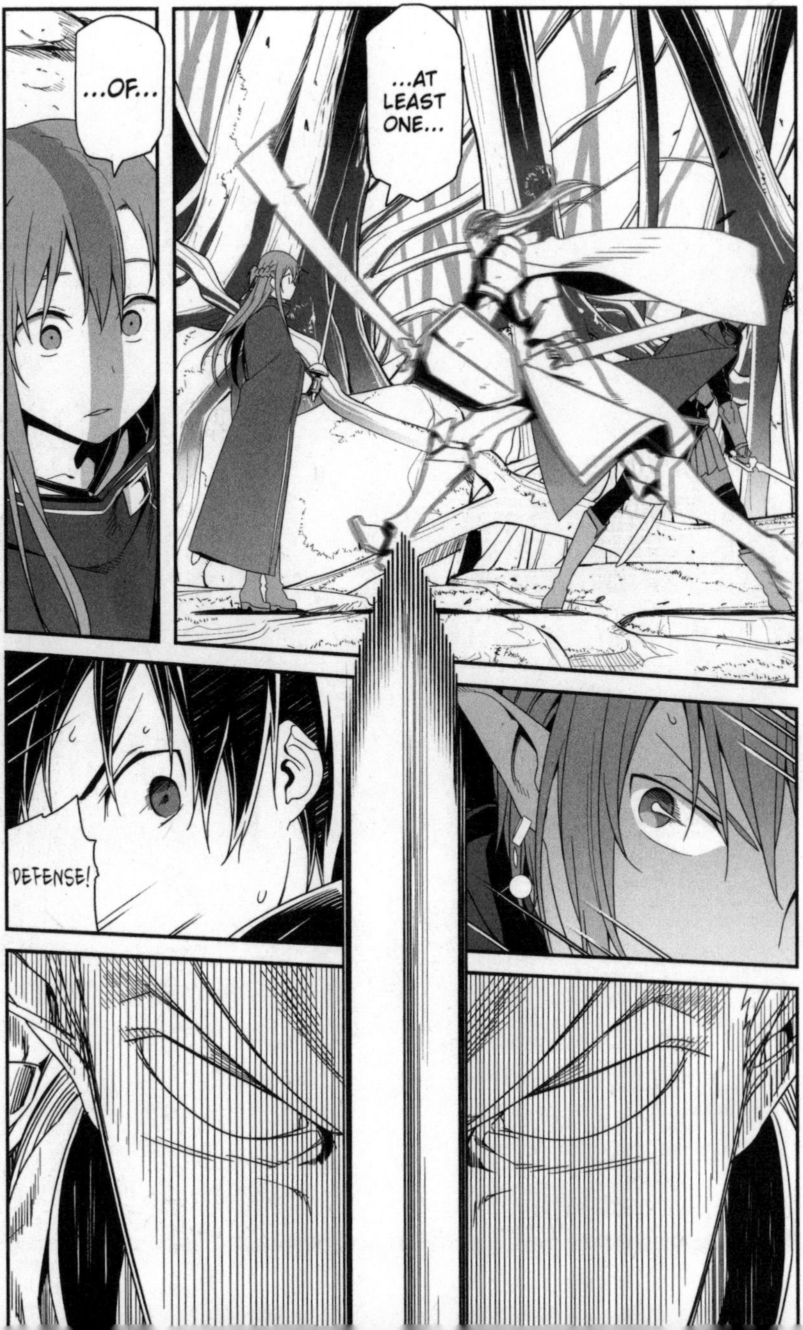
...AT LEAST ONE...
...OF...
DEFENSE!

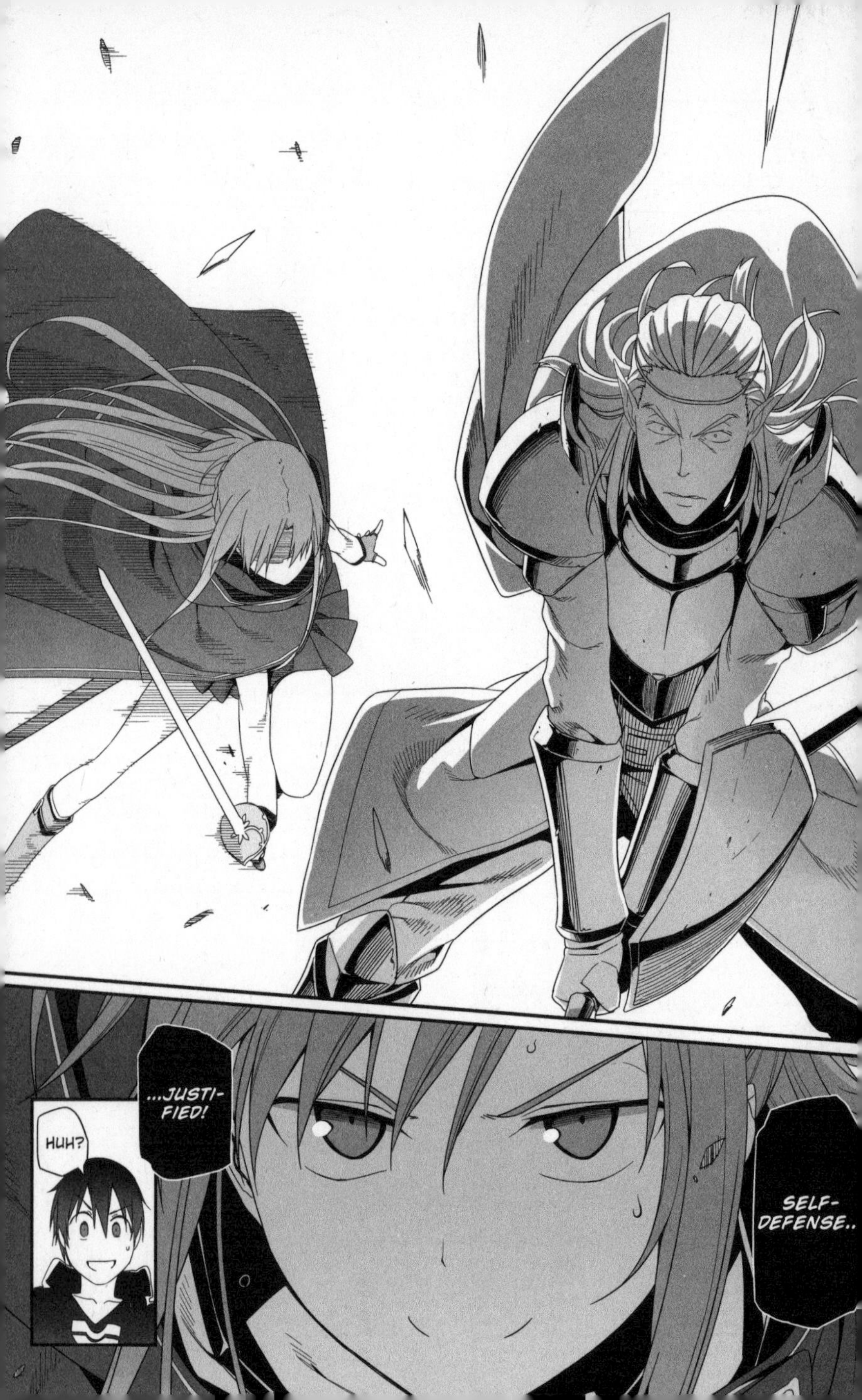
SELF-DEFENSE..
...JUSTIFIED!
HUH?

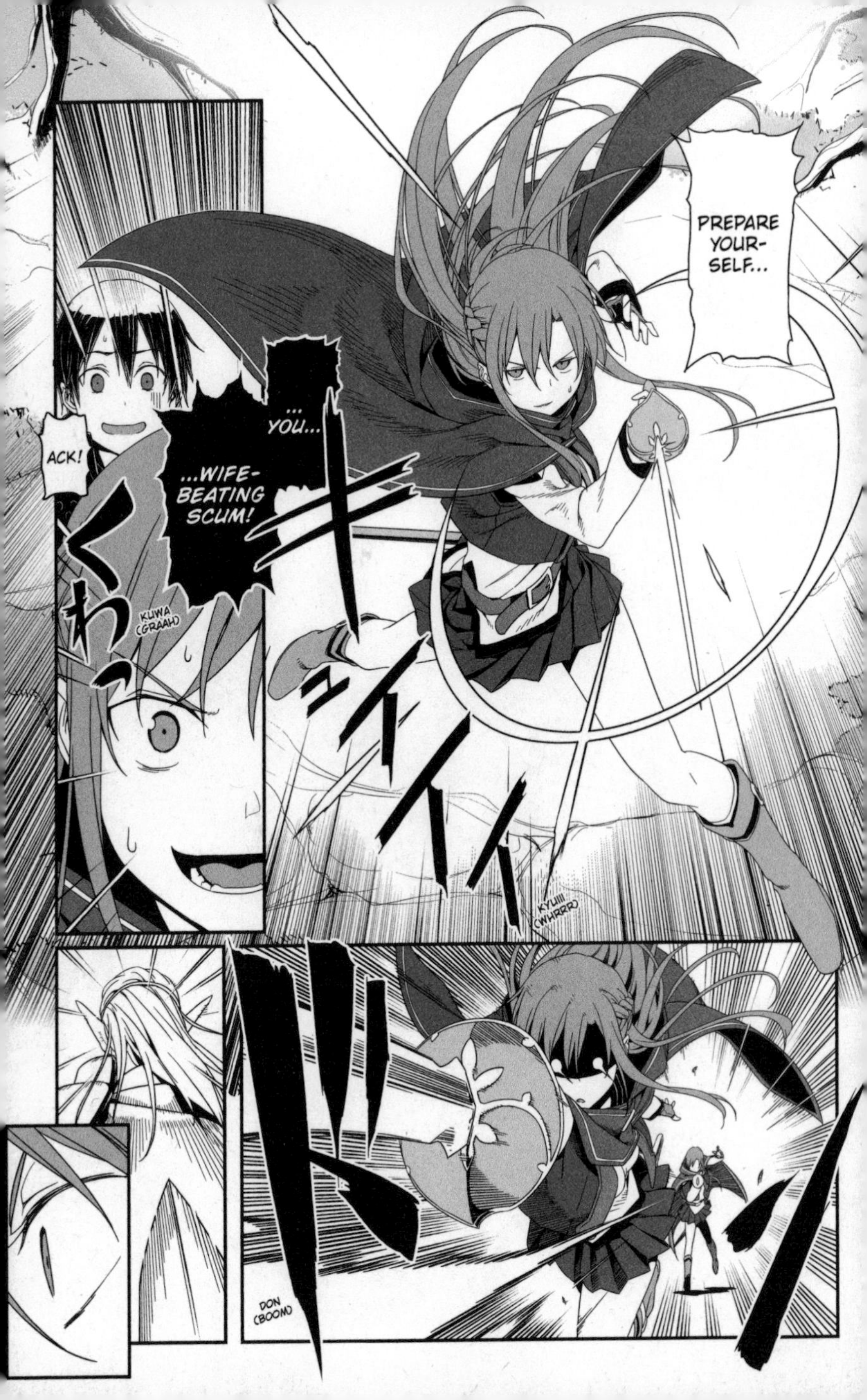
PREPARE YOUR-SELF...
KYUIII (WHRRR)
...YOU...
...WIFE-BEATING SCUM!
ACK!
KUWA (GRAAH)
DON (BOOM)

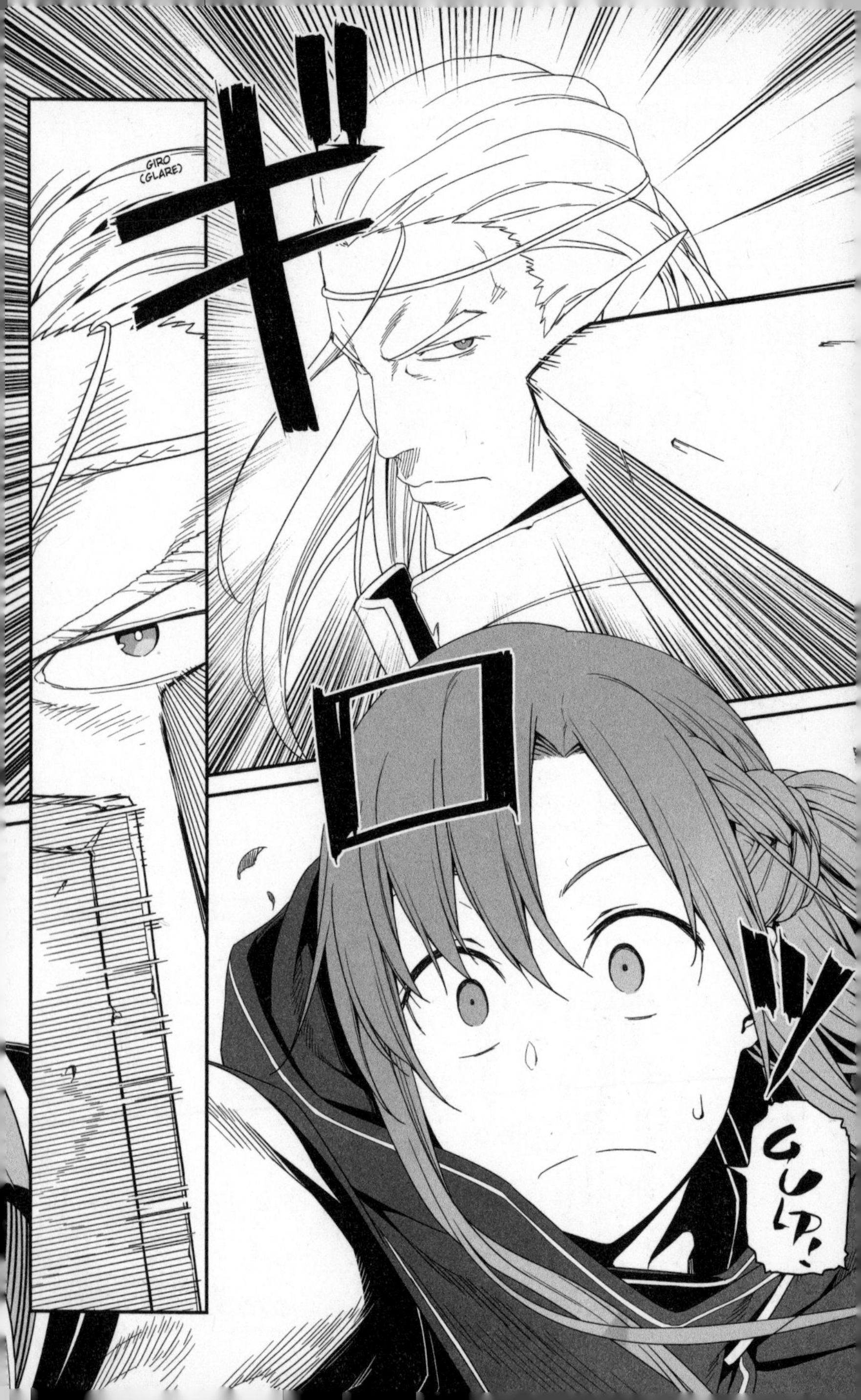
GIRO (GLARE)
GULP!

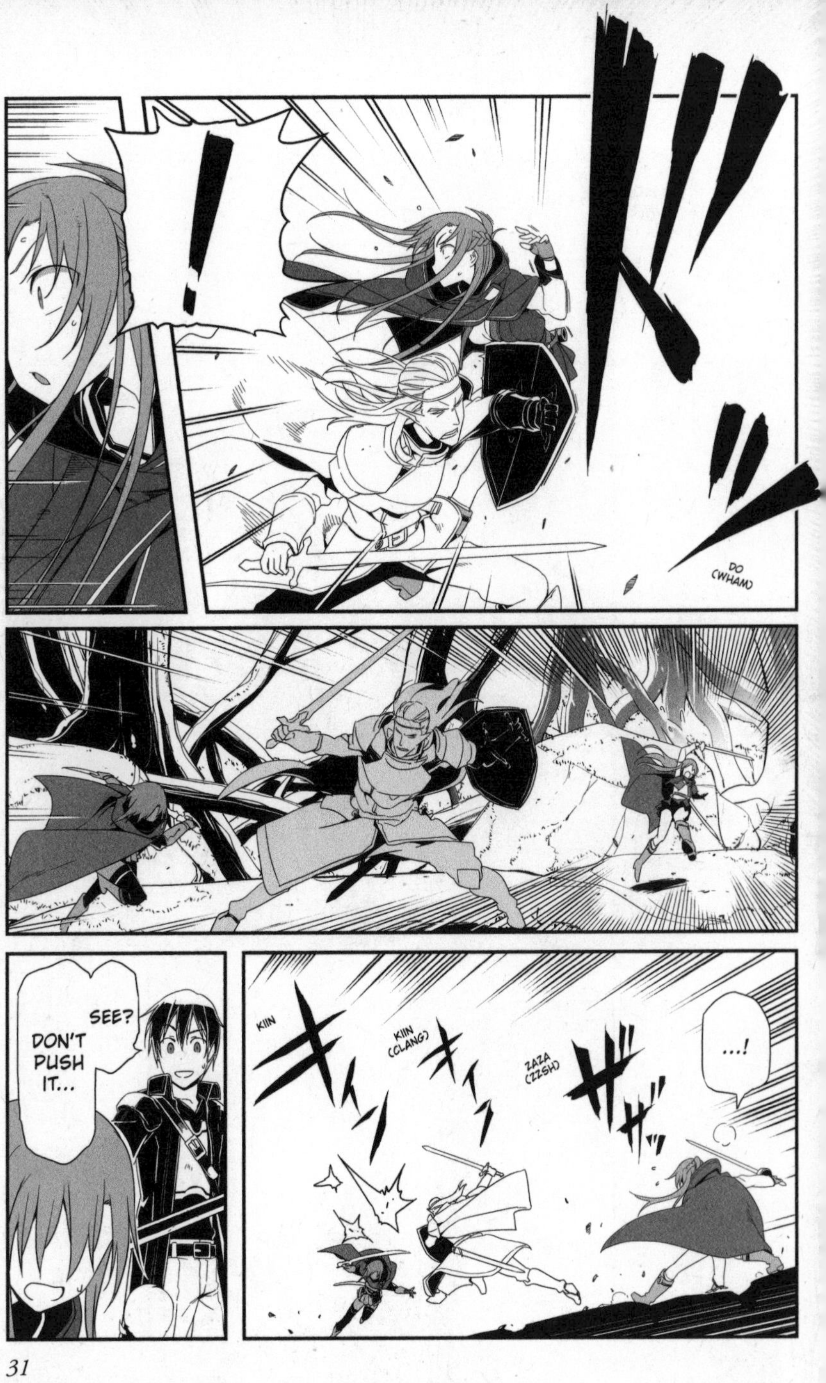
DO (WHAM)
!
...!
ZAZA (ZZSH)
KIIN (CLANG)
KIIN
SEE? DON'T PUSH IT...

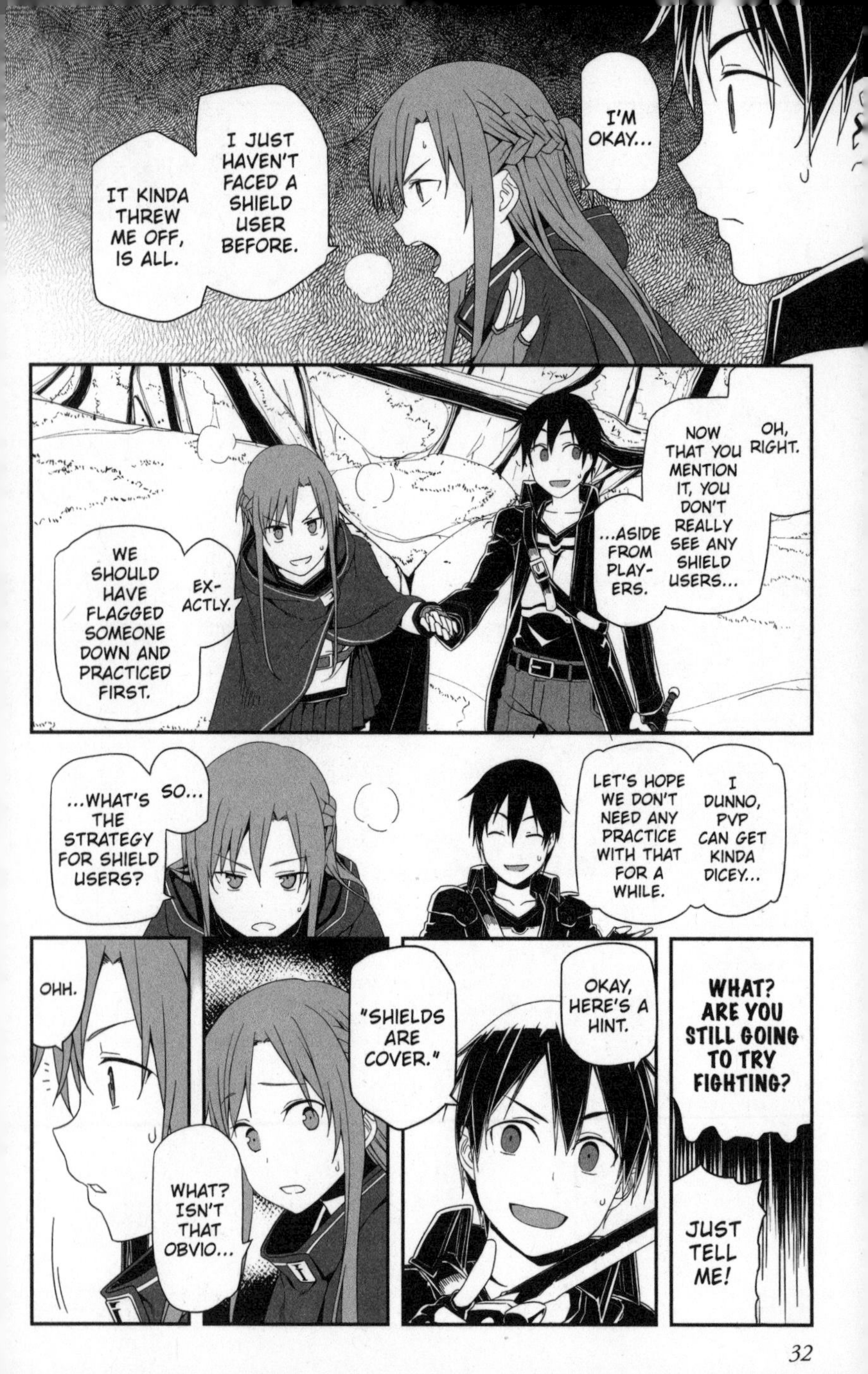

I'M OKAY...
I JUST HAVEN'T FACED A SHIELD USER BEFORE.
IT KINDA THREW ME OFF, IS ALL.
OH, RIGHT.
NOW THAT YOU MENTION IT, YOU DON'T REALLY SEE ANY SHIELD USERS...
...ASIDE FROM PLAY-ERS.
EX-ACTLY.
WE SHOULD HAVE FLAGGED SOMEONE DOWN AND PRACTICED FIRST.
I DUNNO, PVP CAN GET KINDA DICEY...
LET'S HOPE WE DON'T NEED ANY PRACTICE WITH THAT FOR A WHILE.
SO...
...WHAT'S THE STRATEGY FOR SHIELD USERS?
WHAT? ARE YOU STILL GOING TO TRY FIGHTING?
JUST TELL ME!
OKAY, HERE'S A HINT.
"SHIELDS ARE COVER."
WHAT? ISN'T THAT OBVIO...
OHH.

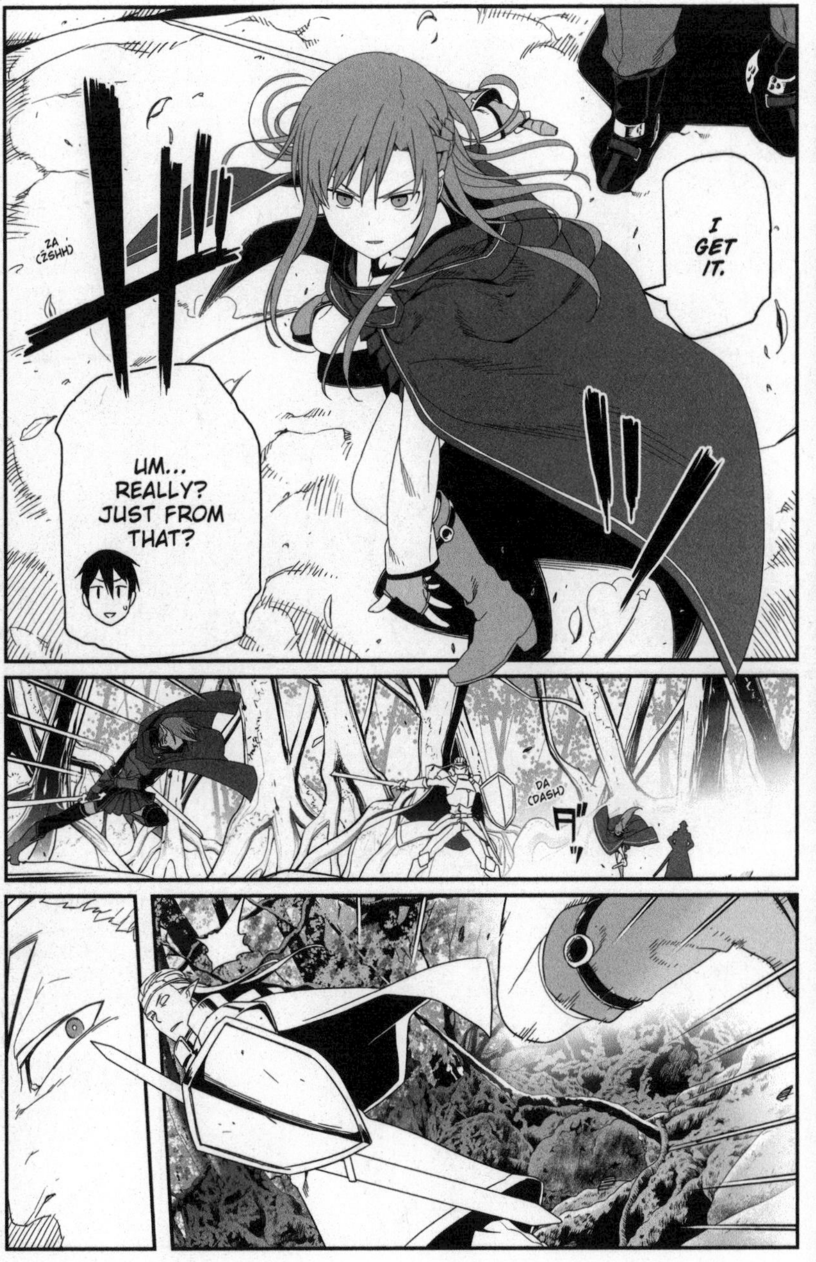
I GET IT.
ZA (ZSHH)
UM... REALLY? JUST FROM THAT?
DA (DASH)

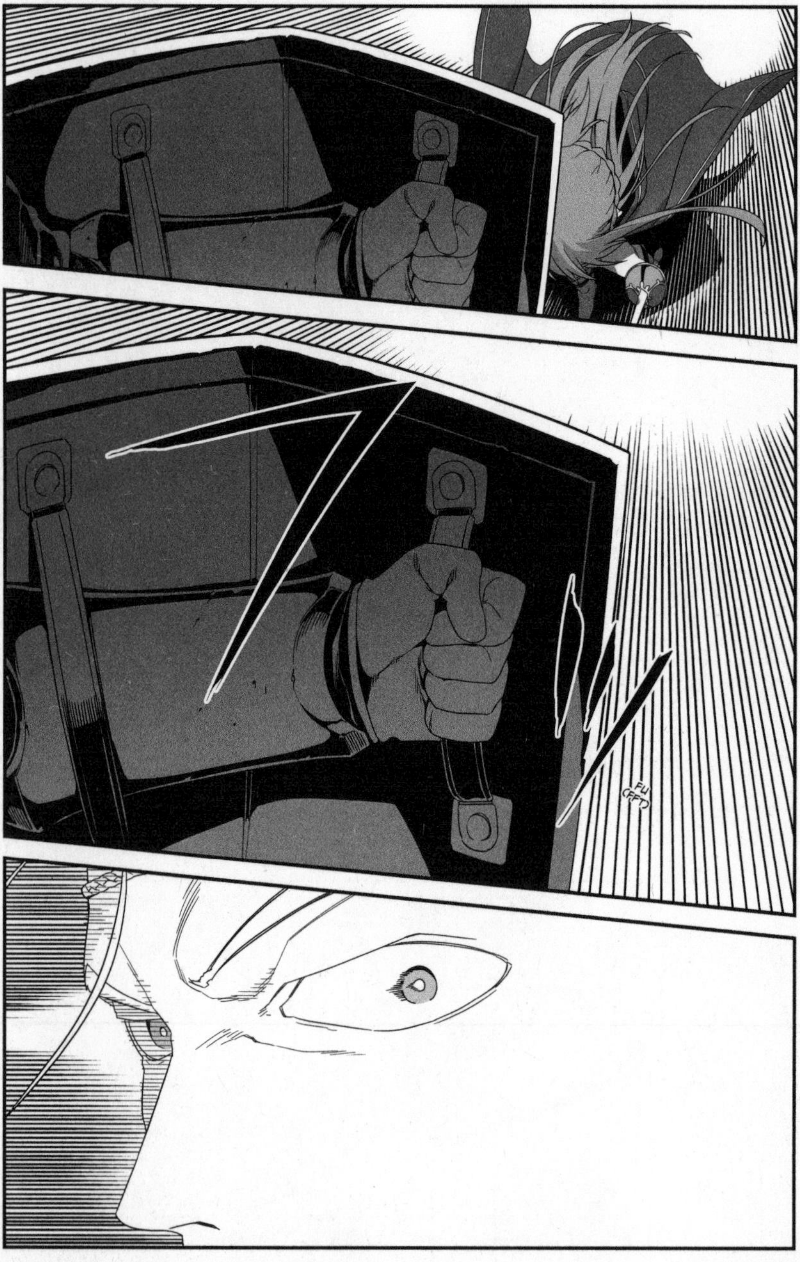
FU
(FFT)

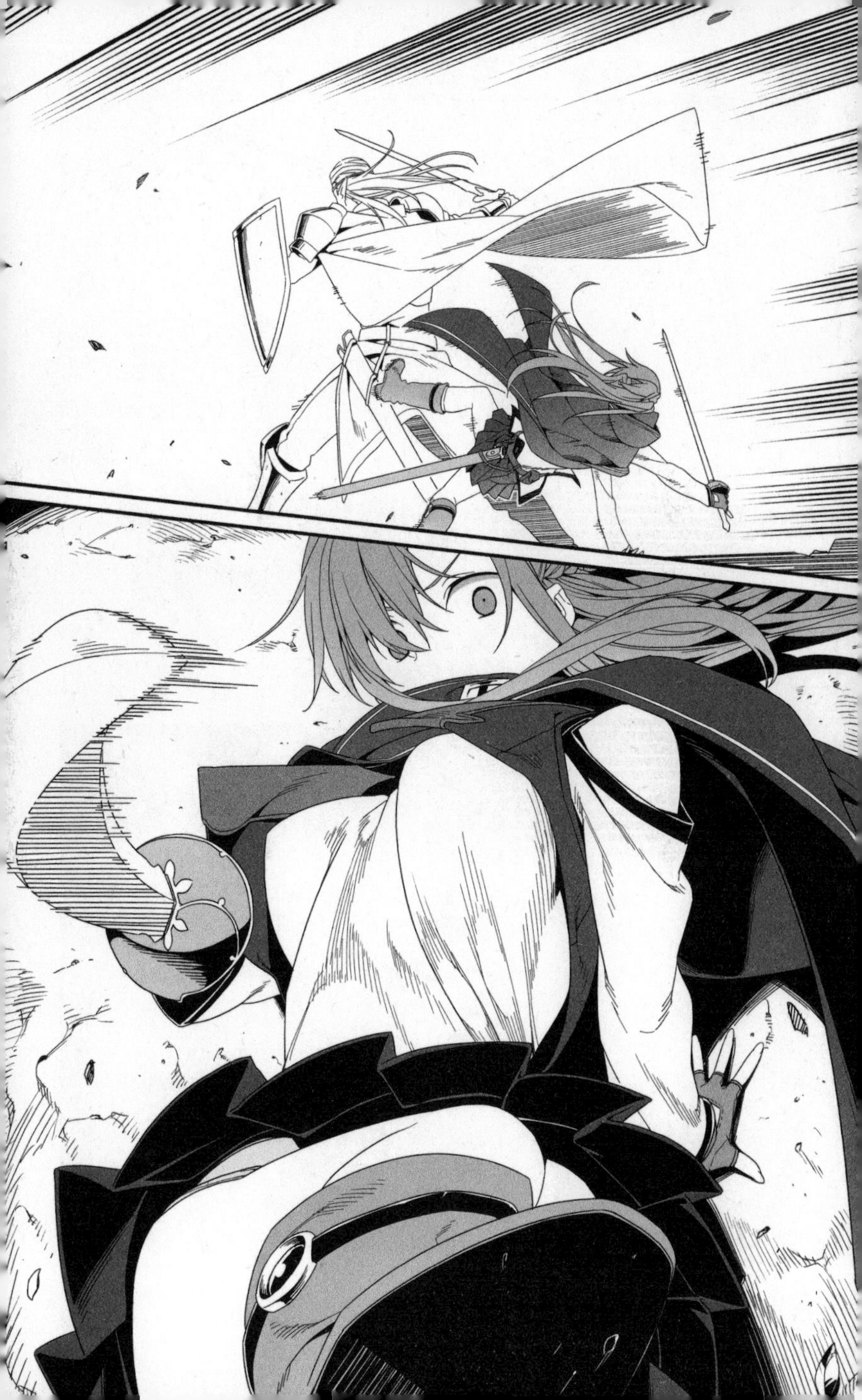

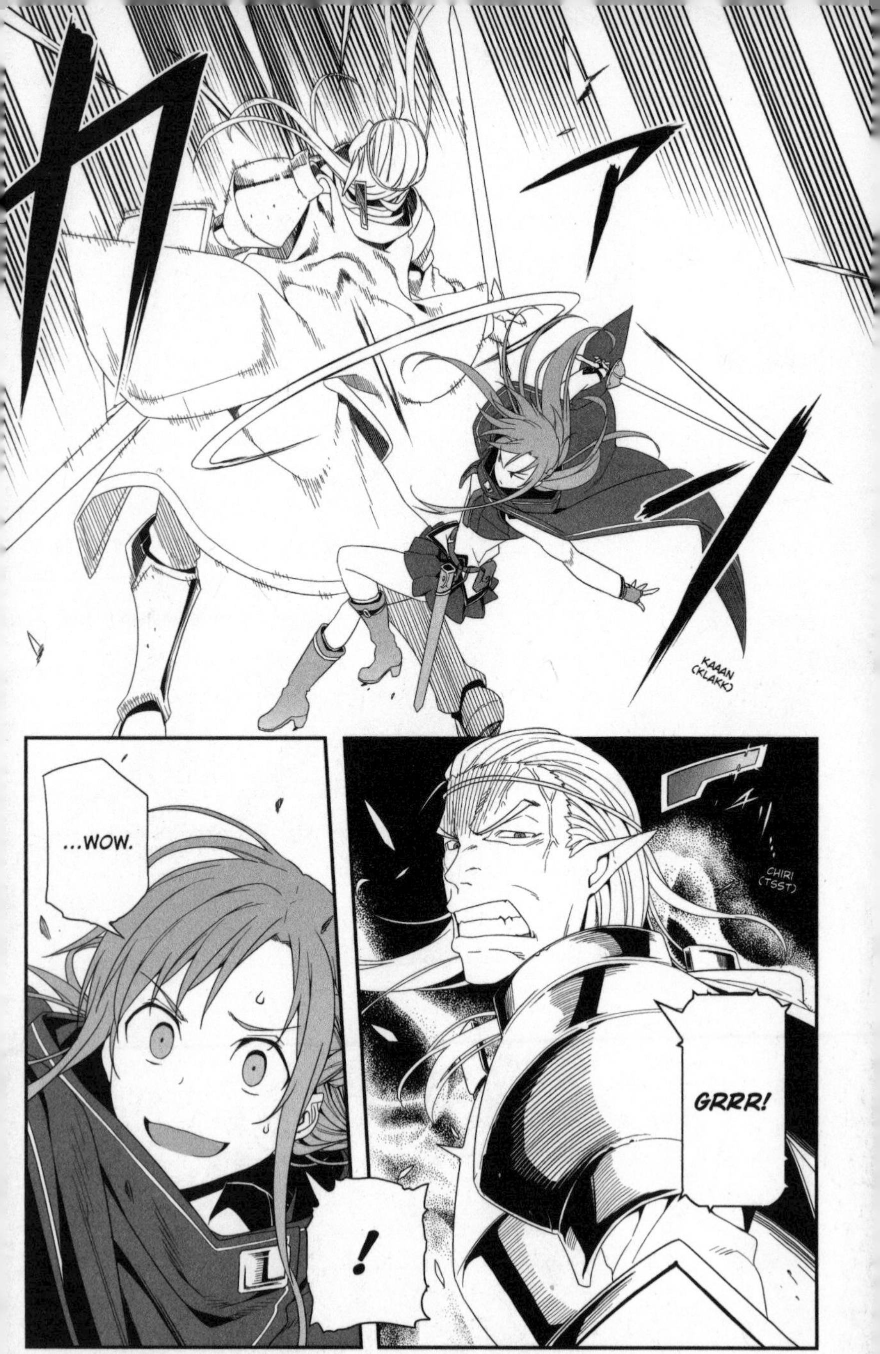
KAAAN
(KLAKK)
CHIRI
(TSST)
GRRR!
...WOW.
!

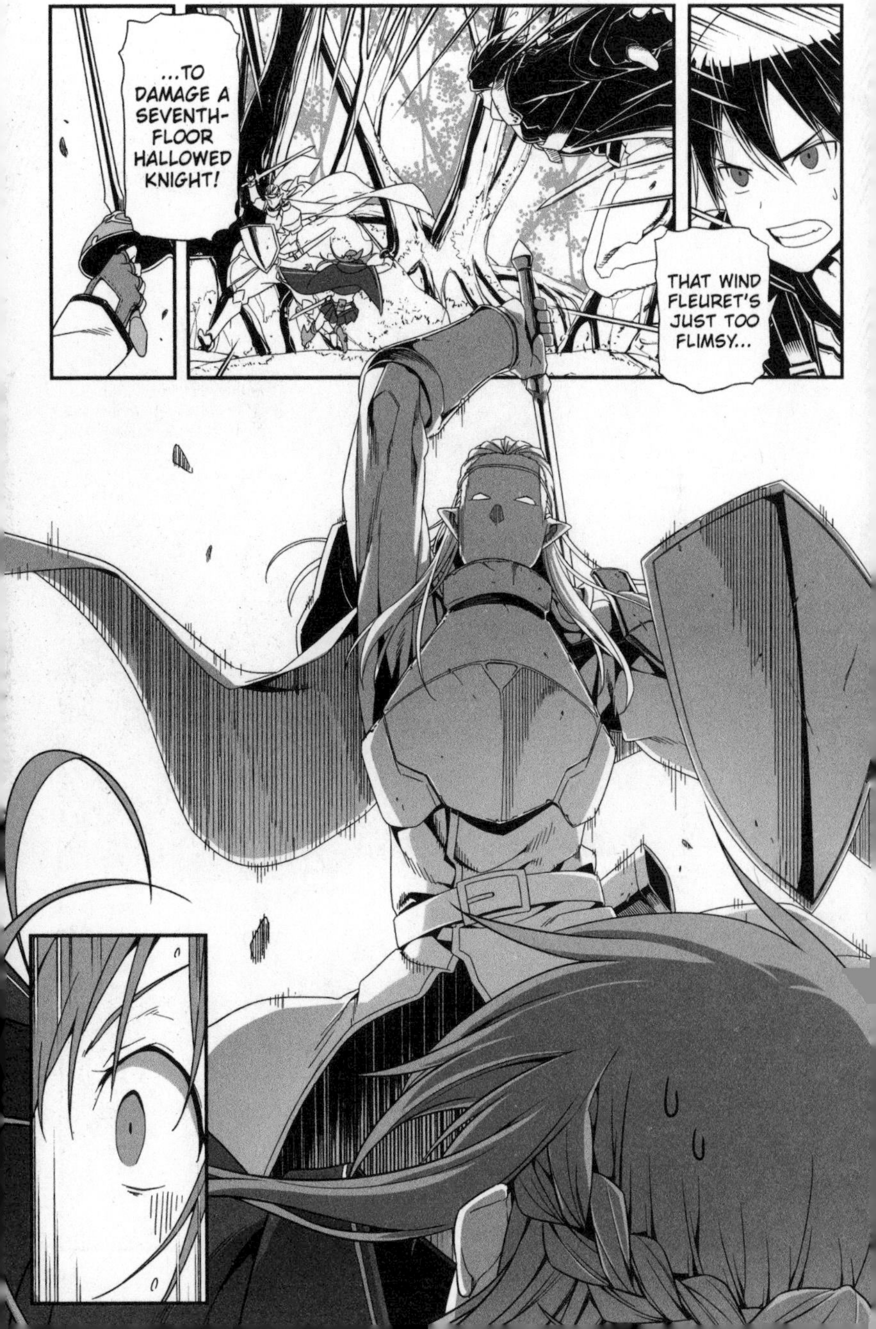
THAT WIND FLEURET'S JUST TOO FLIMSY...
...TO DAMAGE A SEVENTH-FLOOR HALLOWED KNIGHT!

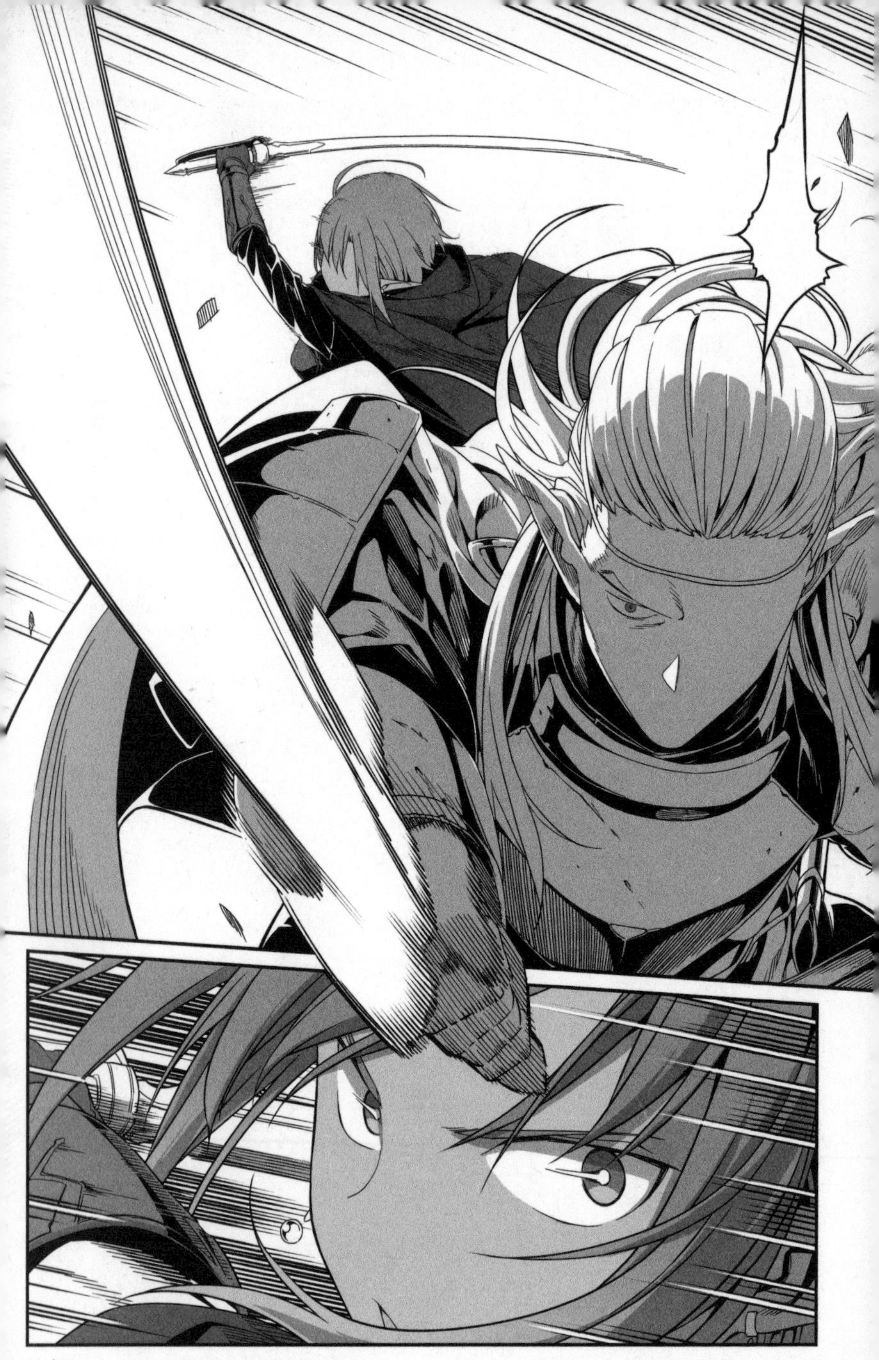

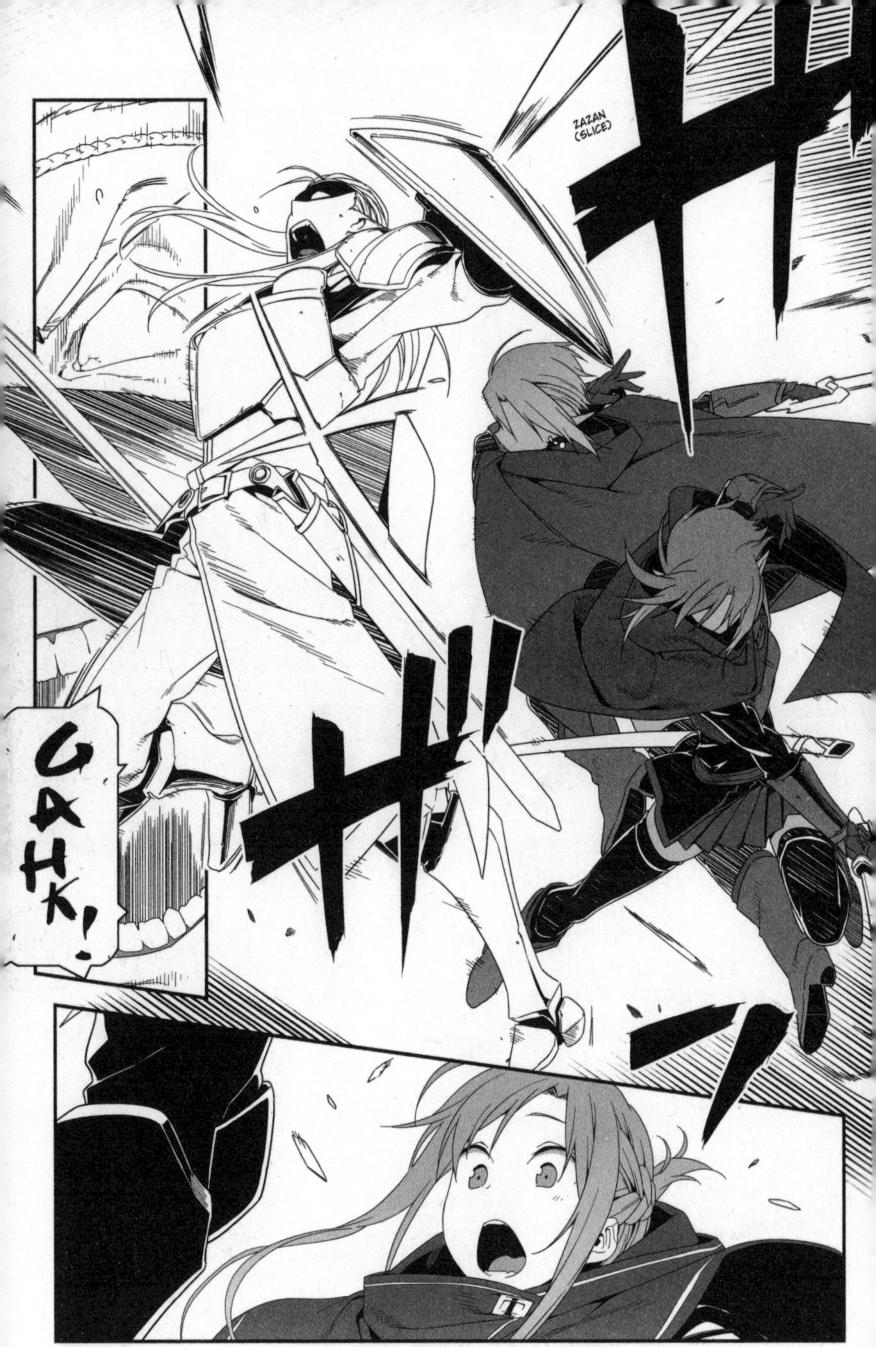
ZAZAN
(SLICE)
GAHK!

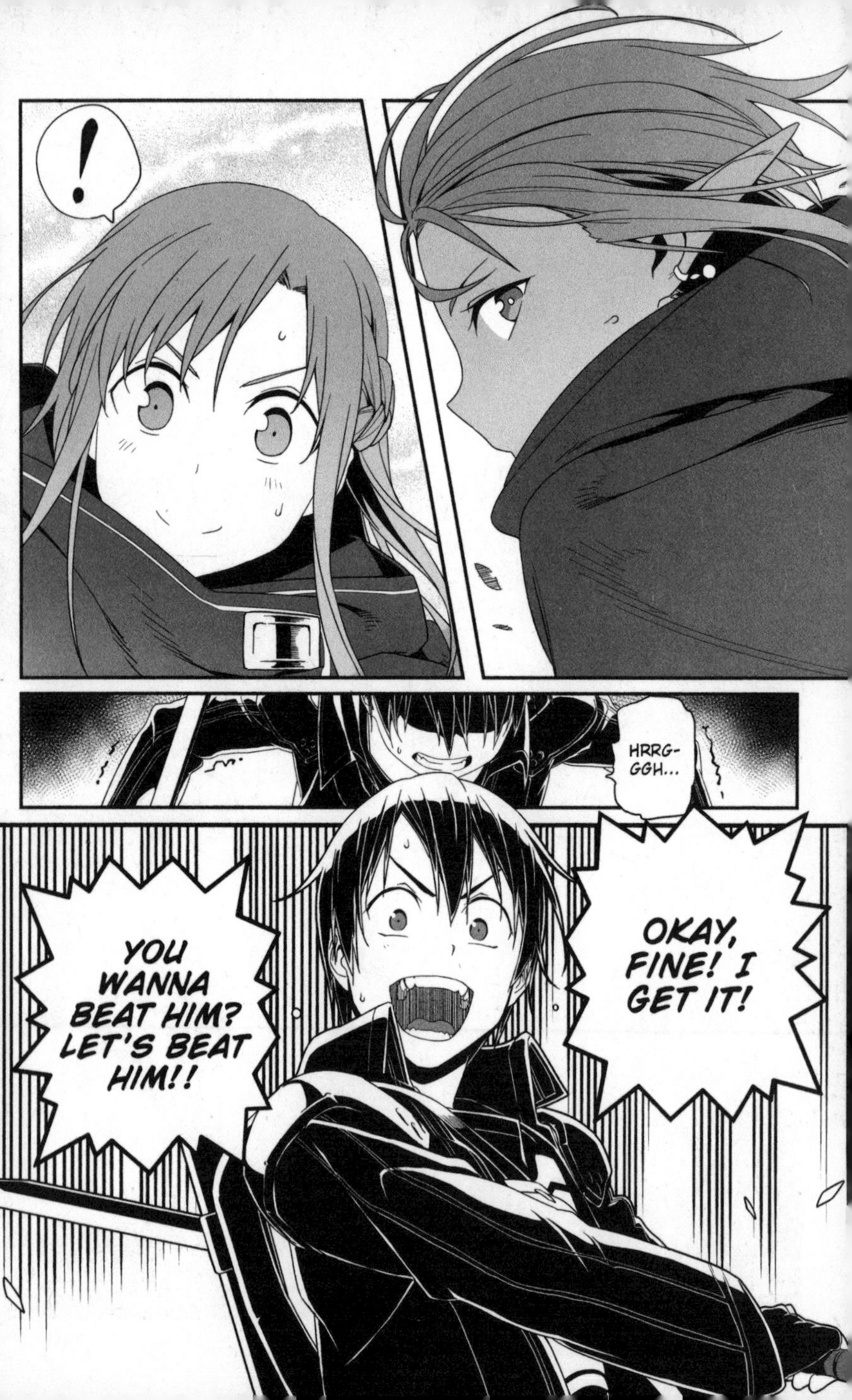
!
HRRG-GGH...
OKAY, FINE! I GET IT!
YOU WANNA BEAT HIM? LET'S BEAT HIM!!

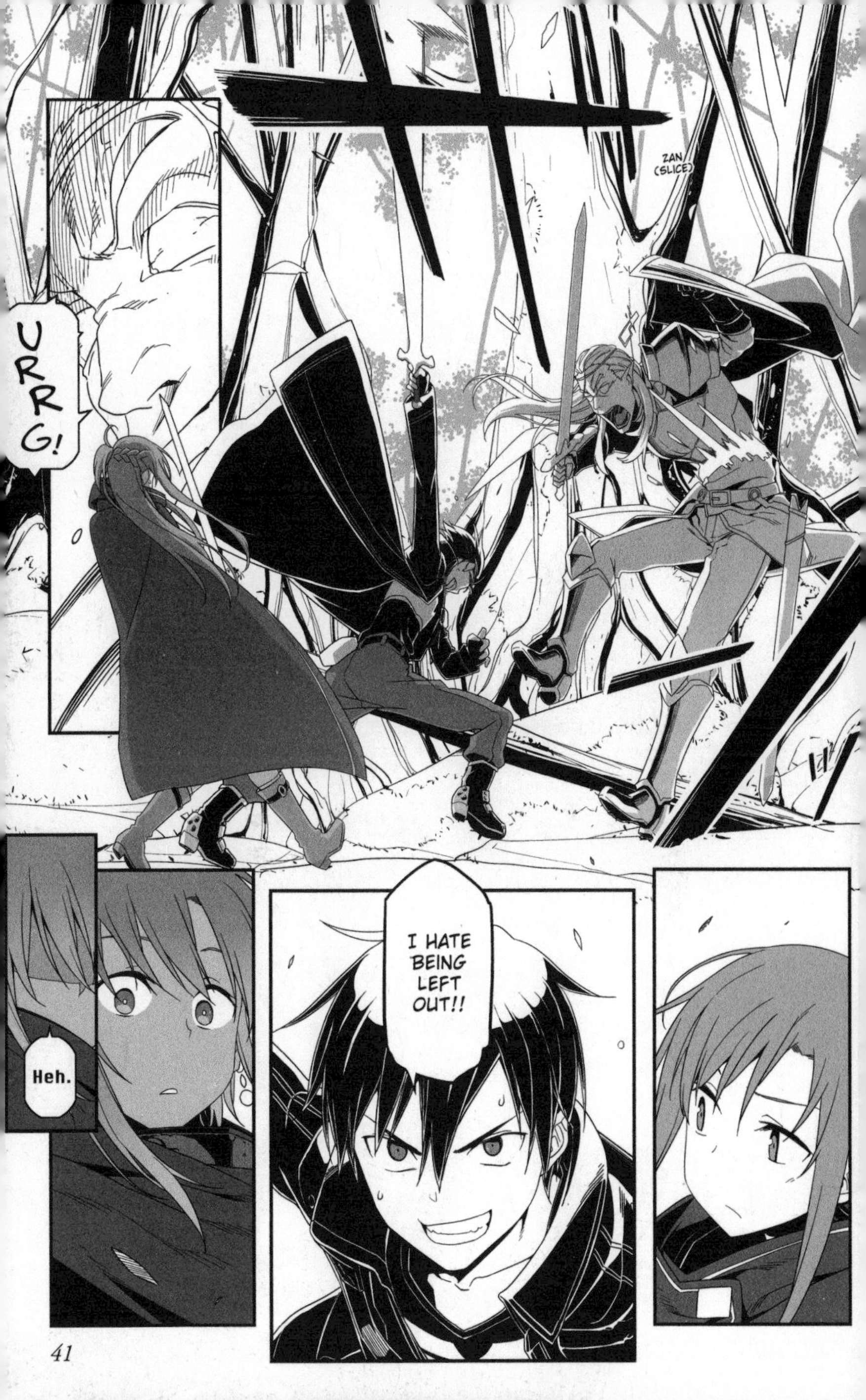
ZAN (SLICE)
URRG!
I HATE BEING LEFT OUT!!
Heh.

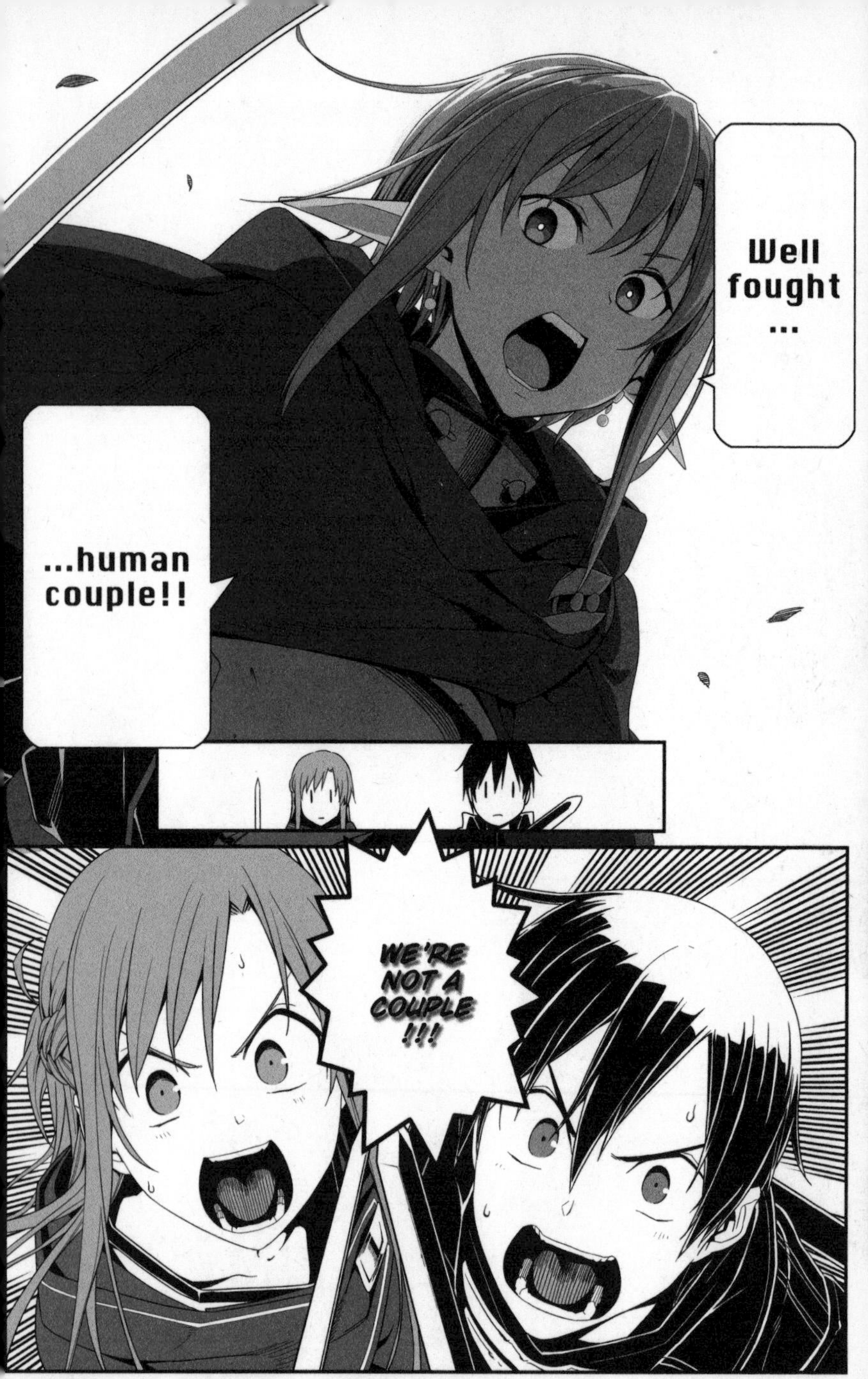
Well fought ...
...human couple!!
WE'RE NOT A COUPLE !!!

#024: Vengeance

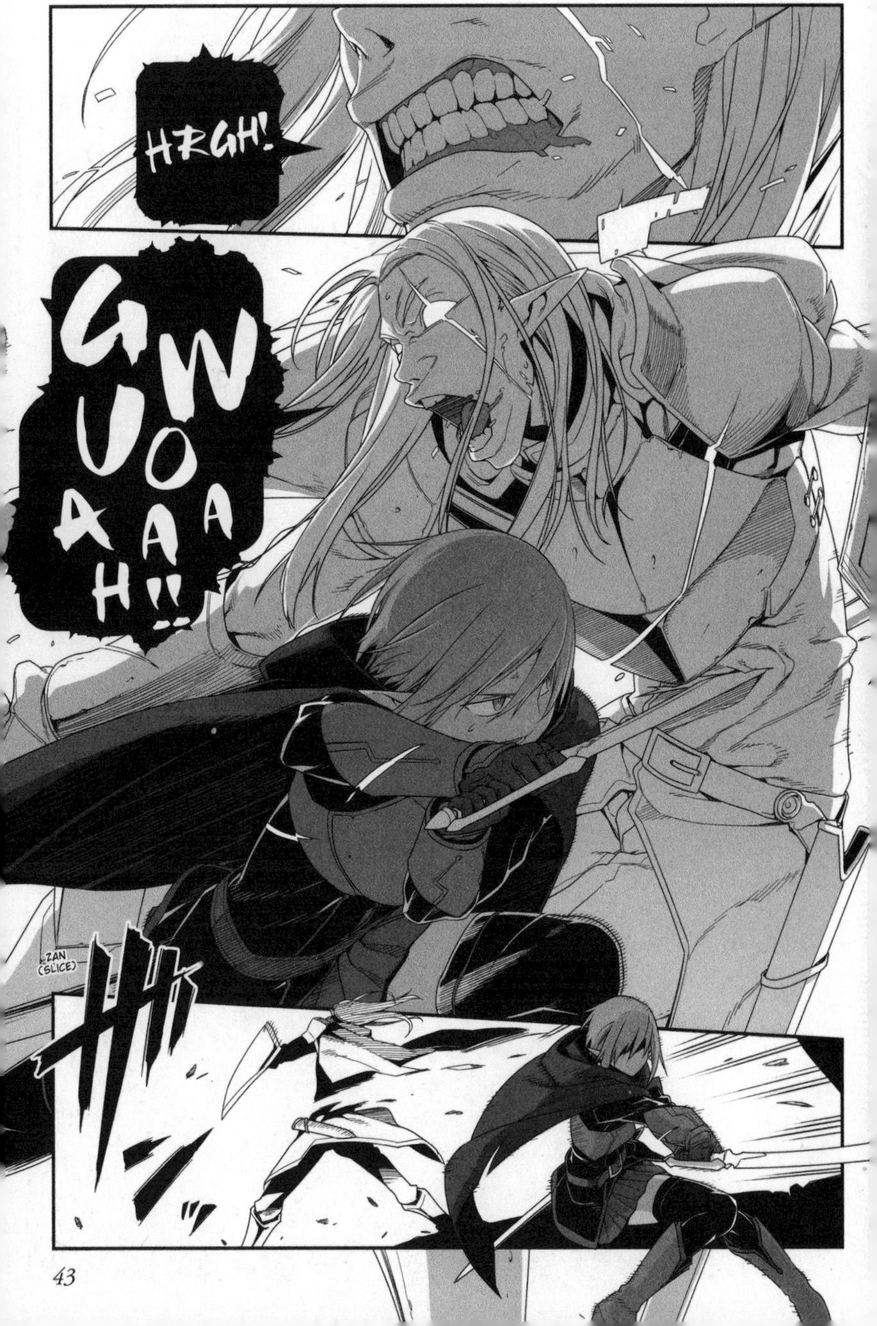
HRGH!
GWUOAAAH!!
ZAN (SLICE)

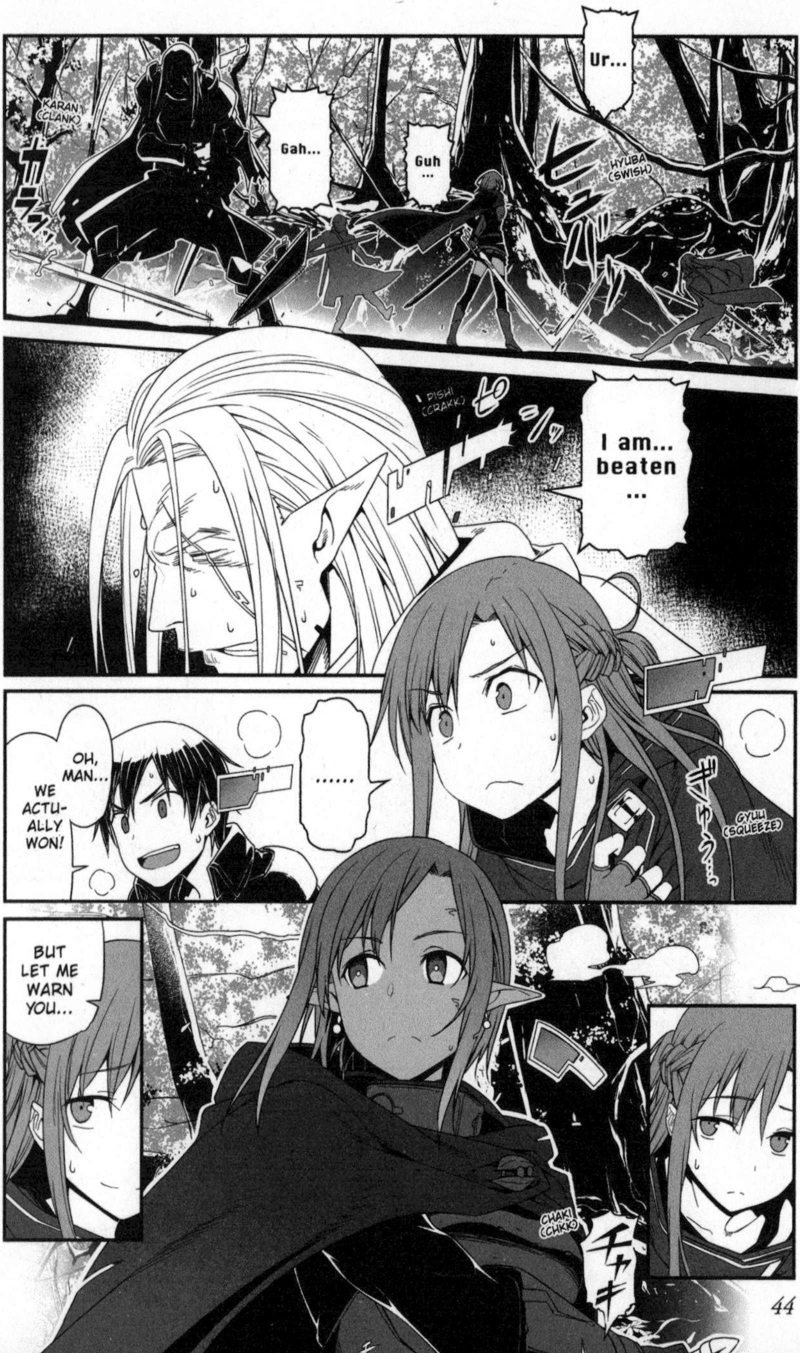
Ur...
HYUBA (SWISH)
Guh...
Gah...
KARAN (CLANK)
I am... beaten...
PISHI (CRAKK)
GYUU (SQUEEZE)
......
OH, MAN... WE ACTU-ALLY WON!
CHAKI (CHKK)
BUT LET ME WARN YOU...

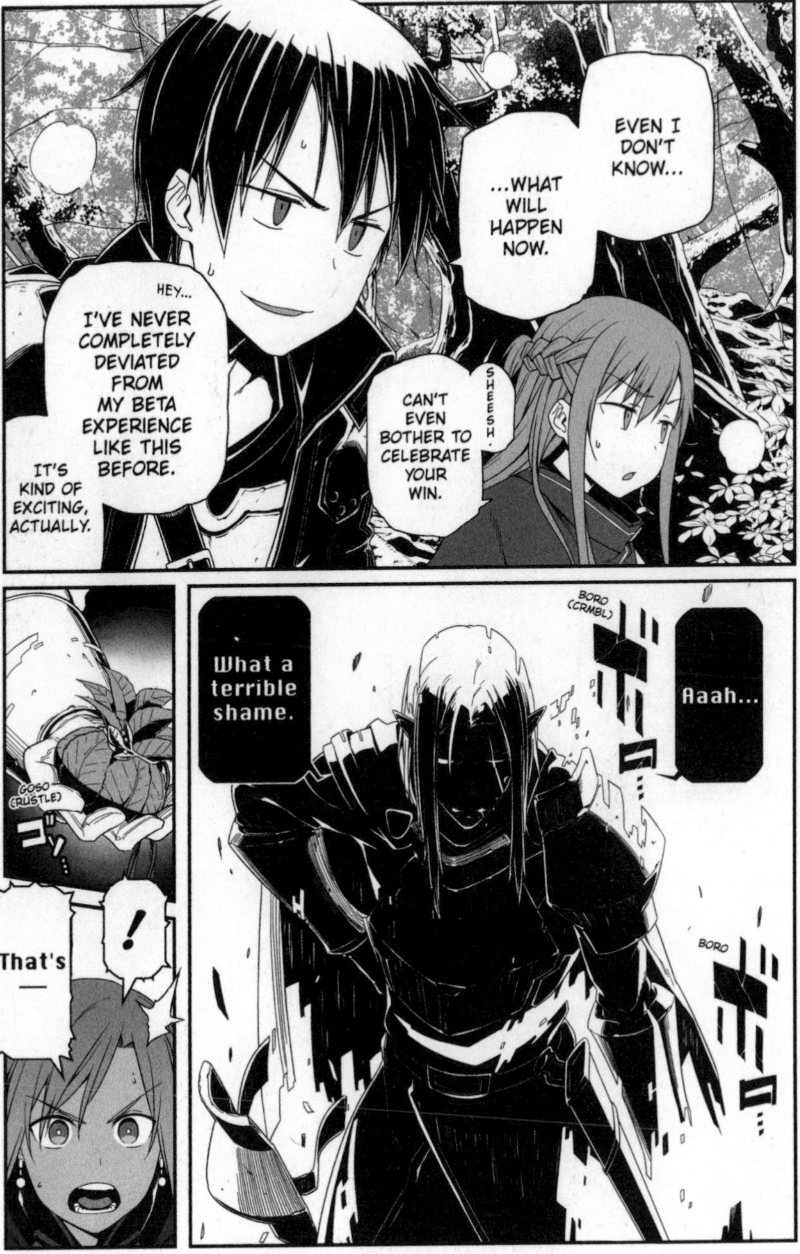
EVEN I DON'T KNOW...
...WHAT WILL HAPPEN NOW.
SHEESH.
CAN'T EVEN BOTHER TO CELEBRATE YOUR WIN.
HEY...
I'VE NEVER COMPLETELY DEVIATED FROM MY BETA EXPERIENCE LIKE THIS BEFORE.
IT'S KIND OF EXCITING, ACTUALLY.
BORO (CRMBL)
Aaah...
What a terrible shame.
BORO
GOSO (RUSTLE)
!
That's —

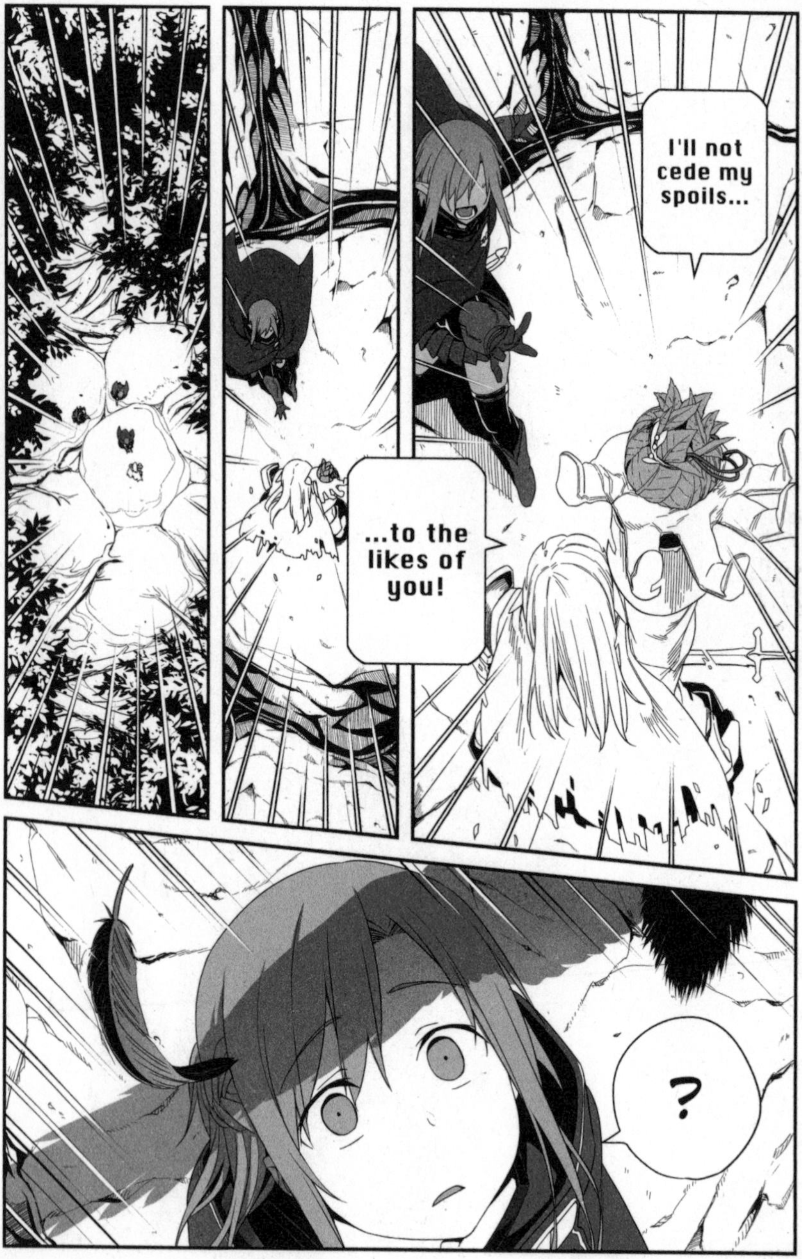
I'll not cede my spoils...
...to the likes of you!
?

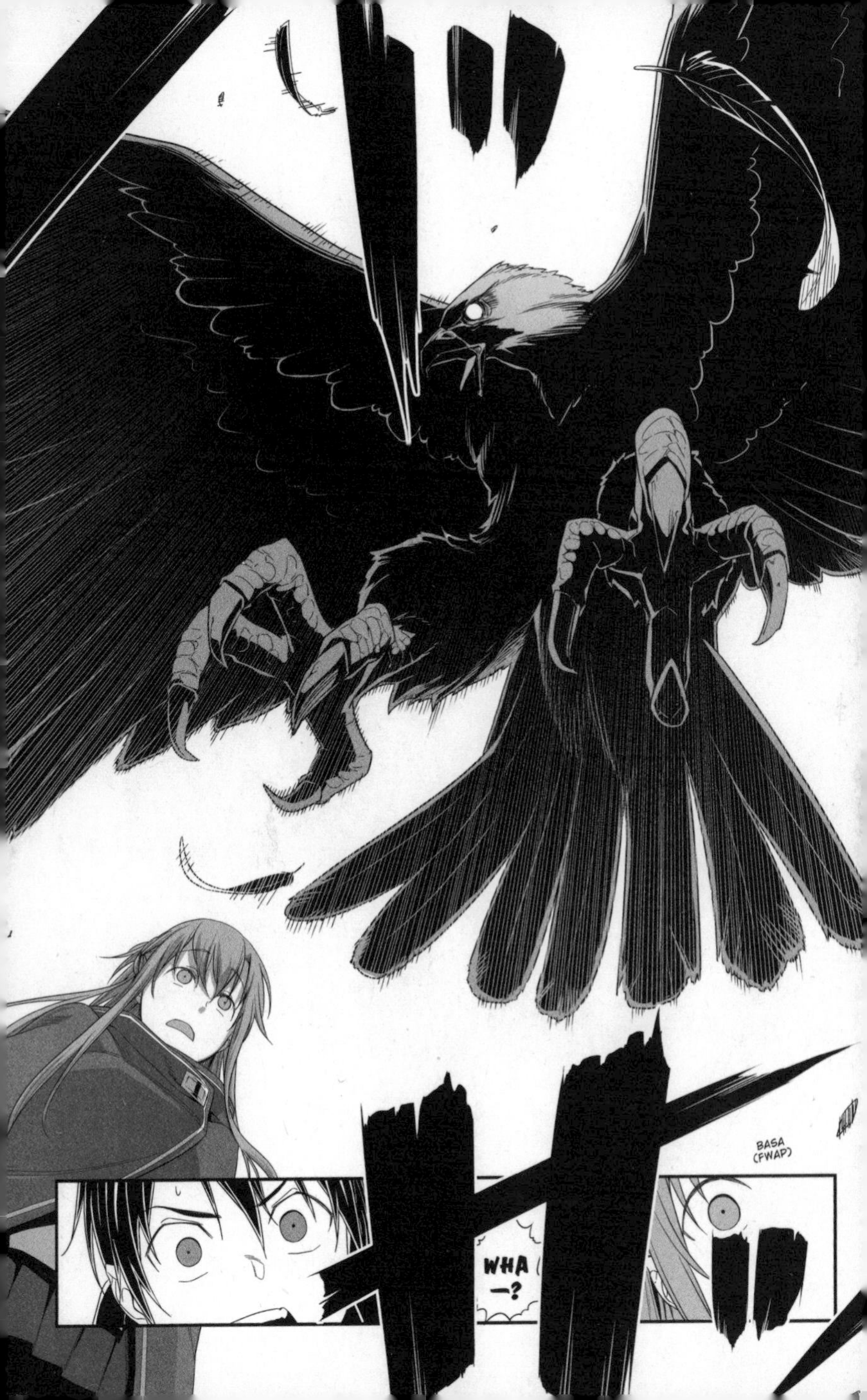
BASA
(FWAP)
WHA
—?

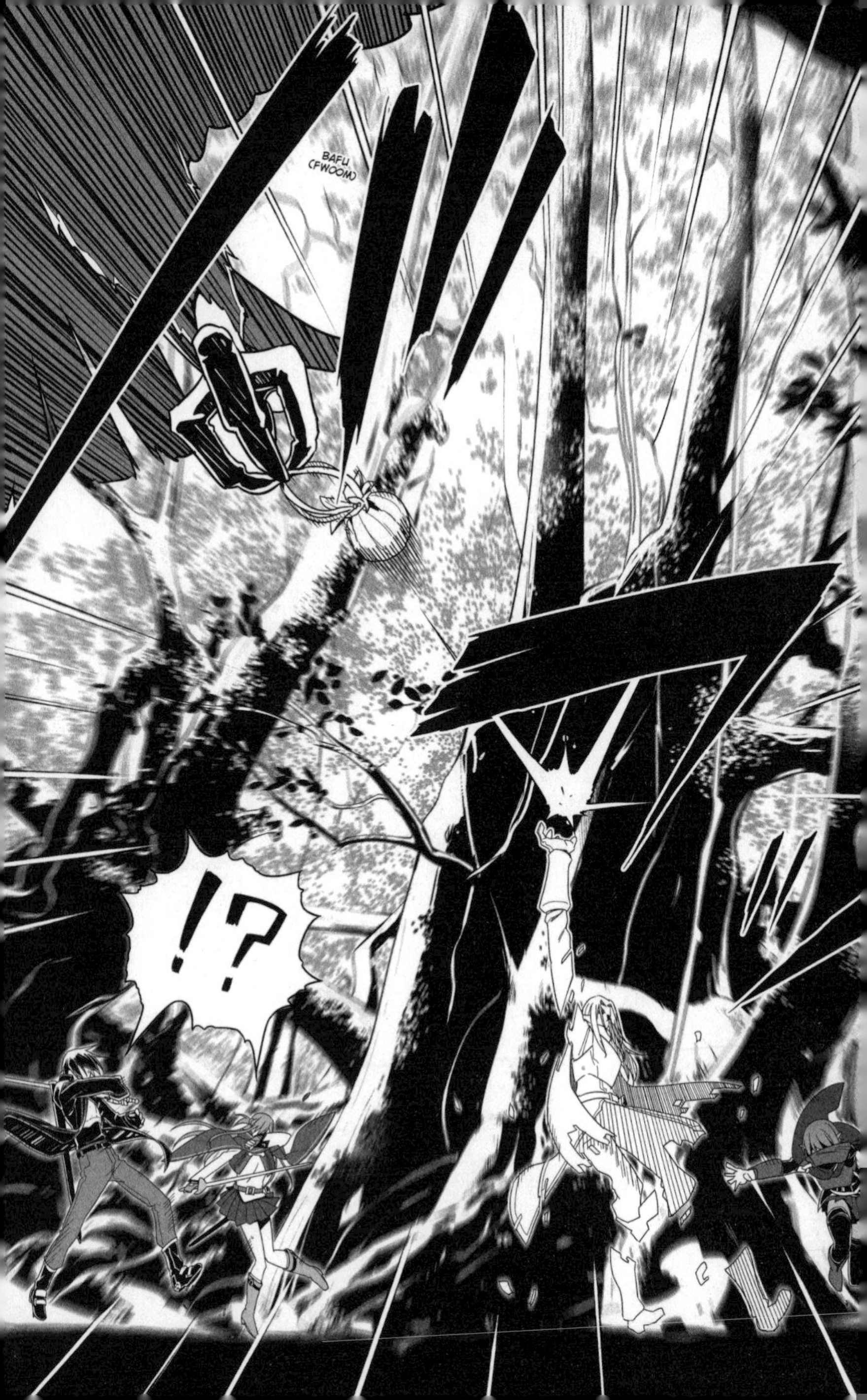
BAFU
(FWOOM)
!?

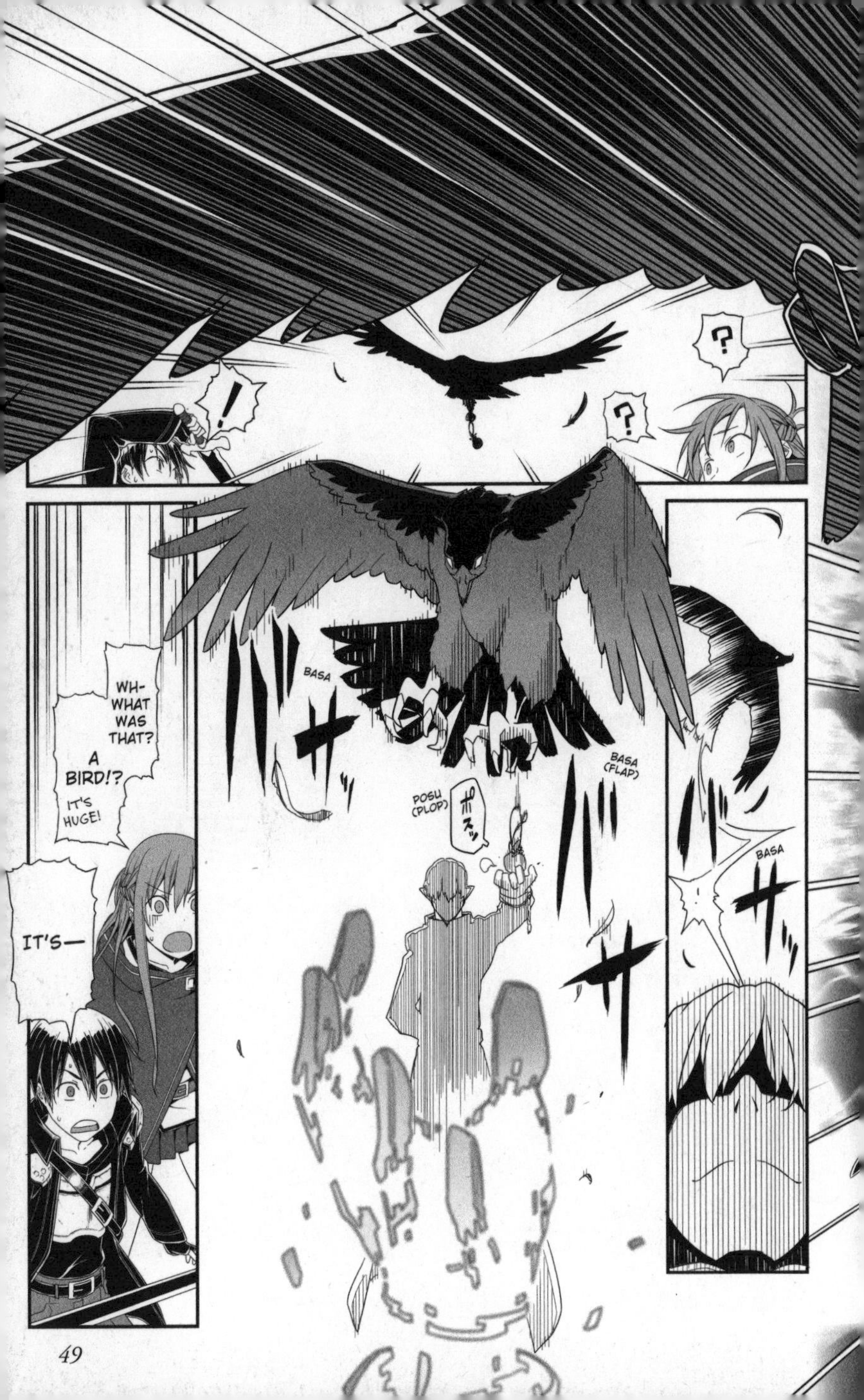
?
?
!
BASA
BASA
BASA (FLAP)
POSU (PLOP)
ポスッ
WH-WHAT WAS THAT?
A BIRD!?
IT'S HUGE!
IT'S—

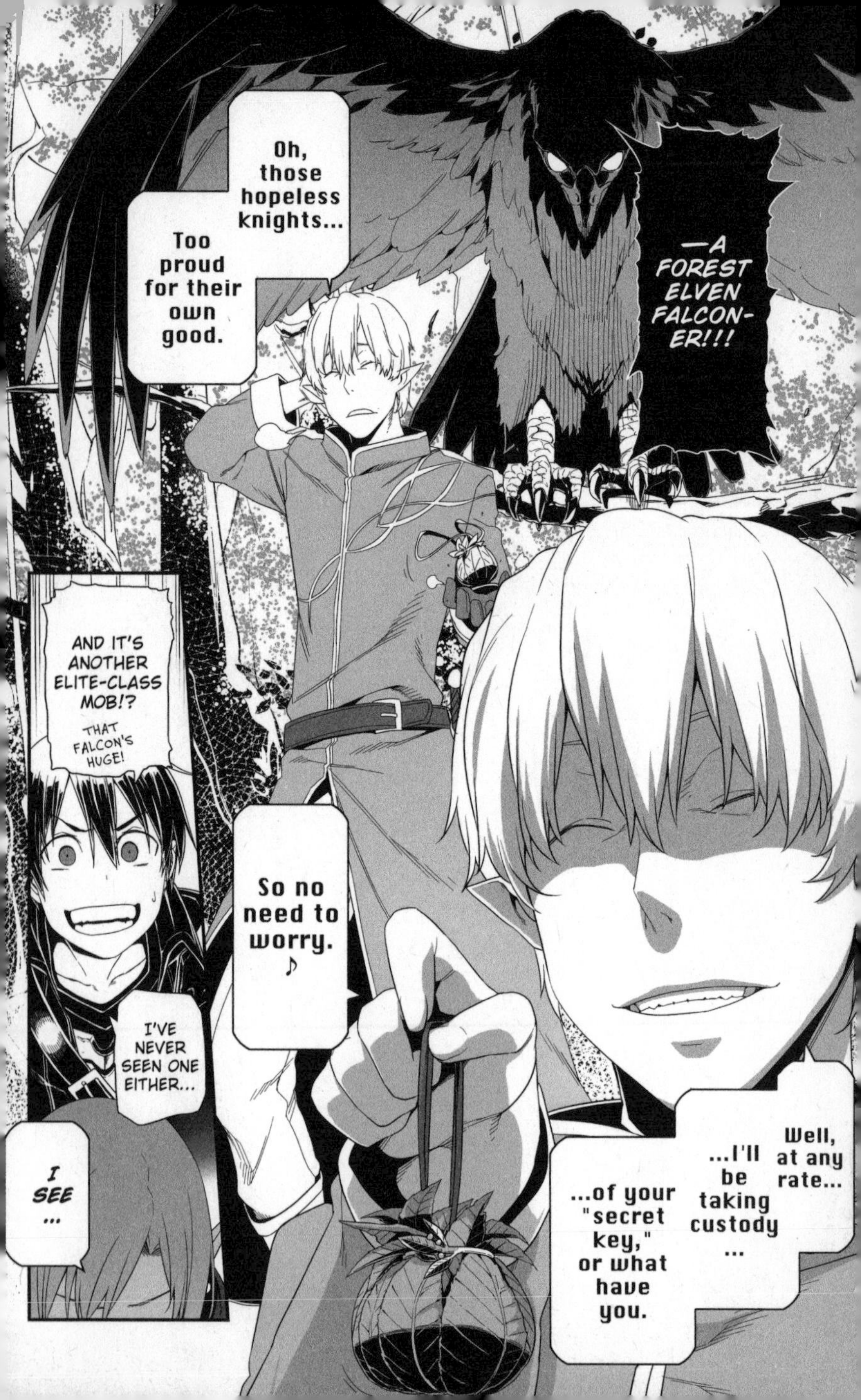
—A FOREST ELVEN FALCON-ER!!!
Oh, those hopeless knights...
Too proud for their own good.
So no need to worry. ♪
Well, at any rate...
...I'll be taking custody...
...of your "secret key," or what have you.
AND IT'S ANOTHER ELITE-CLASS MOB!?
THAT FALCON'S HUGE!
I'VE NEVER SEEN ONE EITHER...
I SEE...

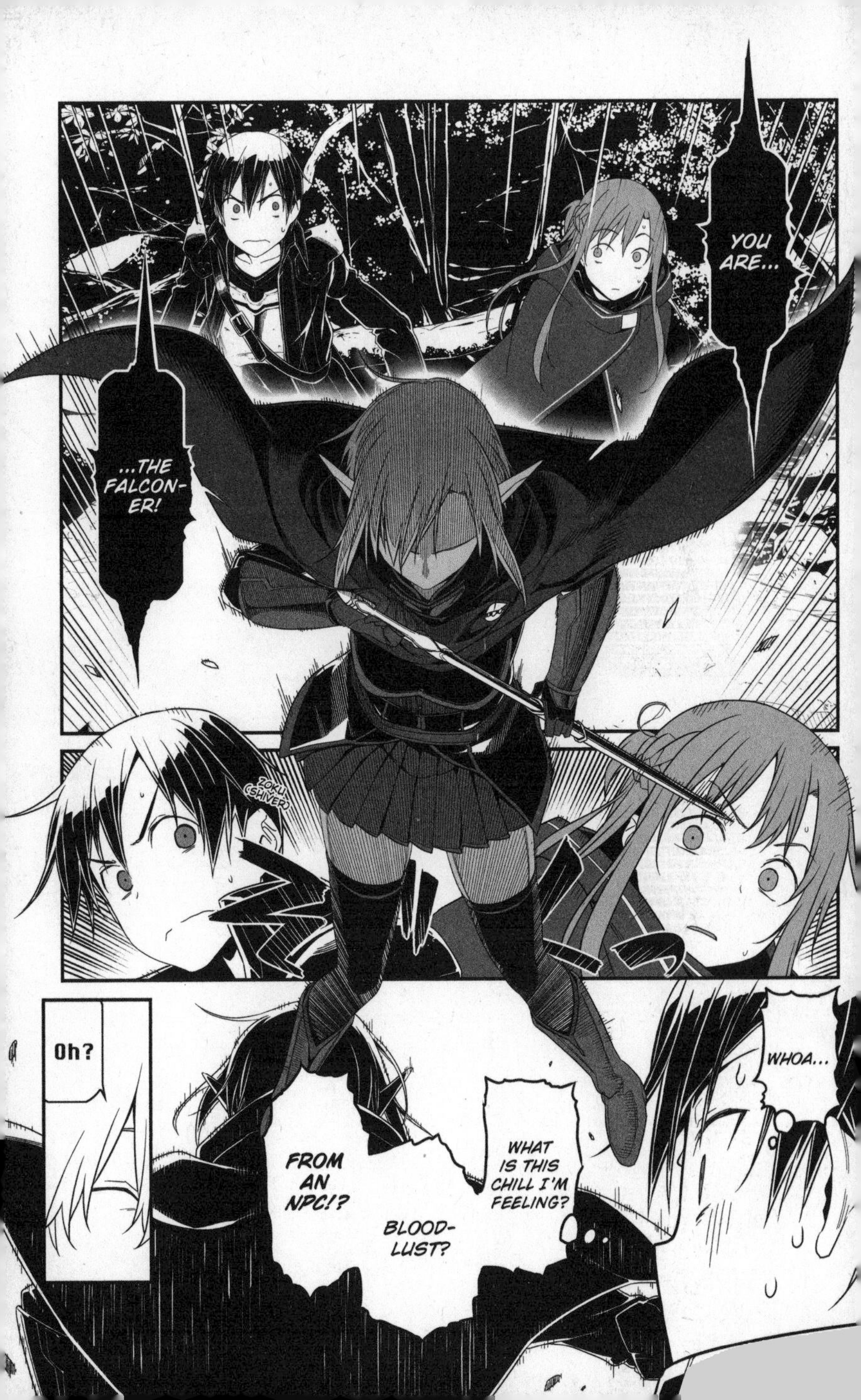
YOU ARE...
...THE FALCON-ER!
ZOKU (SHIVER)
WHOA...
WHAT IS THIS CHILL I'M FEELING?
FROM AN NPC!?
BLOOD-LUST?
Oh?

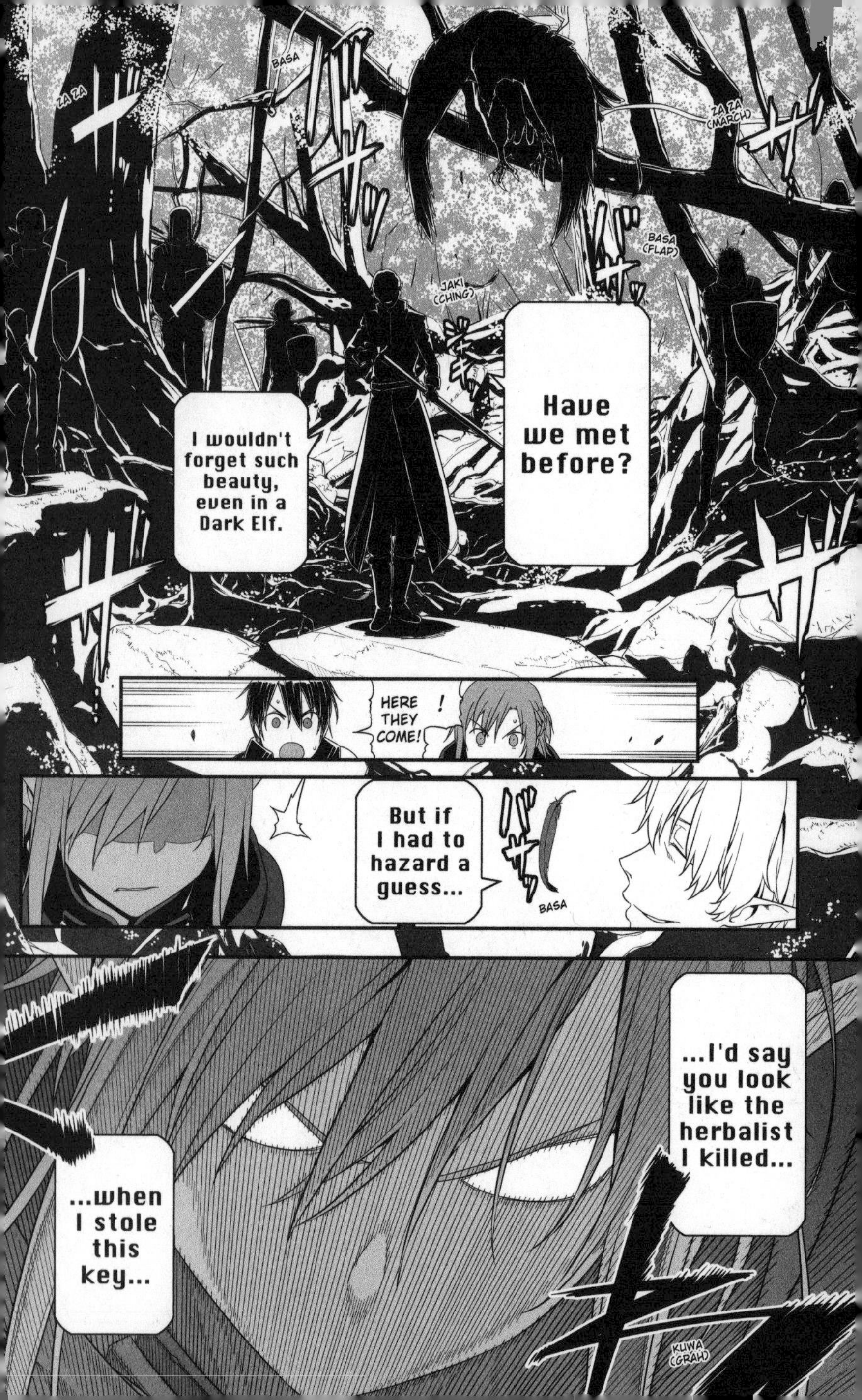
ZA ZA (MARCH)
BASA (FLAP)
BASA
ZA ZA
JAKI (CHING)
Have we met before?
I wouldn't forget such beauty, even in a Dark Elf.
HERE THEY COME!
BASA
But if I had to hazard a guess...
...I'd say you look like the herbalist I killed...
...when I stole this key...
KUWA (GRAH)

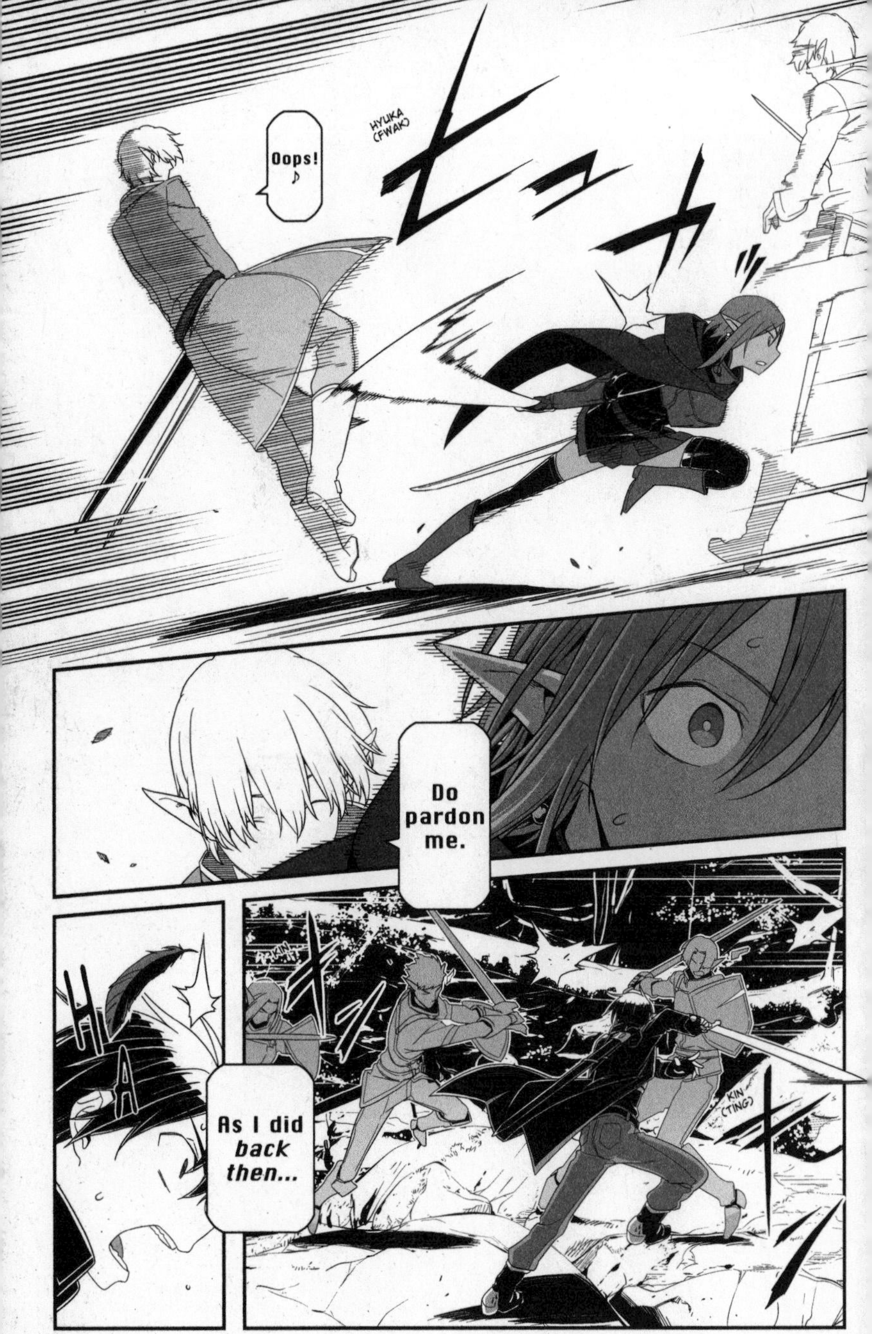
HYUKA (FWAK)
Oops! ♪
Do pardon me.
KIN (TING)
As I did back then...

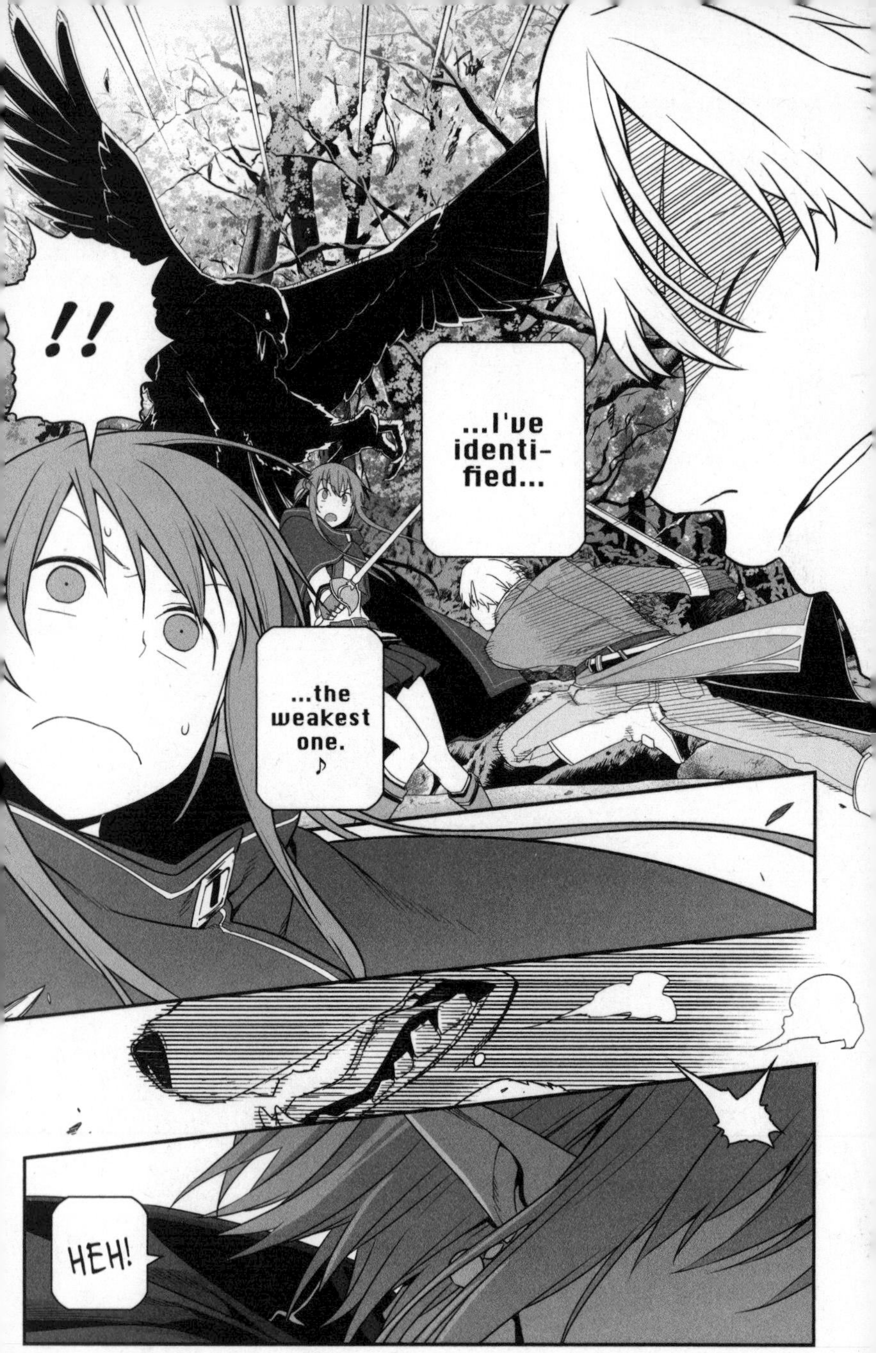
...I've identified...
...the weakest one. ♪
!!
HEH!

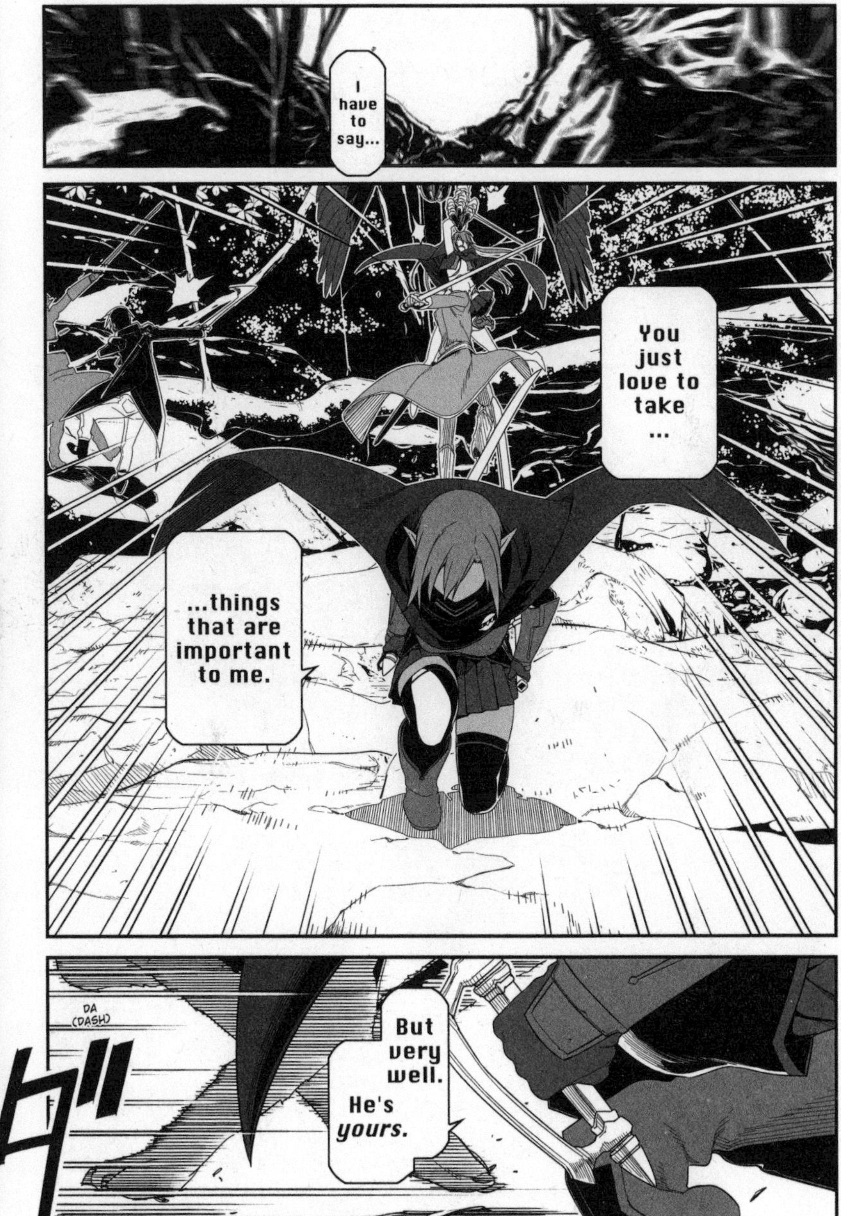
I have to say...
You just love to take ...
...things that are important to me.
But very well. He's *yours.*
DA (DASH)

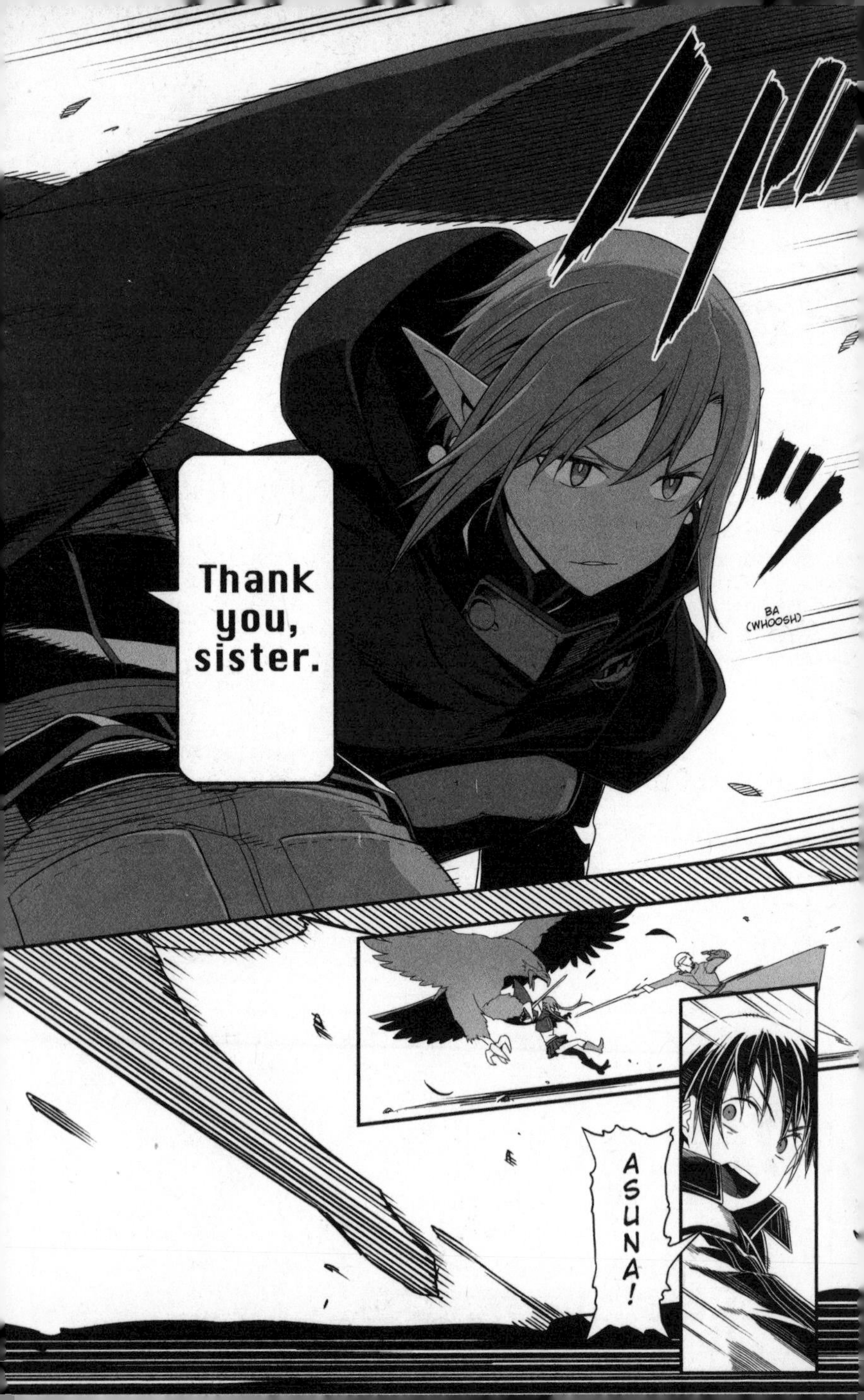

BA (WHOOSH)
Thank you, sister.
ASUNA!

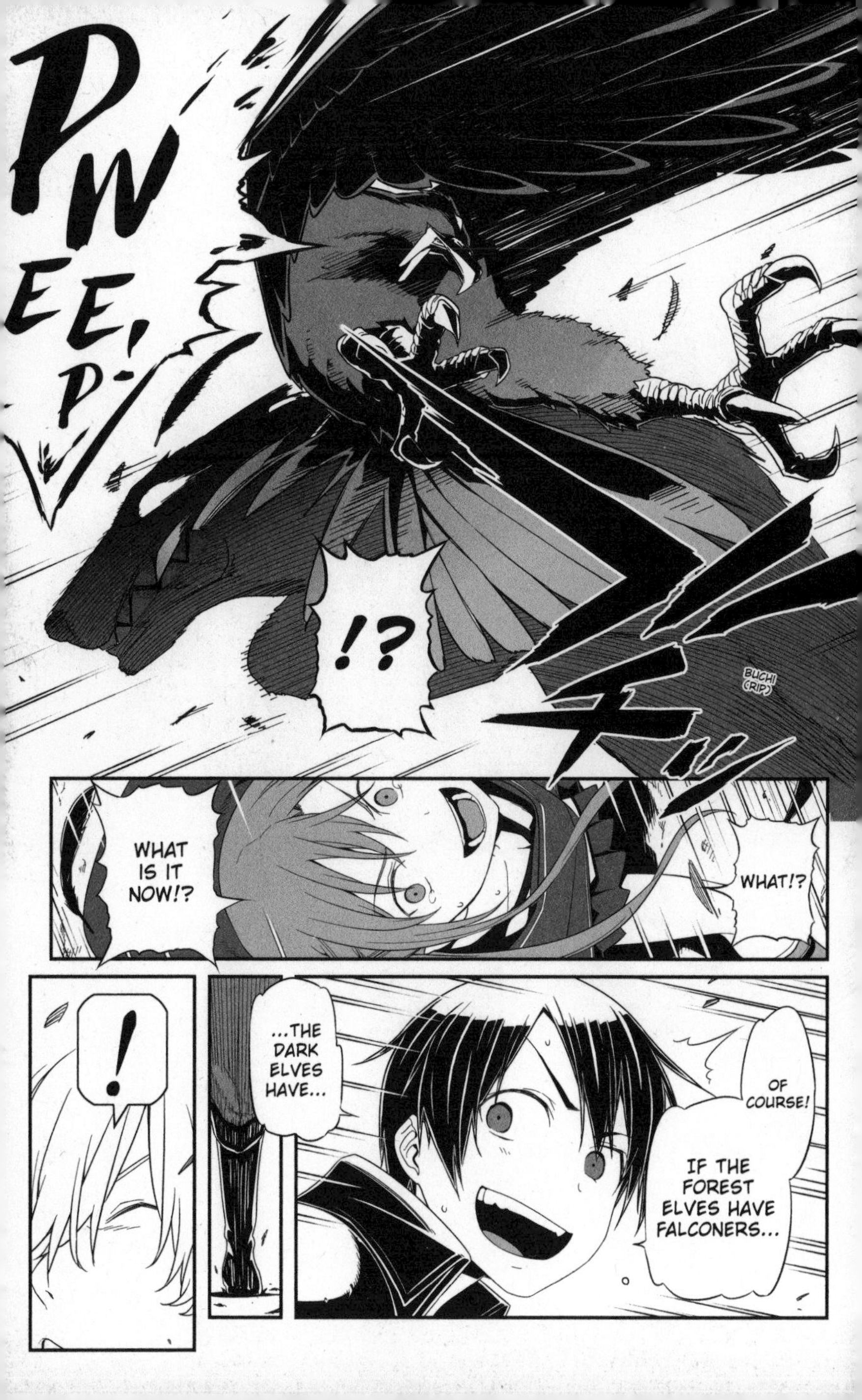
PWEEEP!
BUCHI (RIP)
!?
WHAT!?
WHAT IS IT NOW!?
OF COURSE!
IF THE FOREST ELVES HAVE FALCONERS...
...THE DARK ELVES HAVE...
!

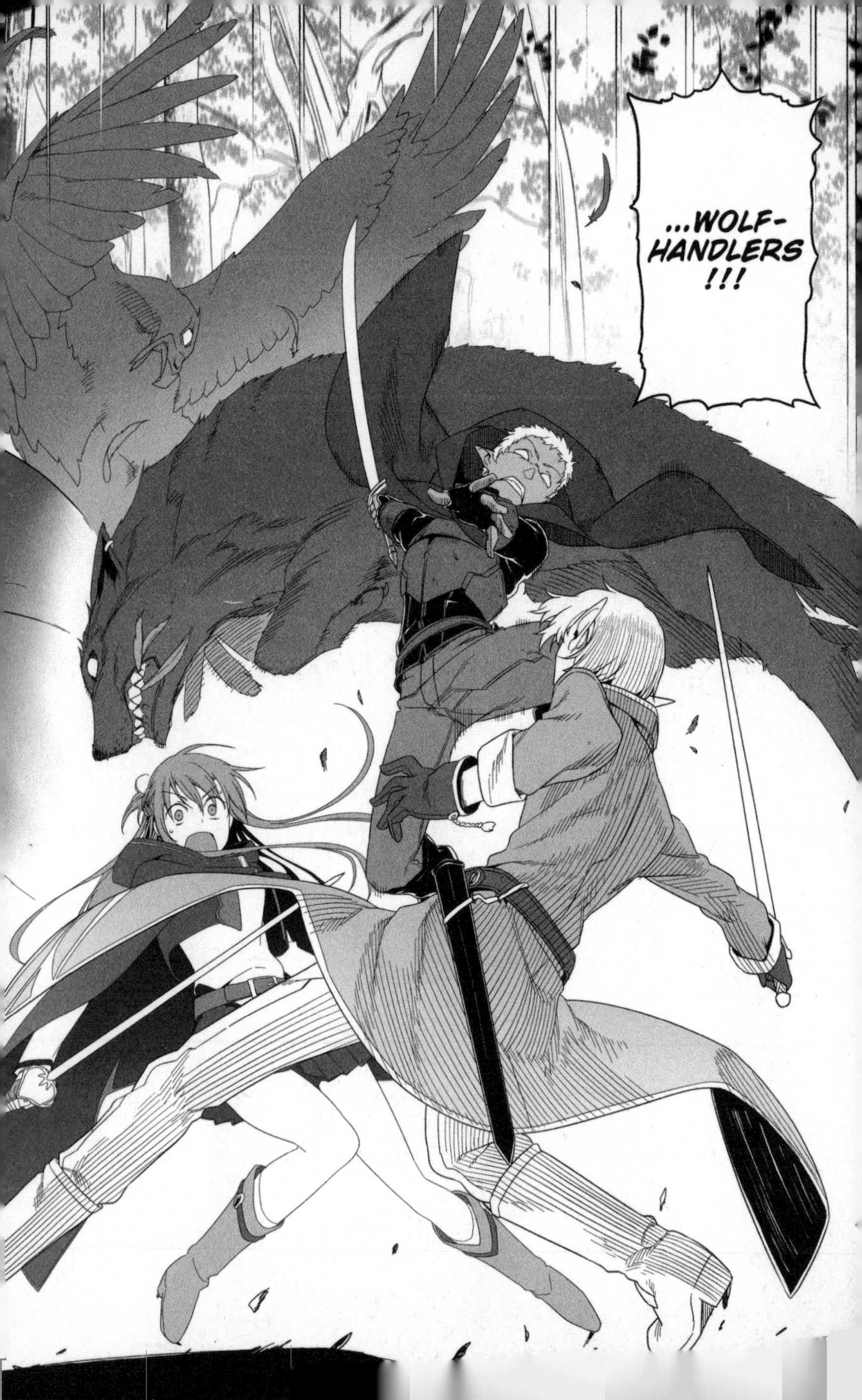
...WOLF-HANDLERS !!!

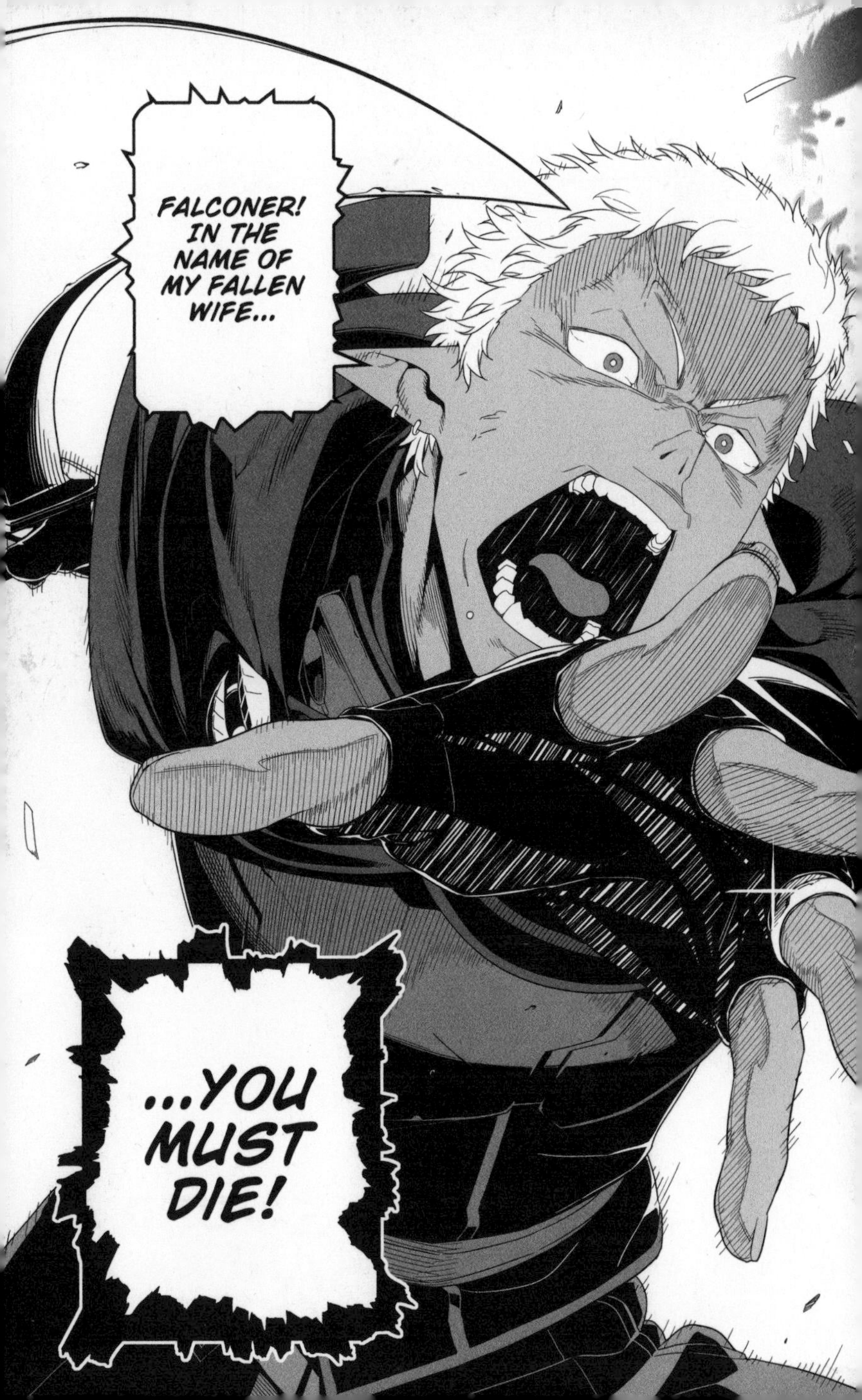
FALCONER! IN THE NAME OF MY FALLEN WIFE...
...YOU MUST DIE!

SWORD
ART
ONLINE
PROGRESSIVE

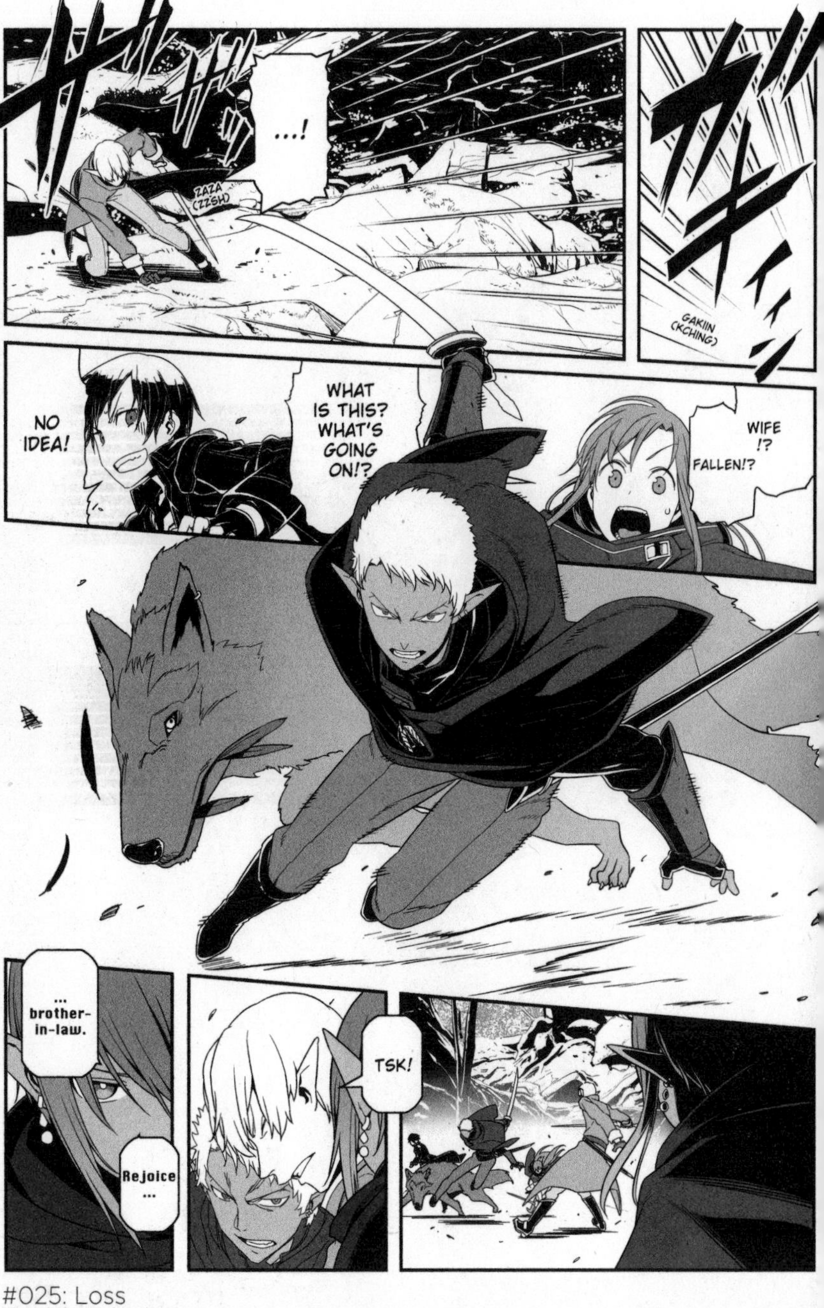
GAKIIN (KCHING)
...!
ZAZA (ZZSH)
WIFE !?
FALLEN!?
WHAT IS THIS? WHAT'S GOING ON!?
NO IDEA!
TSK!
... brother-in-law.
Rejoice ...

#025: Loss

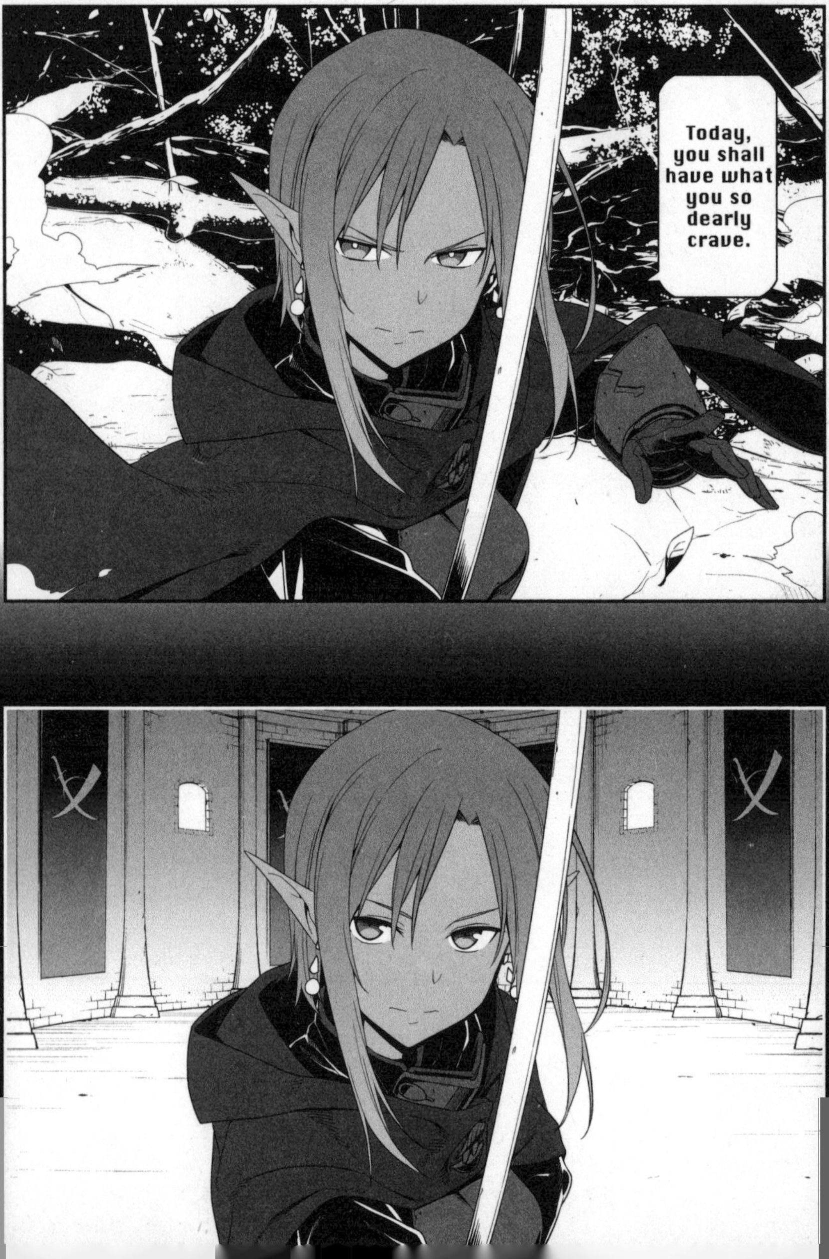
Today, you shall have what you so dearly crave.

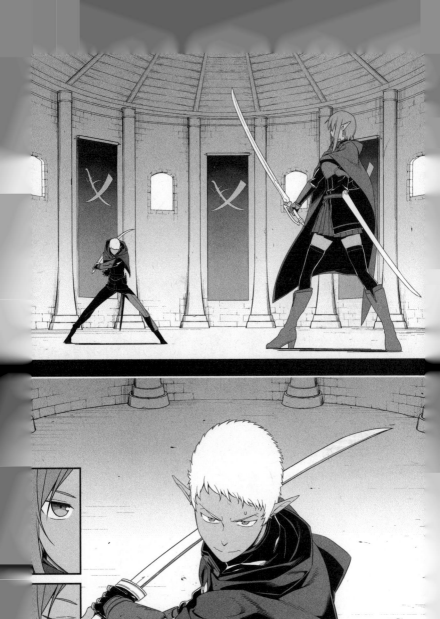

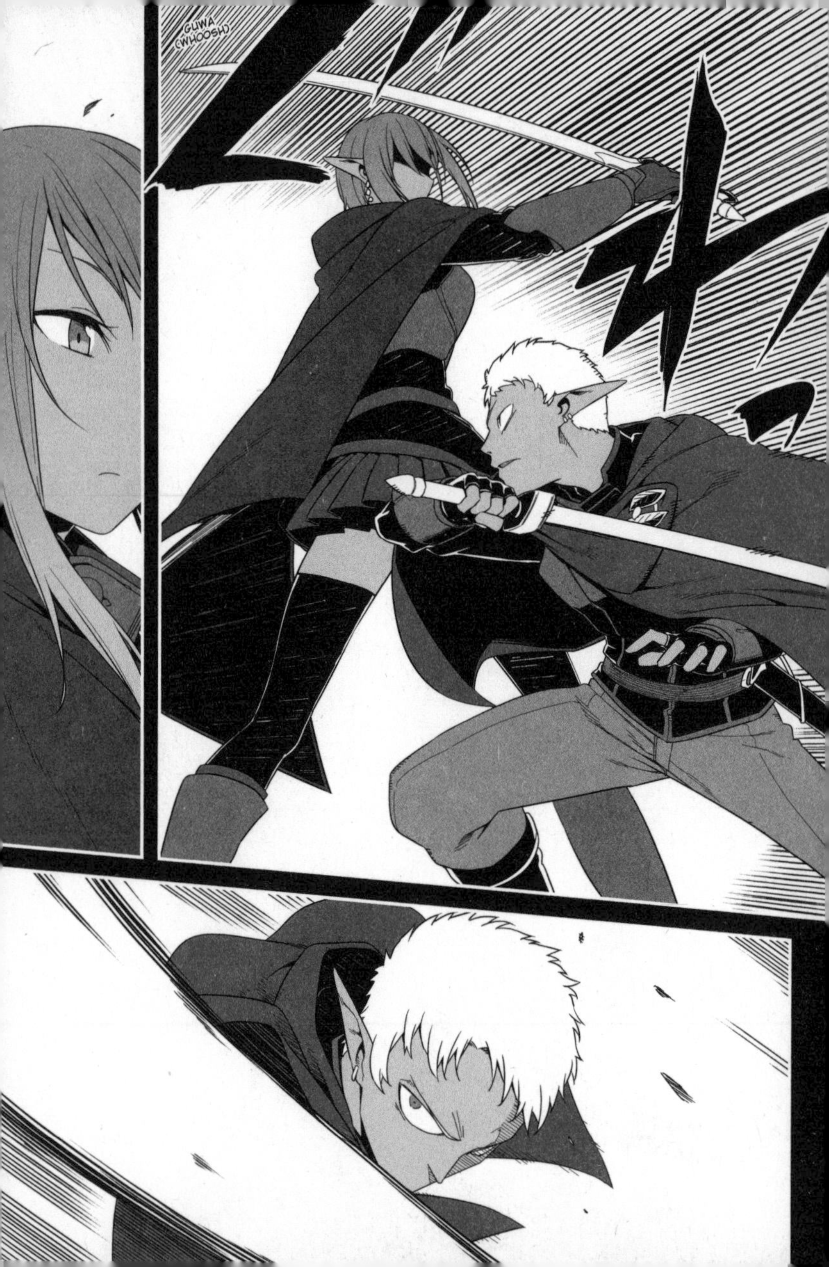
GUWA
(WHOOSH)

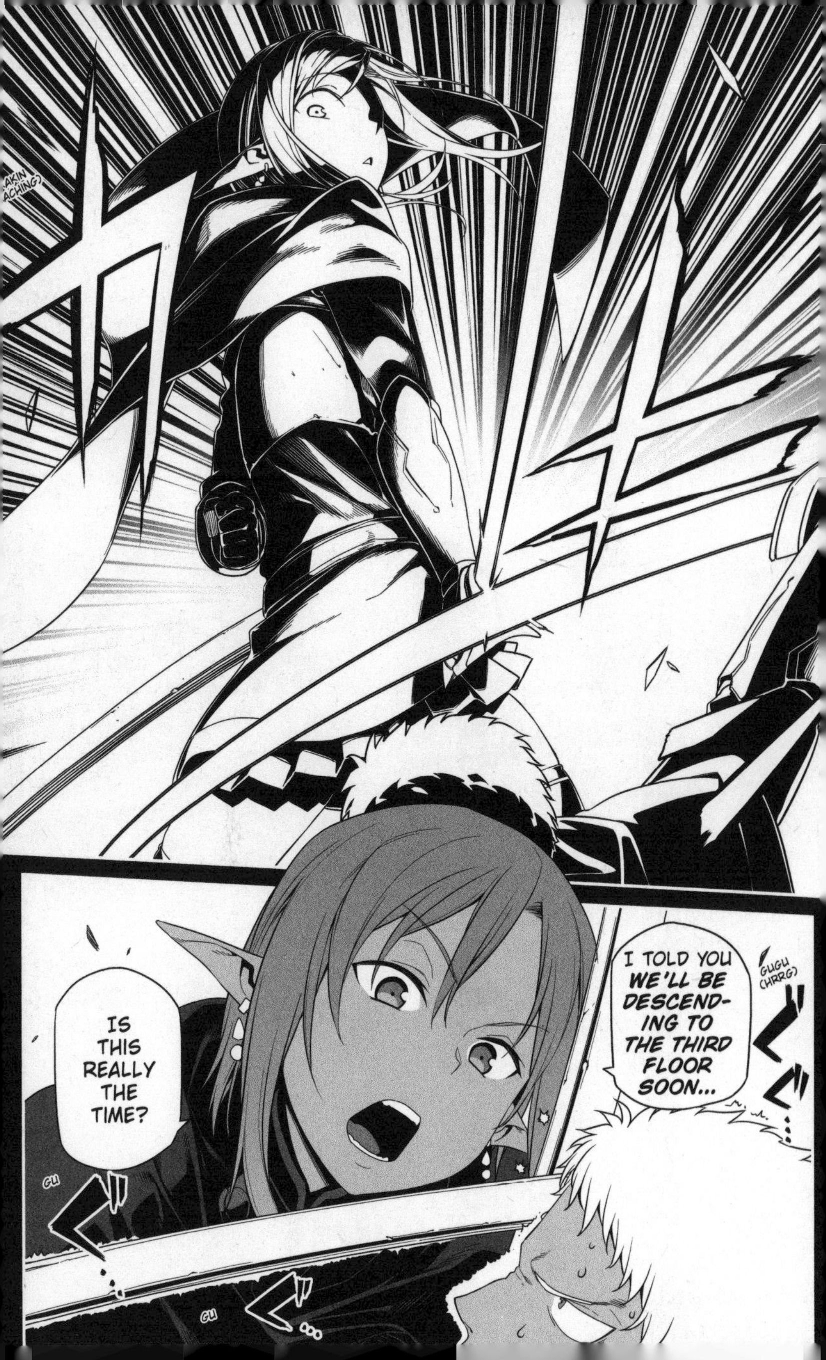
I TOLD YOU WE'LL BE DESCENDING TO THE THIRD FLOOR SOON...
GUGU (HRRG)
IS THIS REALLY THE TIME?
GU
GU

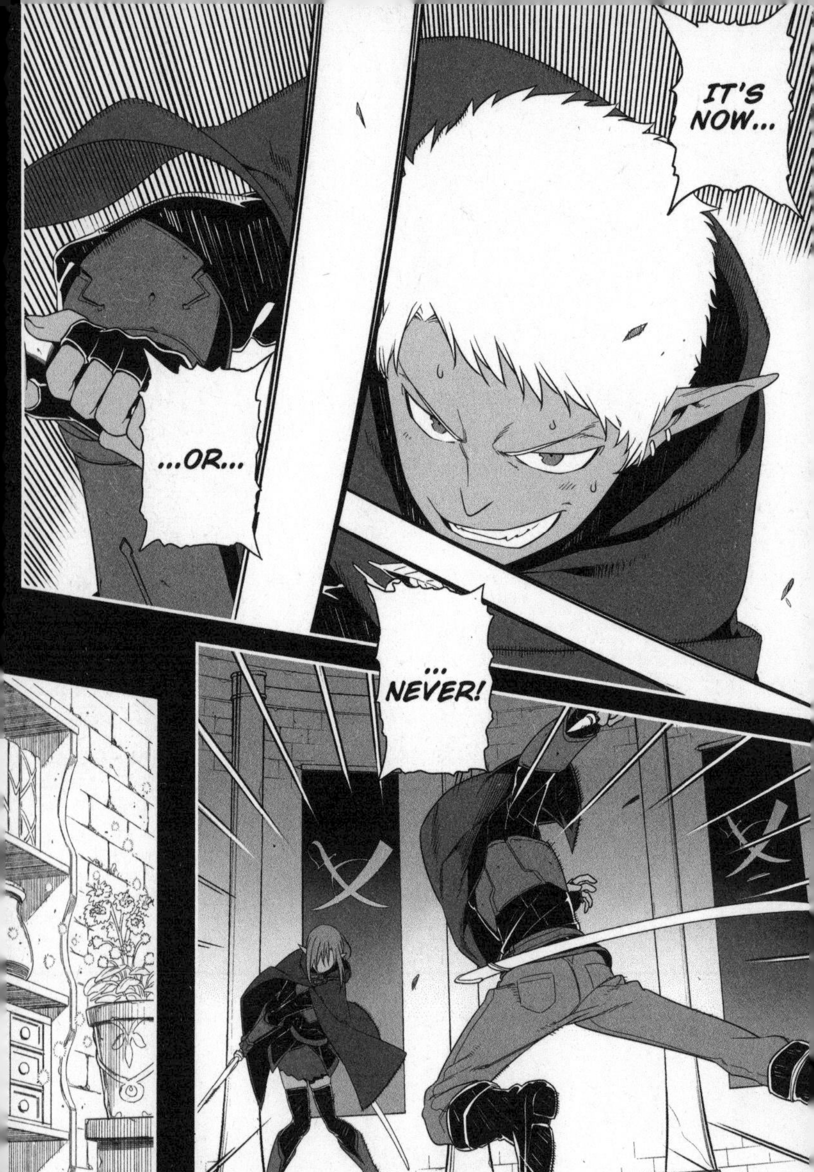
IT'S NOW...
...OR...
... NEVER!

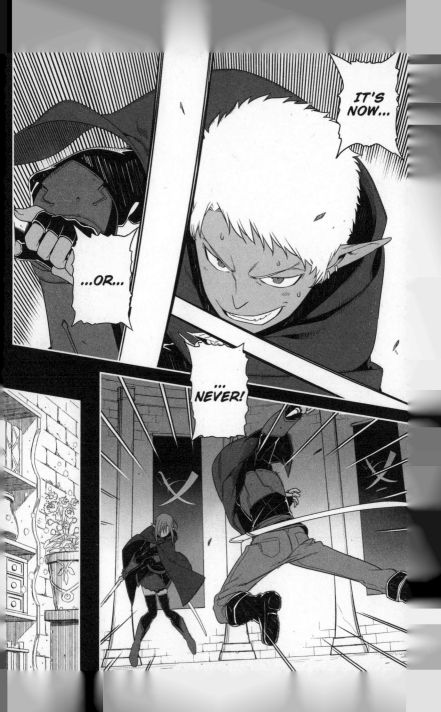

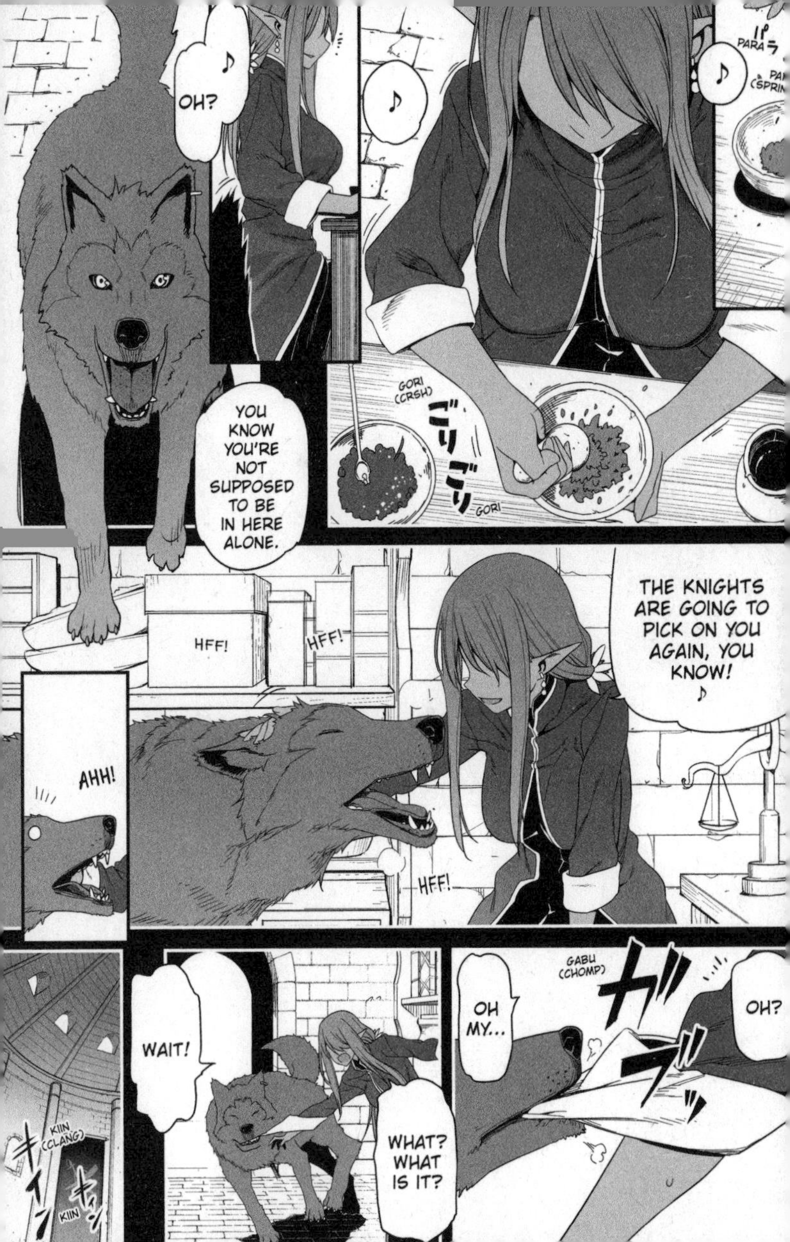

PARA
♪
♪
GORI (CRSH)
GORI
♪
OH?
YOU KNOW YOU'RE NOT SUPPOSED TO BE IN HERE ALONE.
THE KNIGHTS ARE GOING TO PICK ON YOU AGAIN, YOU KNOW! ♪
HFF!
HFF!
HFF!
AHH!
OH?
GABU (CHOMP)
OH MY...
WAIT!
WHAT? WHAT IS IT?
KIIN (CLANG)
KIIN

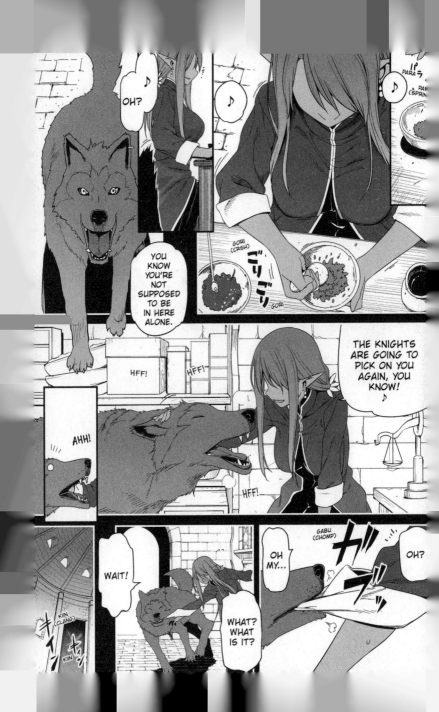

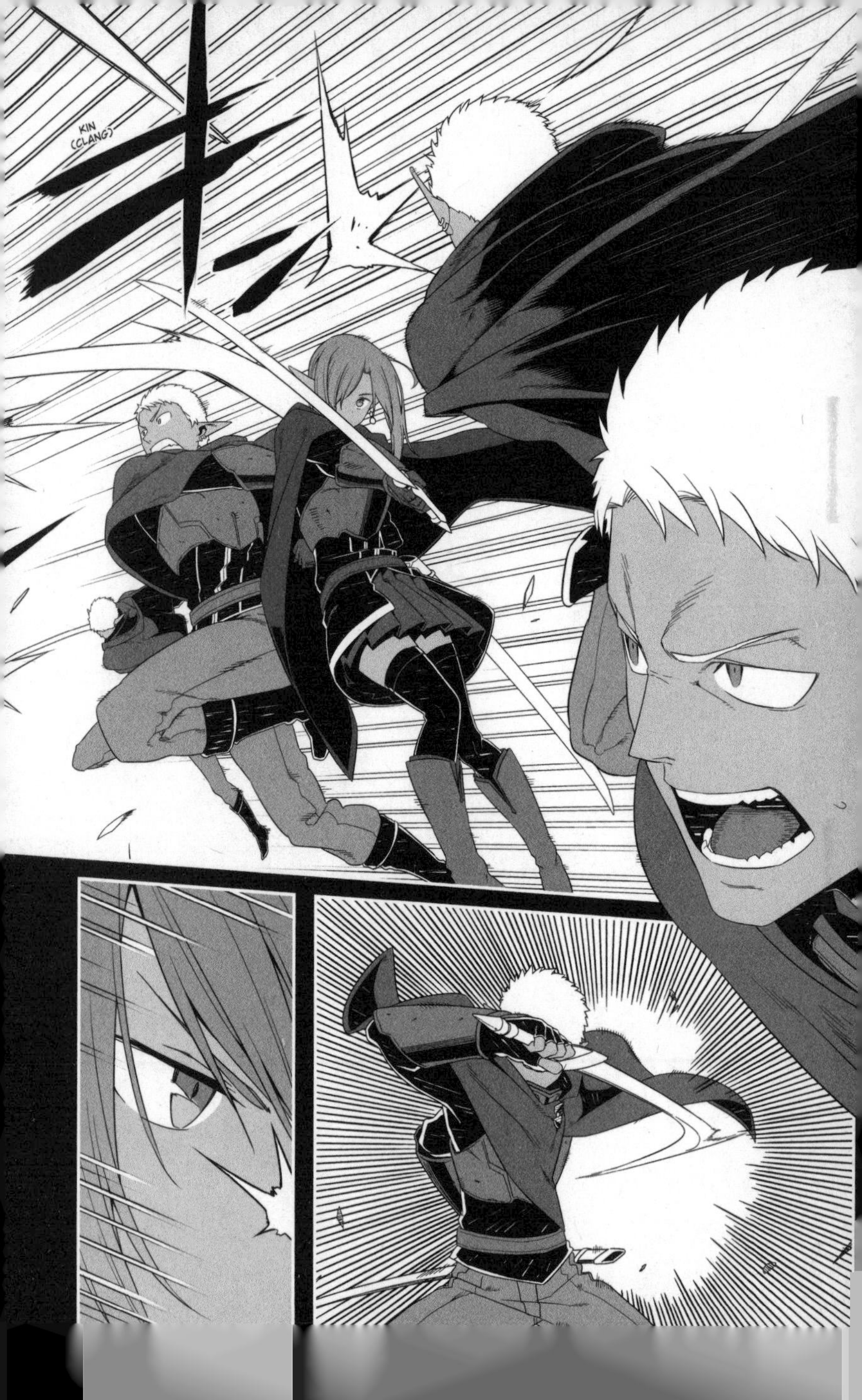
KIN
(CLANG)

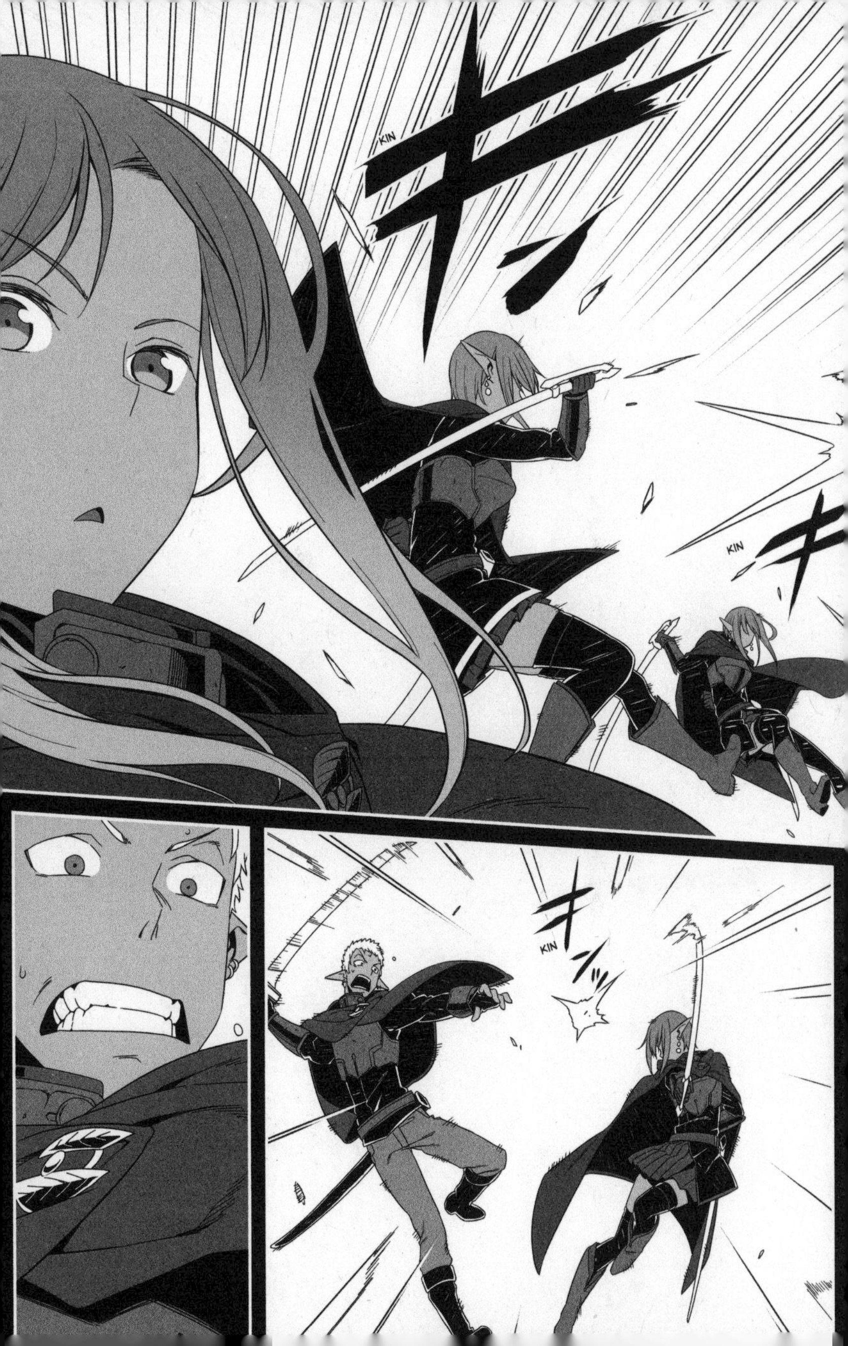
KIN
KIN
KIN

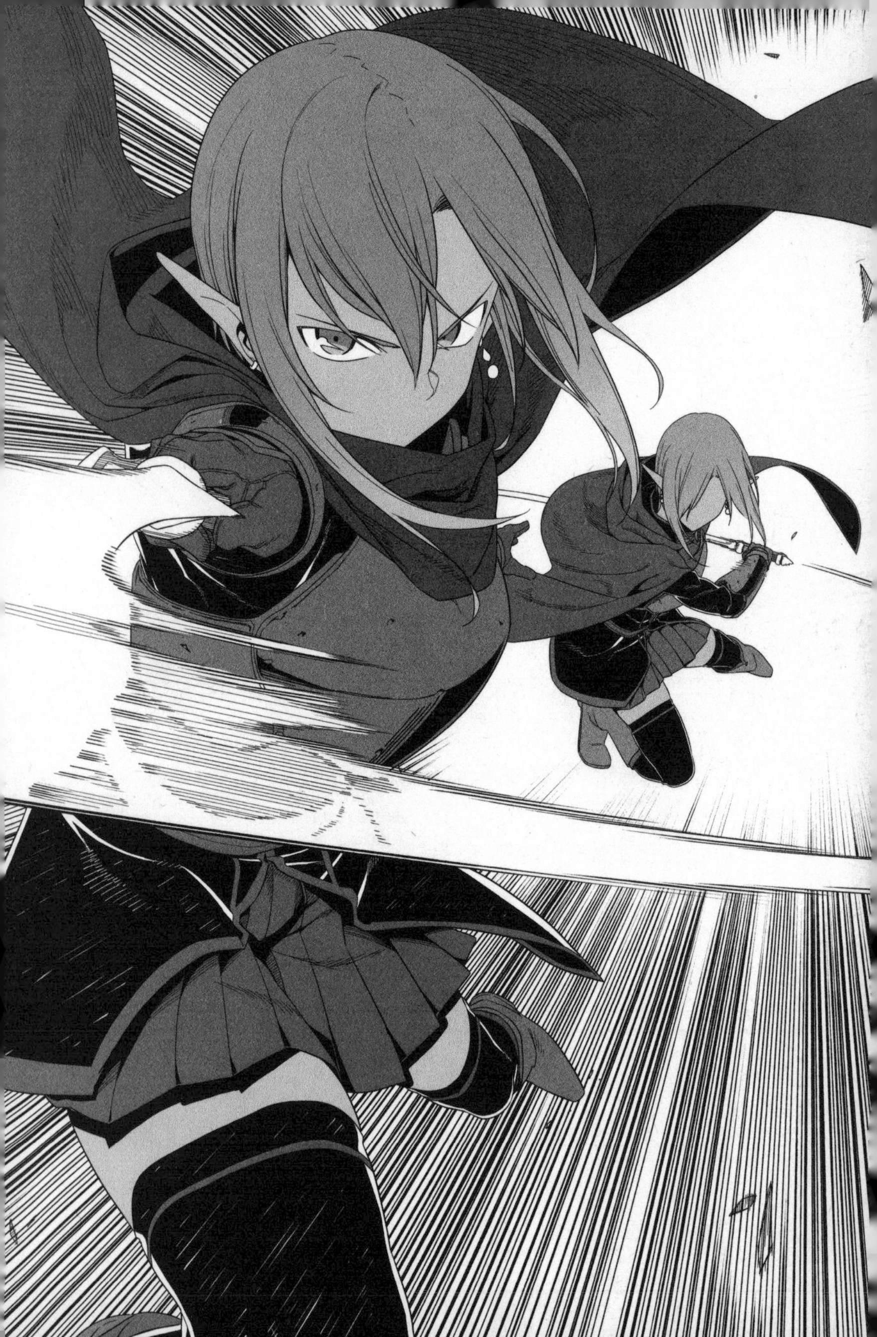

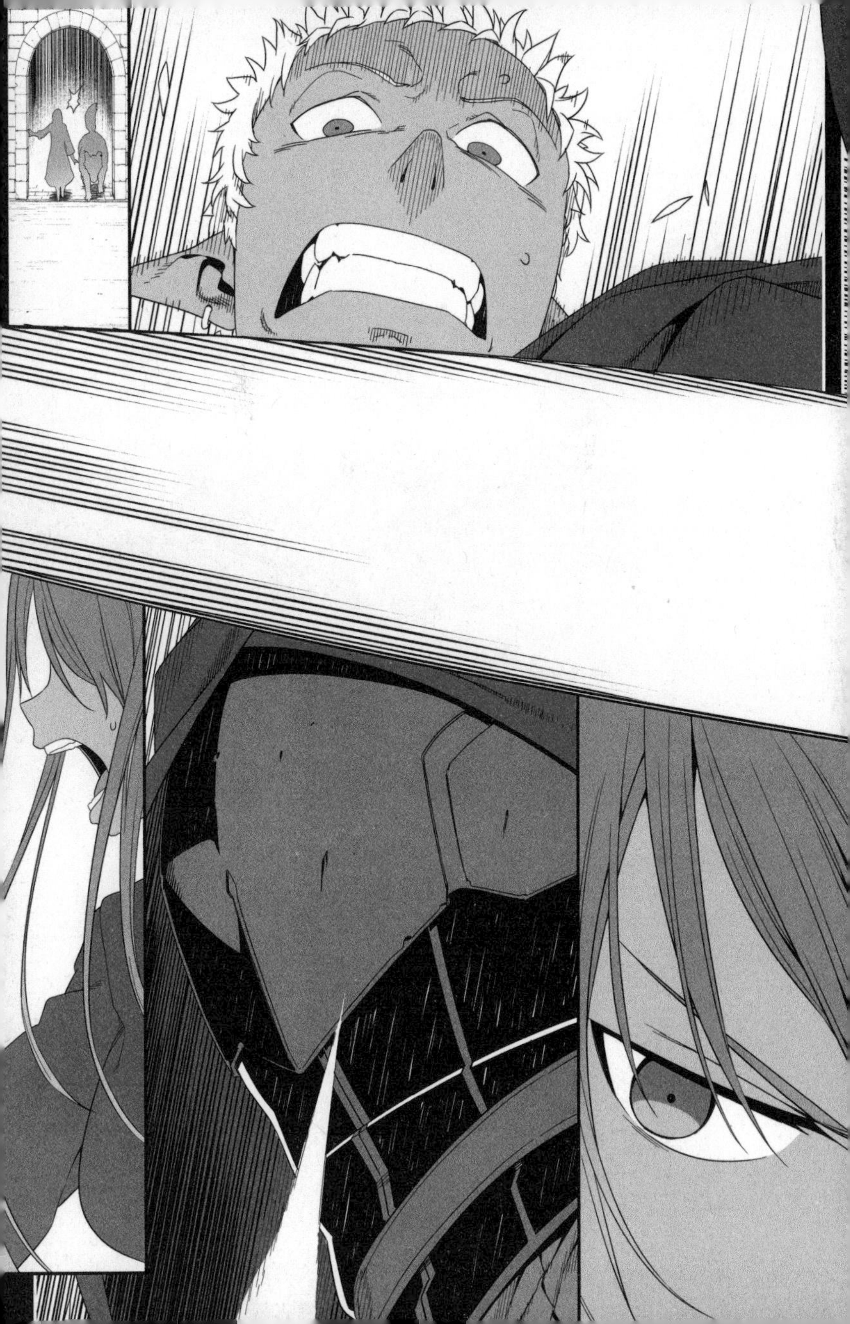

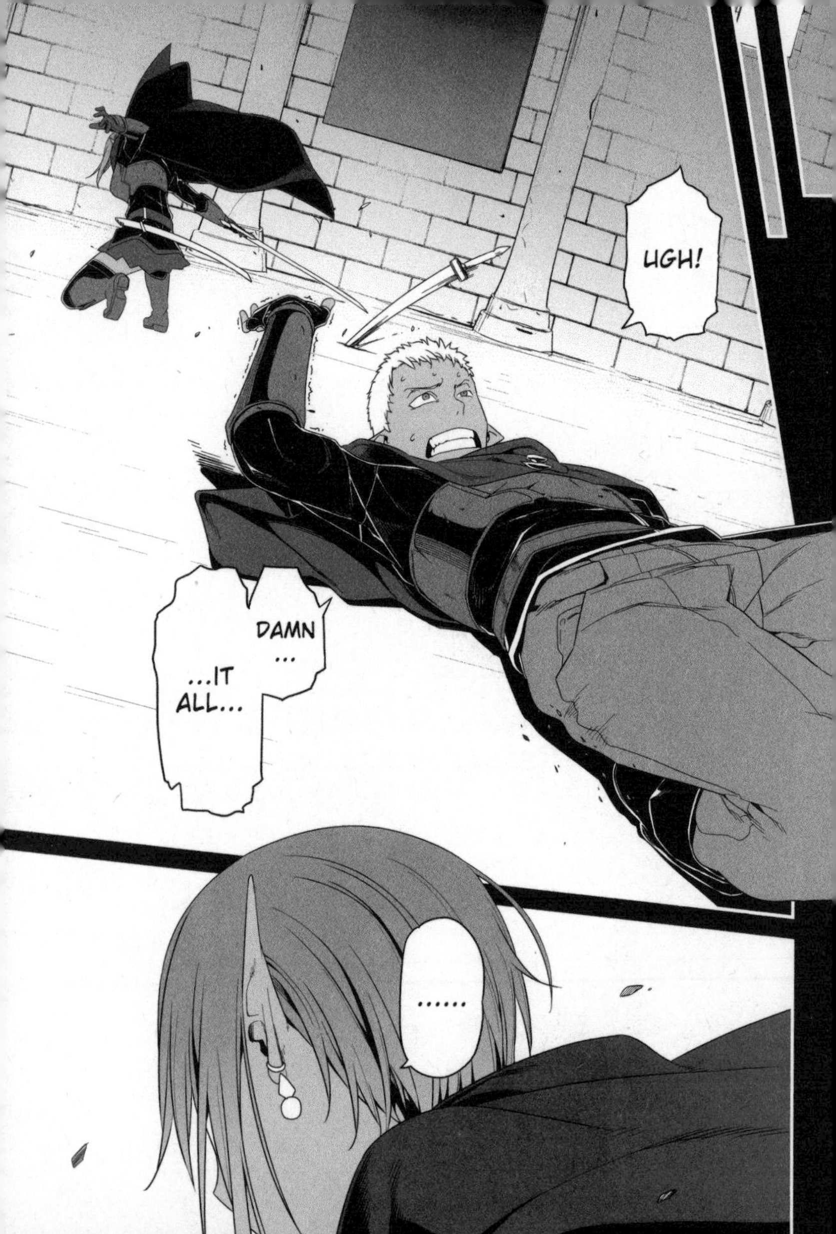
UGH!
DAMN... ...IT ALL...
......

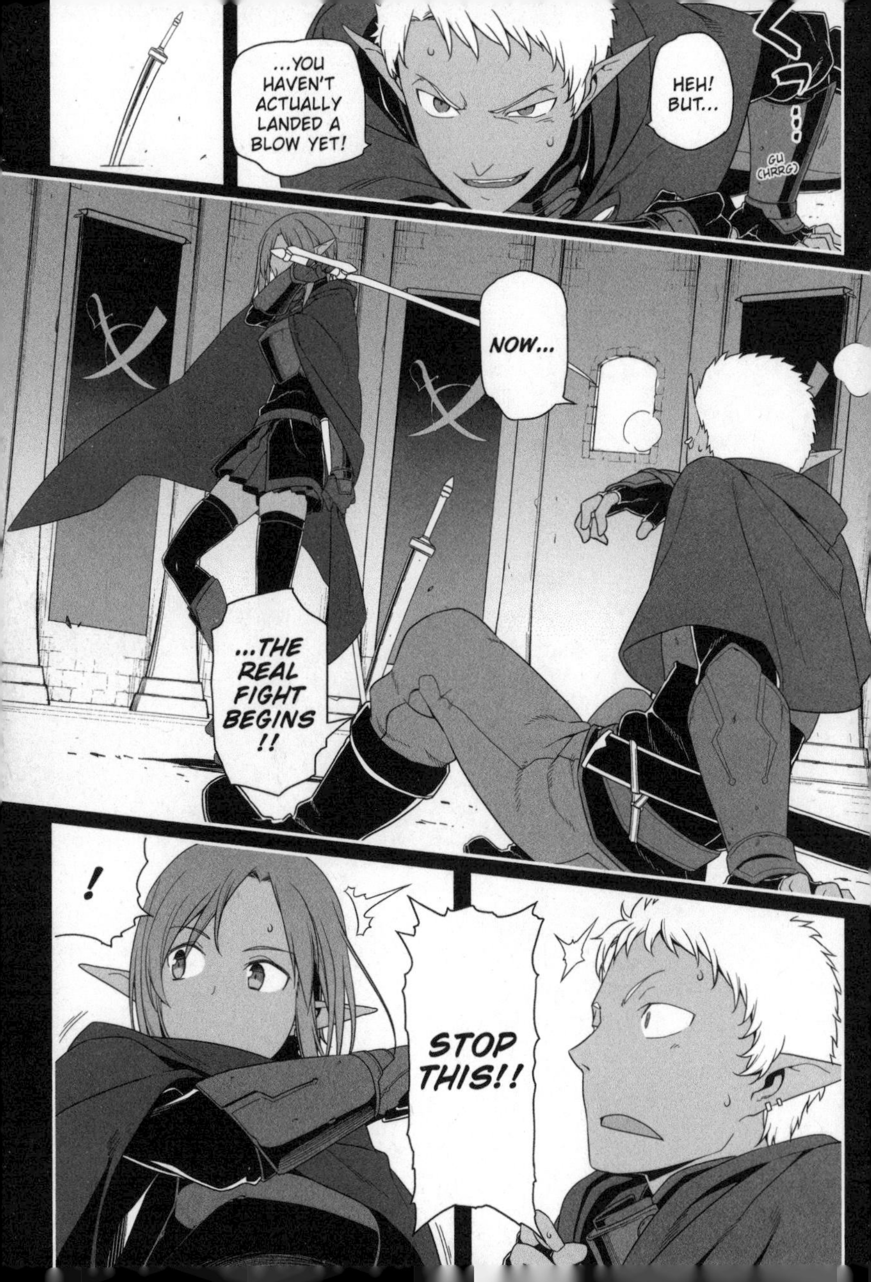
HEH! BUT...
GU (HRRG)
...YOU HAVEN'T ACTUALLY LANDED A BLOW YET!
NOW...
...THE REAL FIGHT BEGINS!!
STOP THIS!!
!

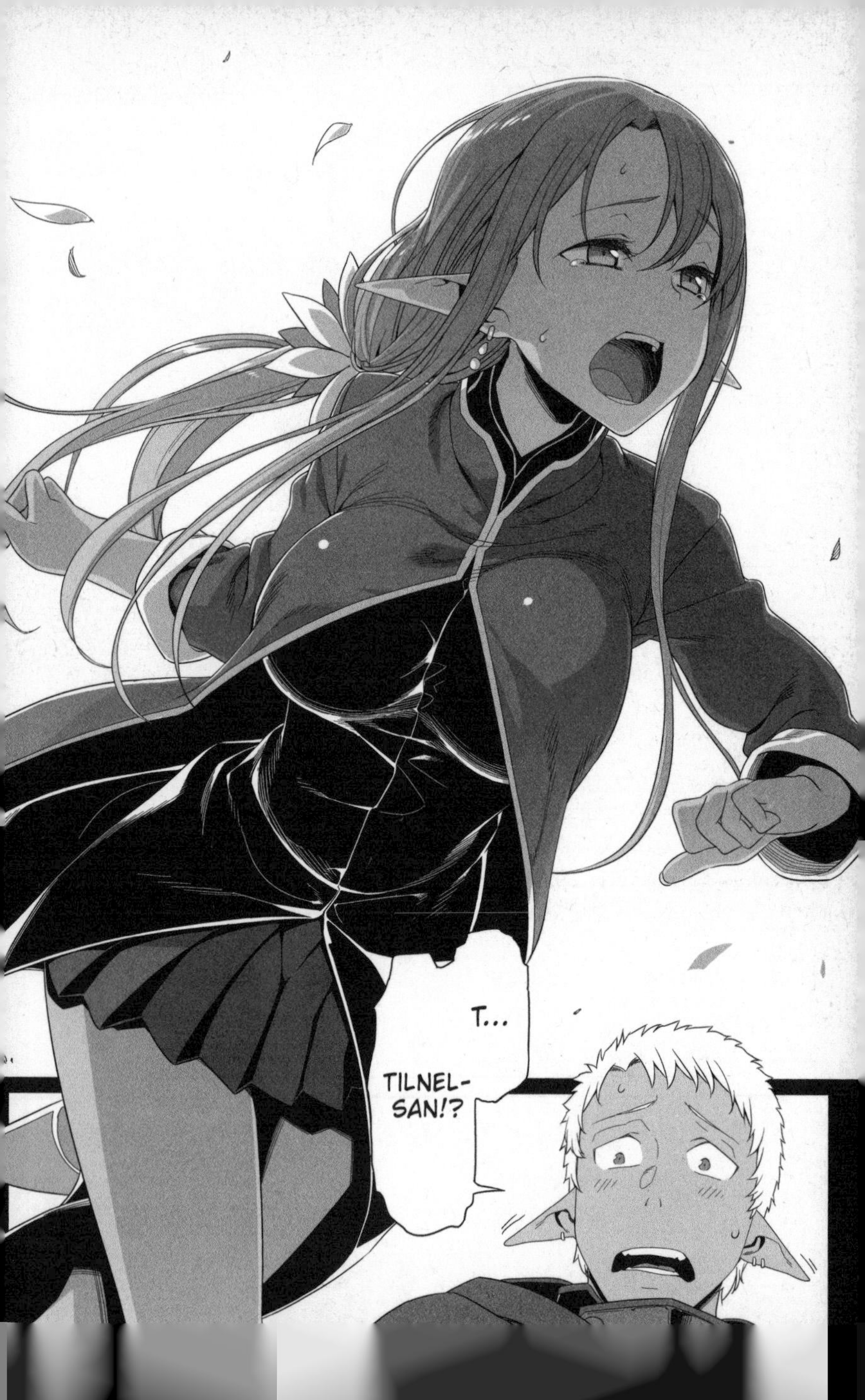
T...
TILNEL-SAN!?

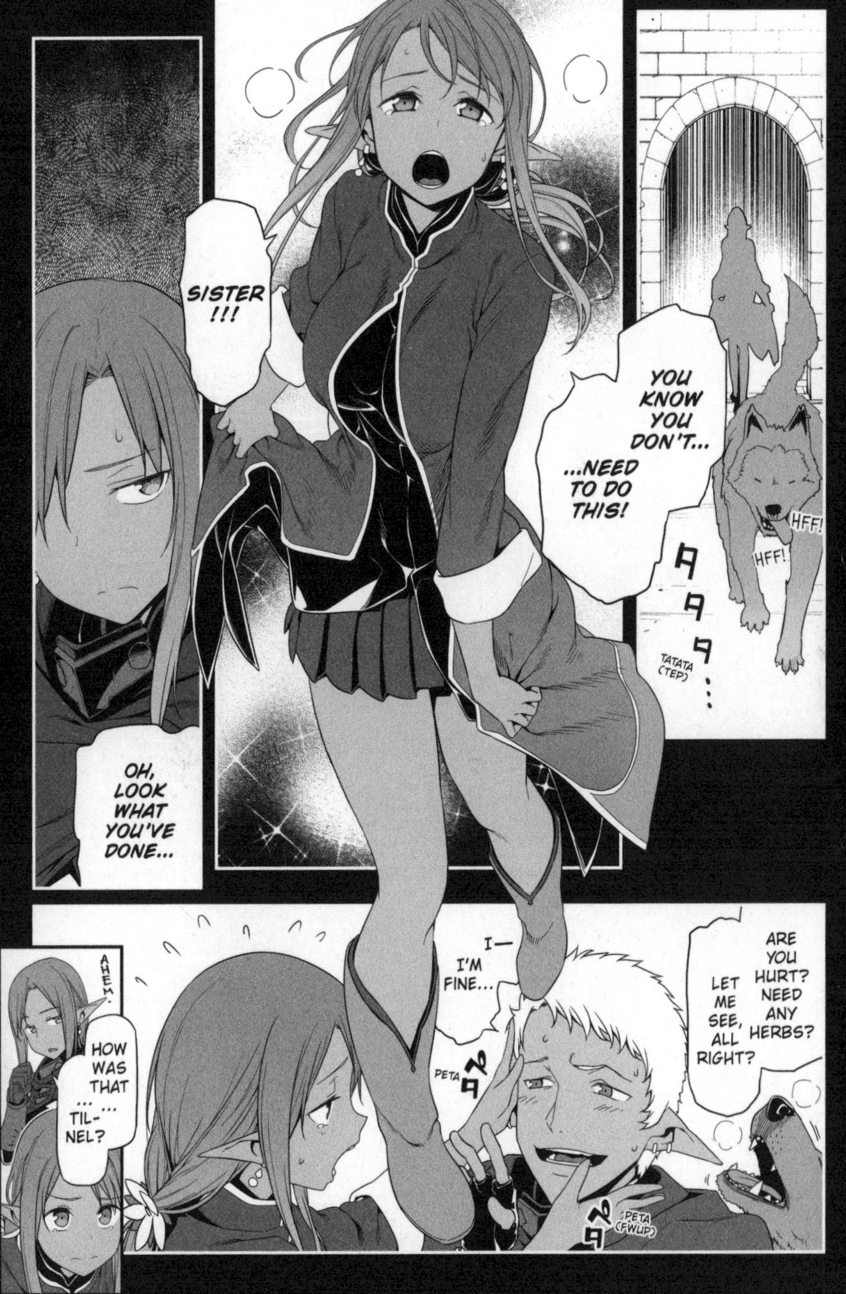
YOU KNOW YOU DON'T...
...NEED TO DO THIS!
HFF!
HFF!
TATATA (TEP)
SISTER!!!
OH, LOOK WHAT YOU'VE DONE...
ARE YOU HURT? NEED ANY HERBS?
LET ME SEE, ALL RIGHT?
PETA (FWUP)
I— I'M FINE...
PETA
AHEM.
HOW WAS THAT... ...TIL-NEL?

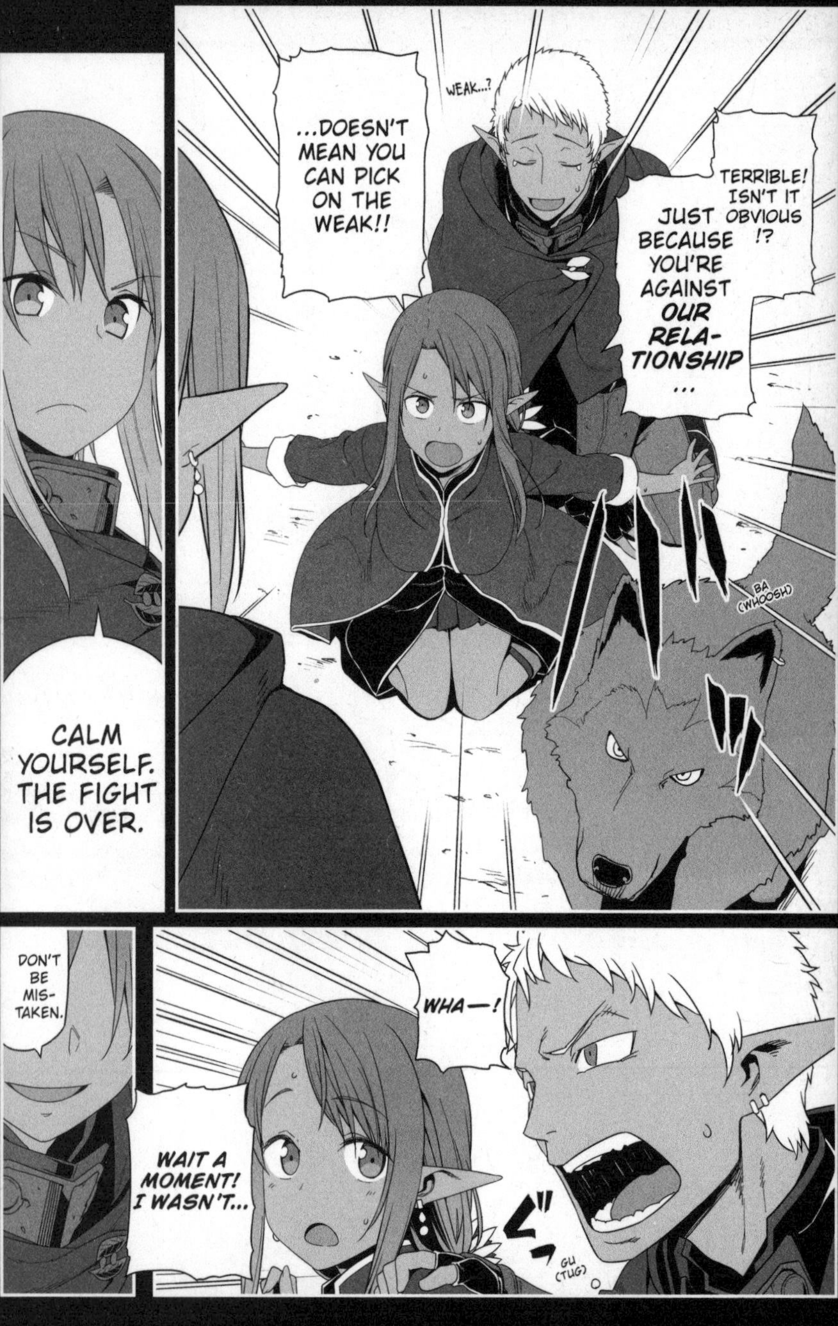
TERRIBLE! ISN'T IT OBVIOUS !?
JUST BECAUSE YOU'RE AGAINST OUR RELATIONSHIP ...
...DOESN'T MEAN YOU CAN PICK ON THE WEAK!!
WEAK...?
BA (WHOOSH)
CALM YOURSELF. THE FIGHT IS OVER.
WHA—!
WAIT A MOMENT! I WASN'T...
GU (TUG)
DON'T BE MIS-TAKEN.

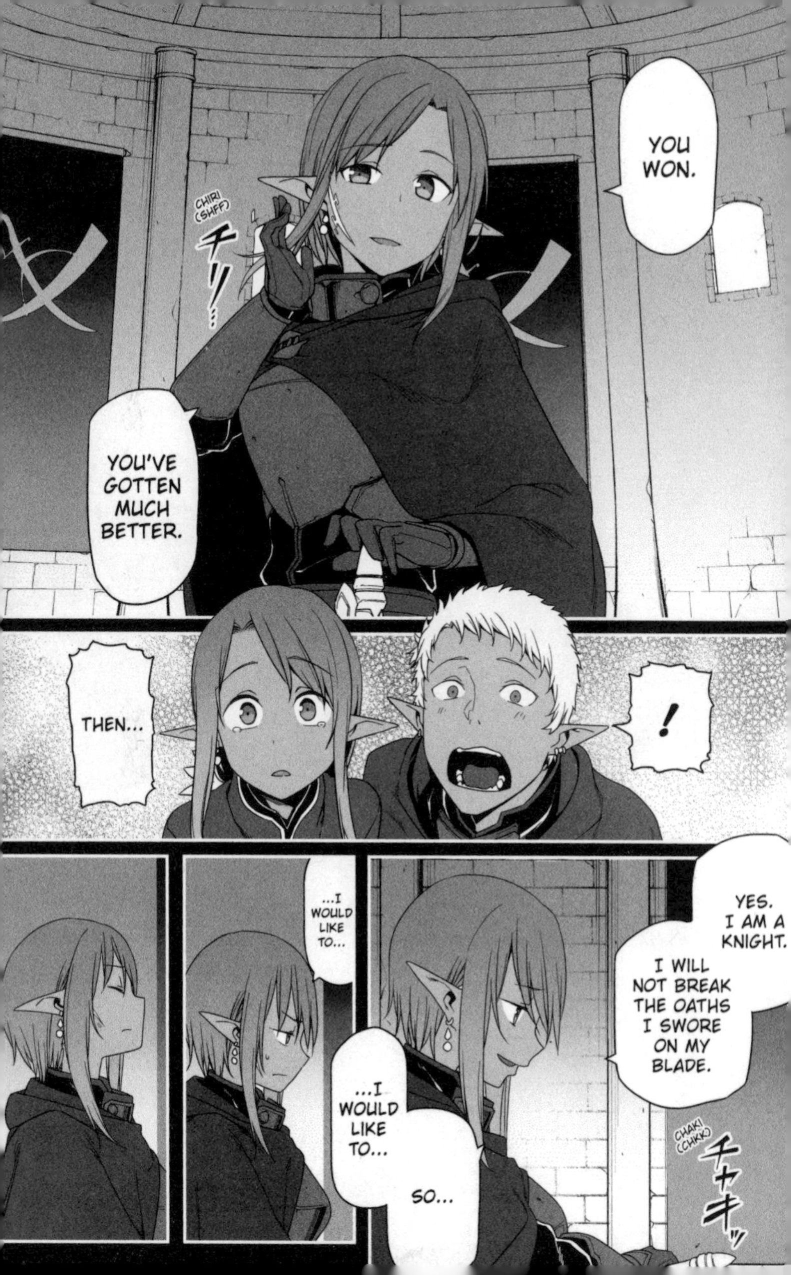
YOU WON.
CHIRI (SHFF)
チリ…
YOU'VE GOTTEN MUCH BETTER.
!
THEN...
YES. I AM A KNIGHT.
I WILL NOT BREAK THE OATHS I SWORE ON MY BLADE.
CHAKI (CHKK)
チャキッ
...I WOULD LIKE TO...
SO...
...I WOULD LIKE TO...

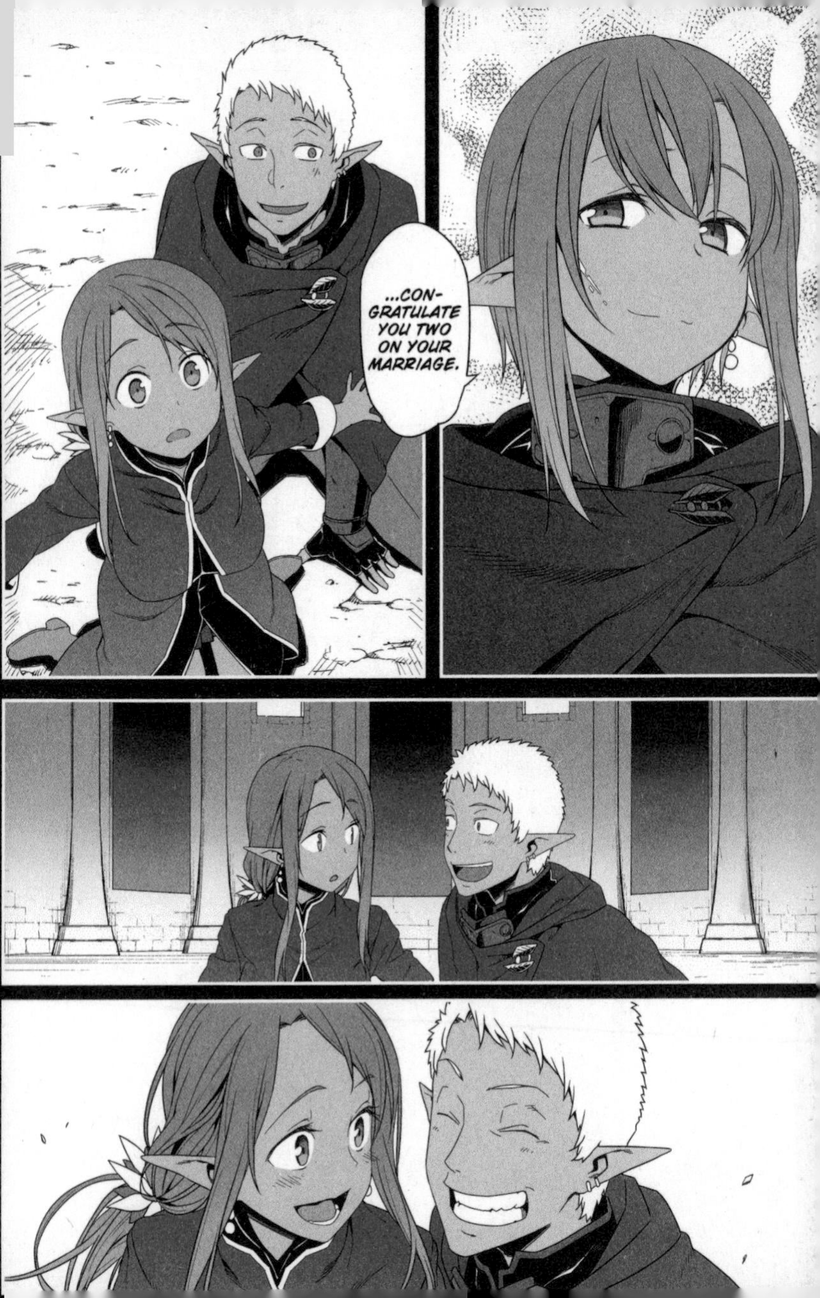
...CON-GRATULATE YOU TWO ON YOUR MARRIAGE.

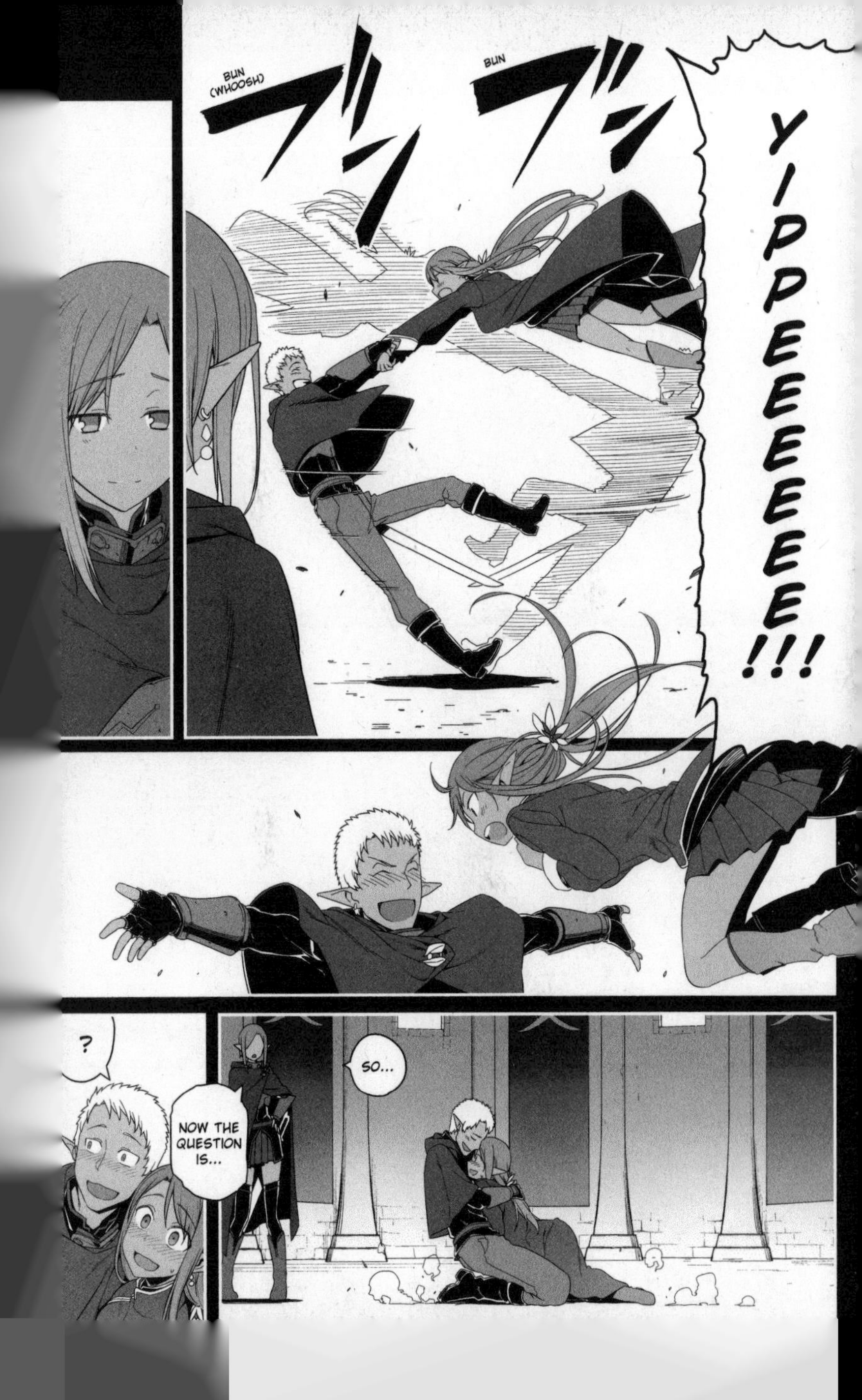
YIPPEEEEEEEE!!!
BUN
BUN (WHOOSH)
SO...
?
NOW THE QUESTION IS...

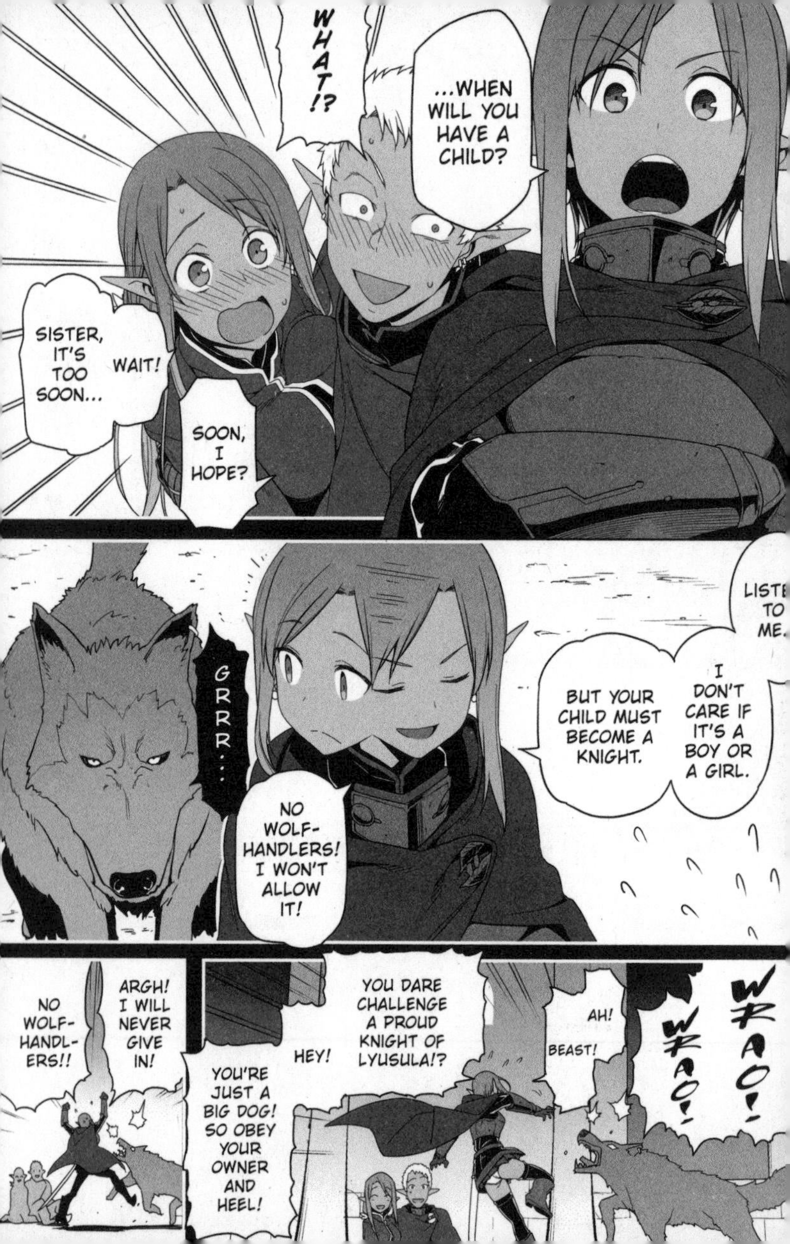
...WHEN WILL YOU HAVE A CHILD?
WHAT!?
WAIT!
SISTER, IT'S TOO SOON...
SOON, I HOPE?
LISTE TO ME.
I DON'T CARE IF IT'S A BOY OR A GIRL.
BUT YOUR CHILD MUST BECOME A KNIGHT.
GRRR...
NO WOLF-HANDLERS! I WON'T ALLOW IT!
WRAO!
WRAO!
AH!
BEAST!
YOU DARE CHALLENGE A PROUD KNIGHT OF LYUSULA!?
HEY!
YOU'RE JUST A BIG DOG! SO OBEY YOUR OWNER AND HEEL!
ARGH! I WILL NEVER GIVE IN!
NO WOLF-HANDL-ERS!!

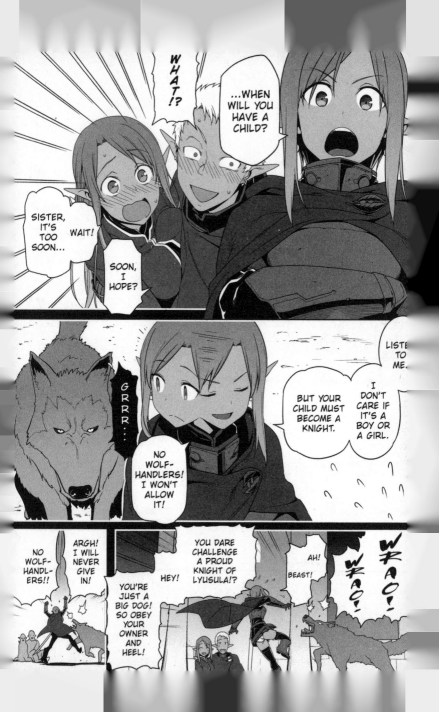

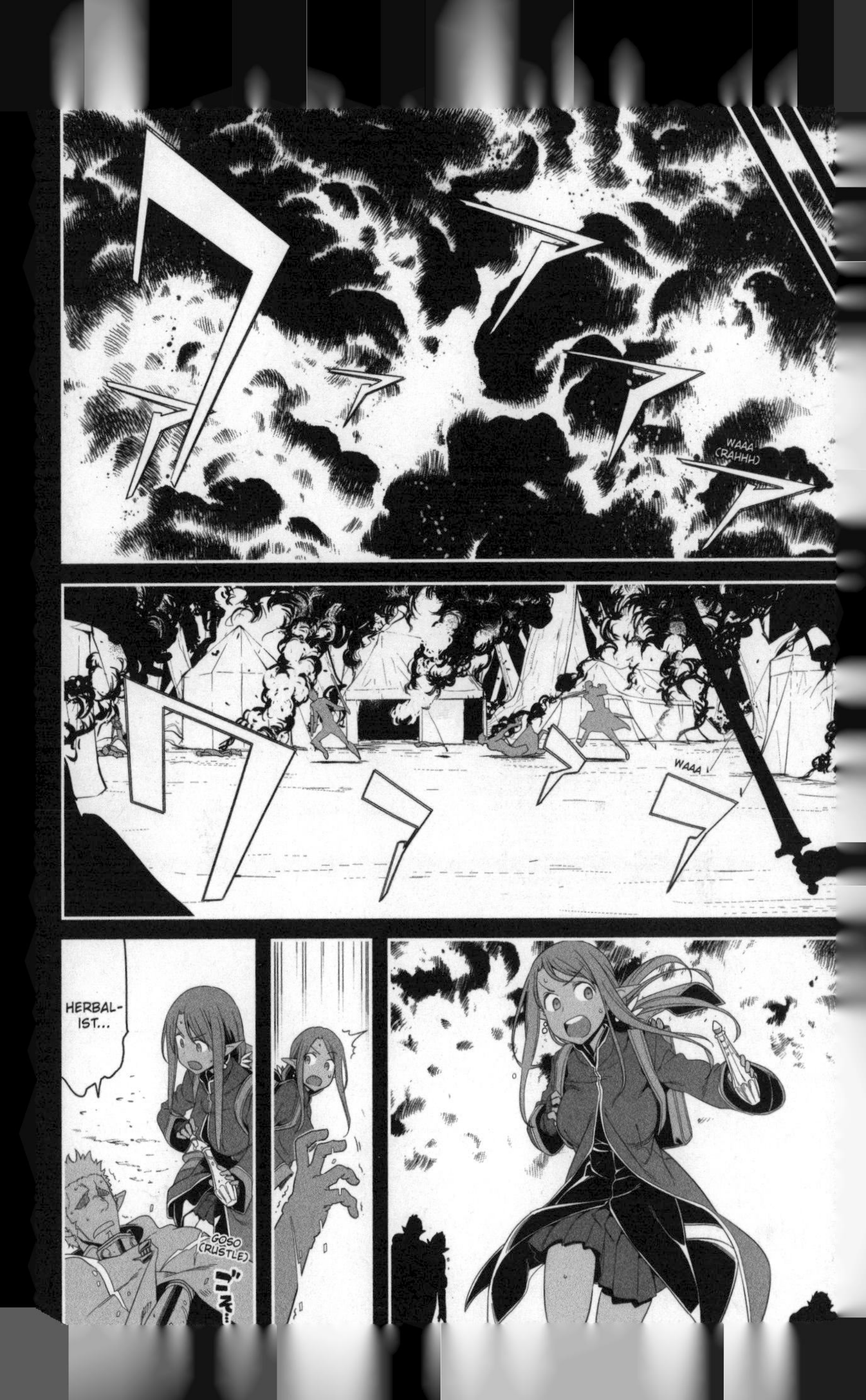
WAAA (RAHHH)
WAAA
HERBAL-IST...
GOSO (RUSTLE)

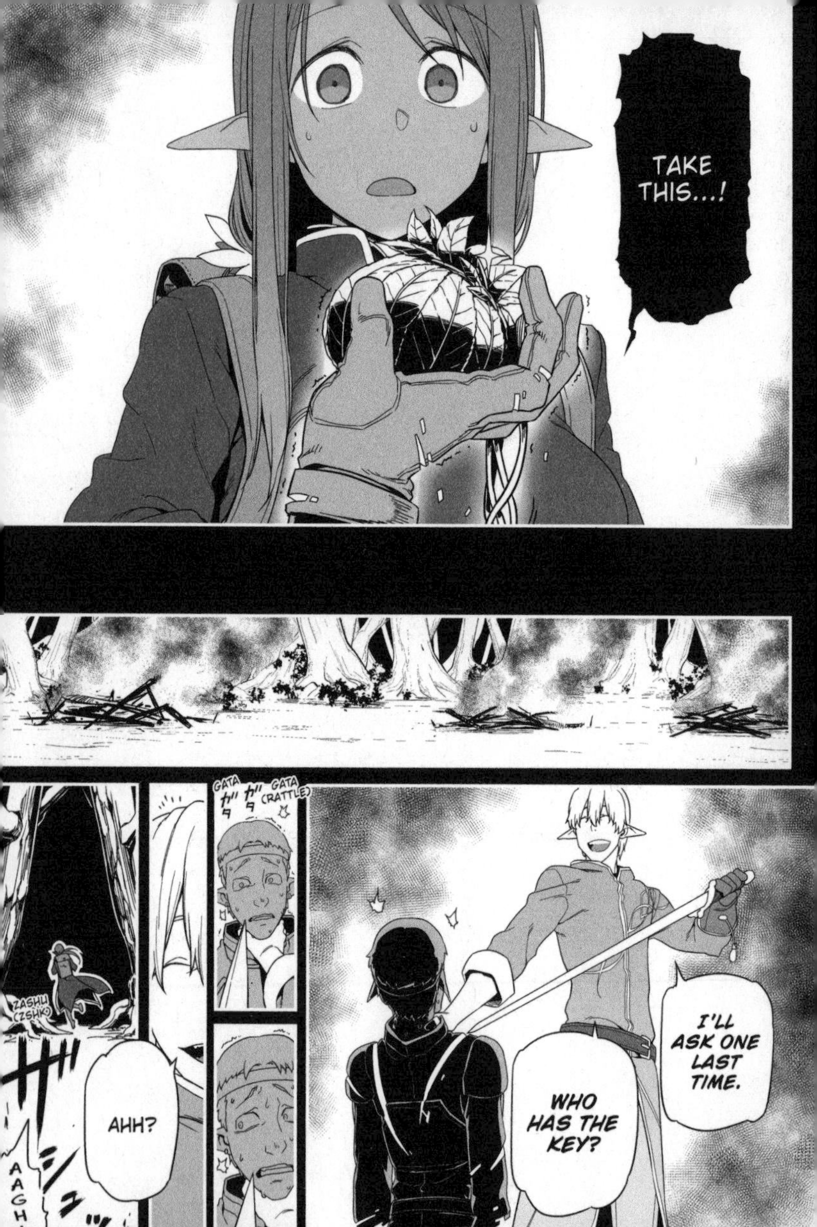
TAKE THIS...!
I'LL ASK ONE LAST TIME.
WHO HAS THE KEY?
GATA GATA (RATTLE)
AHH?
ZASHU (ZSHK)
AAGH!

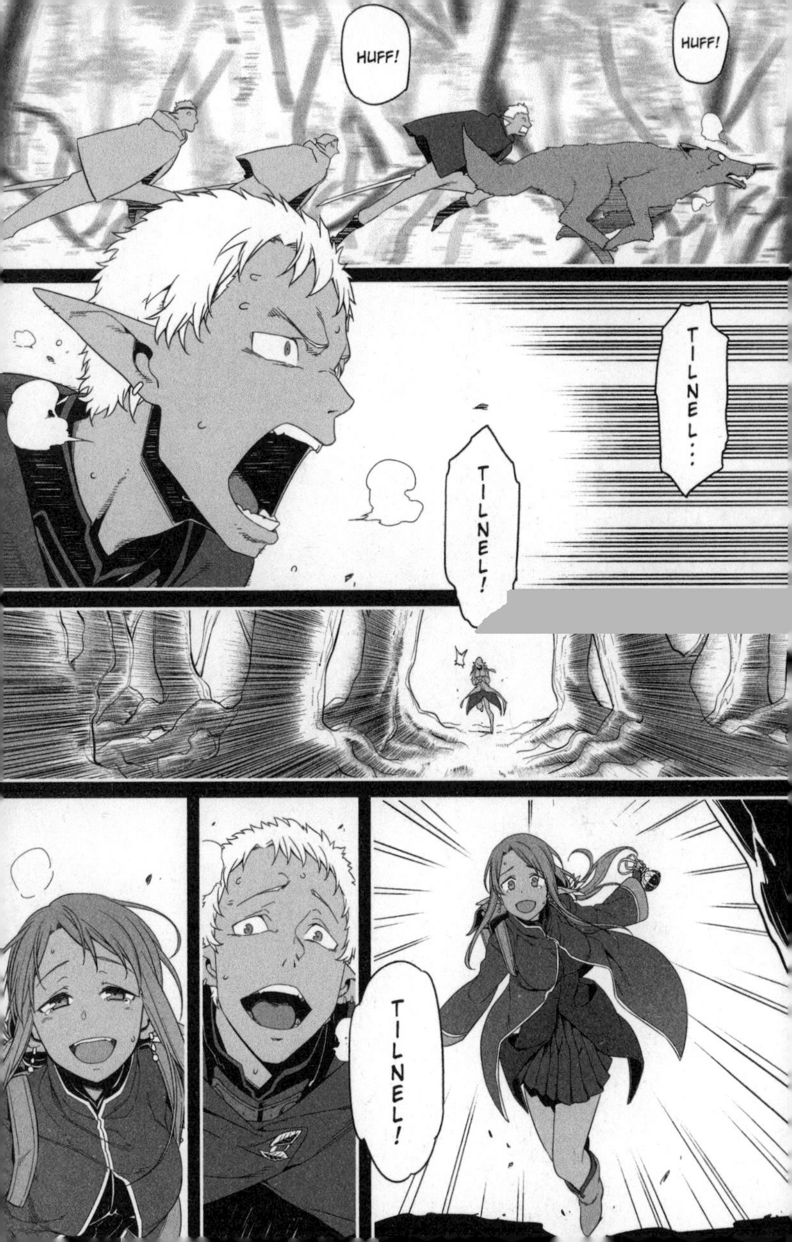
HUFF!
HUFF!
TILNEL...
TILNEL!
TILNEL!

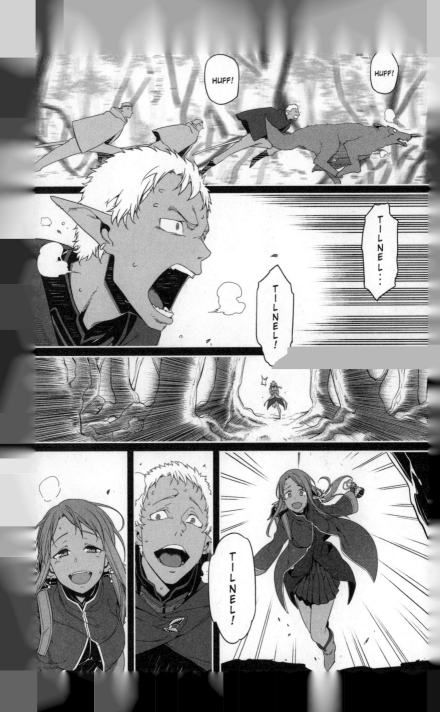

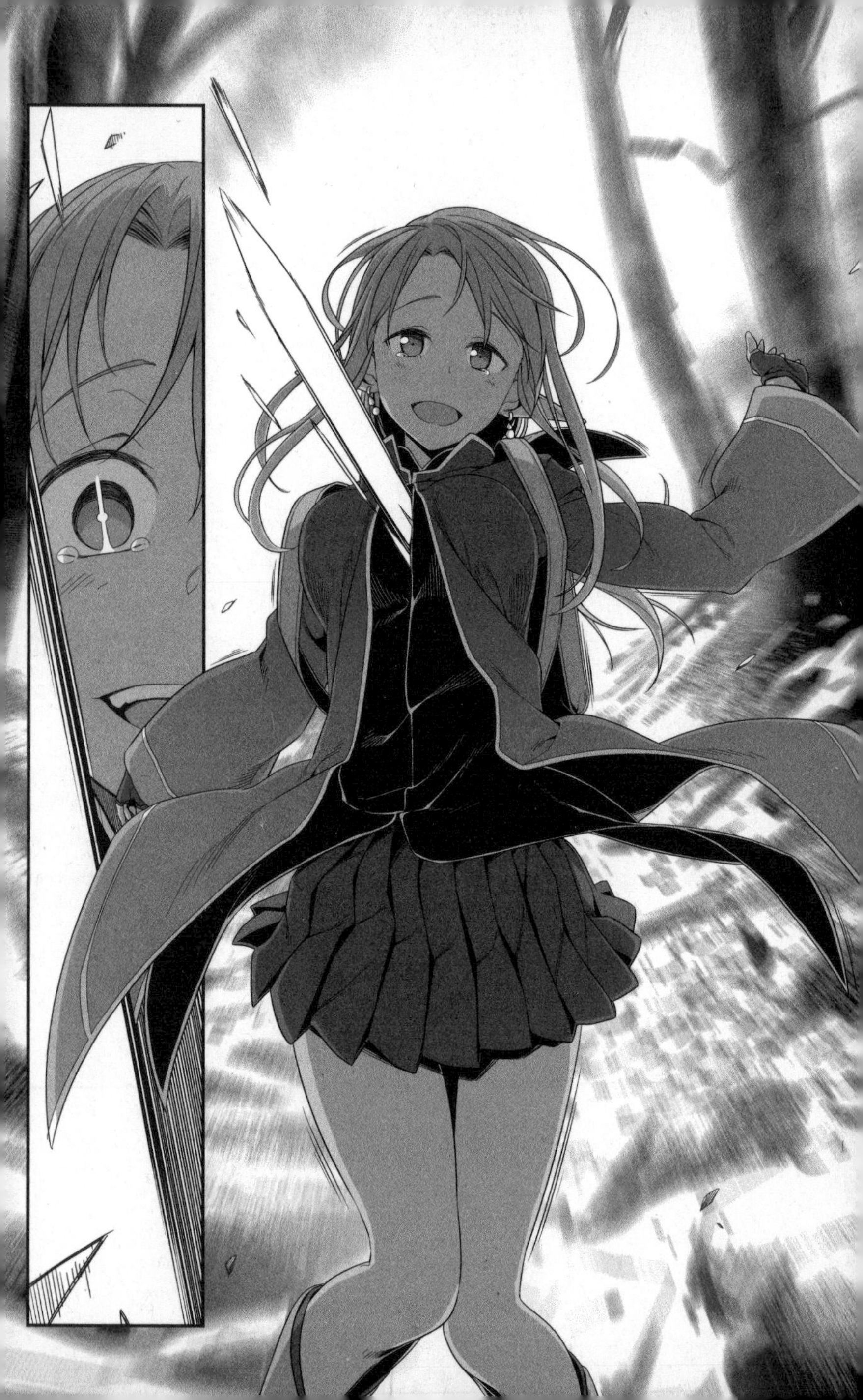

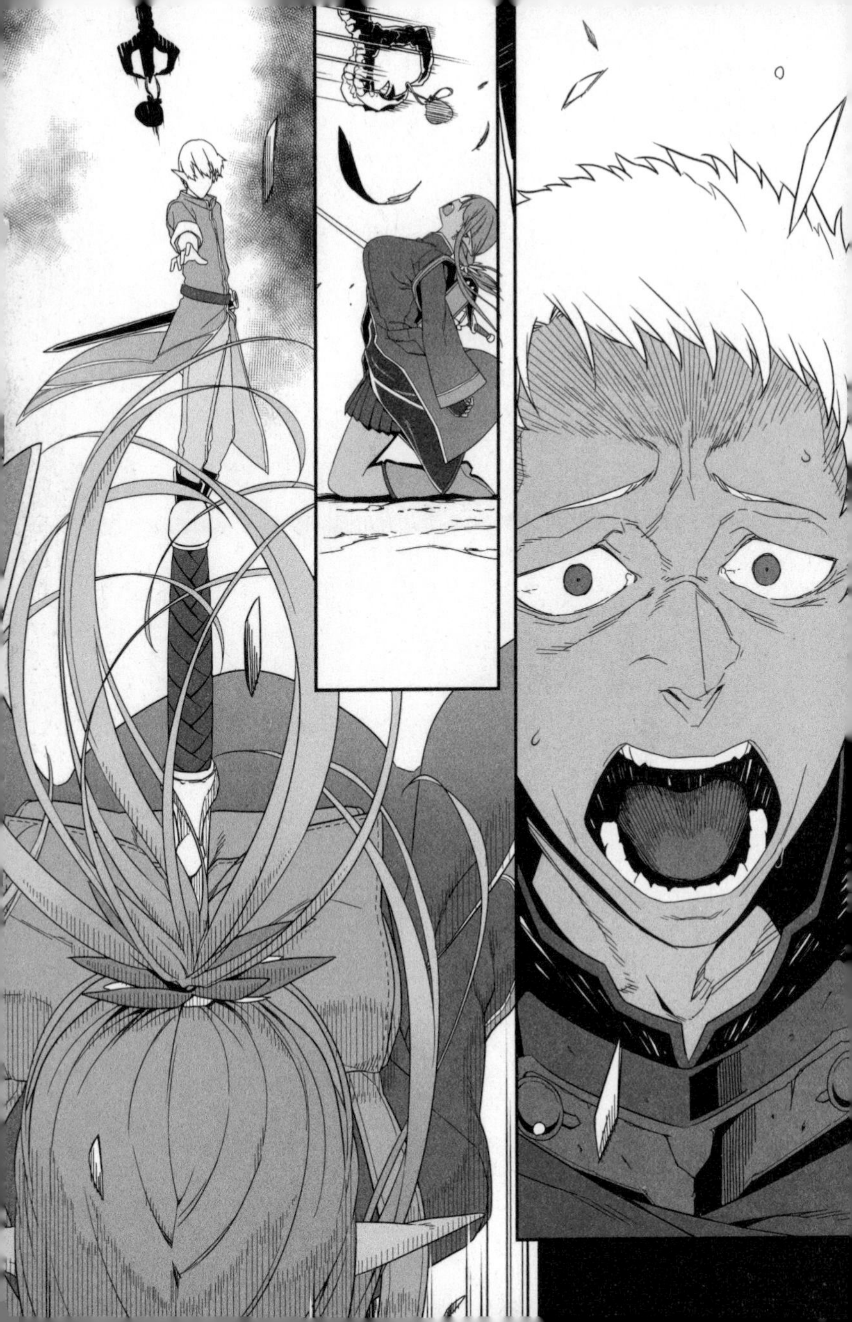

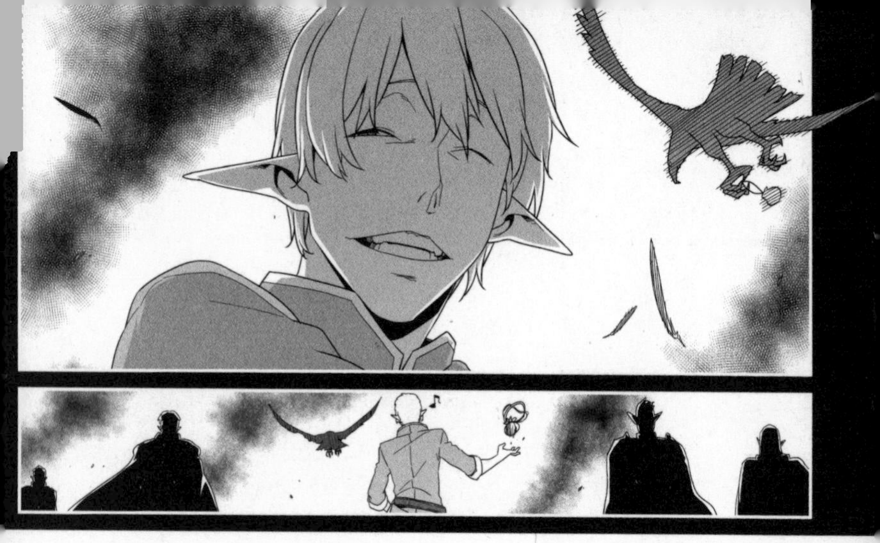

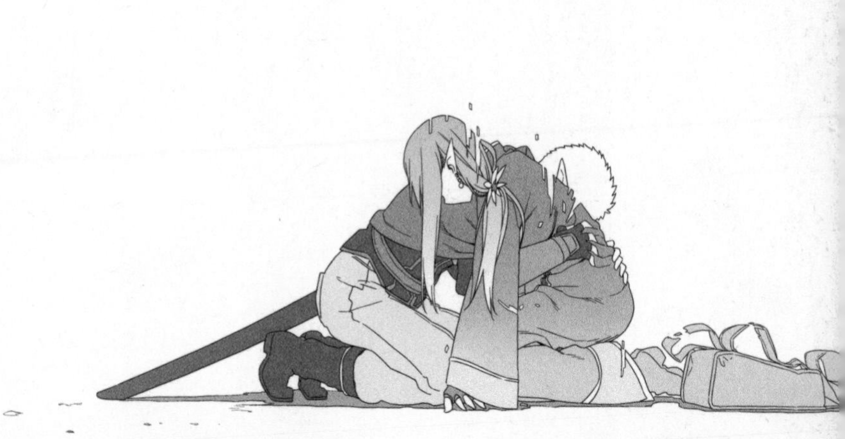

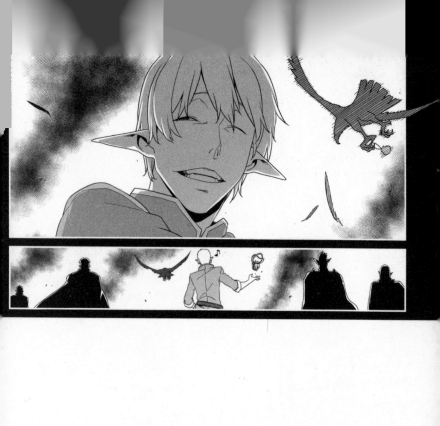

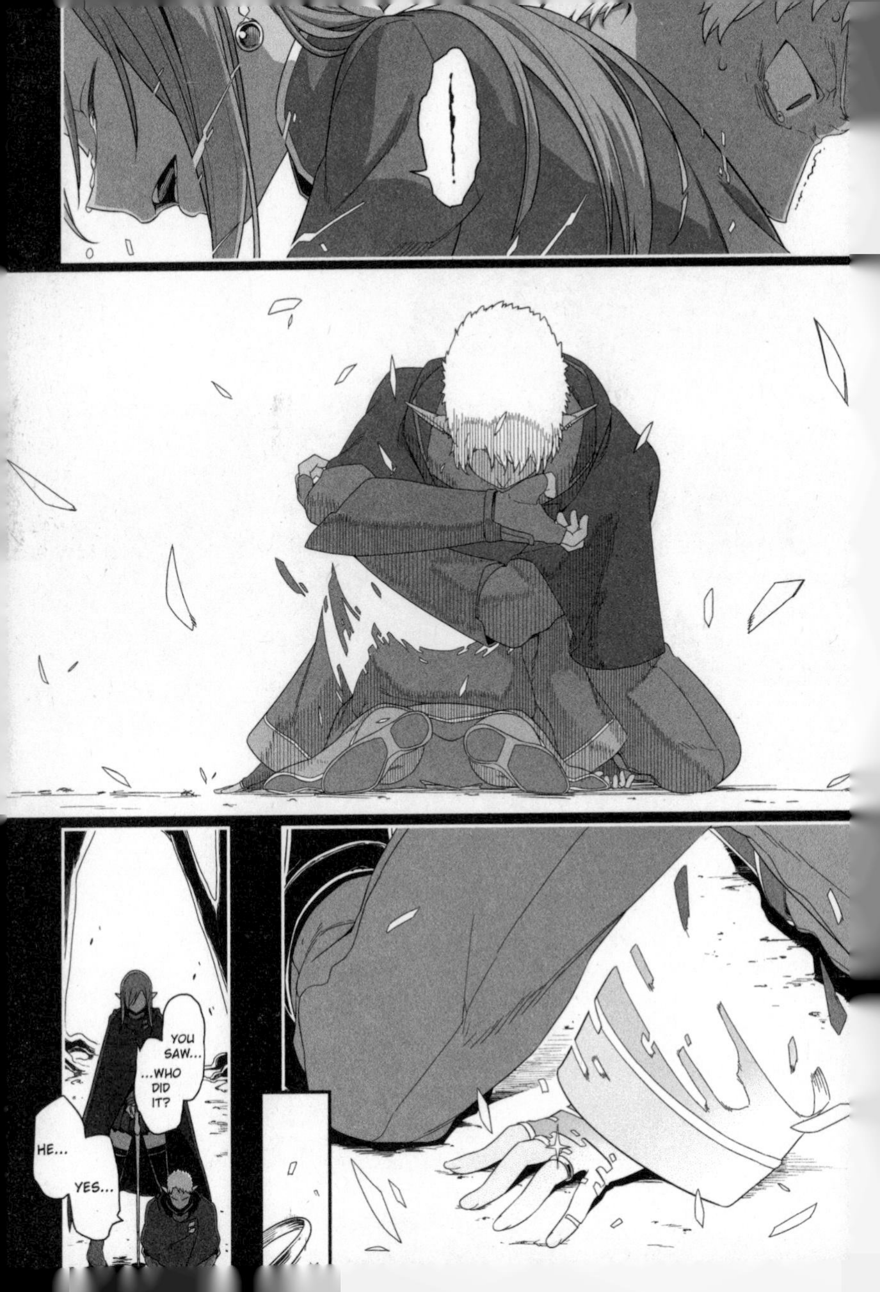
YOU SAW... ...WHO DID IT?
HE... YES...

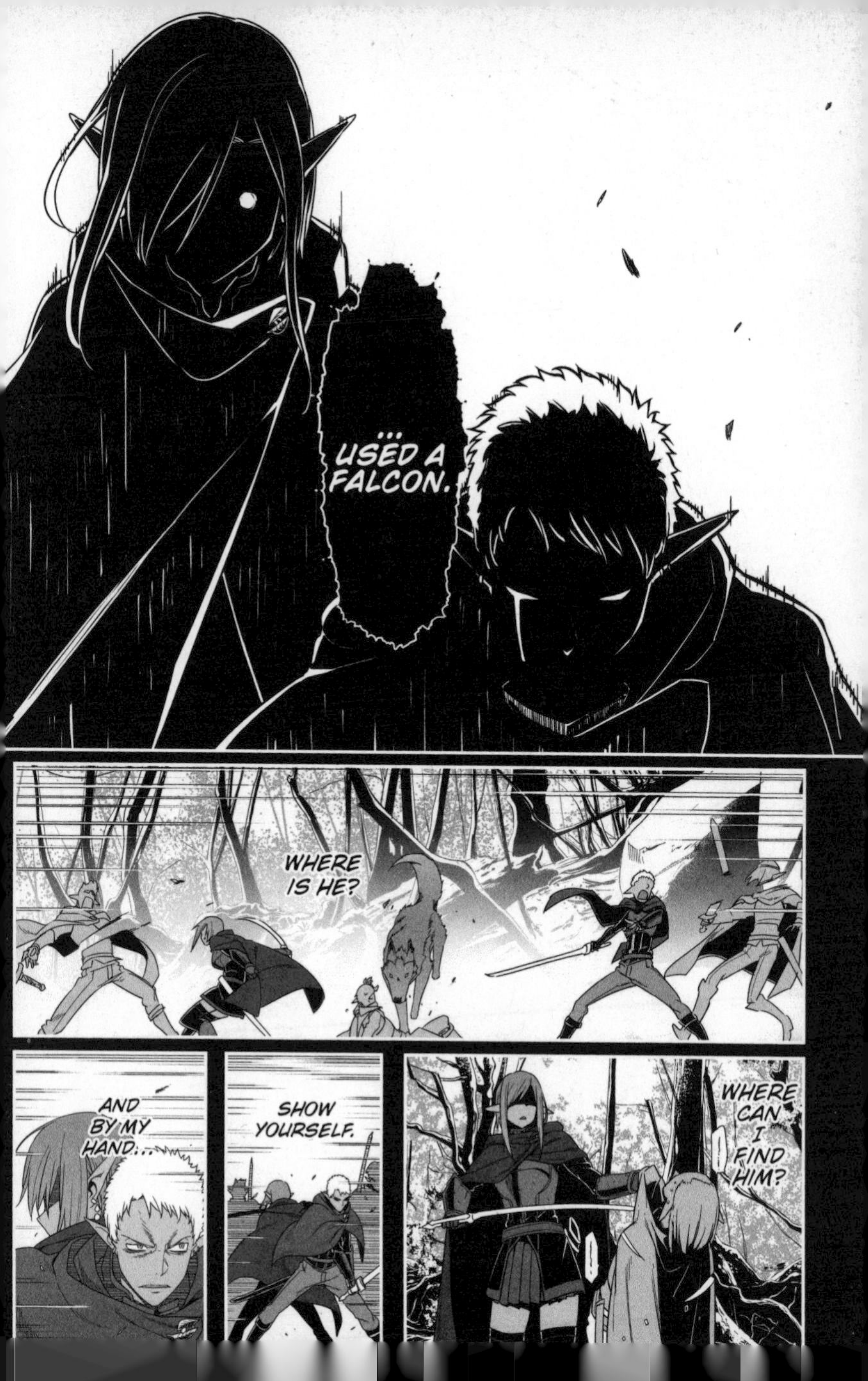
...USED A FALCON.
WHERE IS HE?
WHERE CAN I FIND HIM?
!
!
SHOW YOURSELF.
AND BY MY HAND...

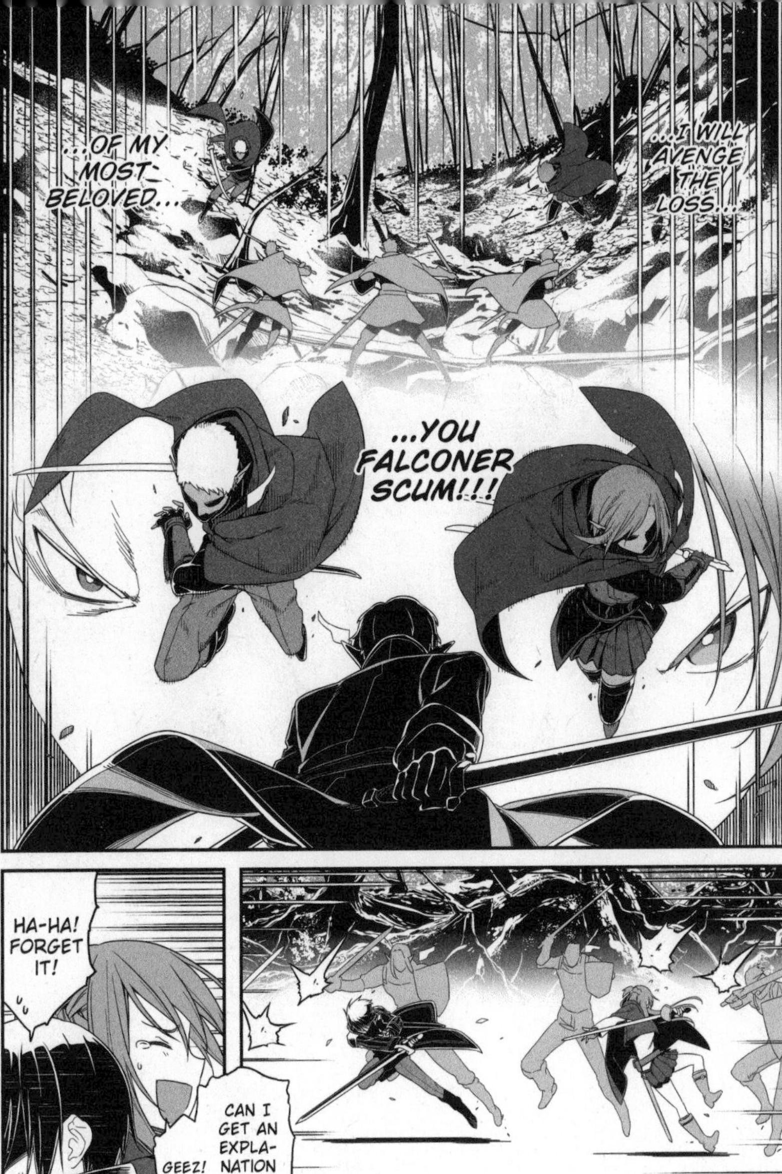
...I WILL AVENGE THE LOSS...
...OF MY MOST BELOVED...
...YOU FALCONER SCUM!!!
CAN I GET AN EXPLA-NATION HERE!?
HA-HA! FORGET IT!
GEEZ!

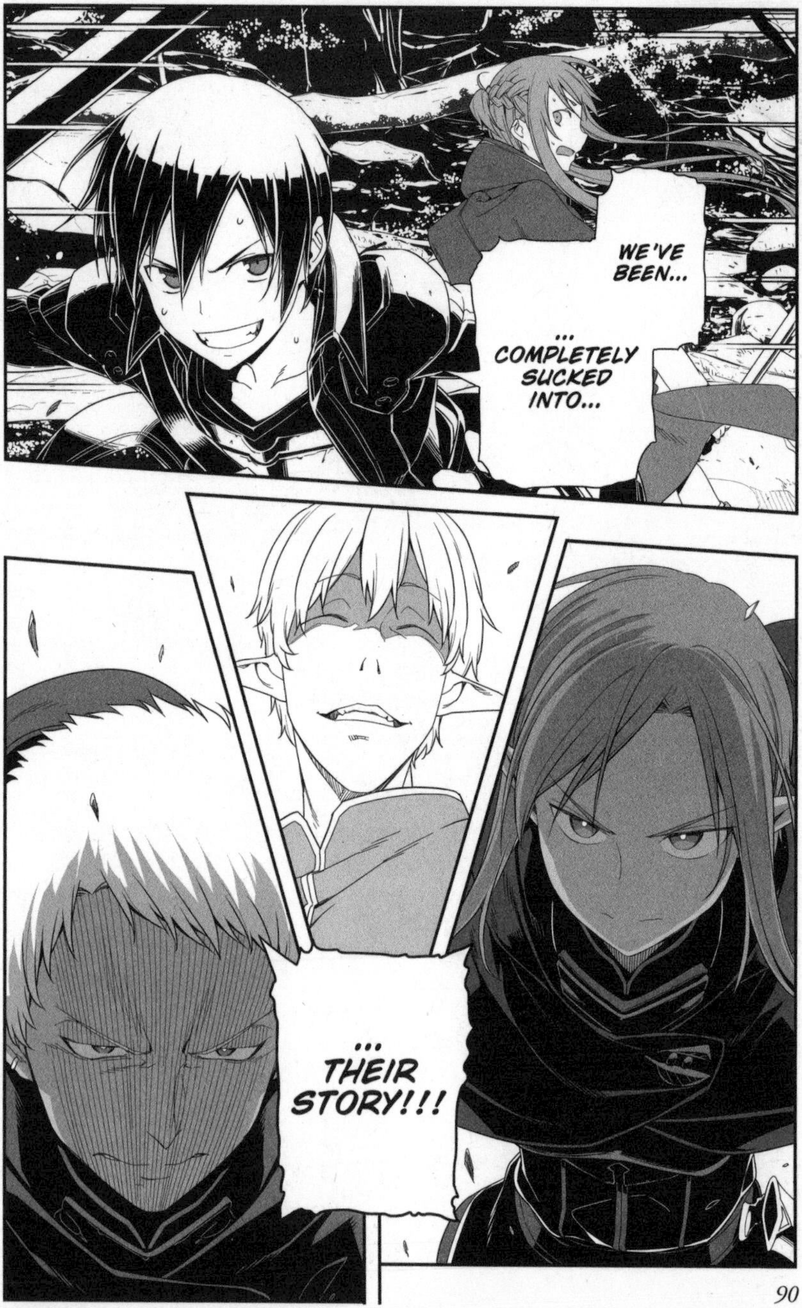
WE'VE BEEN...
... COMPLETELY SUCKED INTO...
... THEIR STORY!!!

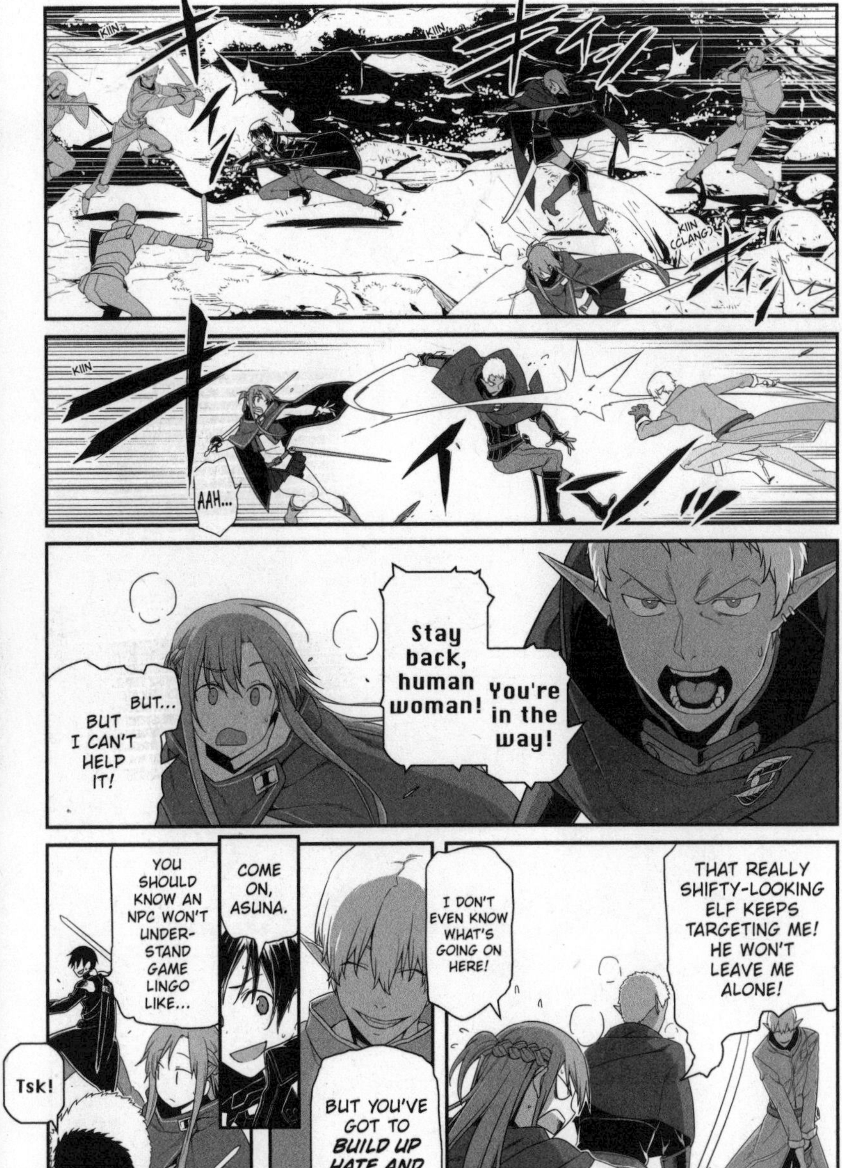
KIIN
KIIN
KIIN (CLANG)
KIIN
AAH...
Stay back, human woman!
You're in the way!
BUT... BUT I CAN'T HELP IT!
THAT REALLY SHIFTY-LOOKING ELF KEEPS TARGETING ME! HE WON'T LEAVE ME ALONE!
I DON'T EVEN KNOW WHAT'S GOING ON HERE!
COME ON, ASUNA.
YOU SHOULD KNOW AN NPC WON'T UNDER-STAND GAME LINGO LIKE...
BUT YOU'VE GOT TO *BUILD UP HATE AND PULL HIS AGGRO!*
Tsk!

#026: Wolfhandler

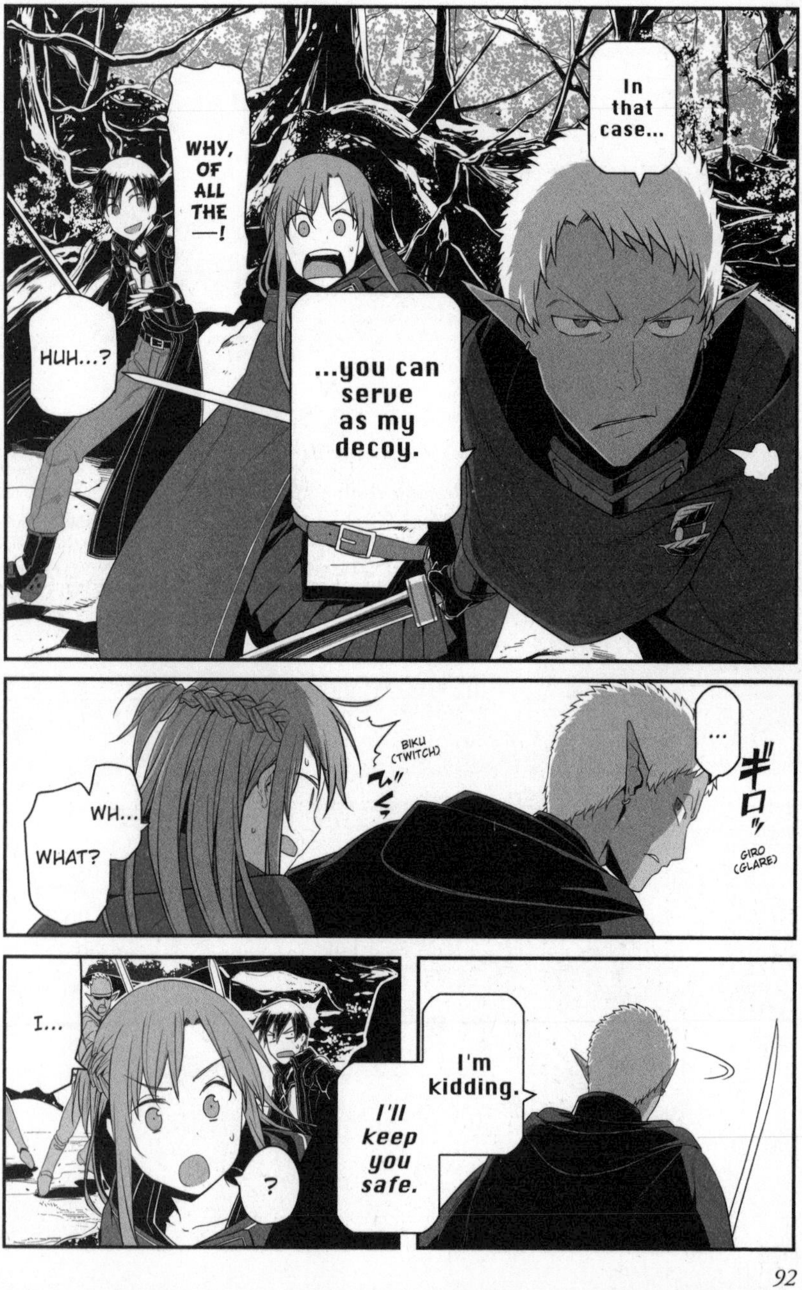
In that case...
...you can serve as my decoy.
WHY, OF ALL THE—!
HUH...?
...
ギロッ
GIRO (GLARE)
ビクッ
BIKU (TWITCH)
WH... WHAT?
I'm kidding.
I'll keep you safe.
?
I...

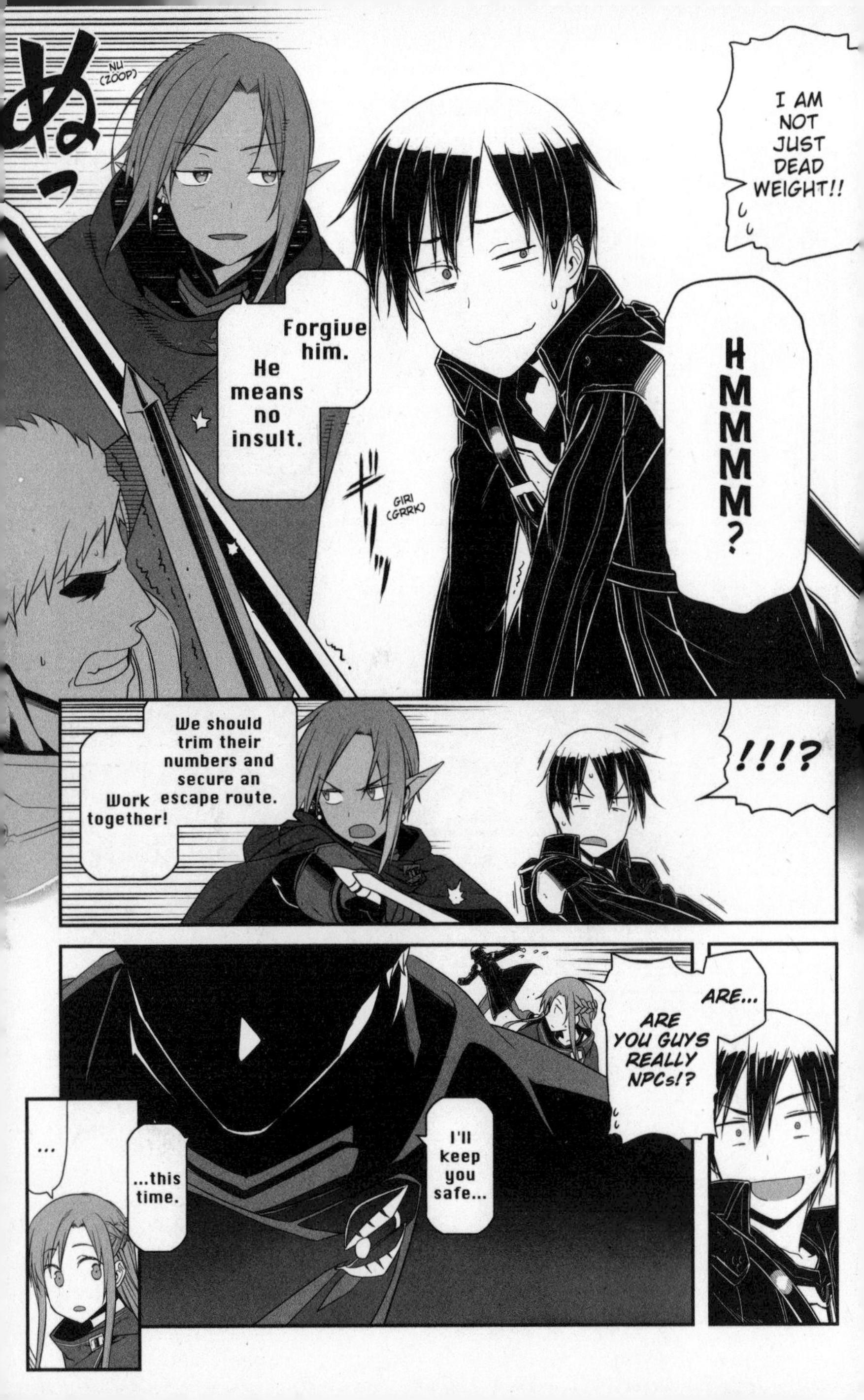
I AM NOT JUST DEAD WEIGHT!!
HMMMM?
Forgive him. He means no insult.
ギリッ
GIRI (GRRK)
ぬっ
NU (ZOOP)
!!!?
We should trim their numbers and secure an escape route.
Work together!
ARE...
ARE YOU GUYS REALLY NPCs!?
I'll keep you safe...
...this time.
...

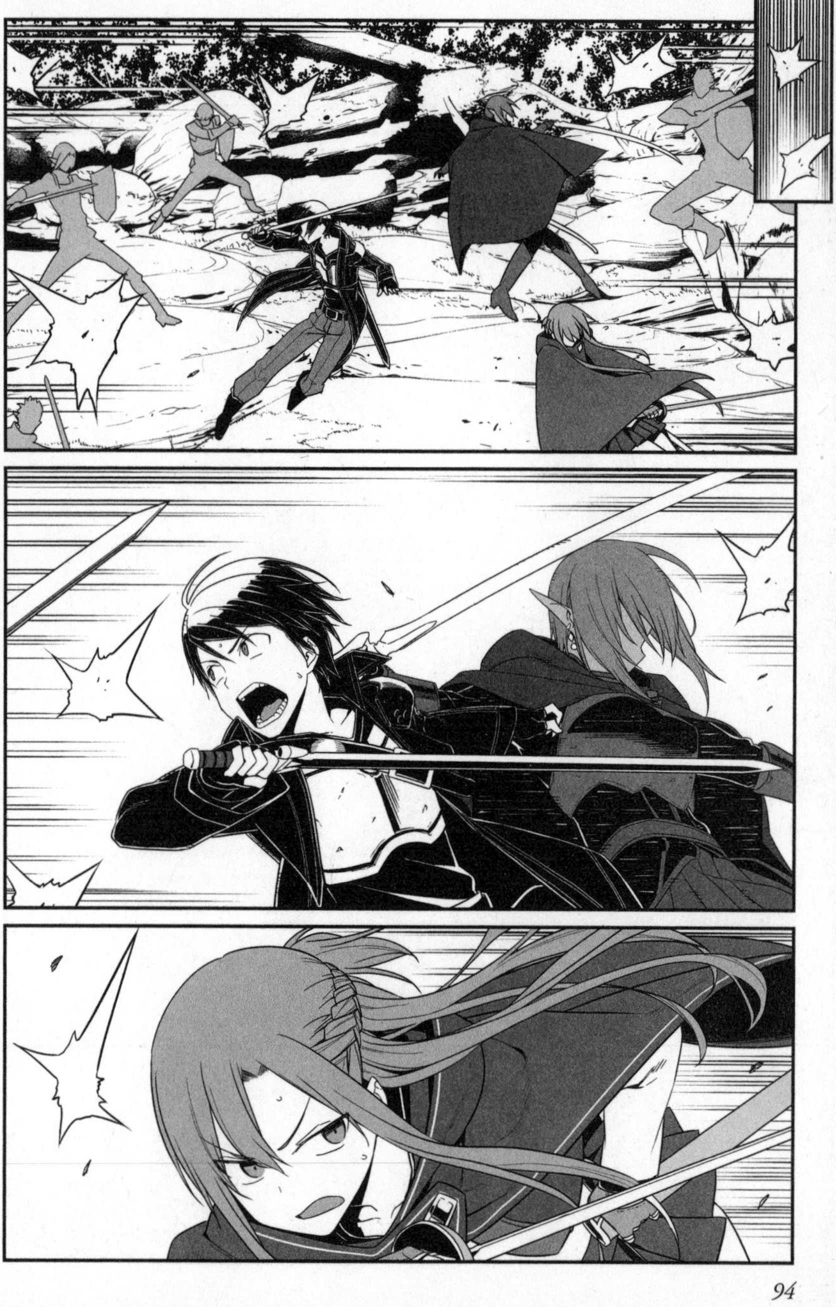

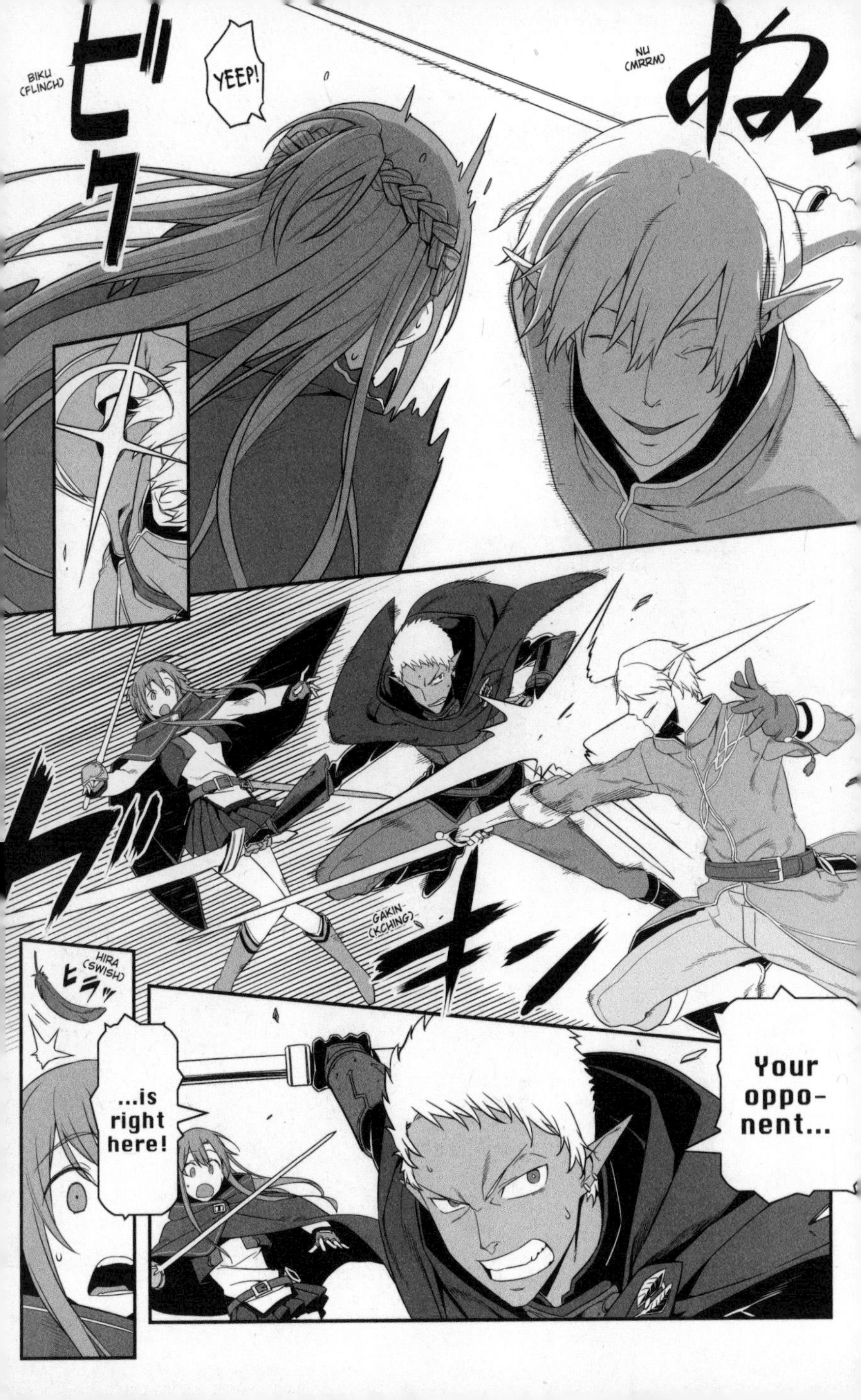

NU (MRRM)
ぬー
YEEP!
BIKU (FLINCH)
ビク
GAKIN (KCHING)
HIRA (SWISH)
ヒラッ
Your oppo-nent...
...is right here!

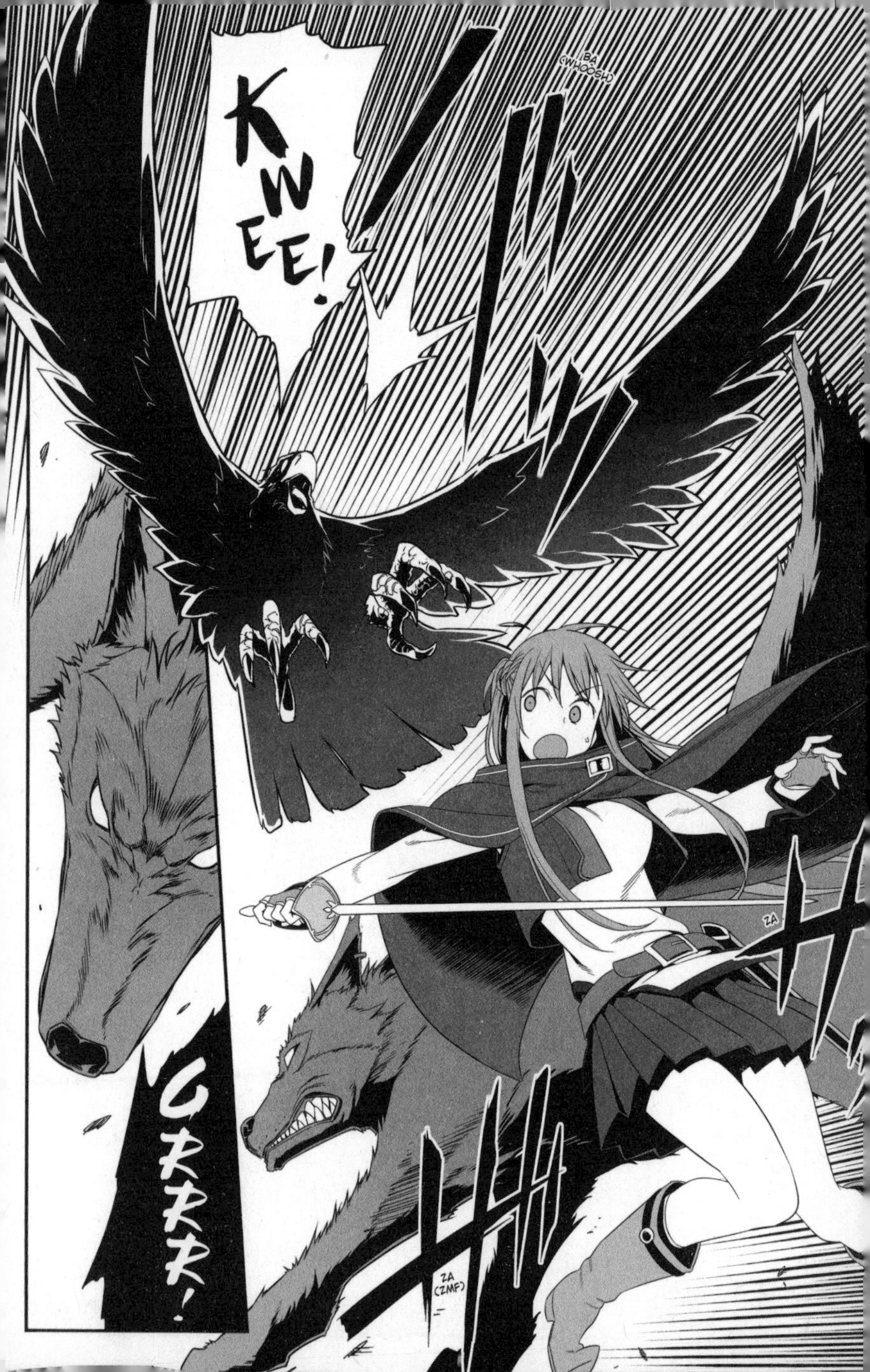
BA (WHOOSH)
KWEE!
ZA
ZA (ZMF)
GRRRR!

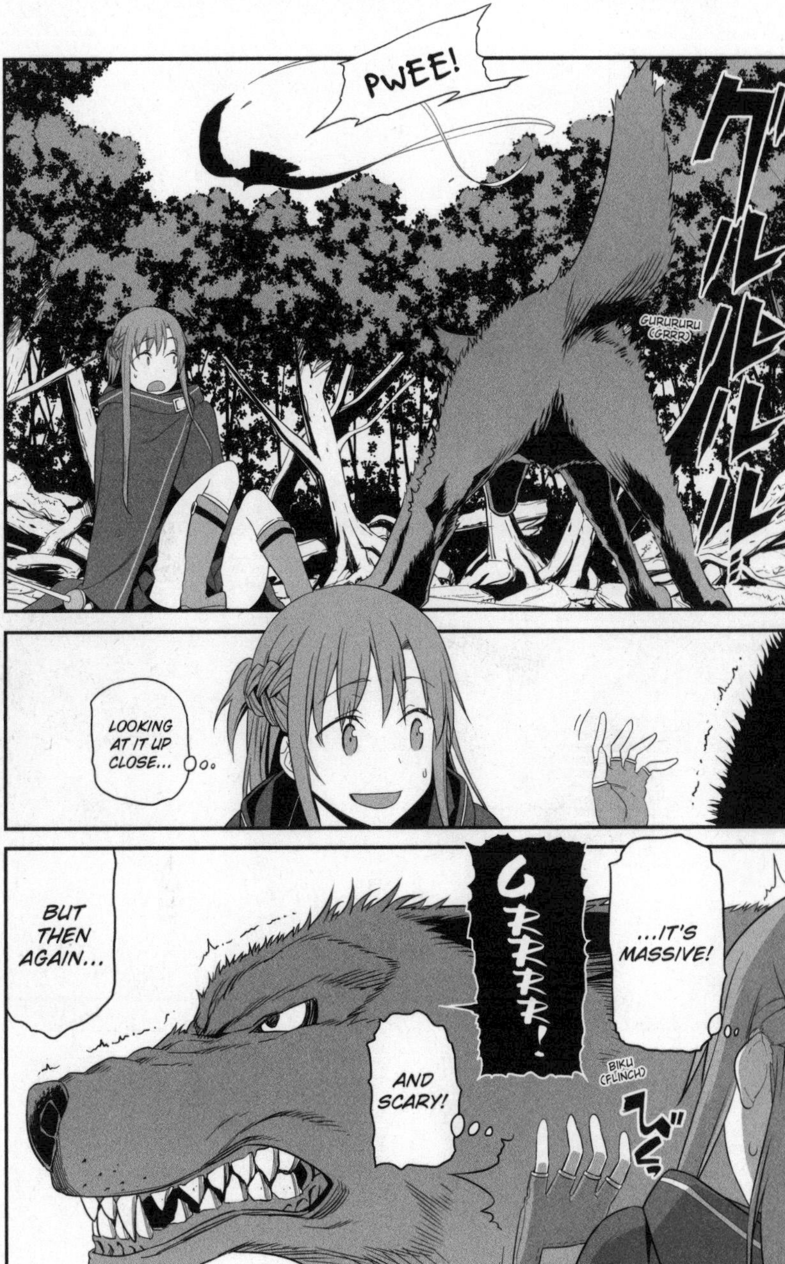
PWEE!
グルルルルル
GURURURU (GRRR)
LOOKING AT IT UP CLOSE...
...IT'S MASSIVE!
GRRRRR!
BUT THEN AGAIN...
AND SCARY!
ビク
BIKU (FLINCH)

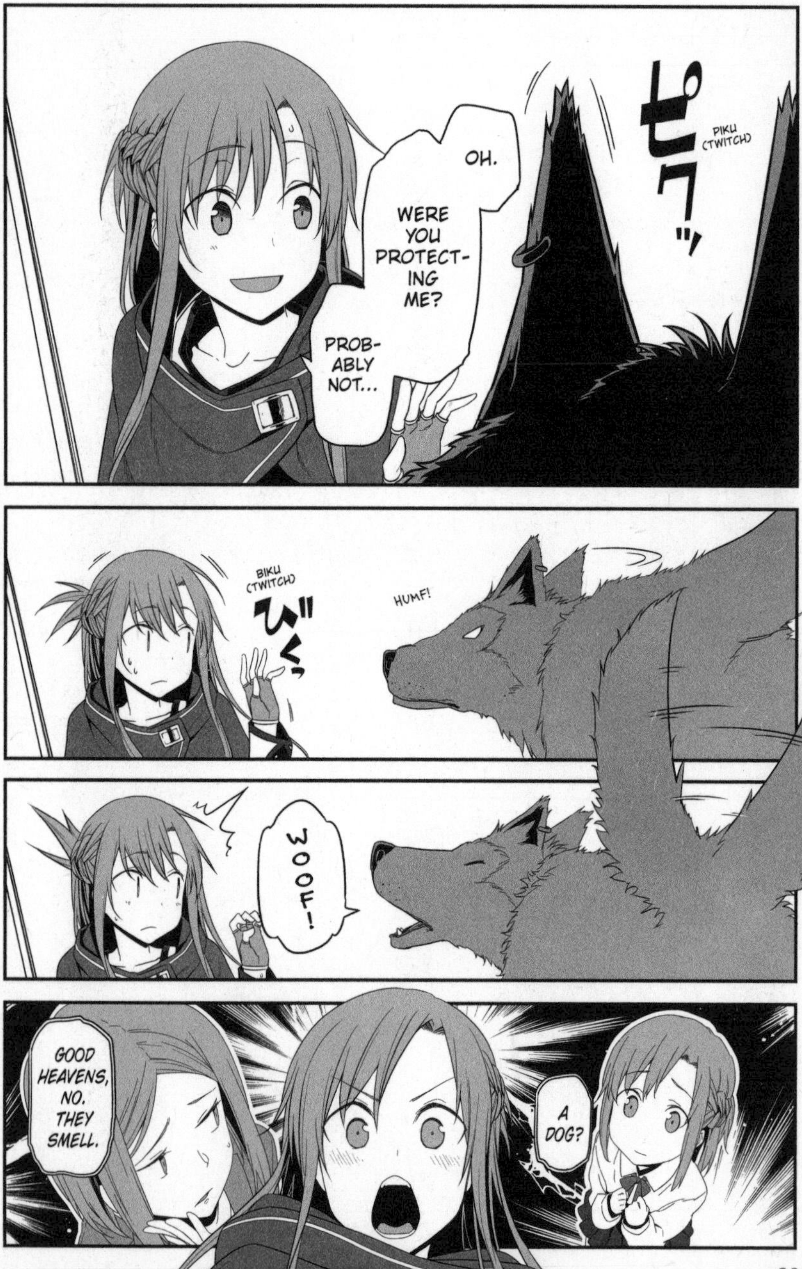
ピクッ
PIKU (TWITCH)
OH.
WERE YOU PROTECTING ME?
PROBABLY NOT...
HUMF!
びくっ
BIKU (TWITCH)
WOOF!
A DOG?
GOOD HEAVENS, NO. THEY SMELL.

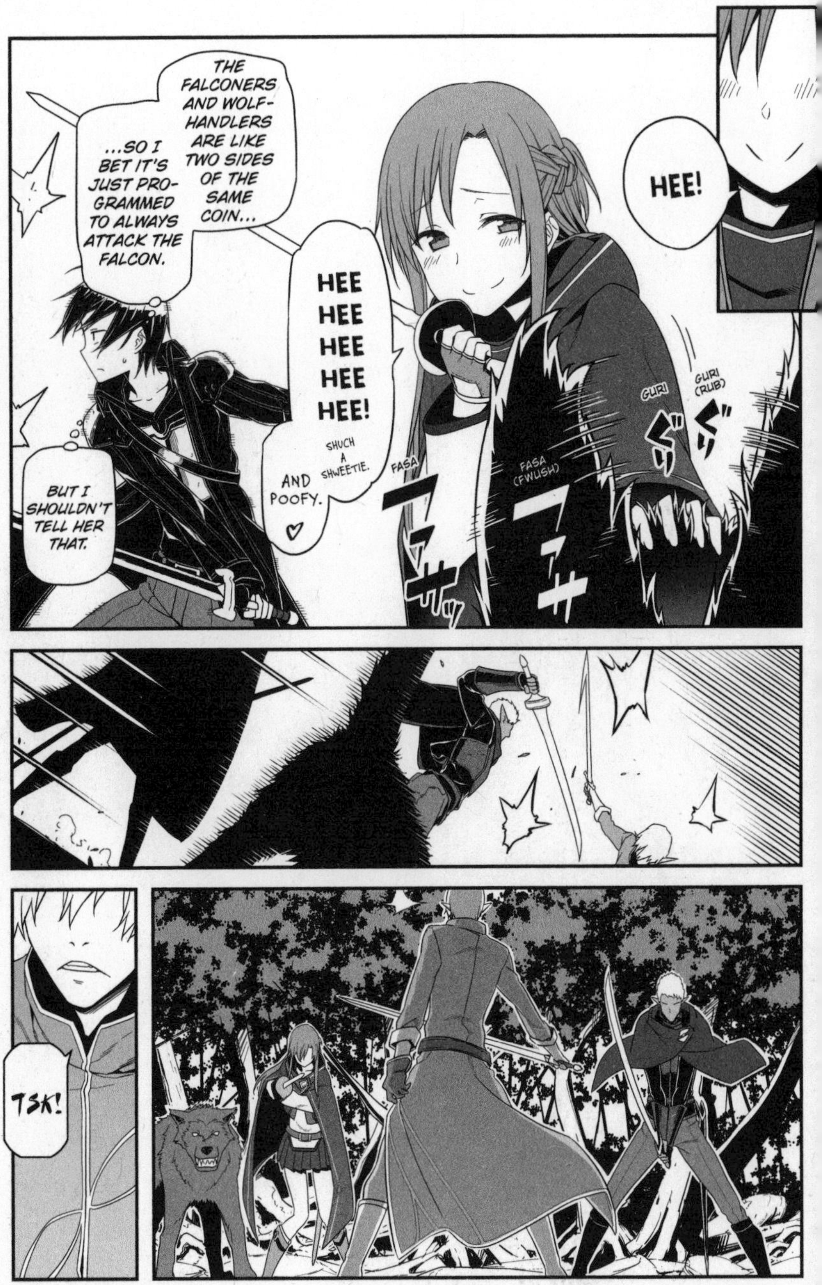
HEE!
GURI (RUB)
GURI
FASA (FWUSH)
FASA
HEE HEE HEE HEE HEE!
SHUCH A SHWEETIE.
AND POOFY. ♡
THE FALCONERS AND WOLF-HANDLERS ARE LIKE TWO SIDES OF THE SAME COIN...
...SO I BET IT'S JUST PRO-GRAMMED TO ALWAYS ATTACK THE FALCON.
BUT I SHOULDN'T TELL HER THAT.
TSK!

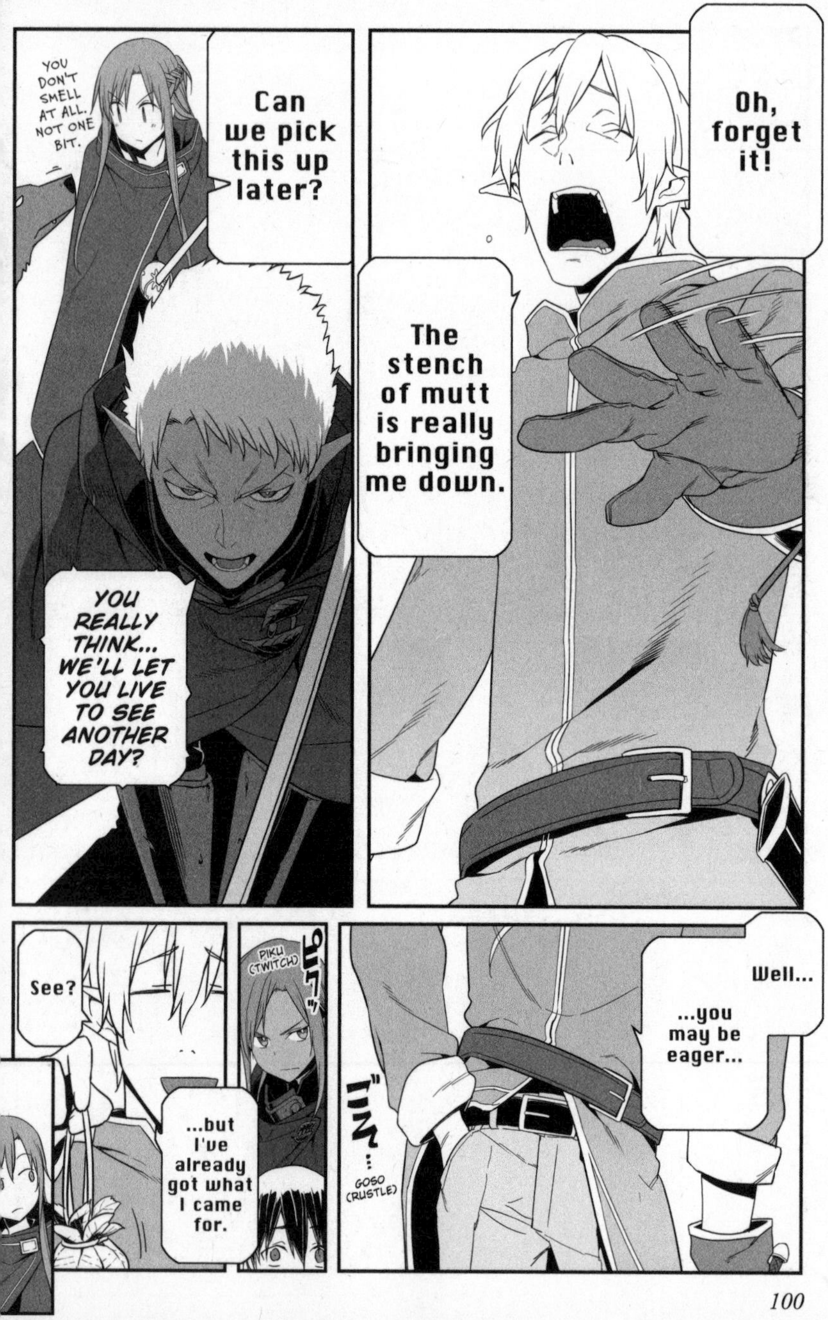
Oh, forget it!
The stench of mutt is really bringing me down.
Can we pick this up later?
YOU DON'T SMELL AT ALL. NOT ONE BIT.
YOU REALLY THINK... WE'LL LET YOU LIVE TO SEE ANOTHER DAY?
Well...
...you may be eager...
GOSO (RUSTLE)
PIKU (TWITCH)
See?
...but I've already got what I came for.

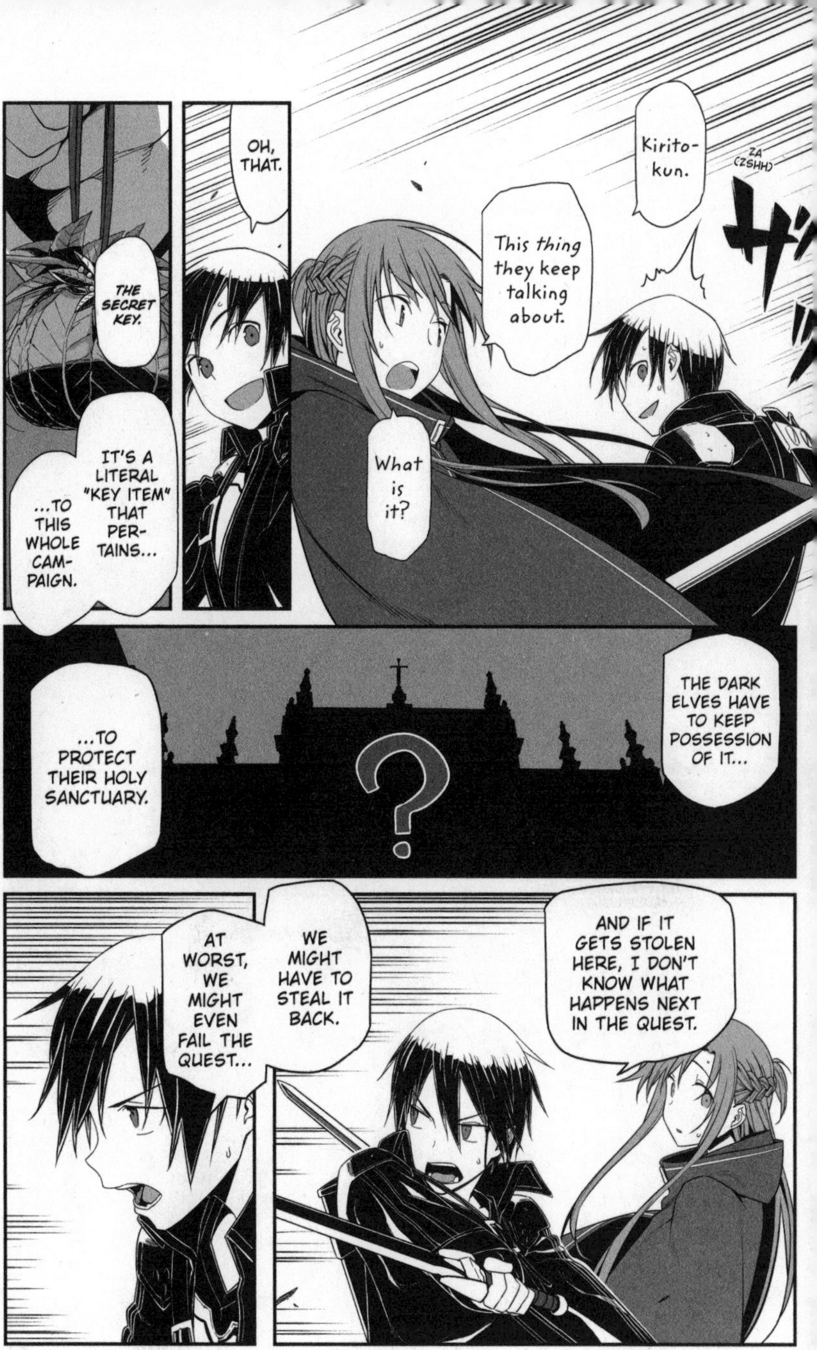
Kirito-kun.
ZA (ZSHH)
This thing they keep talking about.
What is it?
OH, THAT.
THE SECRET KEY.
IT'S A LITERAL "KEY ITEM" THAT PERTAINS...
...TO THIS WHOLE CAMPAIGN.
THE DARK ELVES HAVE TO KEEP POSSESSION OF IT...
...TO PROTECT THEIR HOLY SANCTUARY.
AND IF IT GETS STOLEN HERE, I DON'T KNOW WHAT HAPPENS NEXT IN THE QUEST.
WE MIGHT HAVE TO STEAL IT BACK.
AT WORST, WE MIGHT EVEN FAIL THE QUEST...

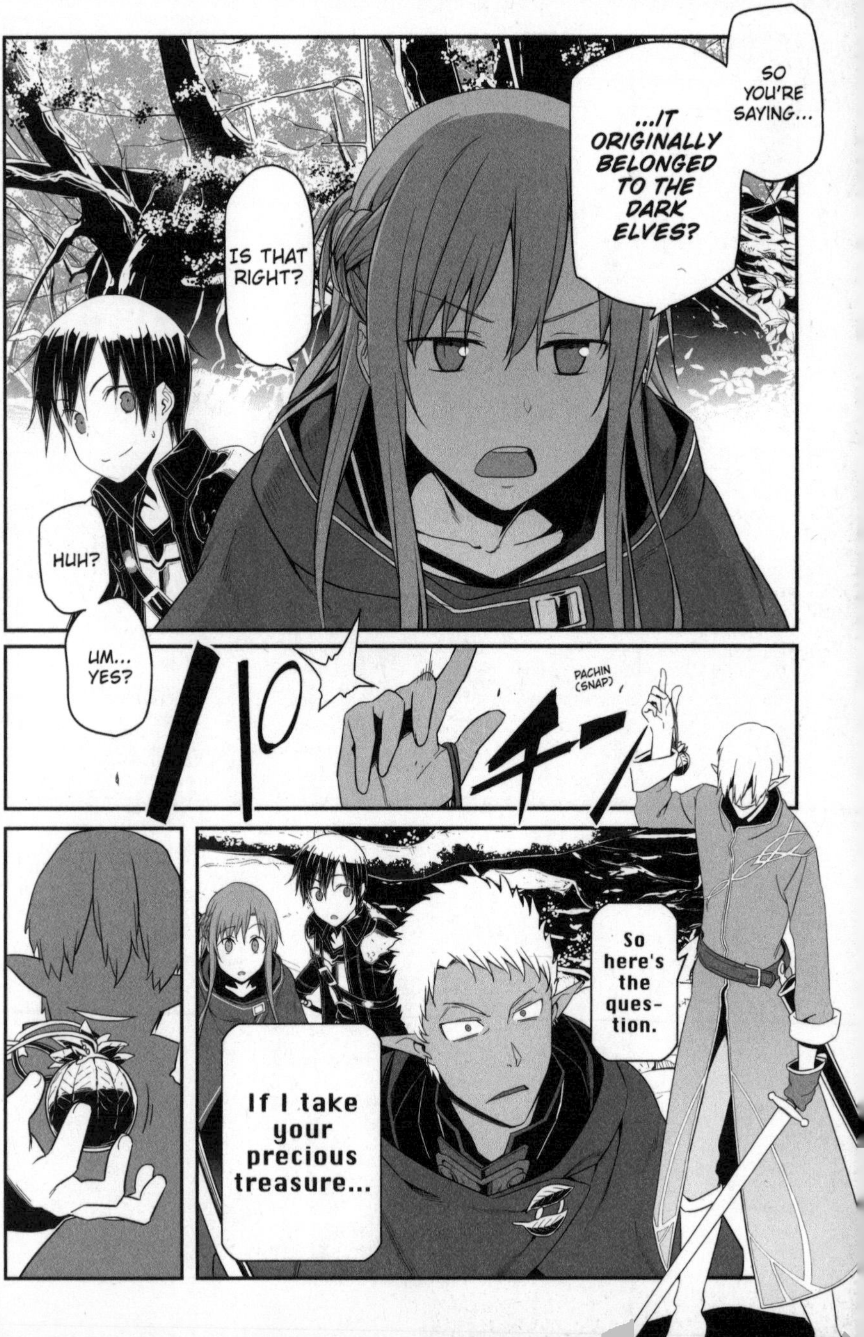
SO YOU'RE SAYING...
...IT ORIGINALLY BELONGED TO THE DARK ELVES?
IS THAT RIGHT?
HUH?
UM... YES?
PACHIN (SNAP)
So here's the ques-tion.
If I take your precious treasure...

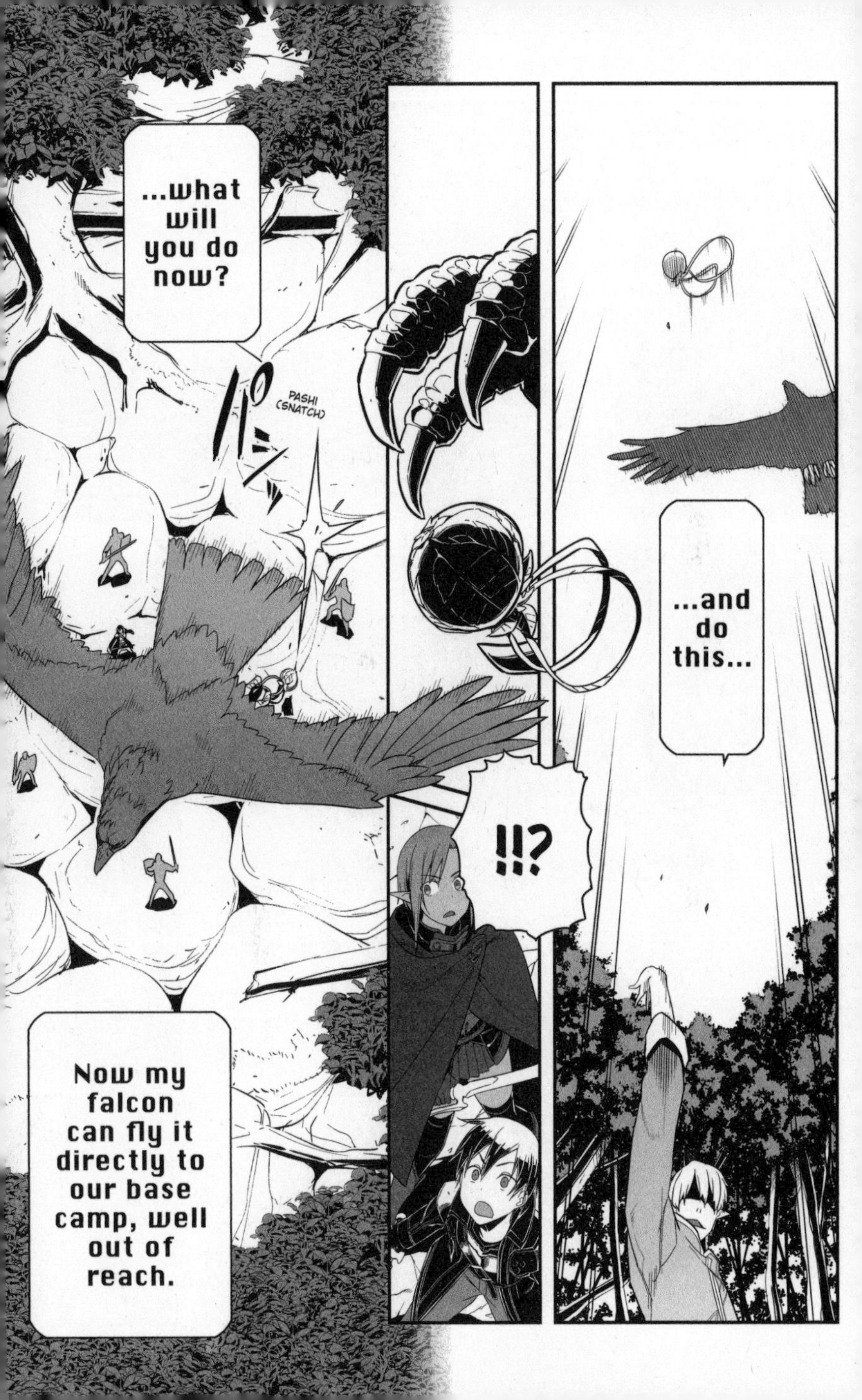
...and do this...
!!?
...what will you do now?
PASHI (SNATCH)
Now my falcon can fly it directly to our base camp, well out of reach.

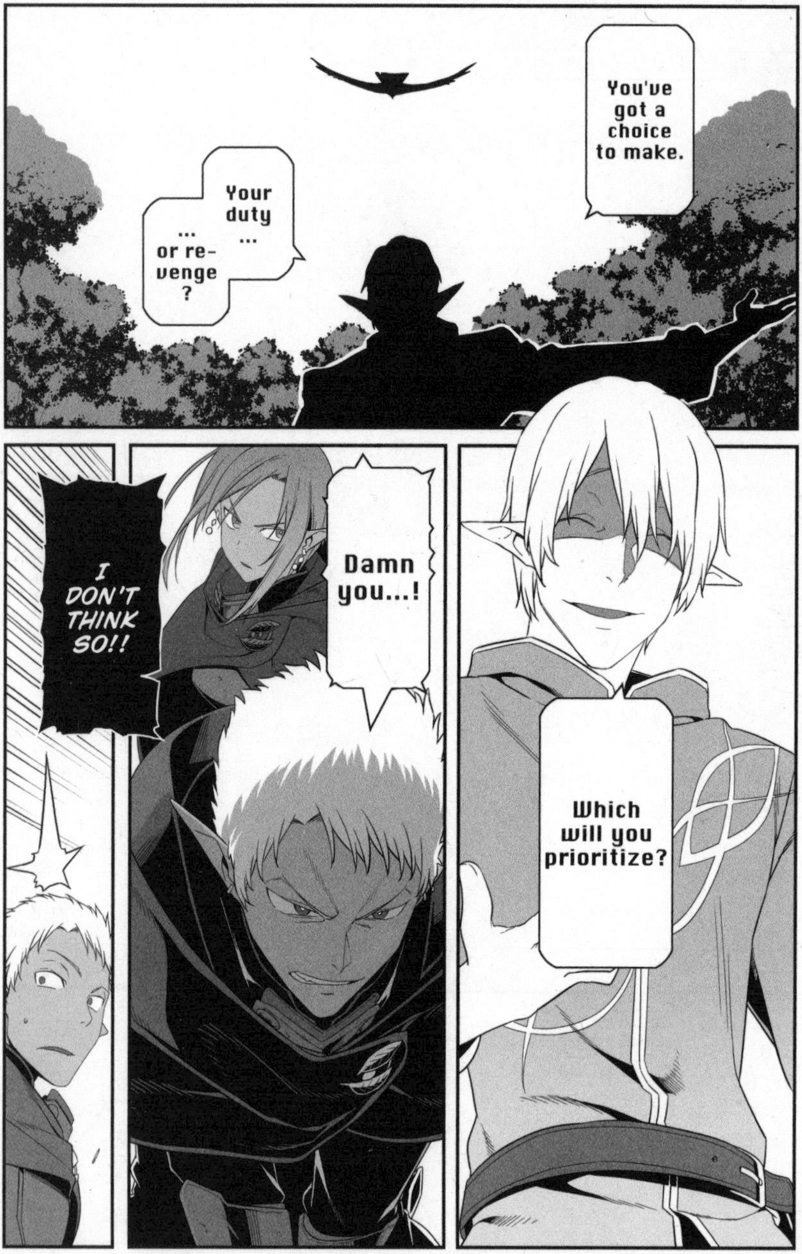
You've got a choice to make.
Your duty ... ... or re-venge?
Which will you prioritize?
Damn you...!
I DON'T THINK SO!!

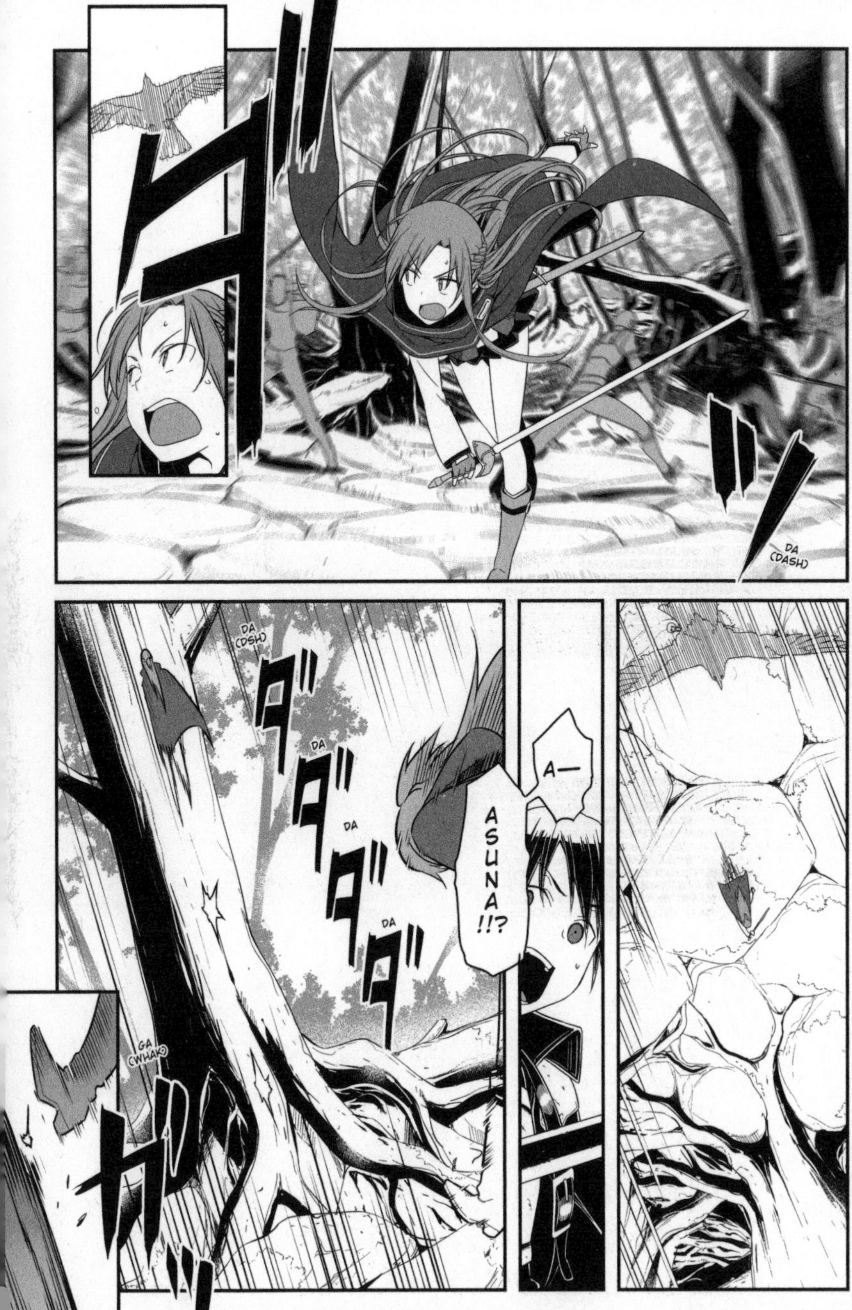
DA (DASH)
A—
ASUNA!!?
DA (DSH)
DA
DA
DA
GA (WHAK)

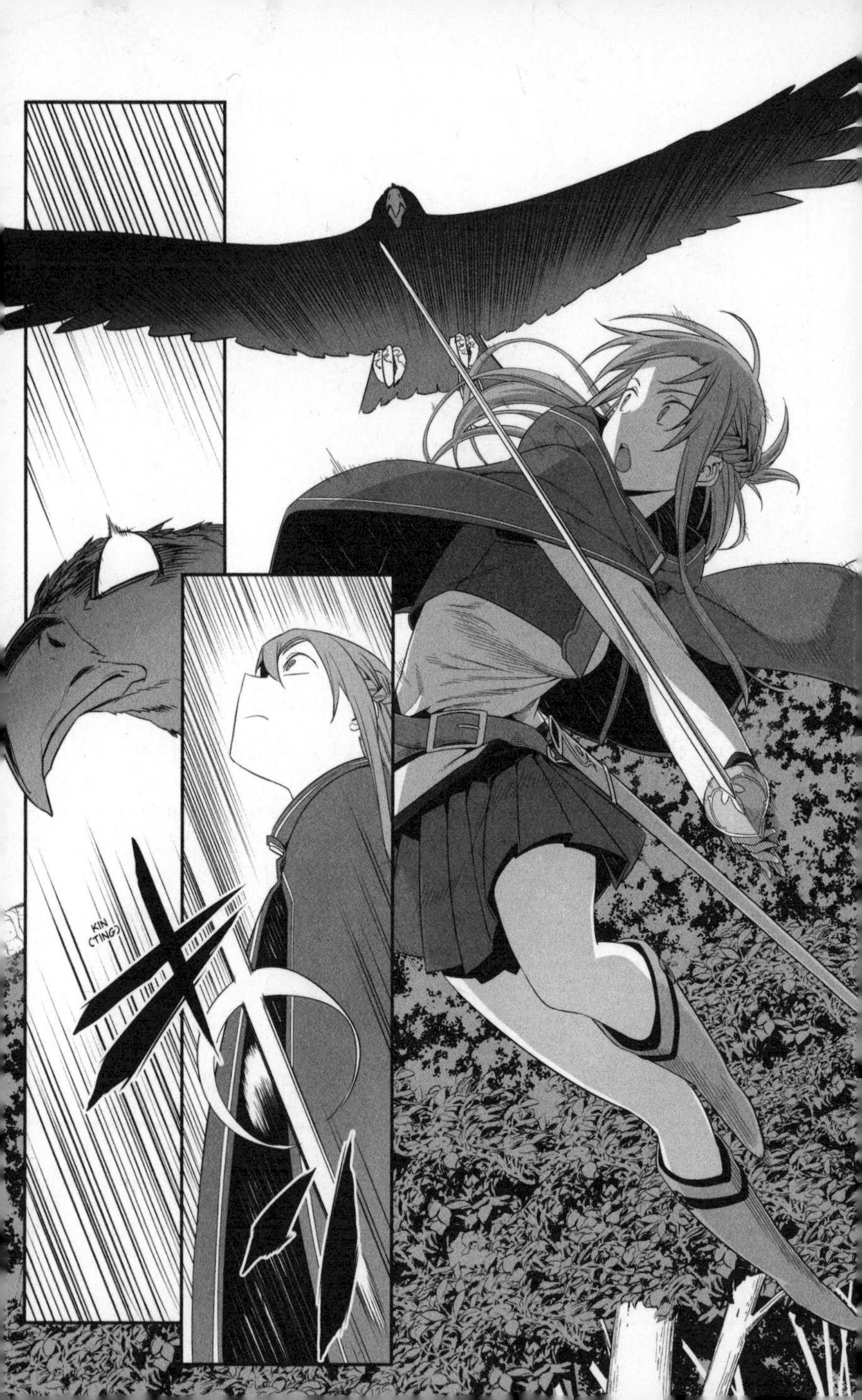
KIN
(TING)

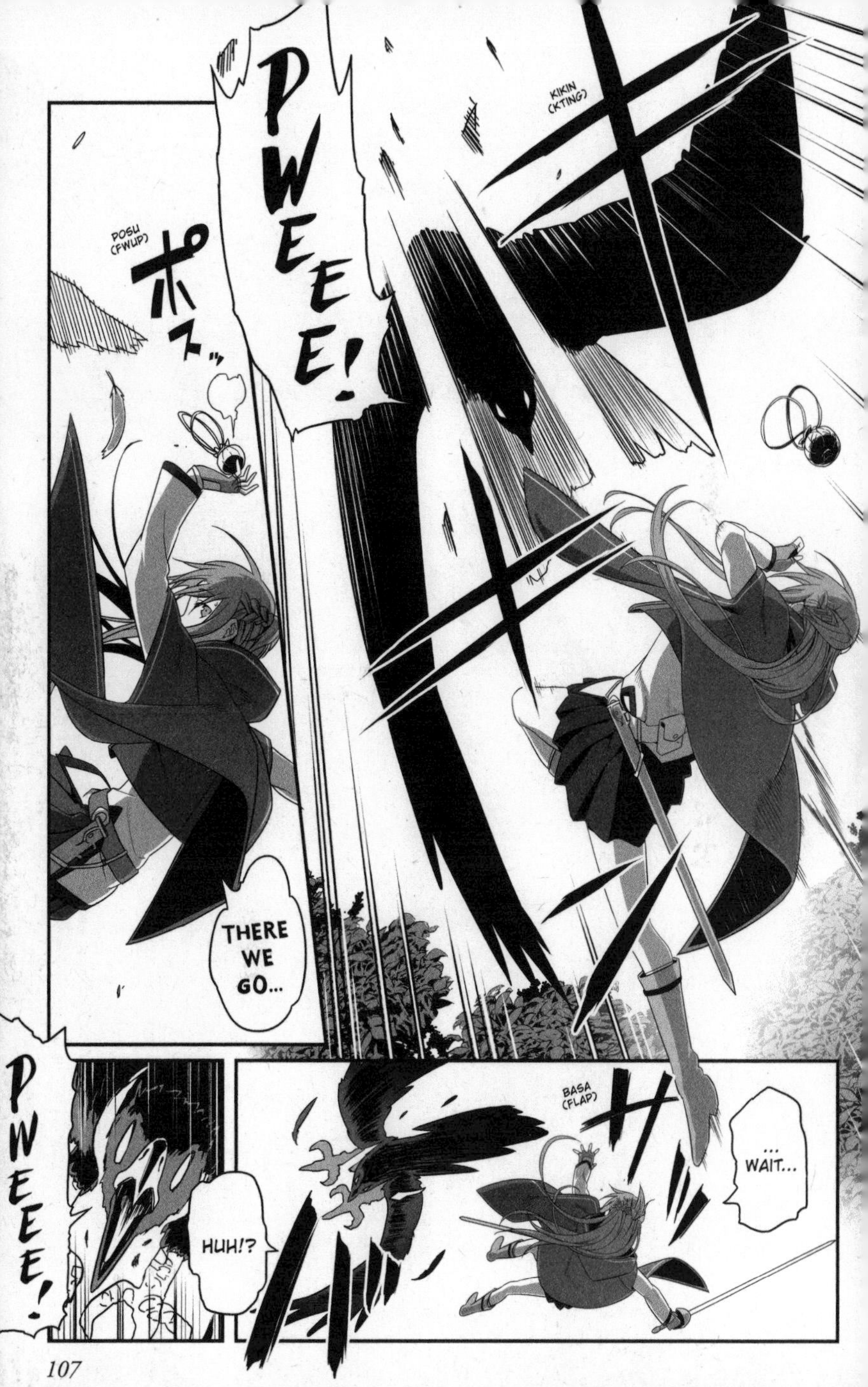

KIKIN (KTING)
PWEEE!
POSU (FWUP)
ポスッ
THERE WE GO...
BASA (FLAP)
... WAIT...
HUH!?
PWEEE!

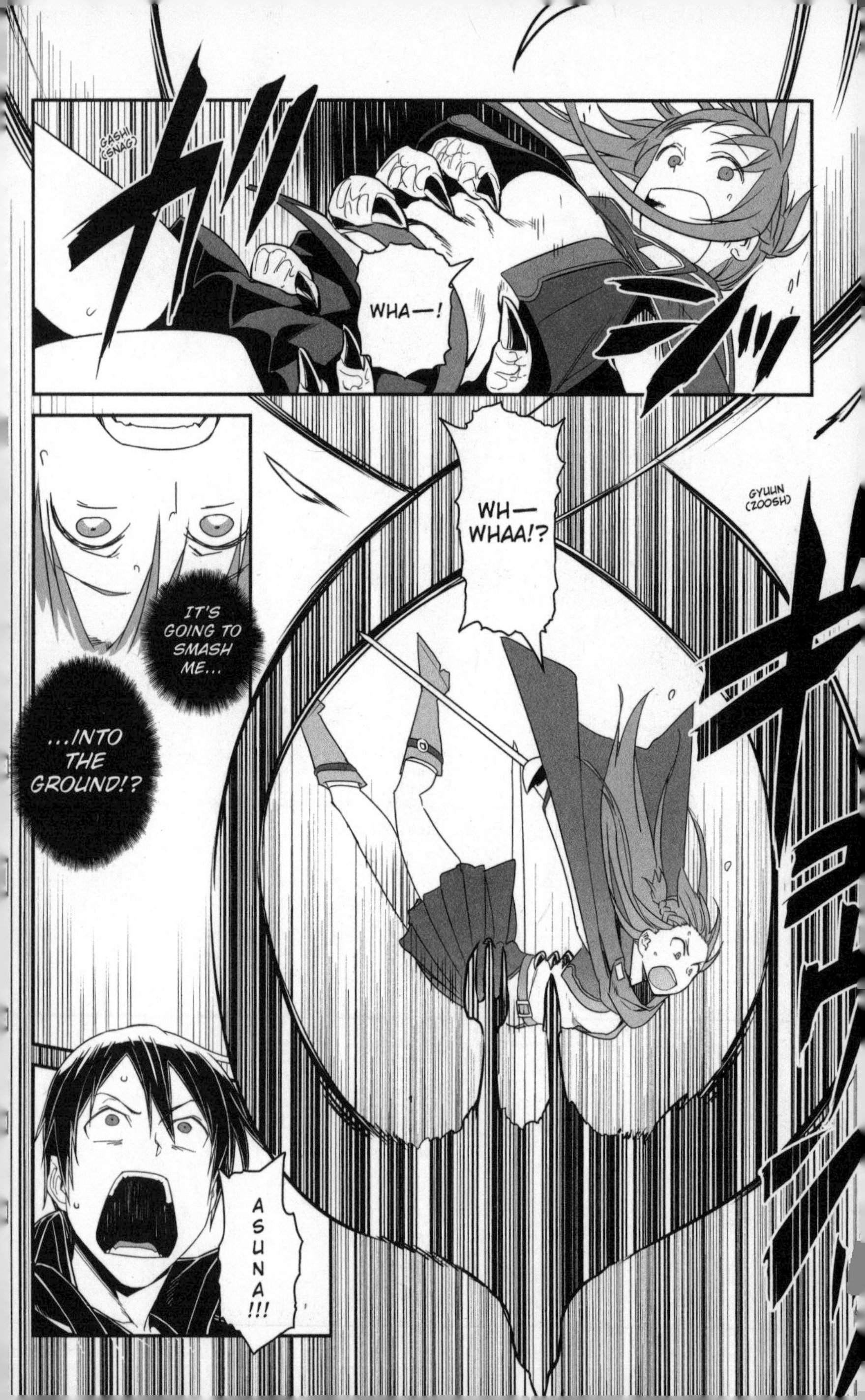
GASHI (SNAG)
WHA—!
GYUUN (ZOOSH)
WH— WHAA!?
IT'S GOING TO SMASH ME...
...INTO THE GROUND!?
ASUNA!!!

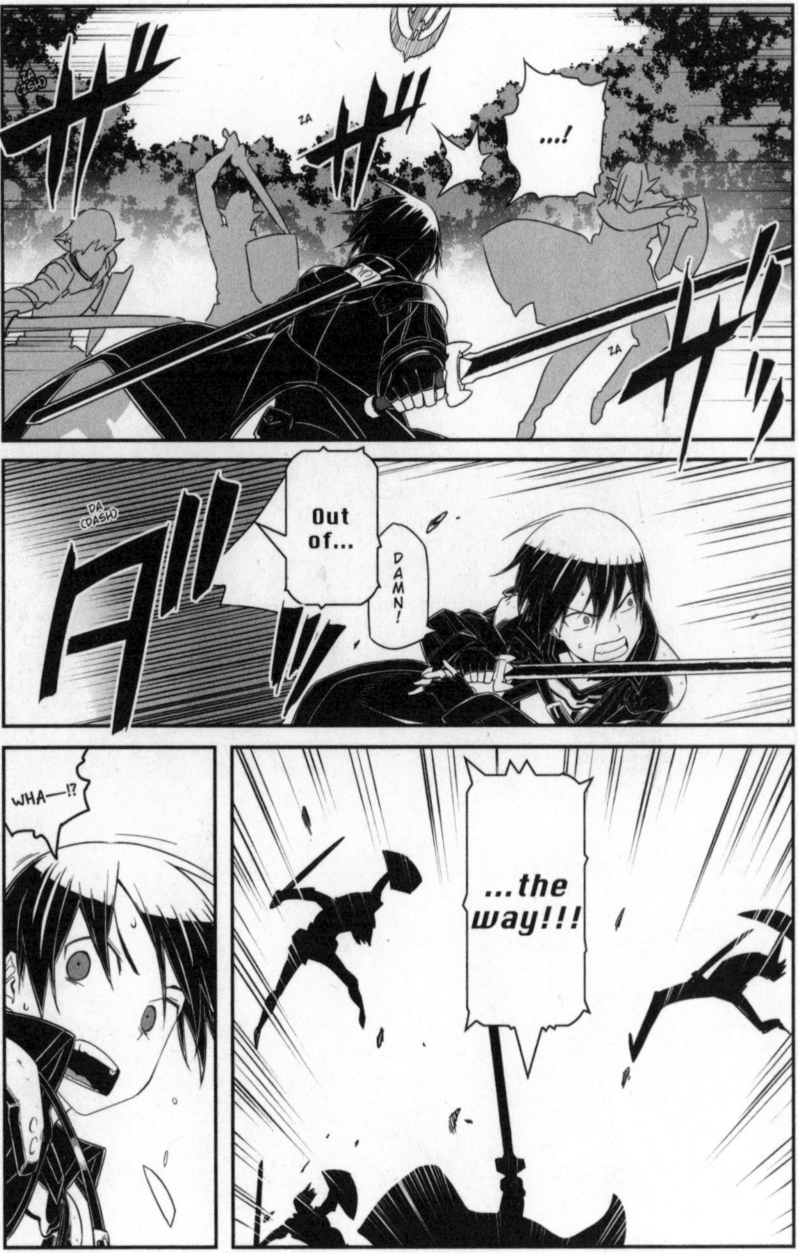
ZA
...!
ZA
ZA (ZSH)
DAMN!
Out of...
DA (DASH)
...the way!!!
WHA—!?

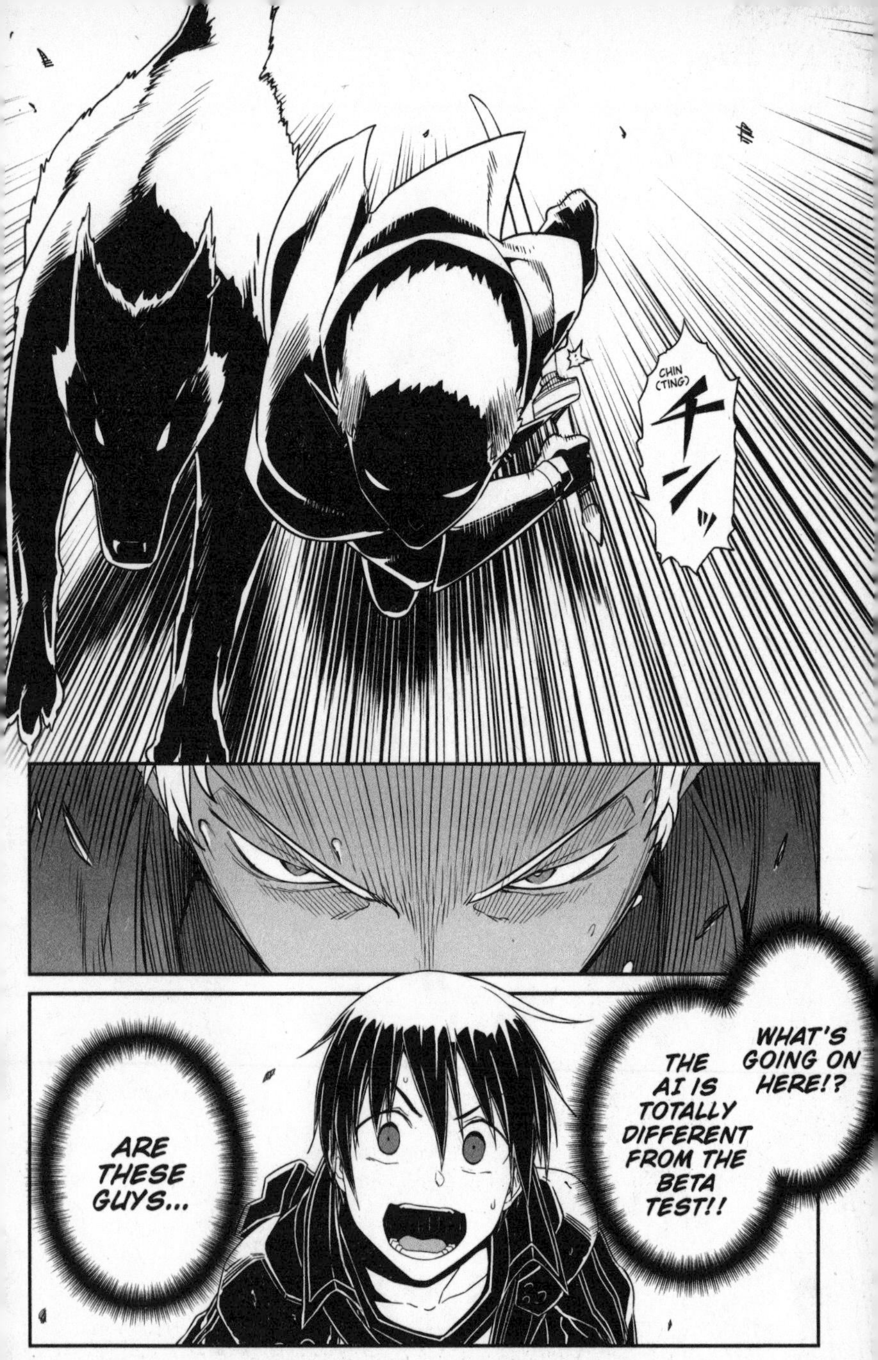
CHIN (TING)
チンッ
WHAT'S GOING ON HERE!?
THE AI IS TOTALLY DIFFERENT FROM THE BETA TEST!!
ARE THESE GUYS...

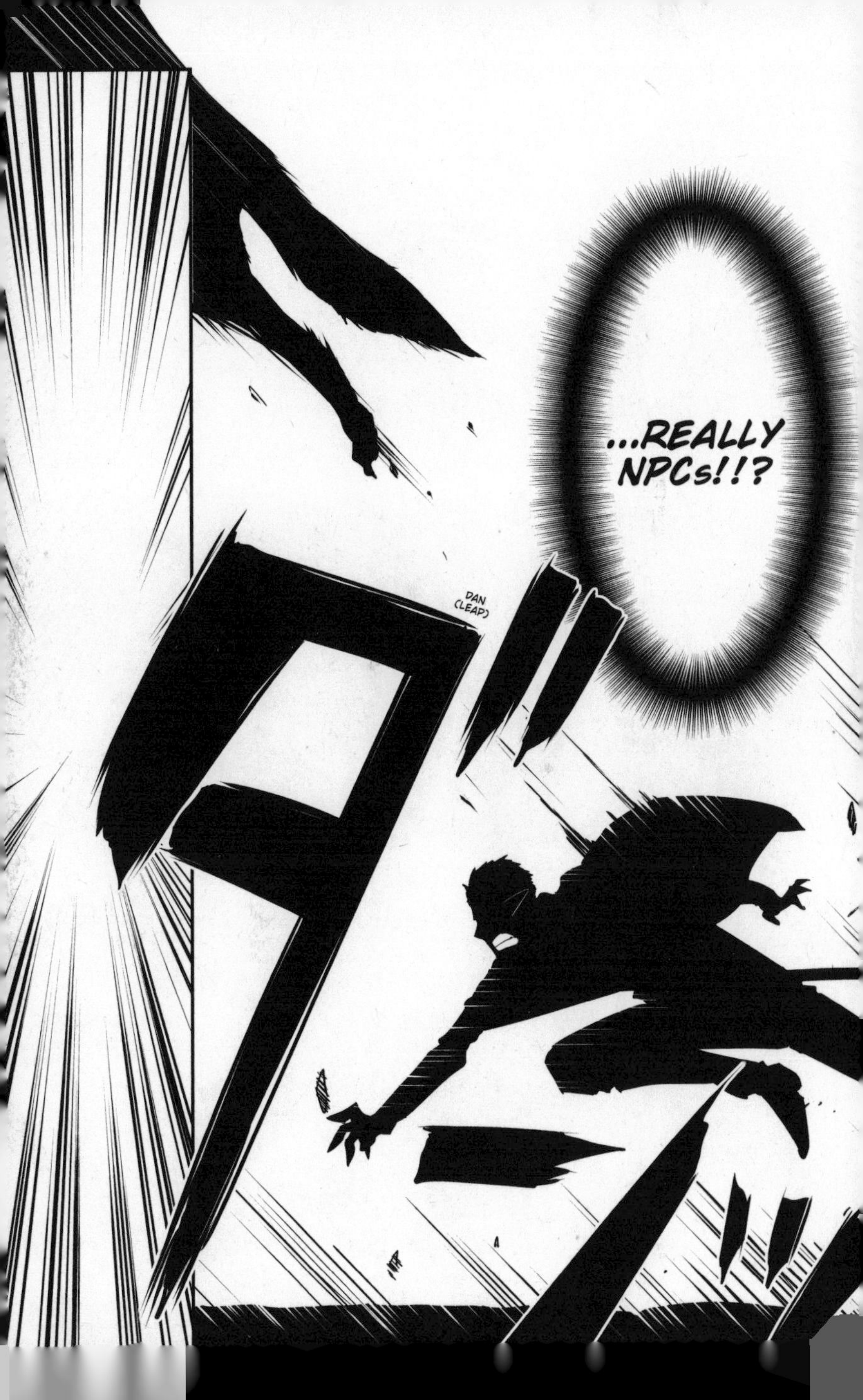
...REALLY NPCs!!?
DAN (LEAP)

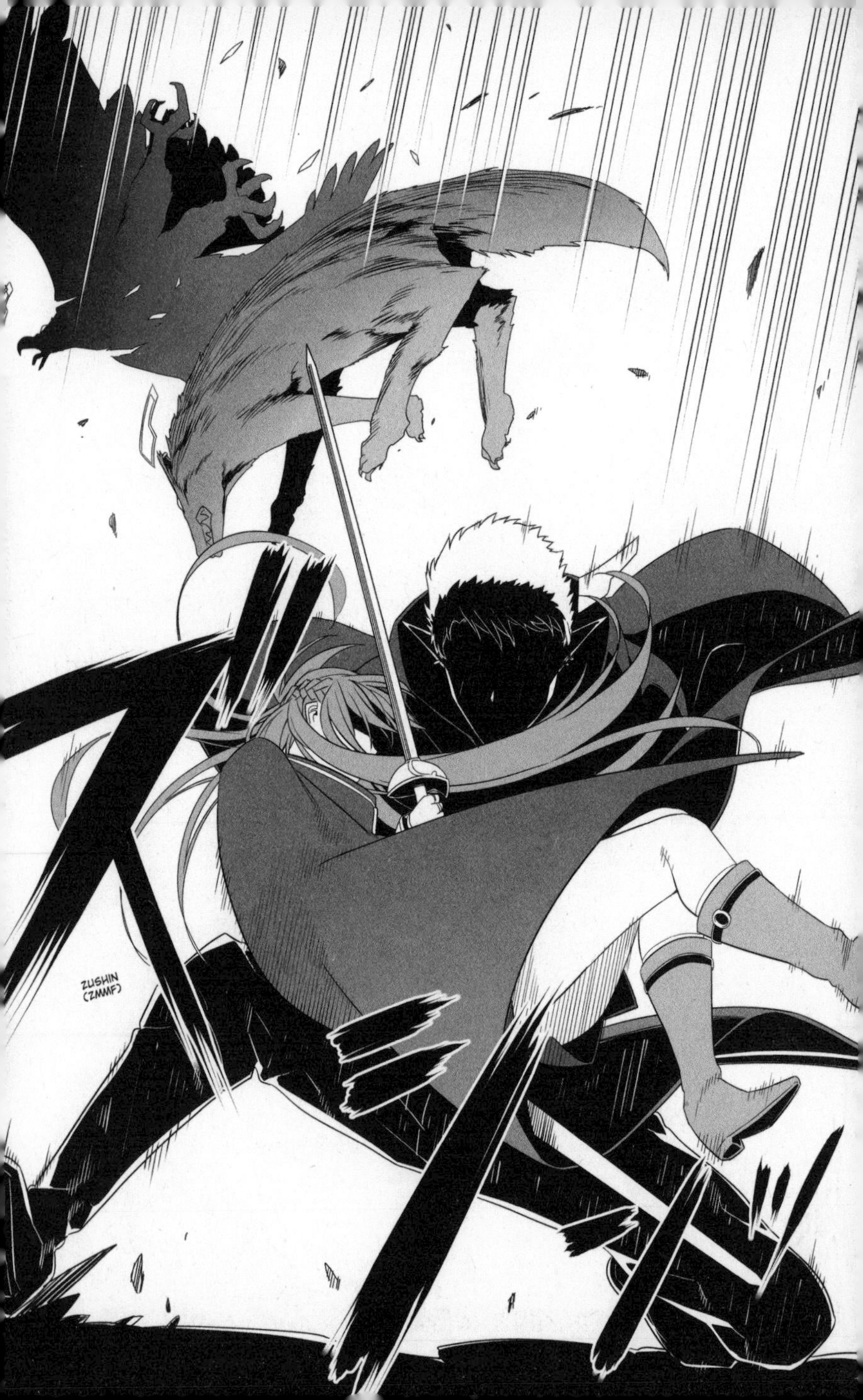
ZUSHIN
(ZMMF)

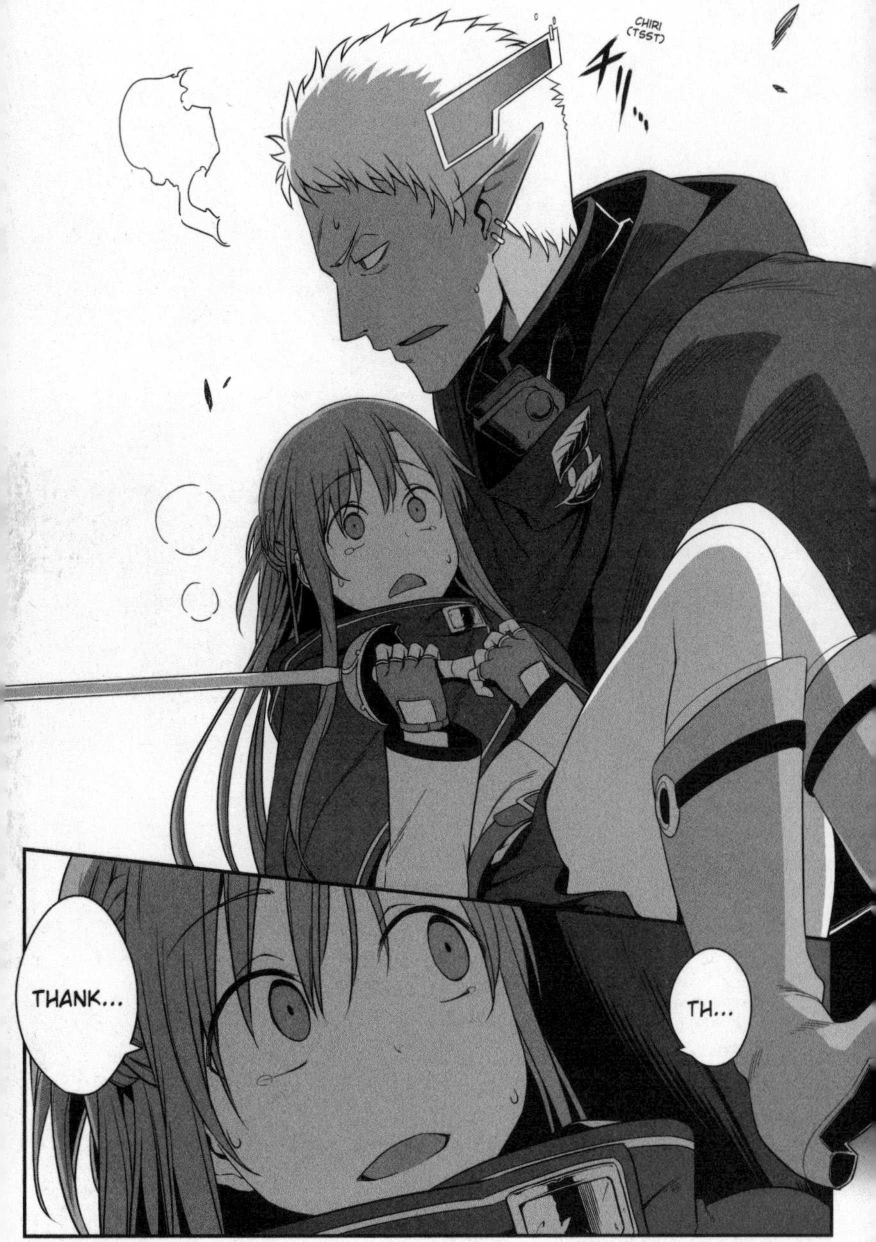
CHIRI (TSST)
チリ…
TH...
THANK...

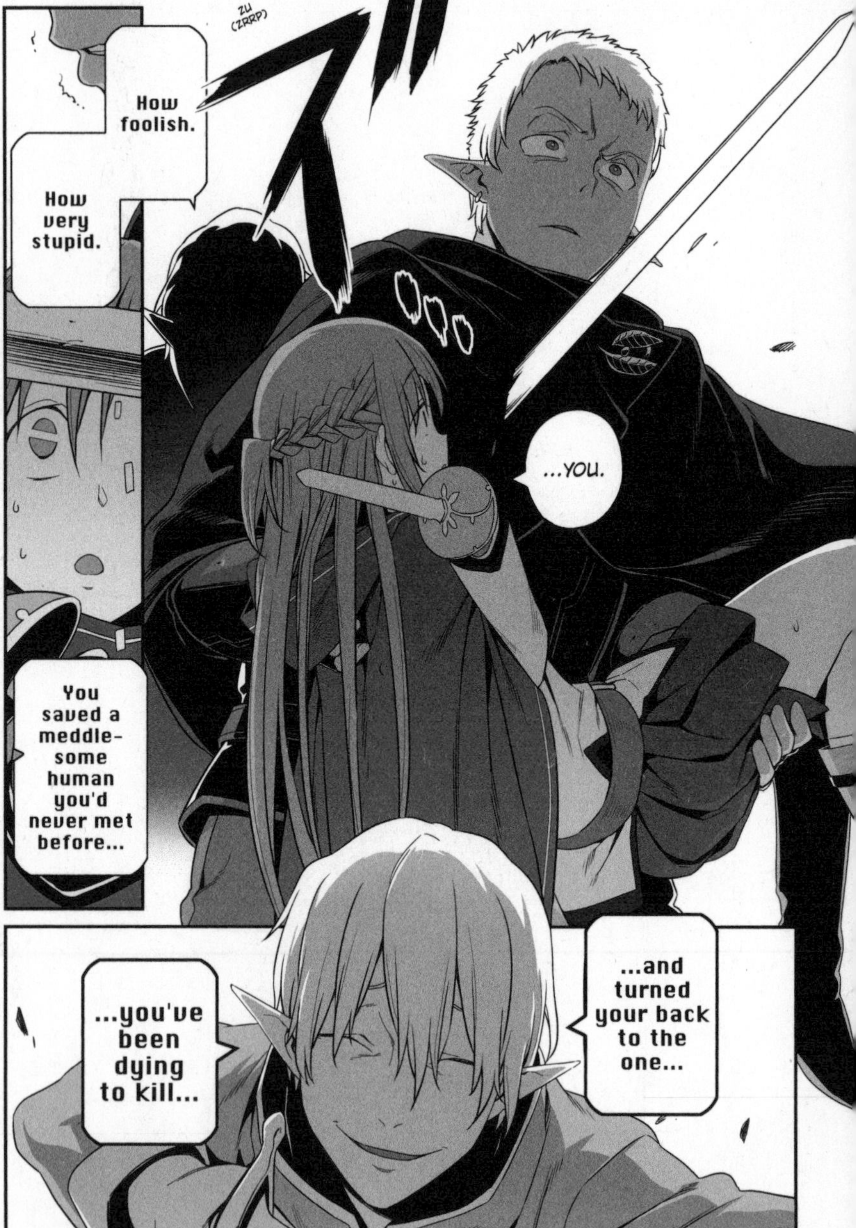

ZU (ZRRP)
...YOU.
How foolish.
How very stupid.
You saved a meddle-some human you'd never met before...
...and turned your back to the one...
...you've been dying to kill...

#027: Loss II

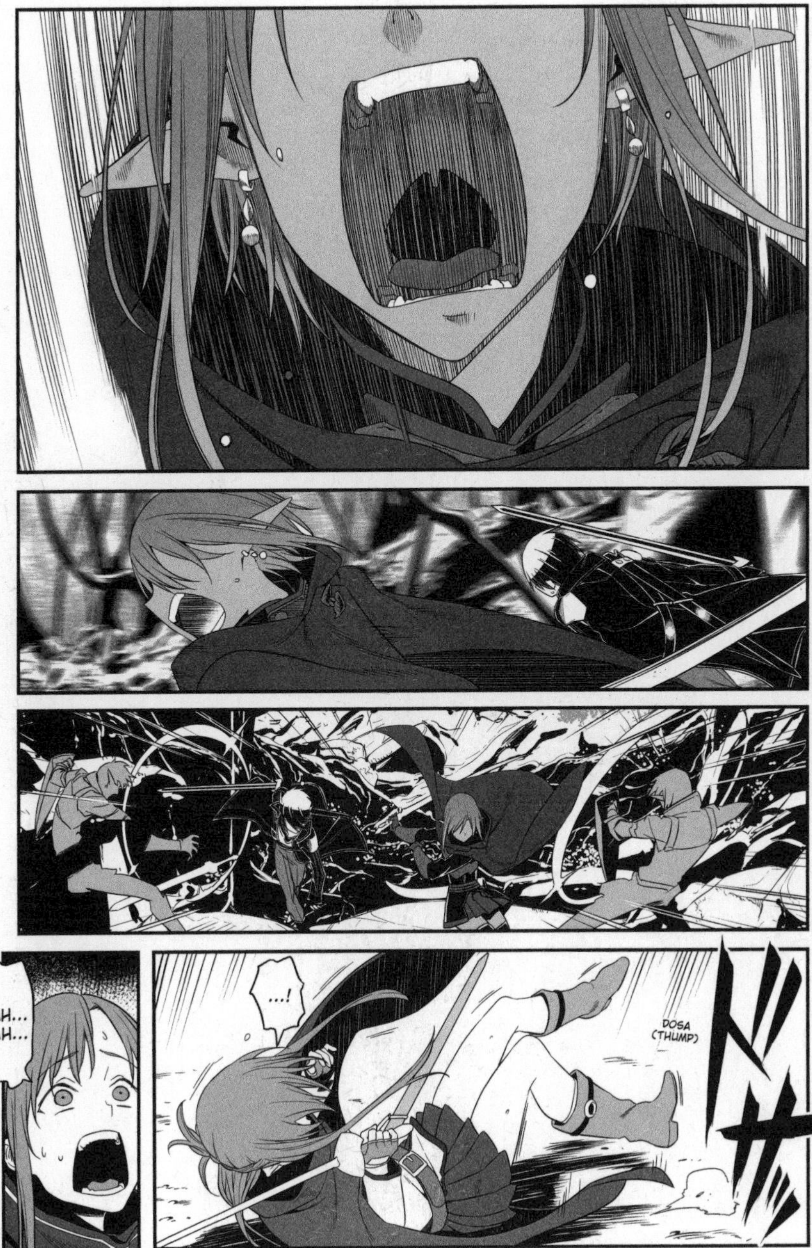
...!
DOSA (THUMP)
AH... AH...

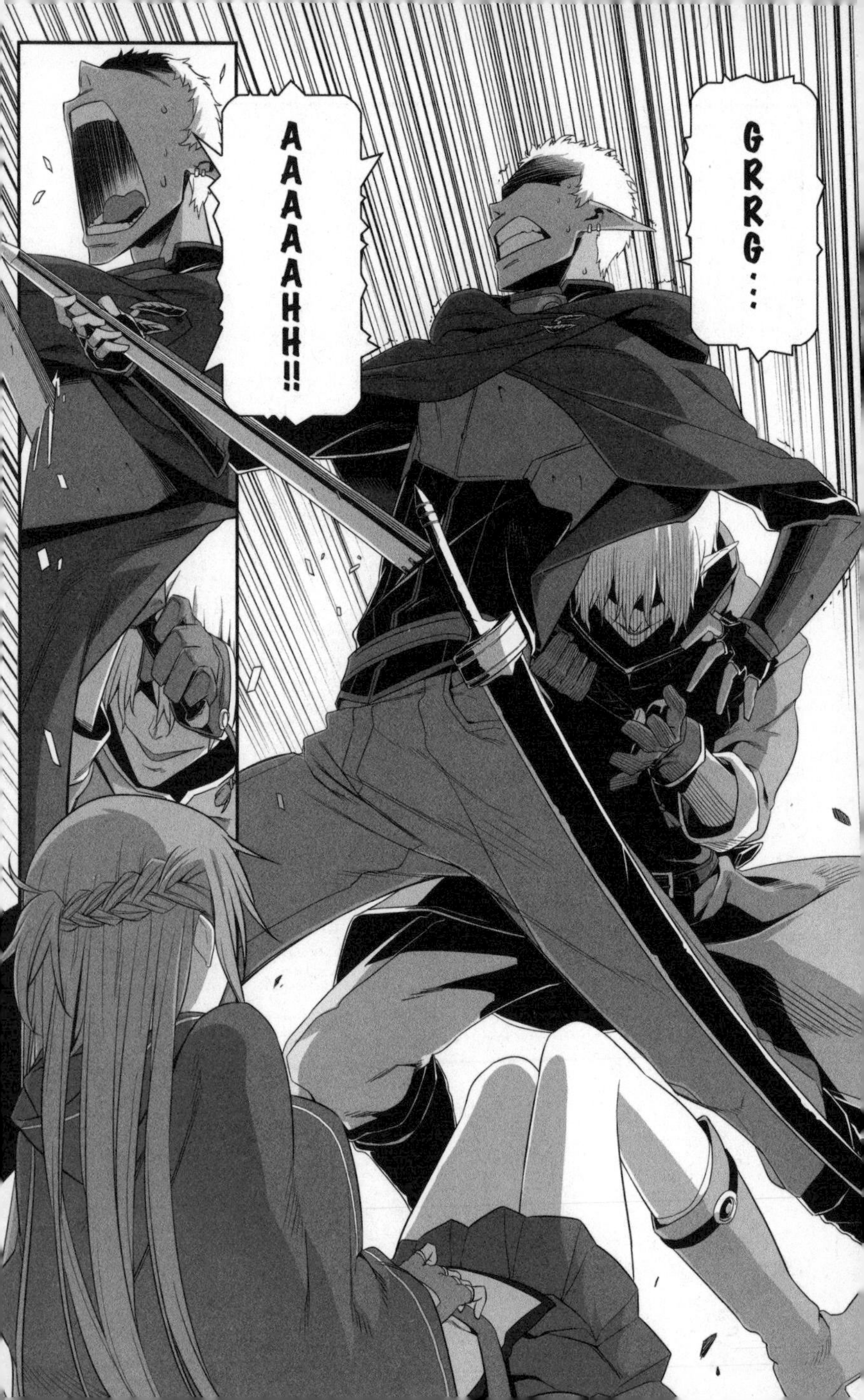
GRRG...
AAAAAAHH!!

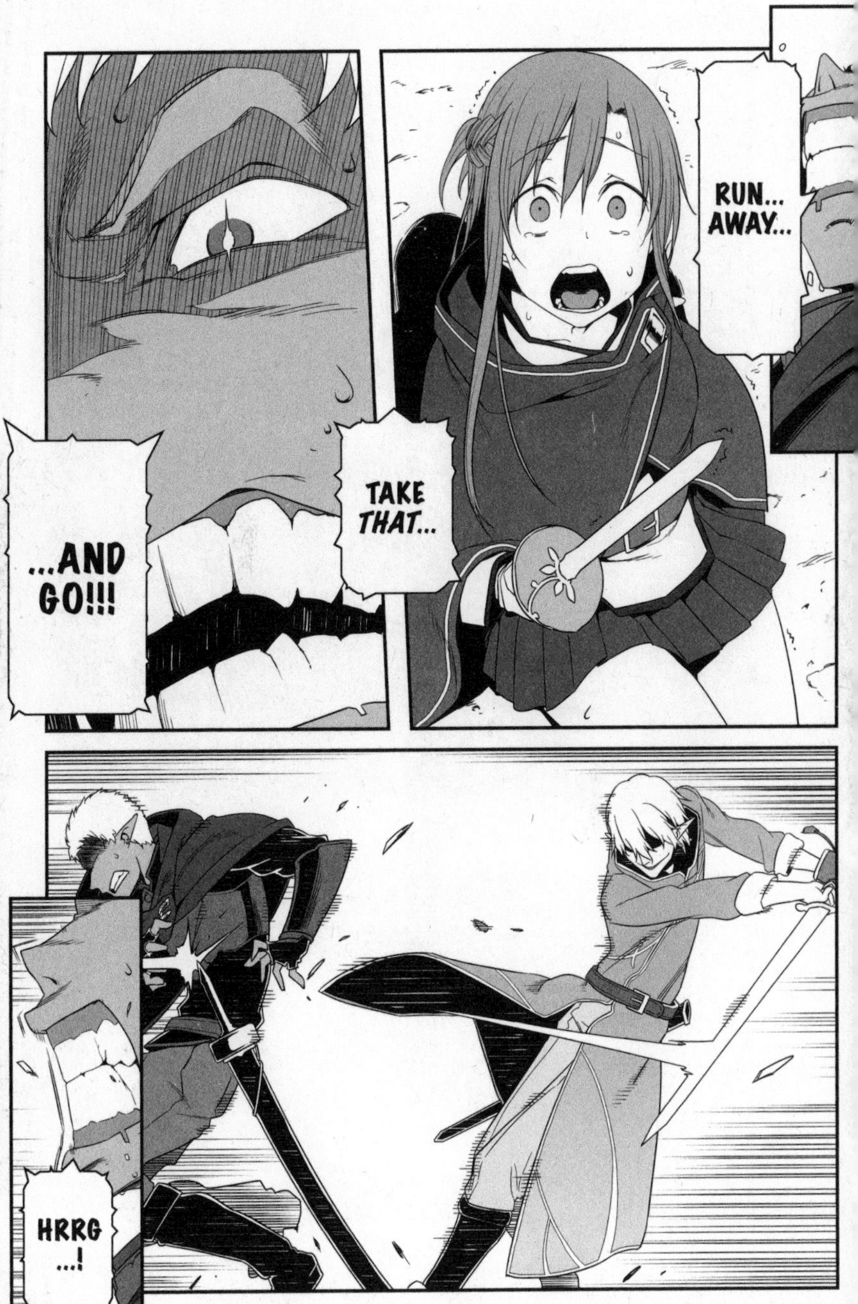
RUN... AWAY...
TAKE THAT...
...AND GO!!!
HRRG ...!

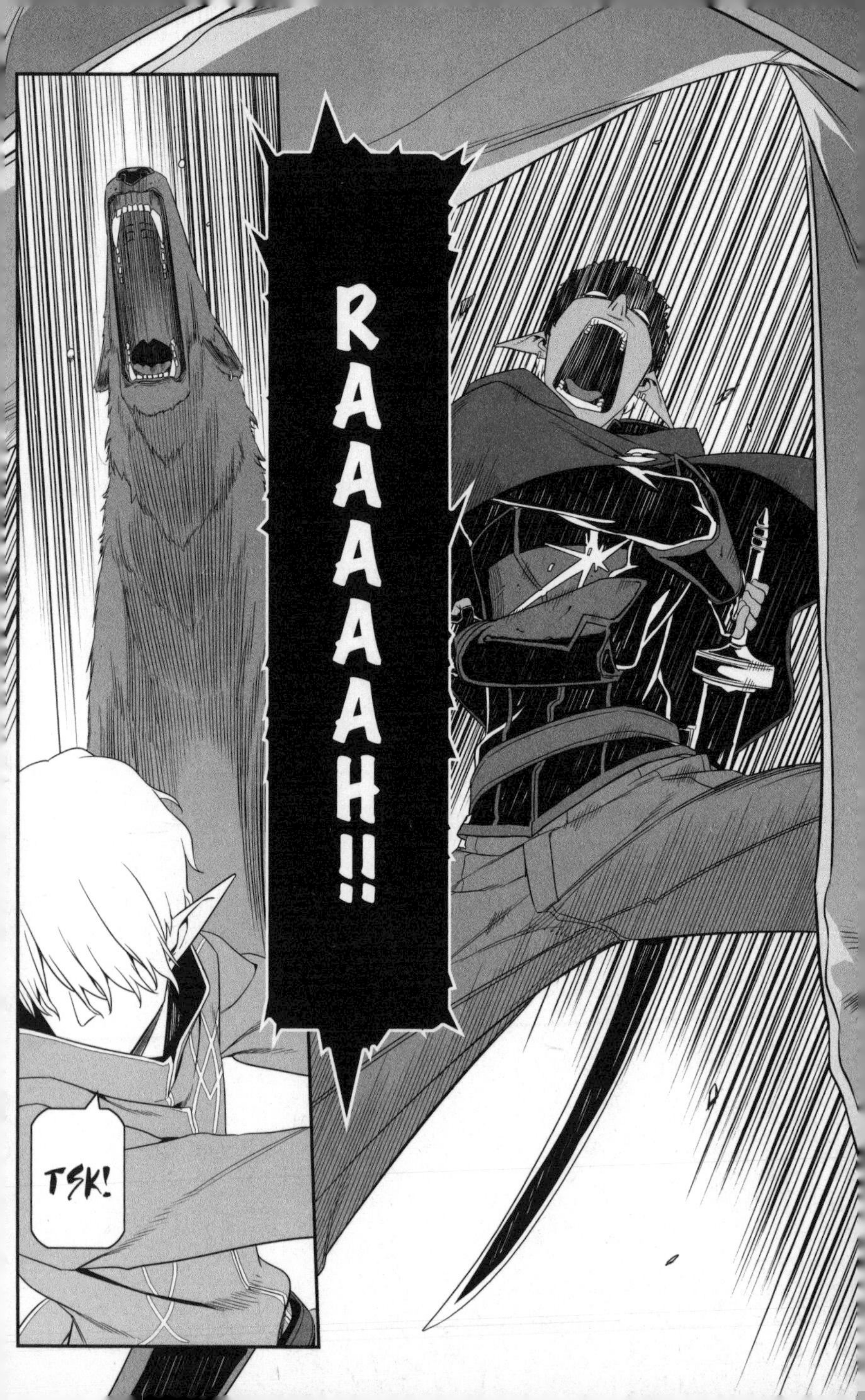
RAAAAAH!!
TSK!

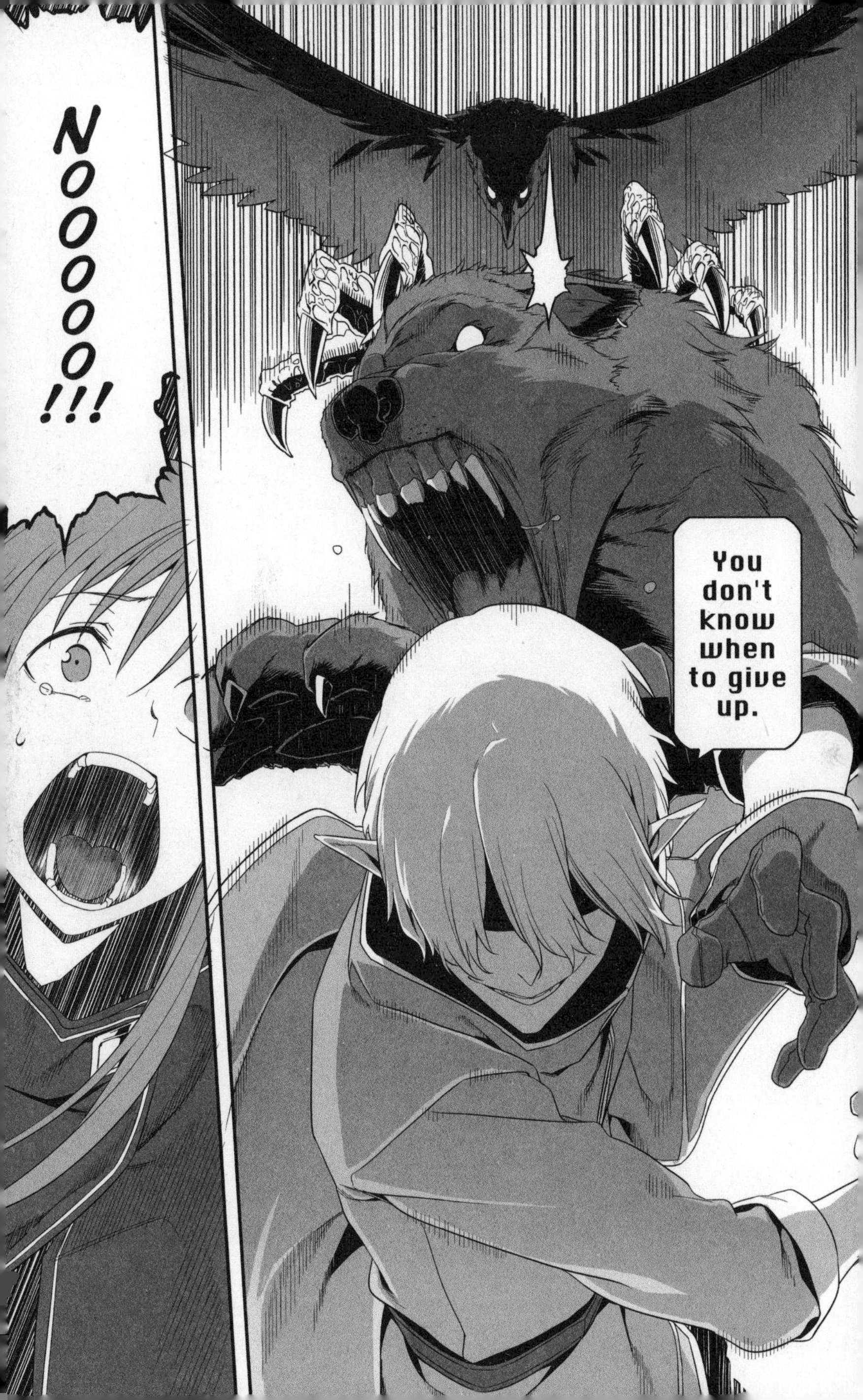
You don't know when to give up.
NOOOOOO!!!

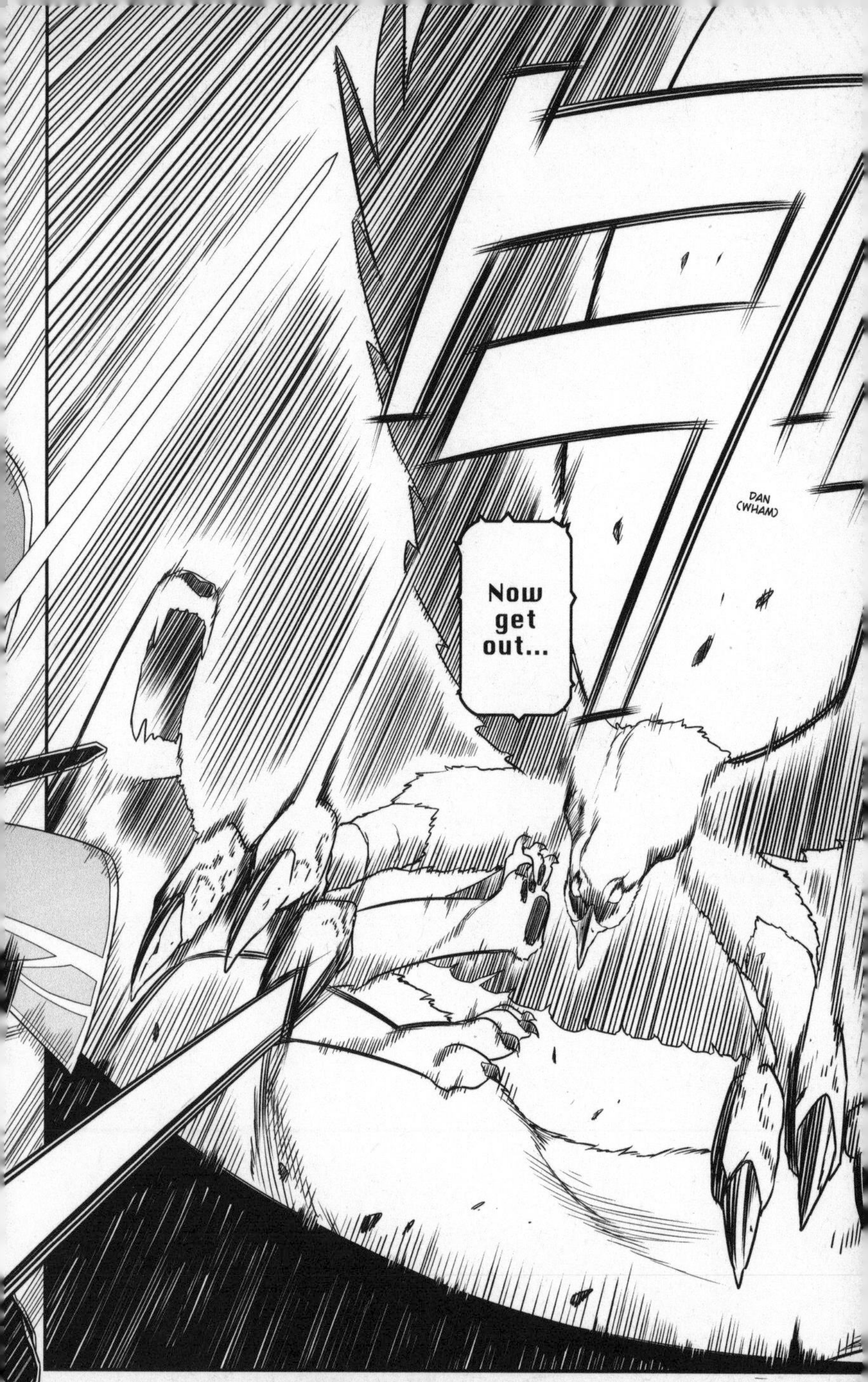
DAN (WHAM)
Now get out...

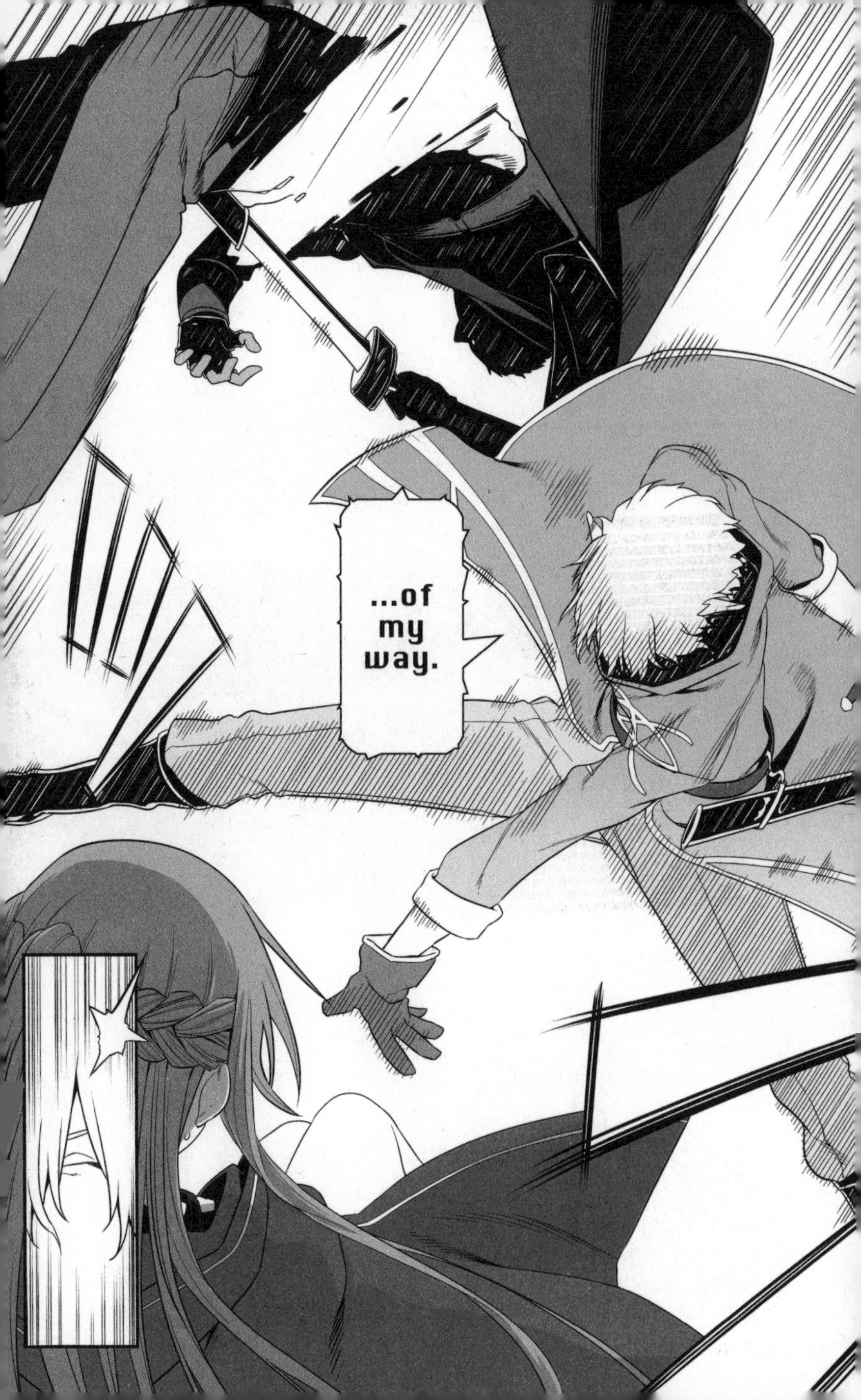
...of my way.

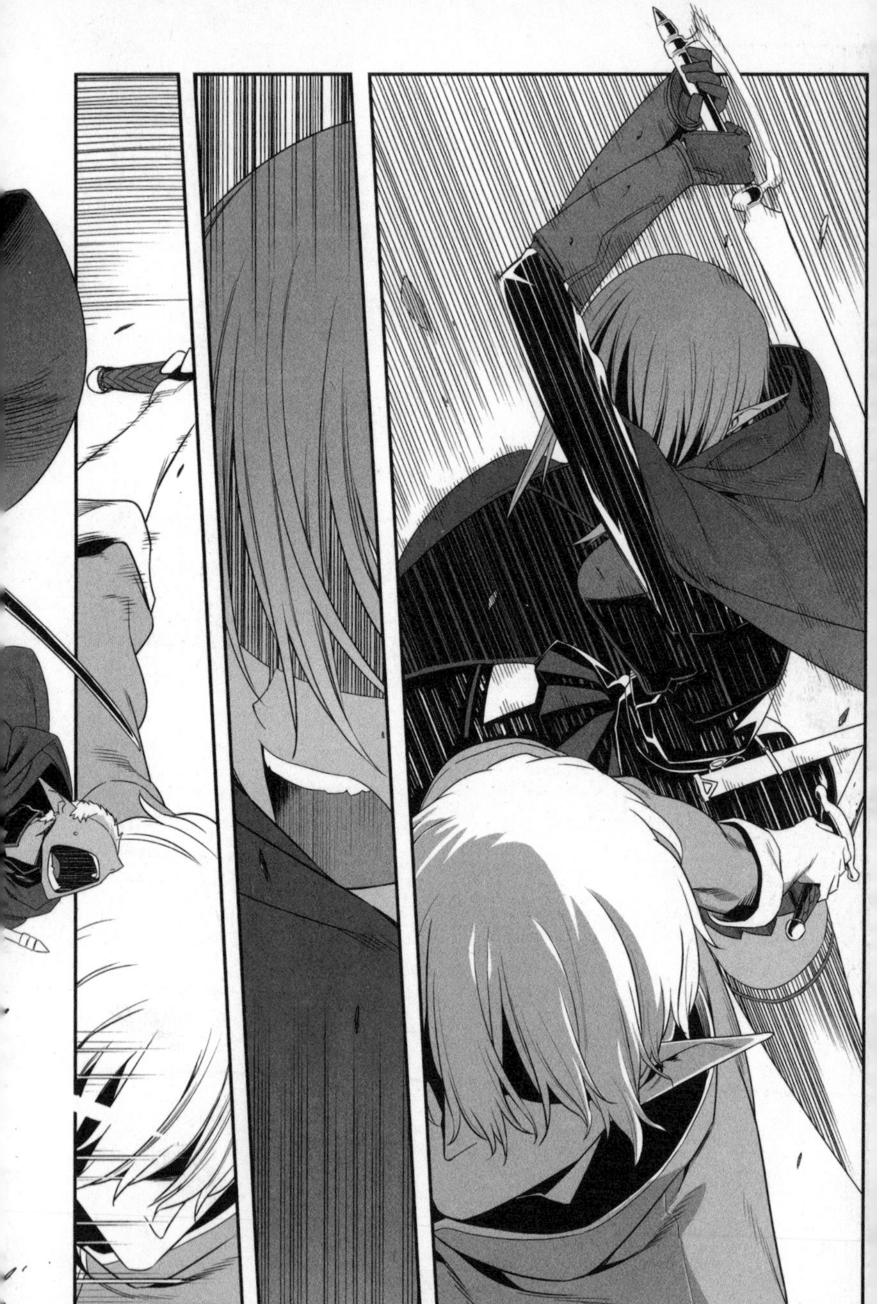

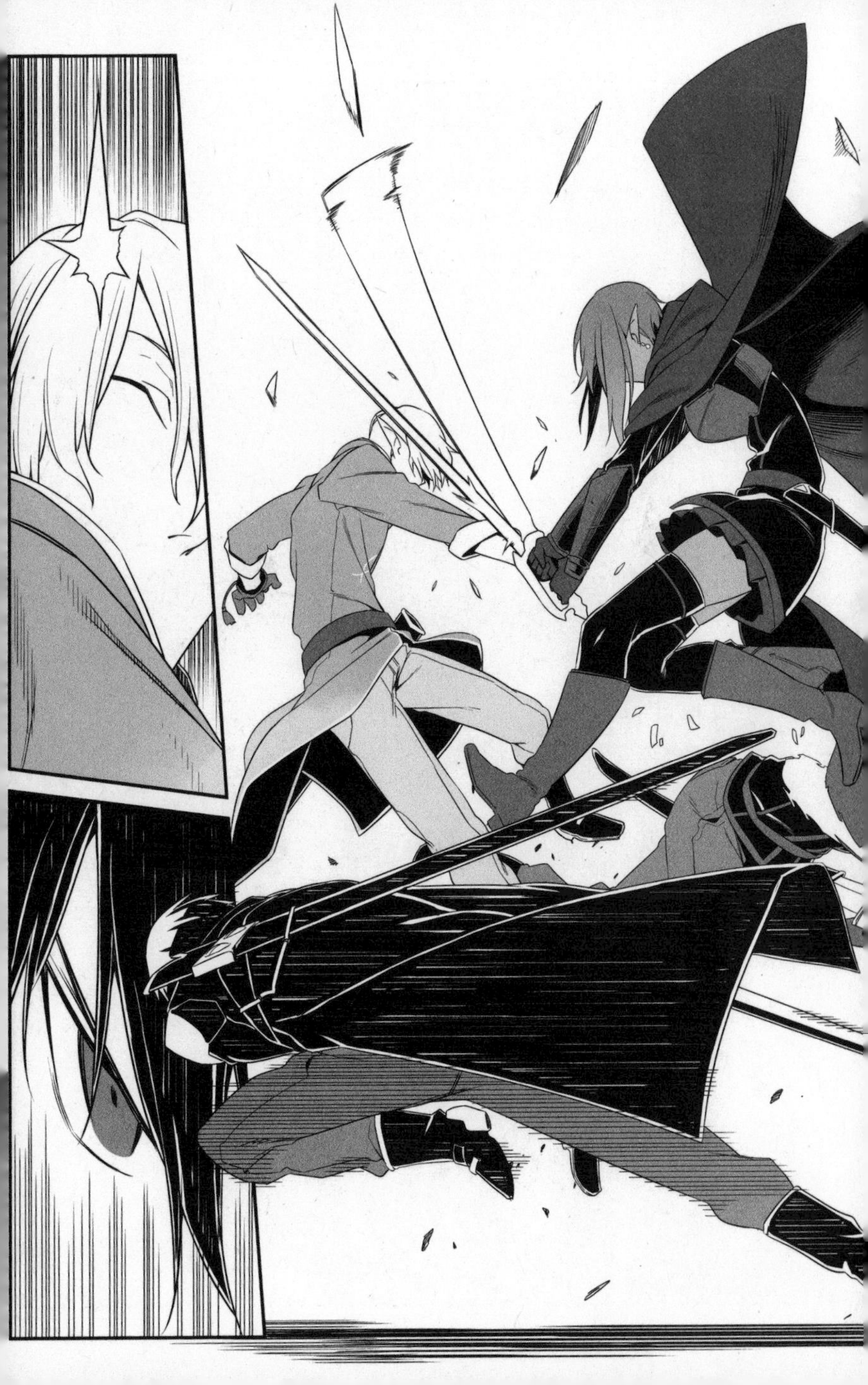

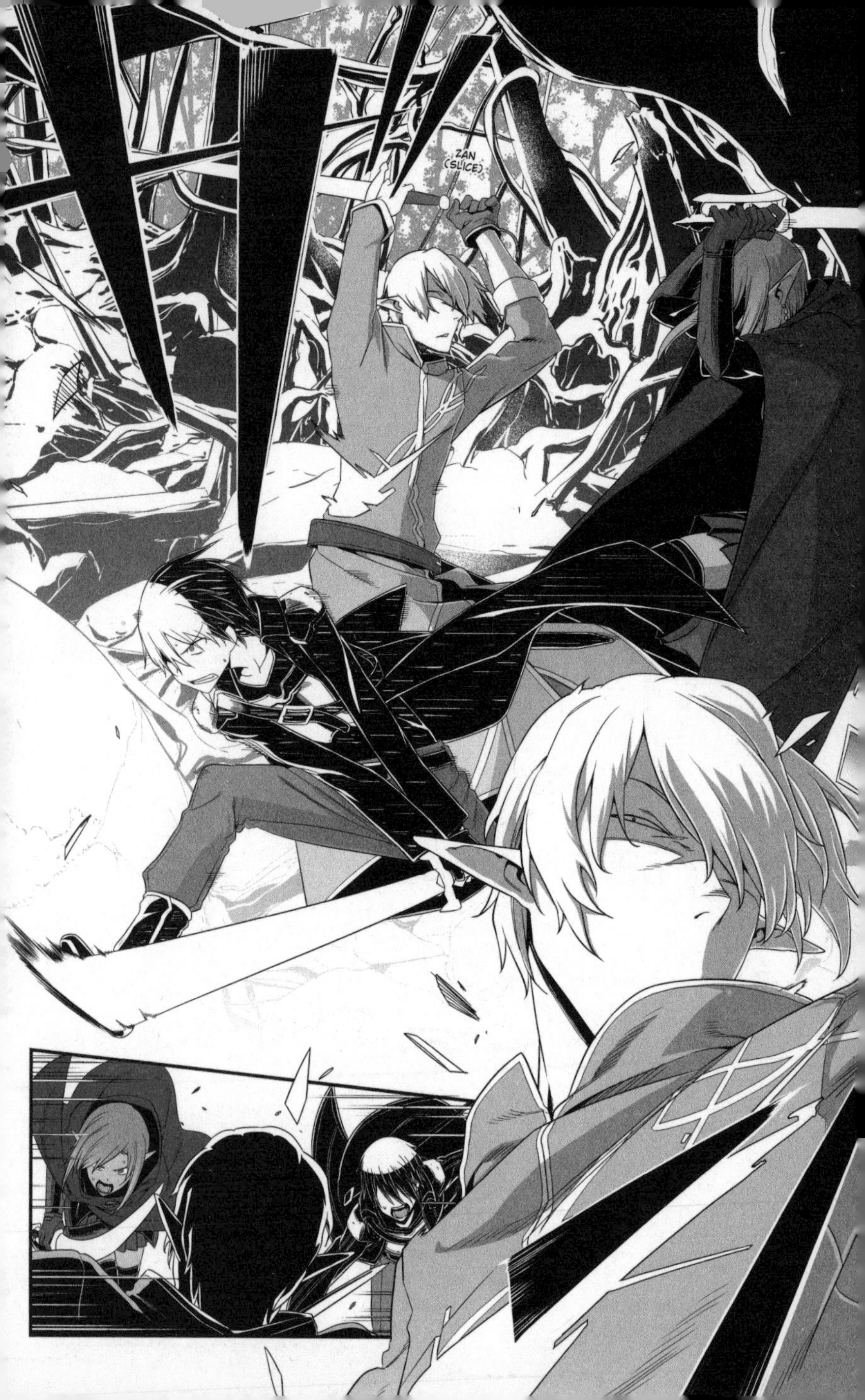
ZAN
(SLICE)

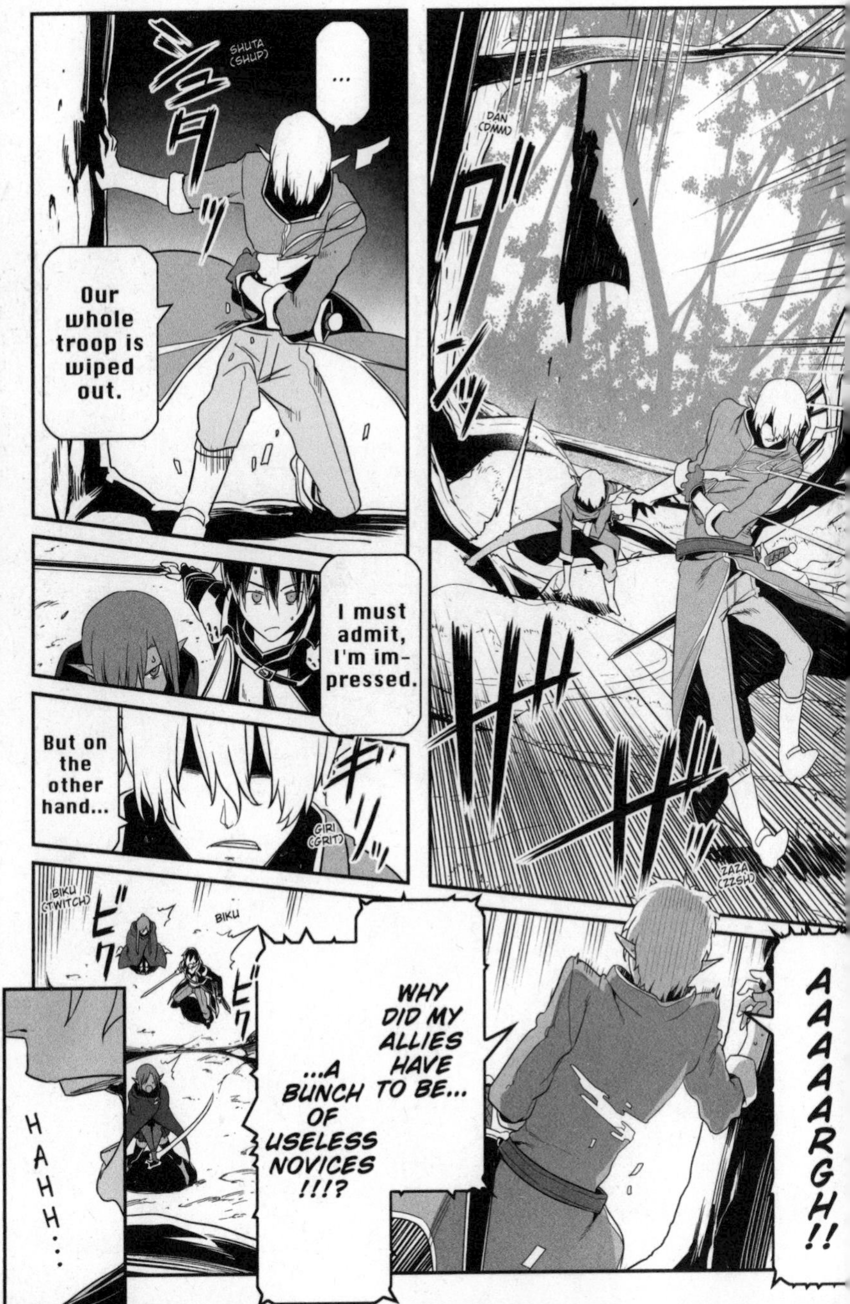
DAN (DMM)
ZAZA (ZZSH)
SHUTA (SHUP)
...
Our whole troop is wiped out.
I must admit, I'm impressed.
But on the other hand...
GIRI (GRIT)
AAAAARGH!!
WHY DID MY ALLIES HAVE TO BE...
BIKU (TWITCH)
BIKU
...A BUNCH OF USELESS NOVICES!!!?
HAHH...

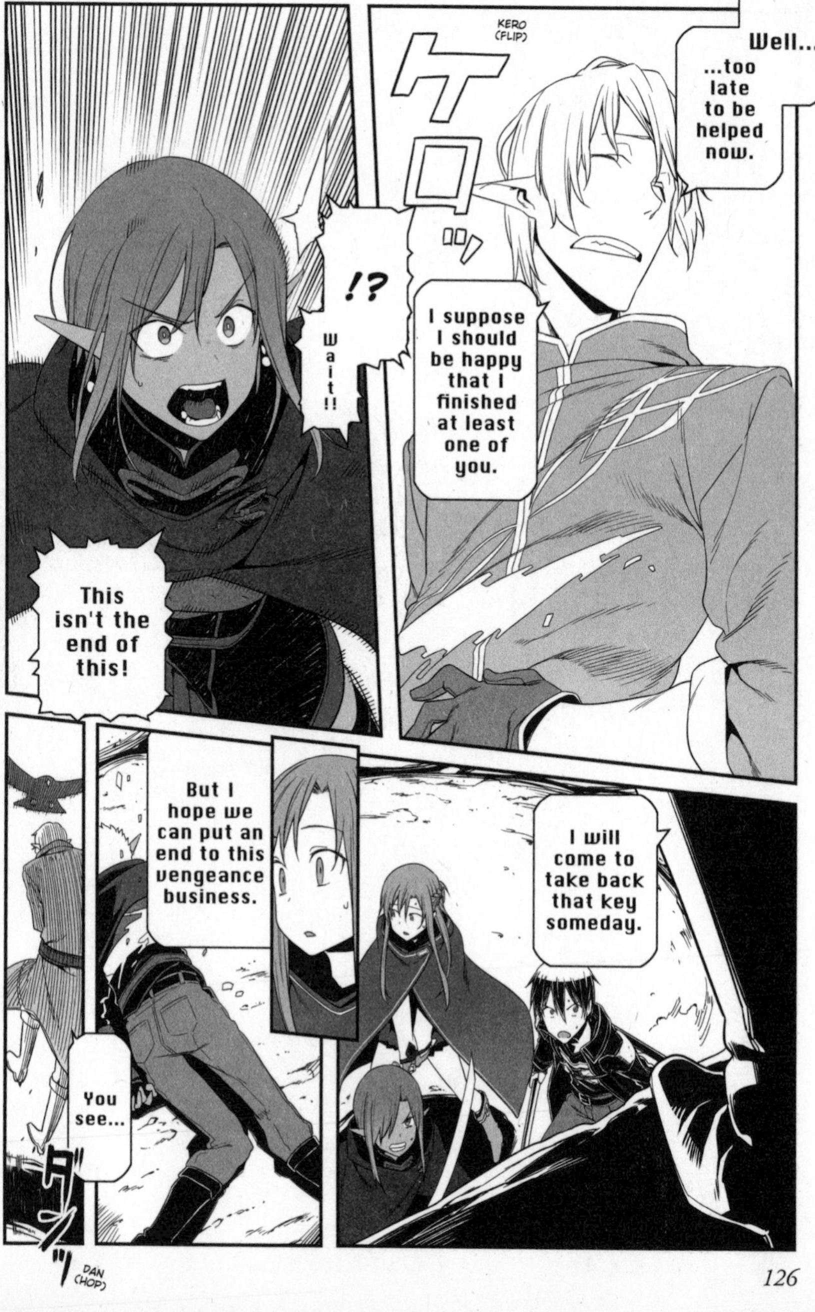
Well...
...too late to be helped now.
KERO (FLIP)
I suppose I should be happy that I finished at least one of you.
!?
Wait!!
This isn't the end of this!
I will come to take back that key someday.
But I hope we can put an end to this vengeance business.
You see...
DAN (HOP)

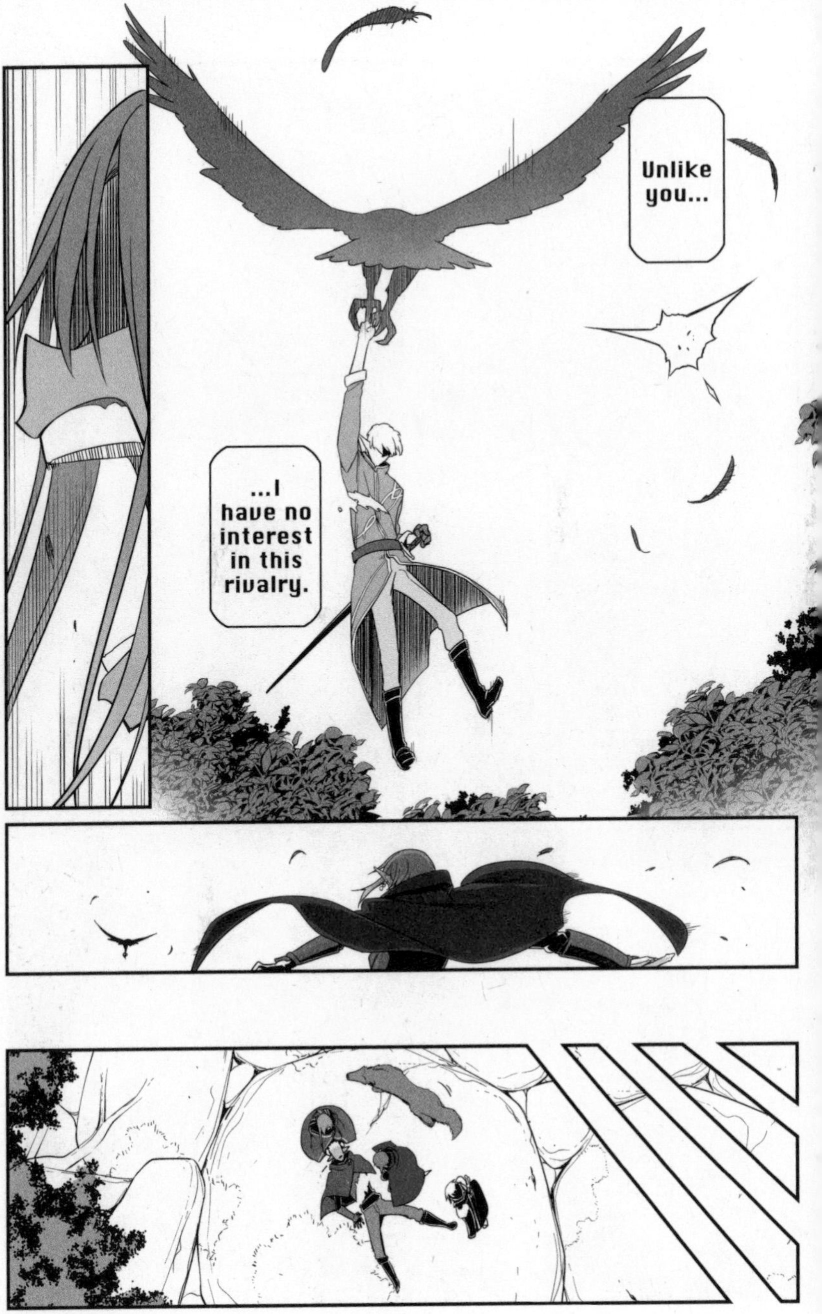
Unlike you...
...I have no interest in this rivalry.

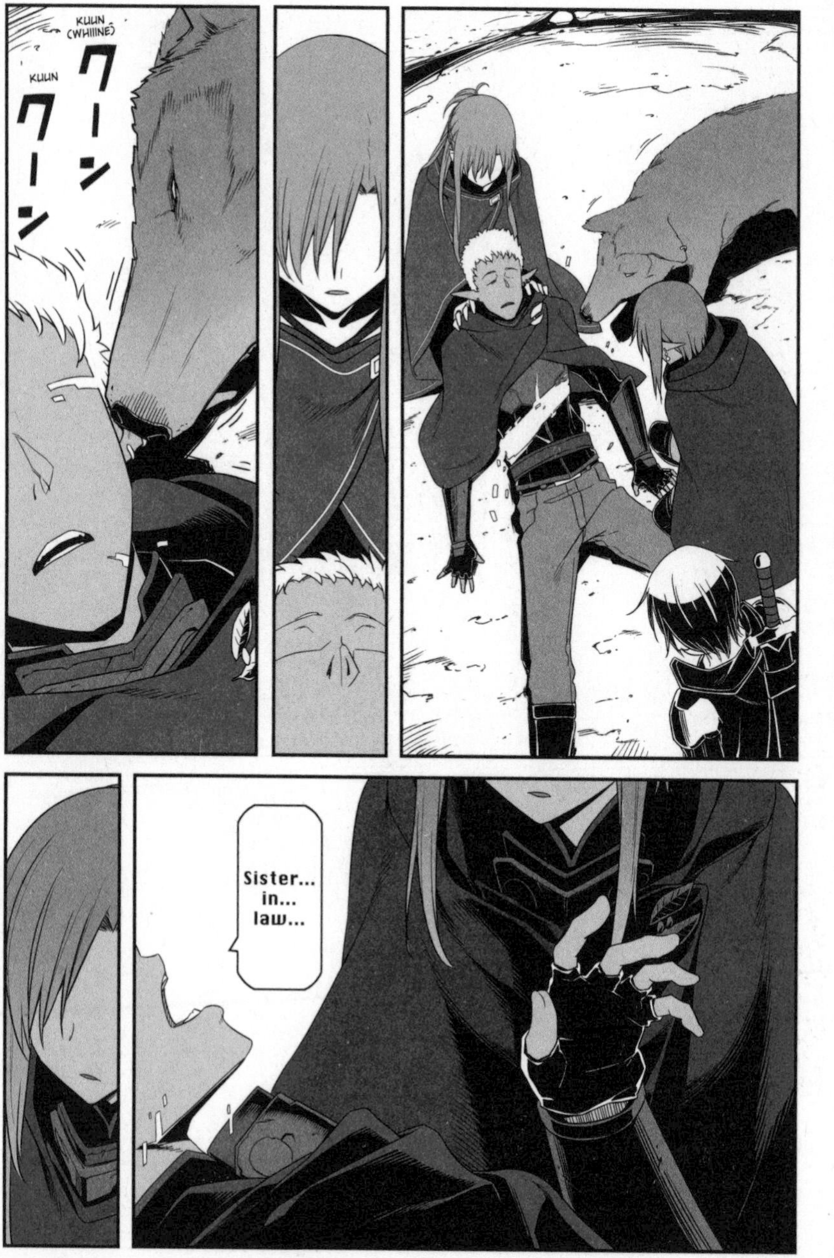

クーン
KUUN (WHIIINE)
クーン
KUUN
Sister... in... law...

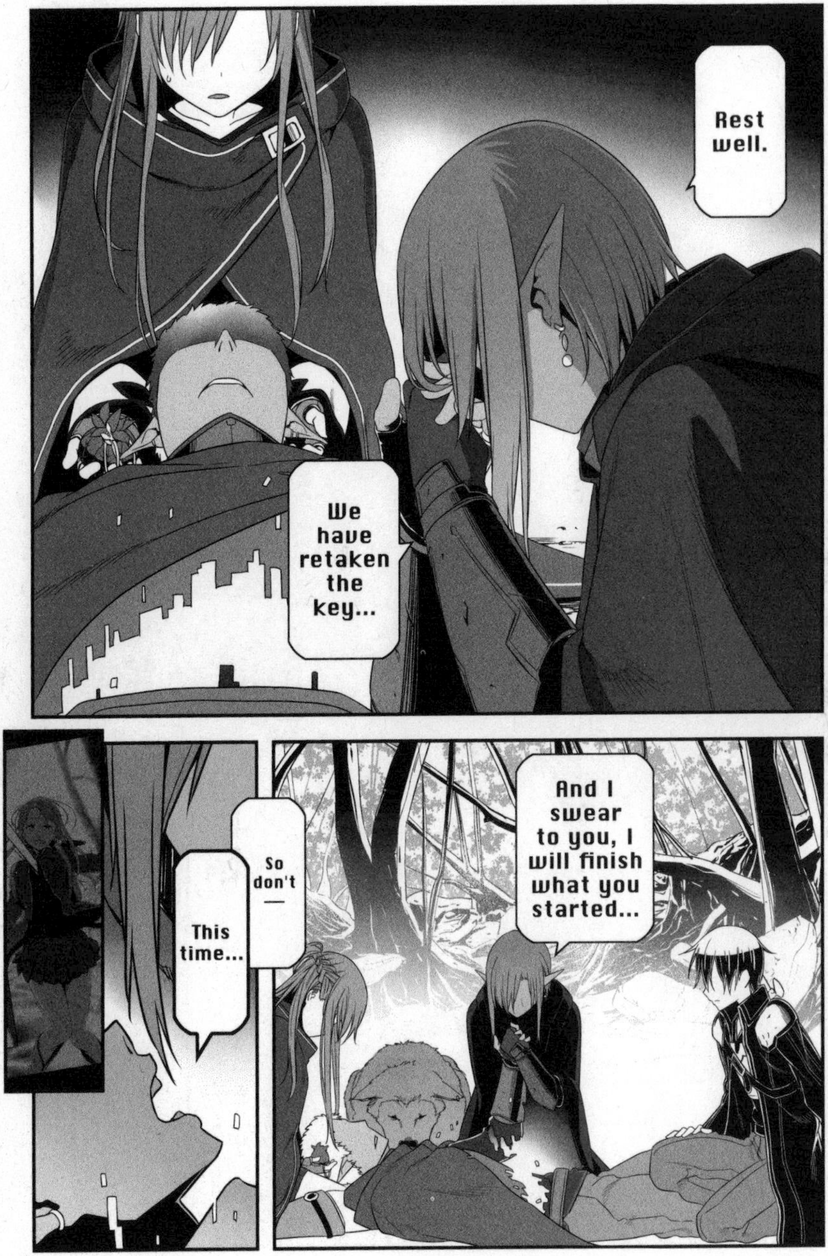
Rest well.
We have retaken the key...
And I swear to you, I will finish what you started...
So don't—
This time...

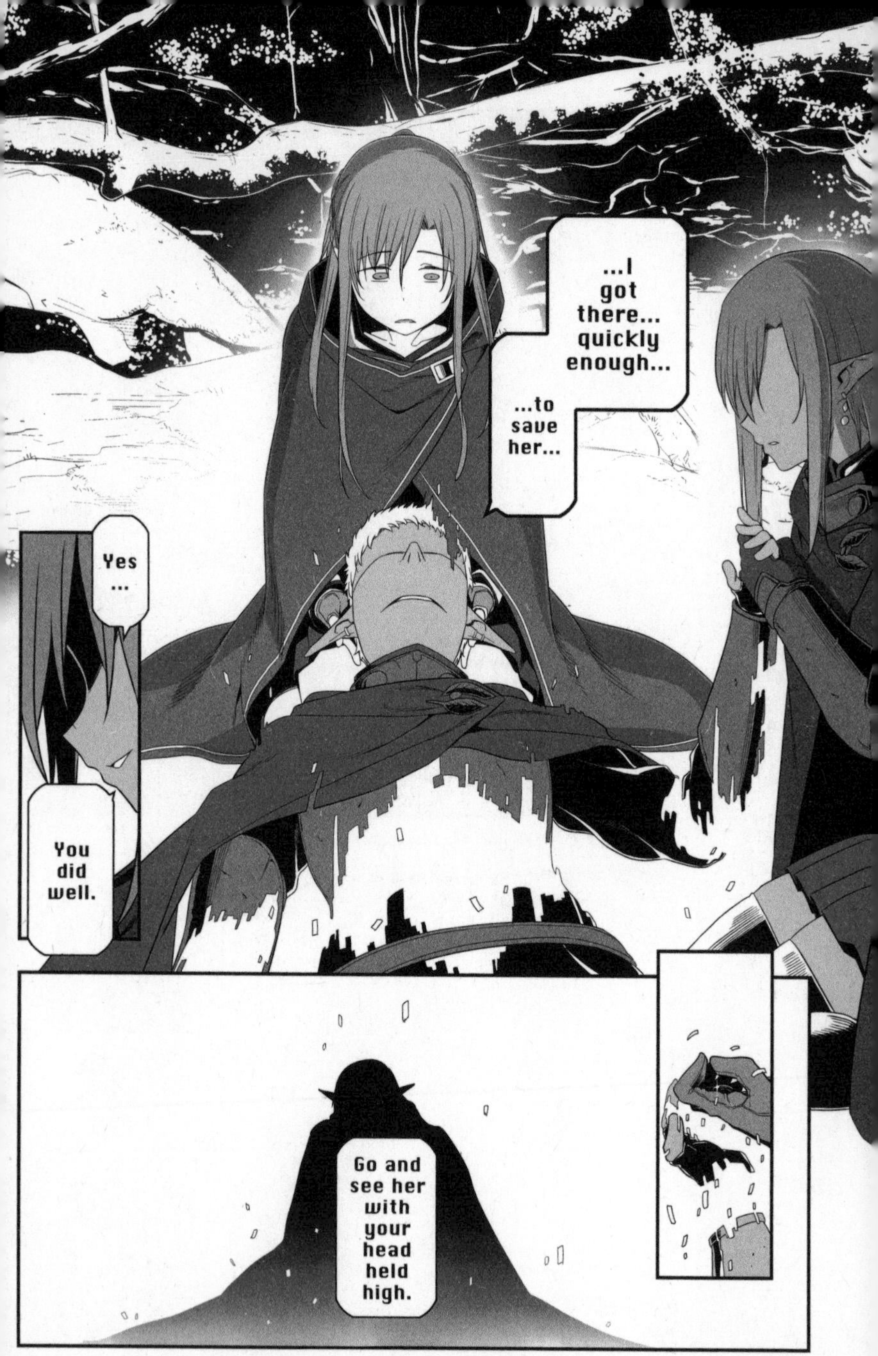
...I got there... quickly enough...
...to save her...
Yes...
You did well.
Go and see her with your head held high.

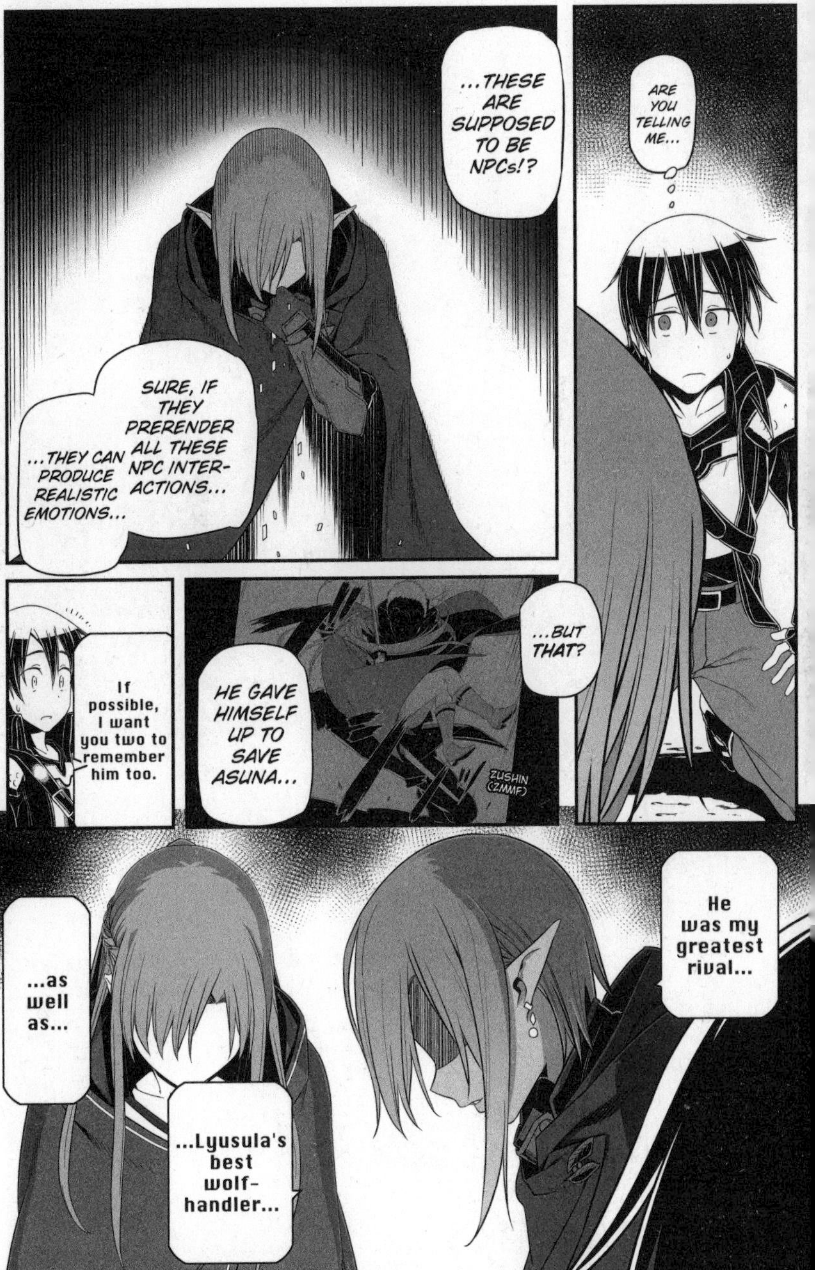
ARE YOU TELLING ME...
...THESE ARE SUPPOSED TO BE NPCs!?
SURE, IF THEY PRERENDER ALL THESE NPC INTER-ACTIONS...
...THEY CAN PRODUCE REALISTIC EMOTIONS...
...BUT THAT?
HE GAVE HIMSELF UP TO SAVE ASUNA...
ZUSHIN (ZMMF)
If possible, I want you two to remember him too.
He was my greatest rival...
...as well as...
...Lyusula's best wolf-handler...

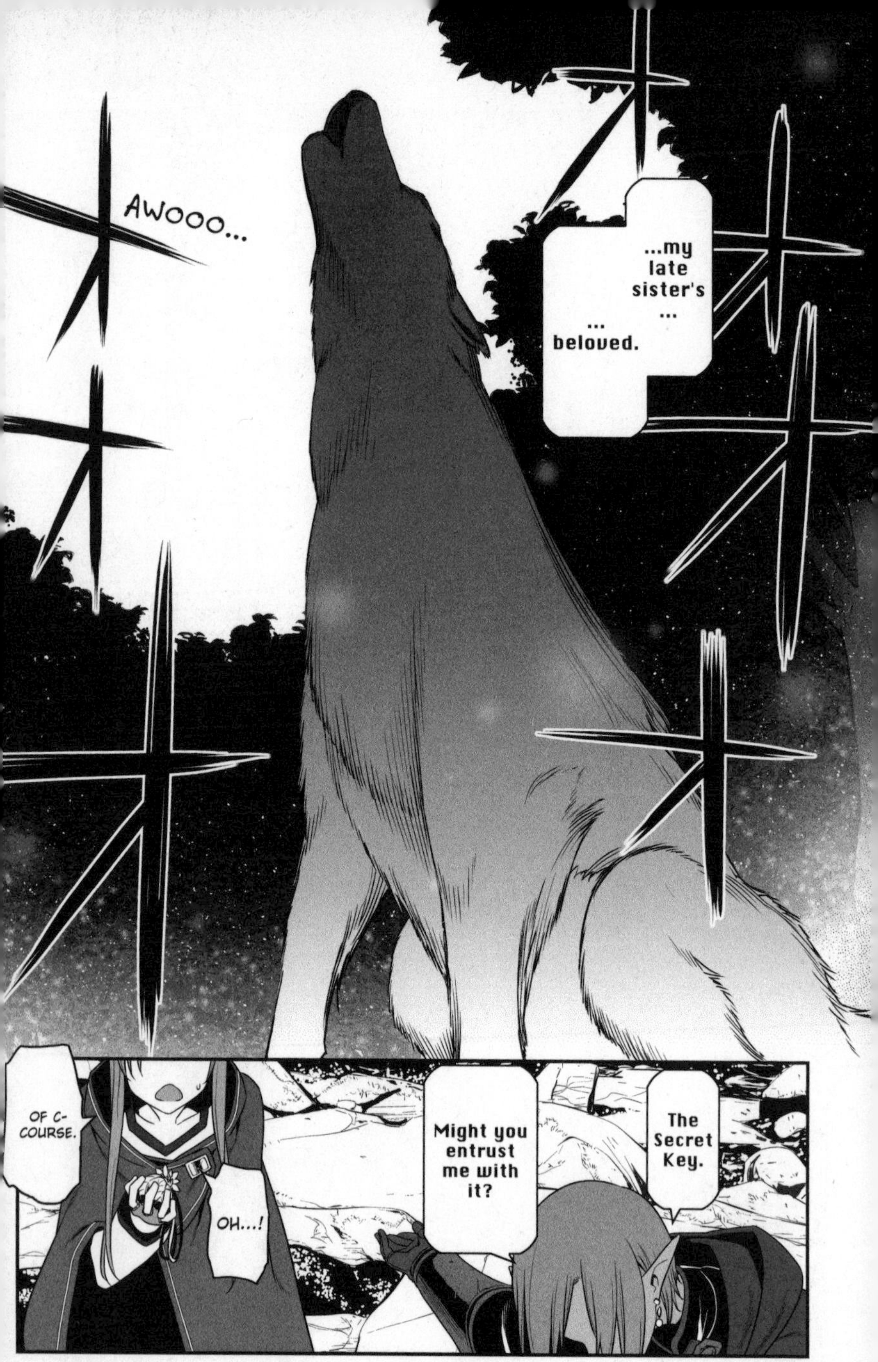
...my late sister's ... ... beloved.
AWOOO...
The Secret Key.
Might you entrust me with it?
OH...!
OF C-COURSE.

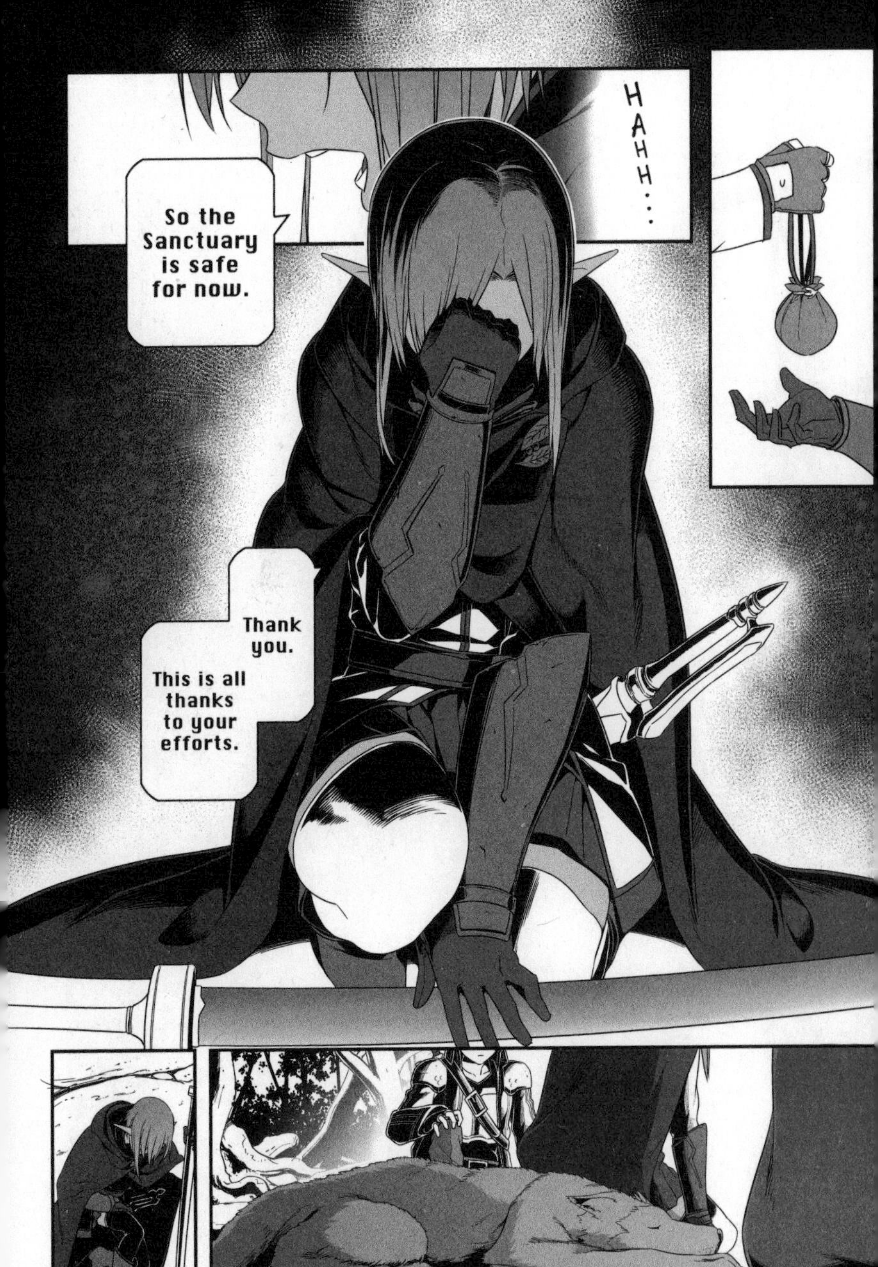
HAHH...
So the Sanctuary is safe for now.
Thank you.
This is all thanks to your efforts.

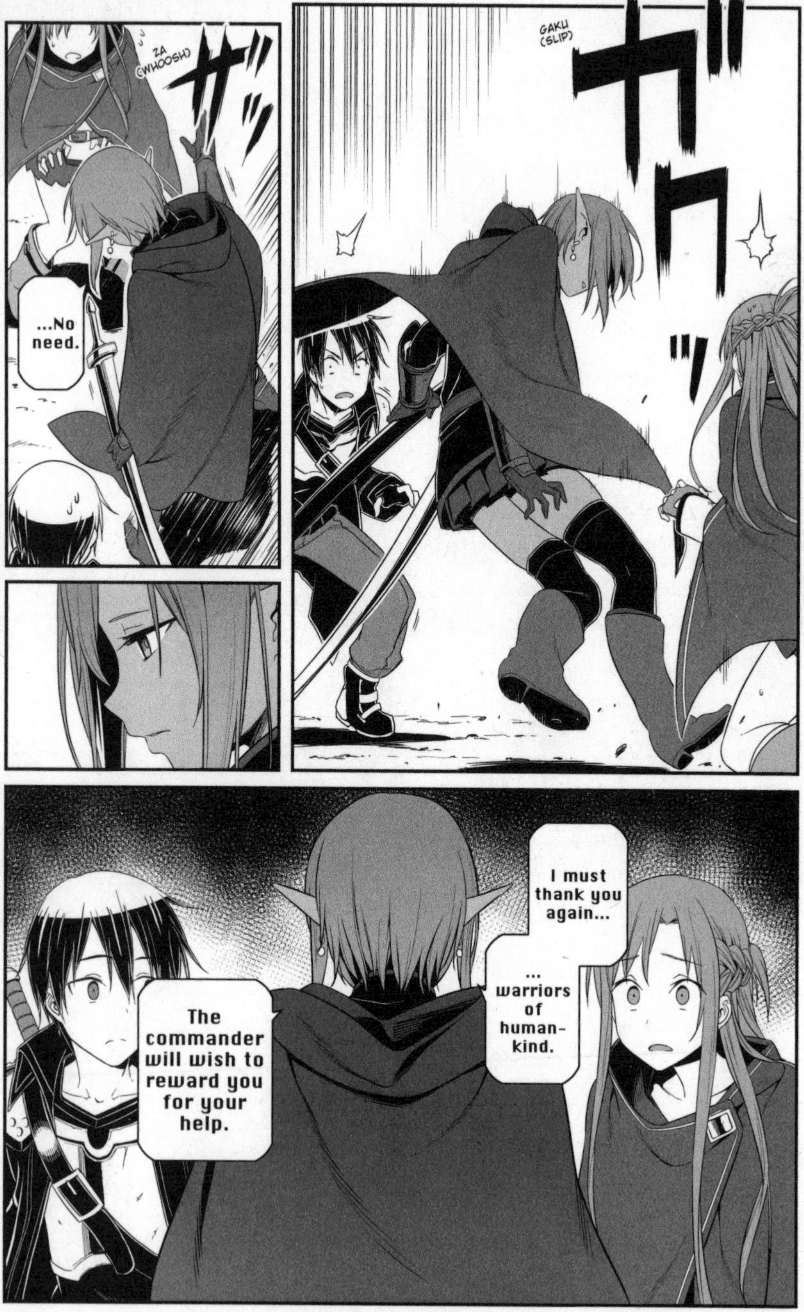
GAKU (SLIP)
ガクッ
ZA (WHOOSH)
ザッ
...No need.
I must thank you again...
...warriors of human-kind.
The commander will wish to reward you for your help.

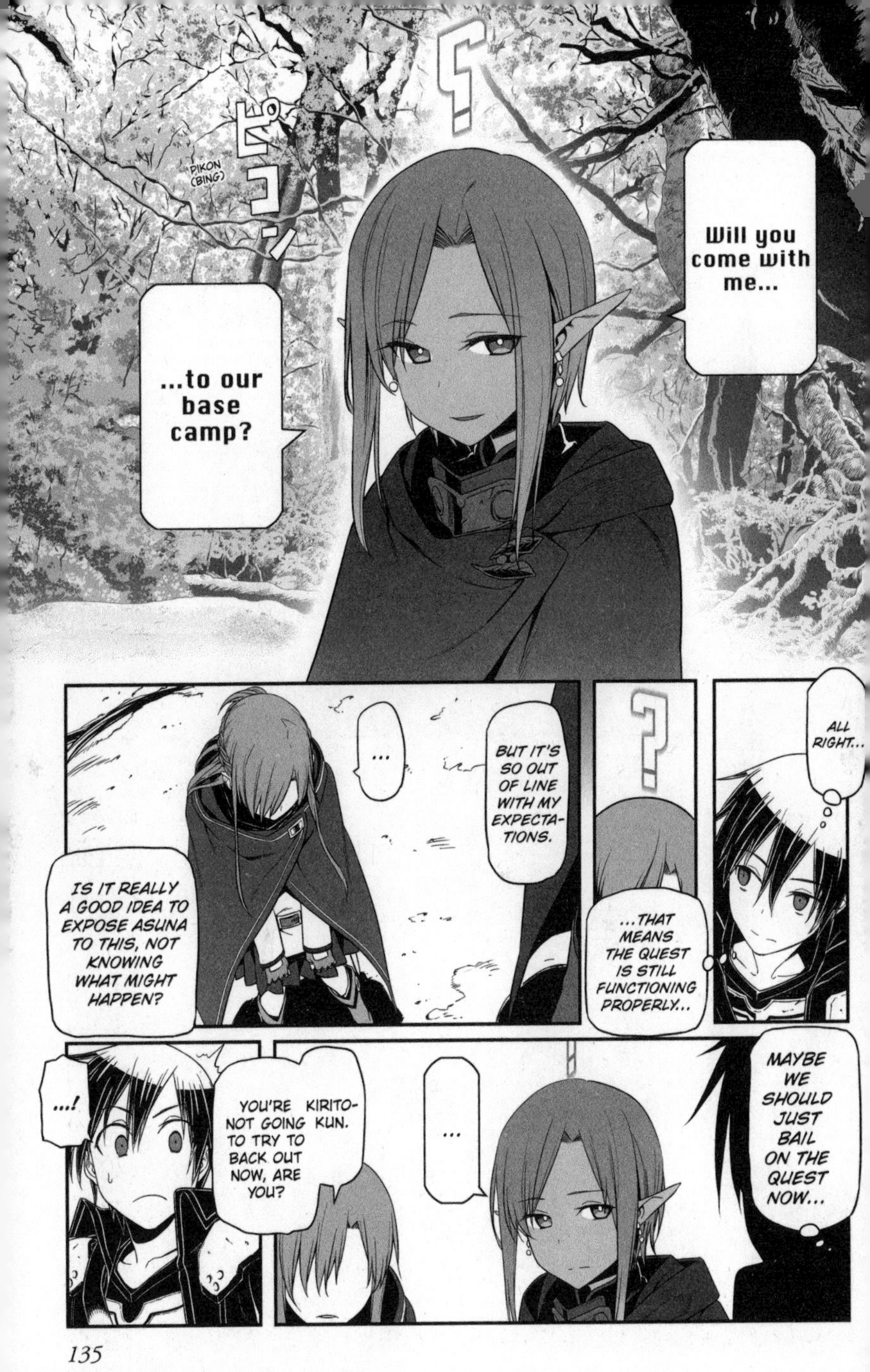
PIKON (BING)
Will you come with me...
...to our base camp?
ALL RIGHT...
...THAT MEANS THE QUEST IS STILL FUNCTIONING PROPERLY...
?
BUT IT'S SO OUT OF LINE WITH MY EXPECTATIONS.
...
IS IT REALLY A GOOD IDEA TO EXPOSE ASUNA TO THIS, NOT KNOWING WHAT MIGHT HAPPEN?
MAYBE WE SHOULD JUST BAIL ON THE QUEST NOW...
...
KIRITO-KUN. YOU'RE NOT GOING TO TRY TO BACK OUT NOW, ARE YOU?
...!

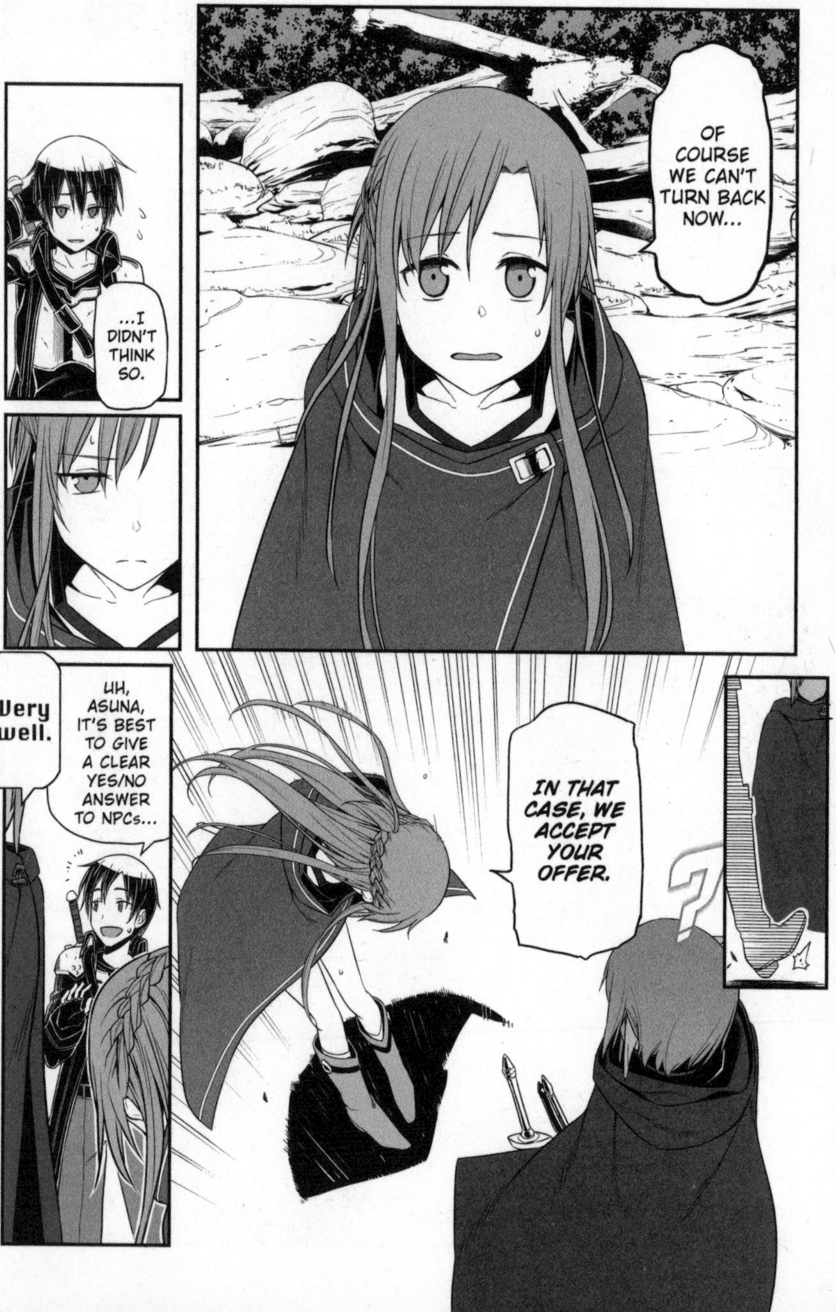
OF COURSE WE CAN'T TURN BACK NOW...
...I DIDN'T THINK SO.
IN THAT CASE, WE ACCEPT YOUR OFFER.
UH, ASUNA, IT'S BEST TO GIVE A CLEAR YES/NO ANSWER TO NPCs...
Very well.

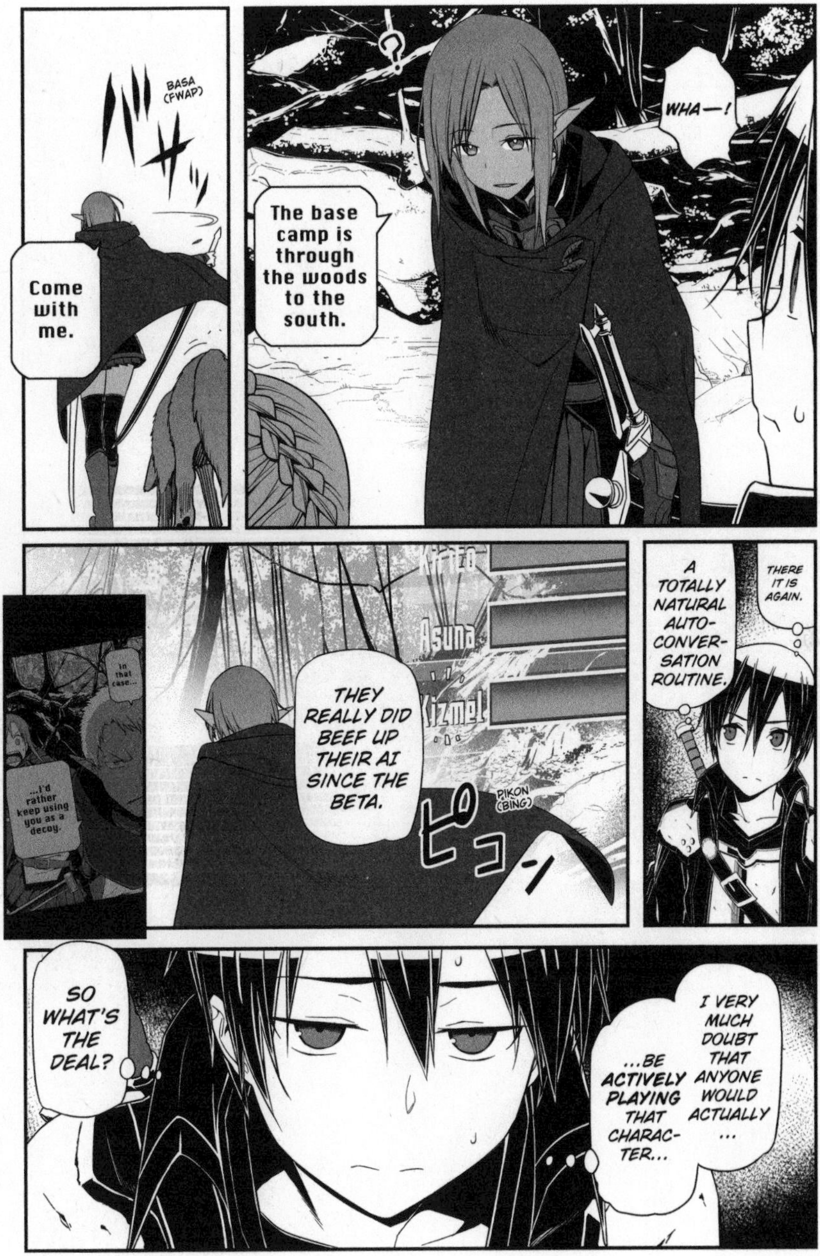
WHA—!
The base camp is through the woods to the south.
BASA (FWAP)
Come with me.
THERE IT IS AGAIN.
A TOTALLY NATURAL AUTO-CONVERSATION ROUTINE.
Kirito
Asuna
Kizmel
THEY REALLY DID BEEF UP THEIR AI SINCE THE BETA.
PIKON (BING)
In that case...
...I'd rather keep using you as a decoy.
I VERY MUCH DOUBT THAT ANYONE WOULD ACTUALLY...
...BE ACTIVELY PLAYING THAT CHARACTER...
SO WHAT'S THE DEAL?

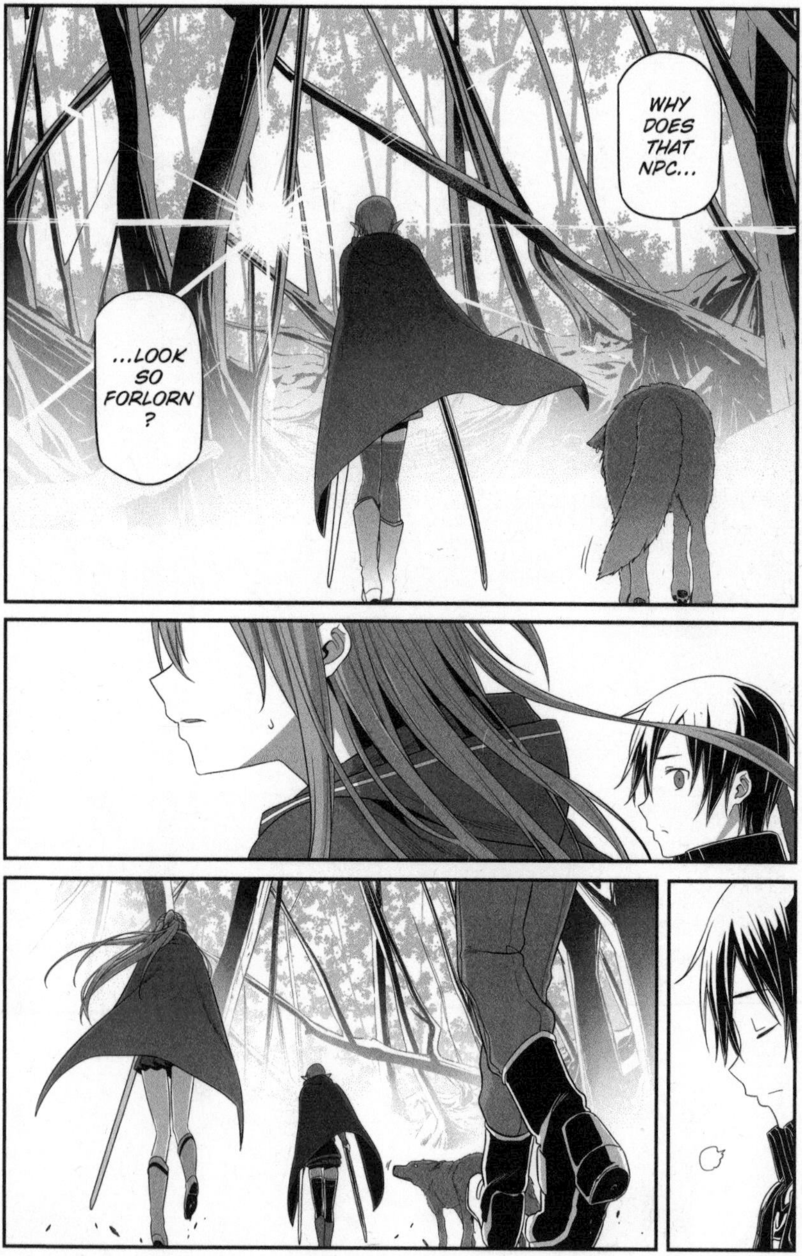
WHY DOES THAT NPC...
...LOOK SO FORLORN ?

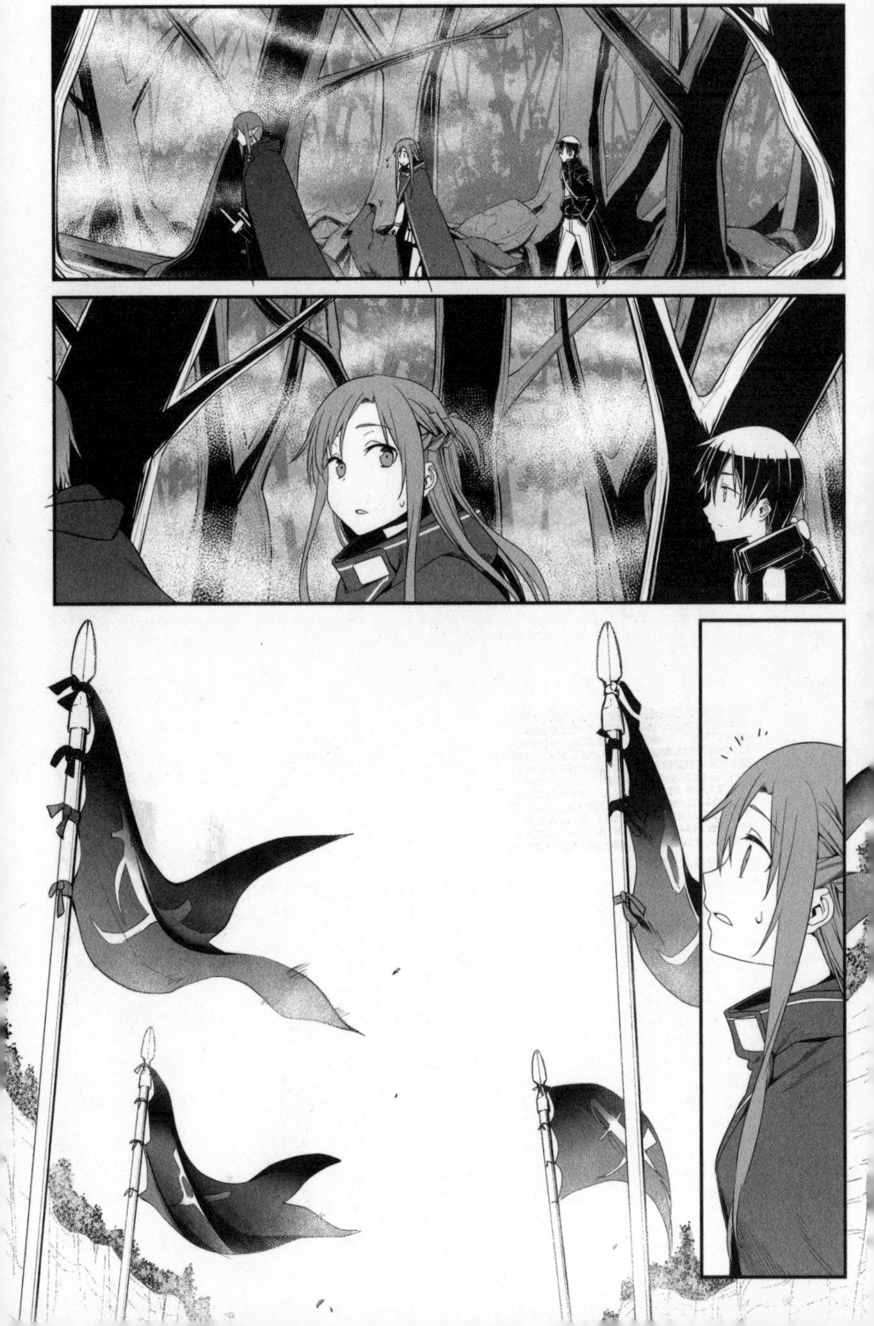

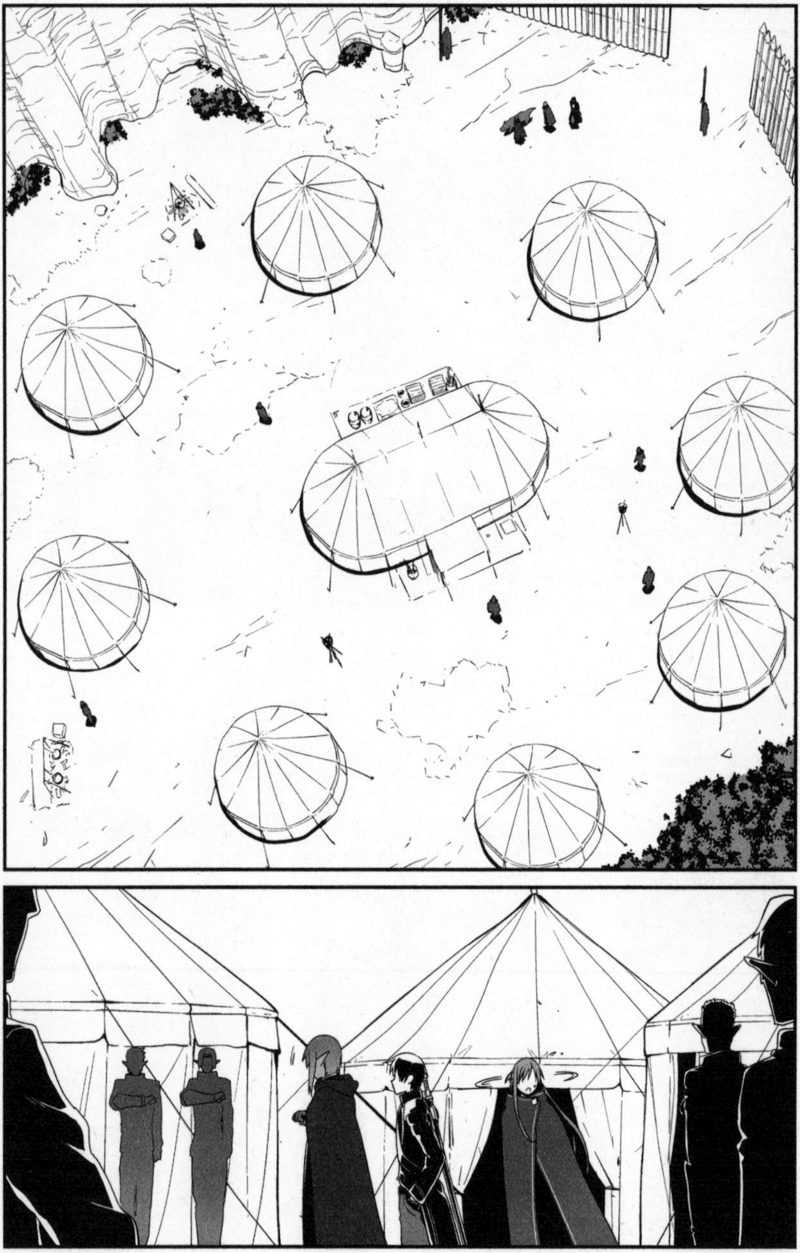

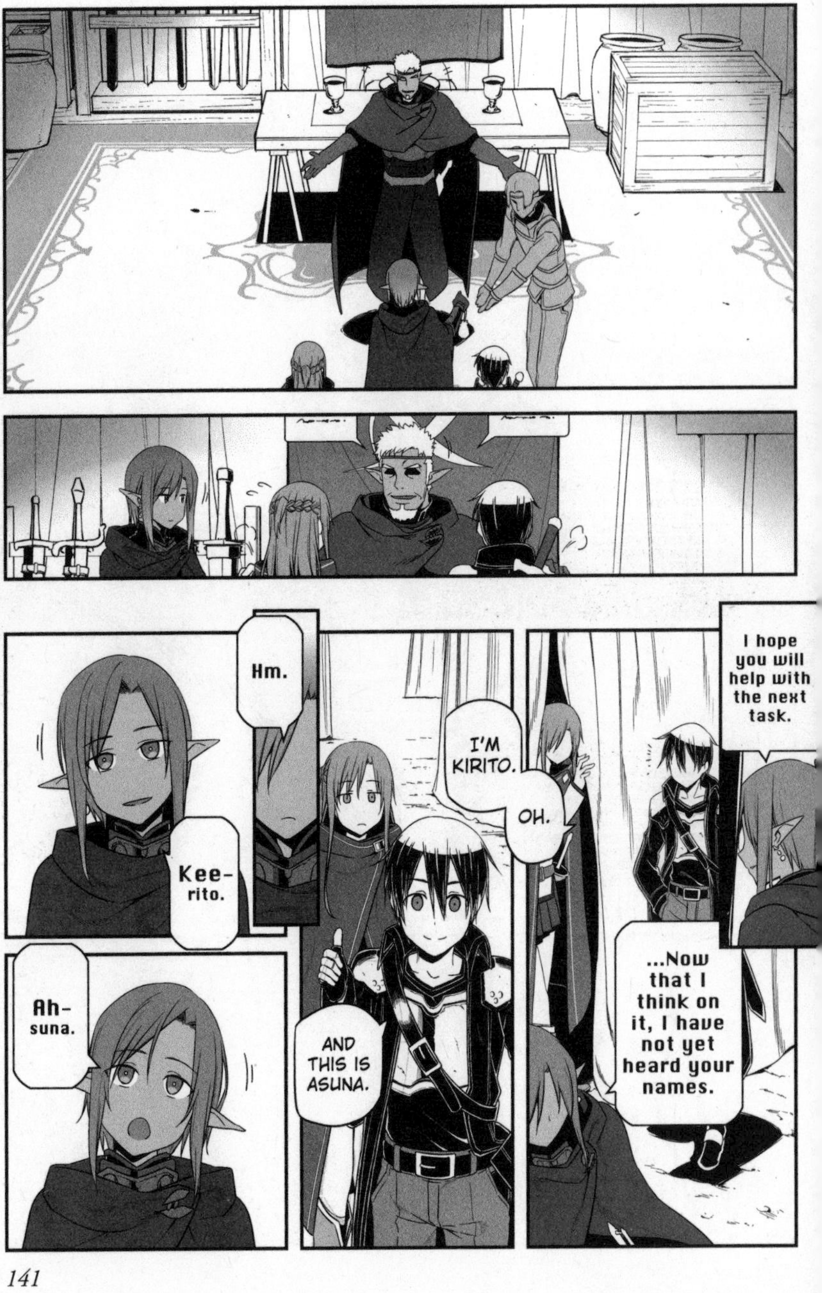
I hope you will help with the next task.
...Now that I think on it, I have not yet heard your names.
I'M KIRITO.
OH.
AND THIS IS ASUNA.
Hm.
Kee-rito.
Ah-suna.

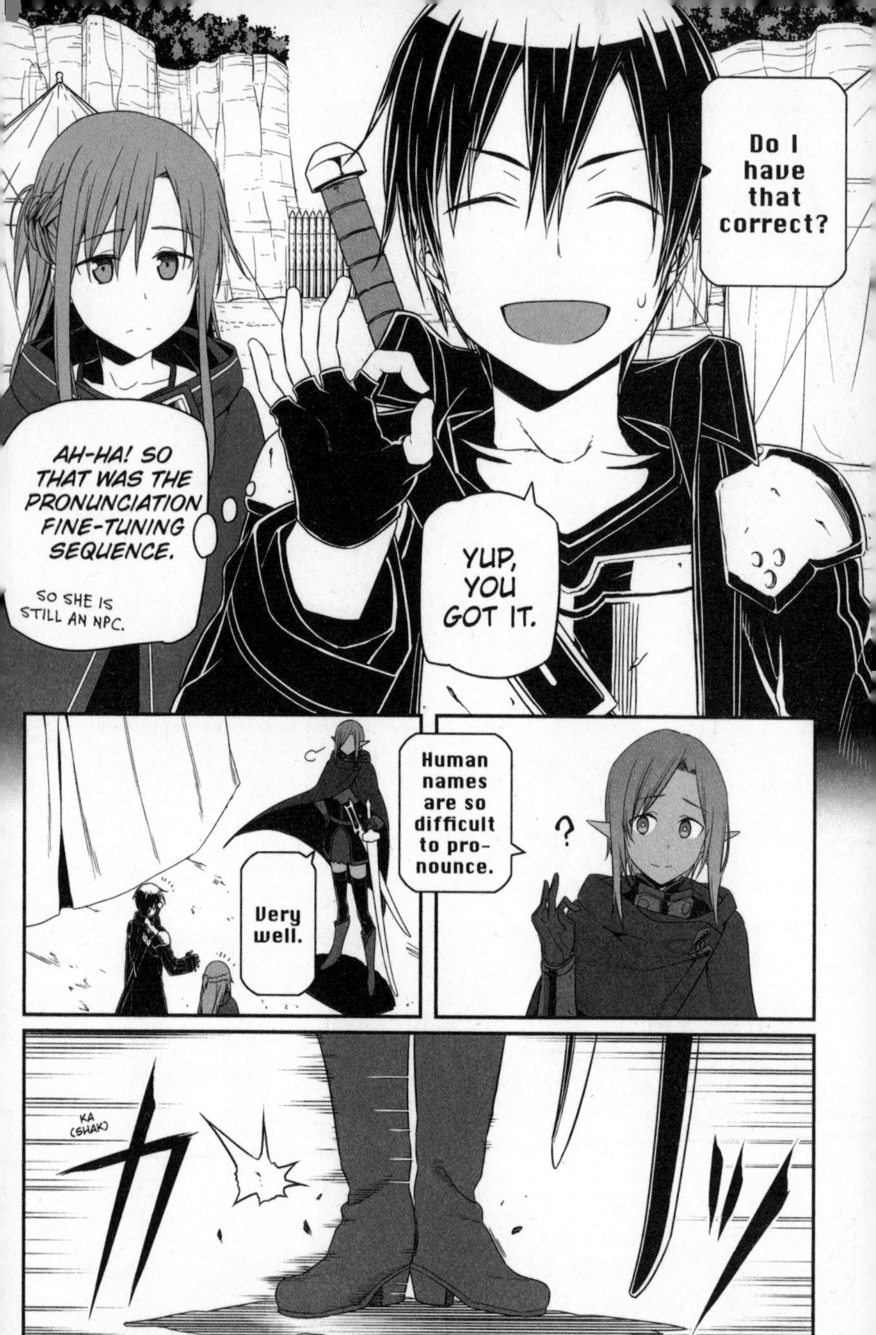
Do I have that correct?
YUP, YOU GOT IT.
AH-HA! SO THAT WAS THE PRONUNCIATION FINE-TUNING SEQUENCE.
SO SHE IS STILL AN NPC.
?
Human names are so difficult to pronounce.
Very well.
KA (SHAK)

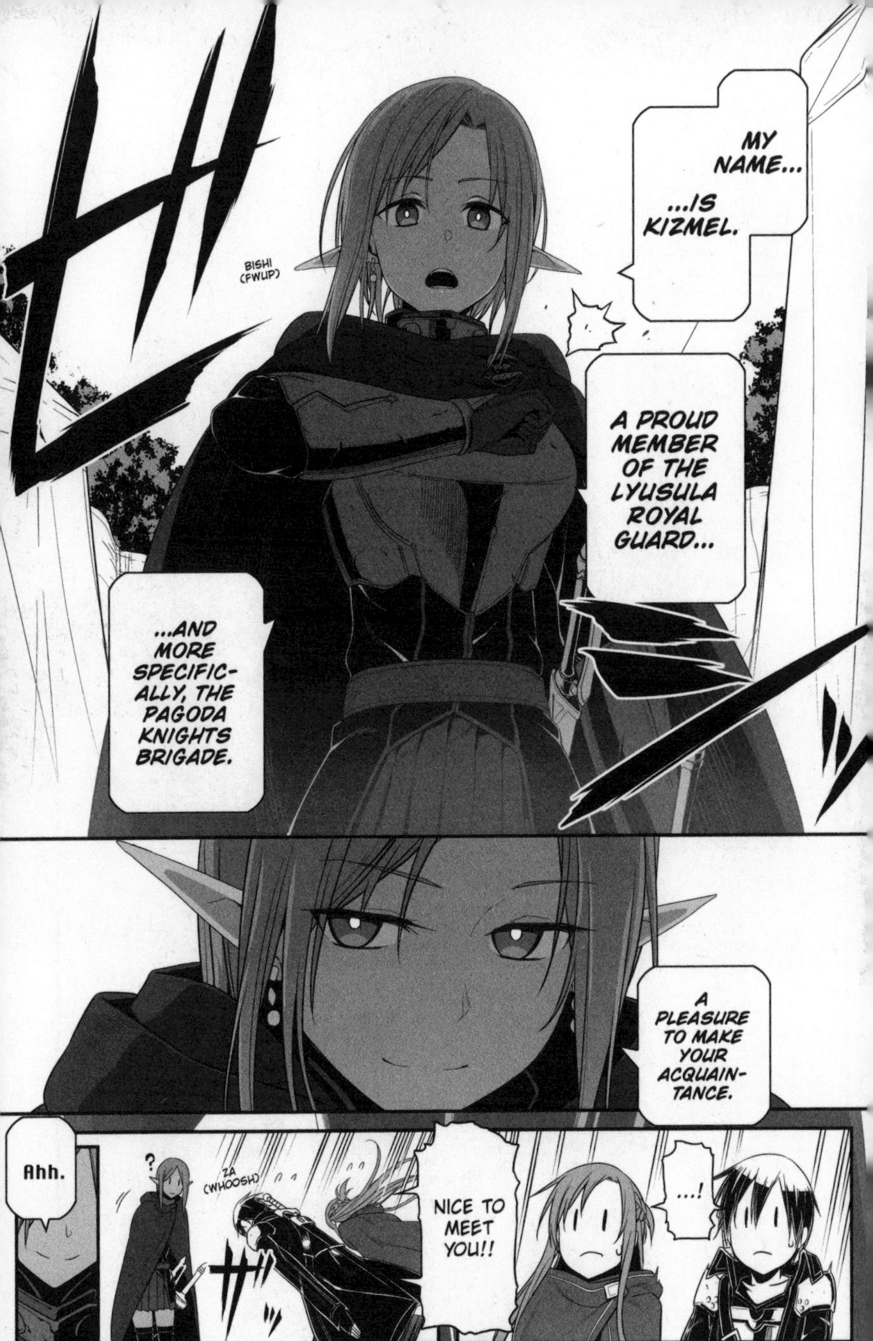

MY NAME...
...IS KIZMEL.
BISHI (FWUP)
A PROUD MEMBER OF THE LYUSULA ROYAL GUARD...
...AND MORE SPECIFIC-ALLY, THE PAGODA KNIGHTS BRIGADE.
A PLEASURE TO MAKE YOUR ACQUAIN-TANCE.
...!
NICE TO MEET YOU!!
ZA (WHOOSH)
Ahh.

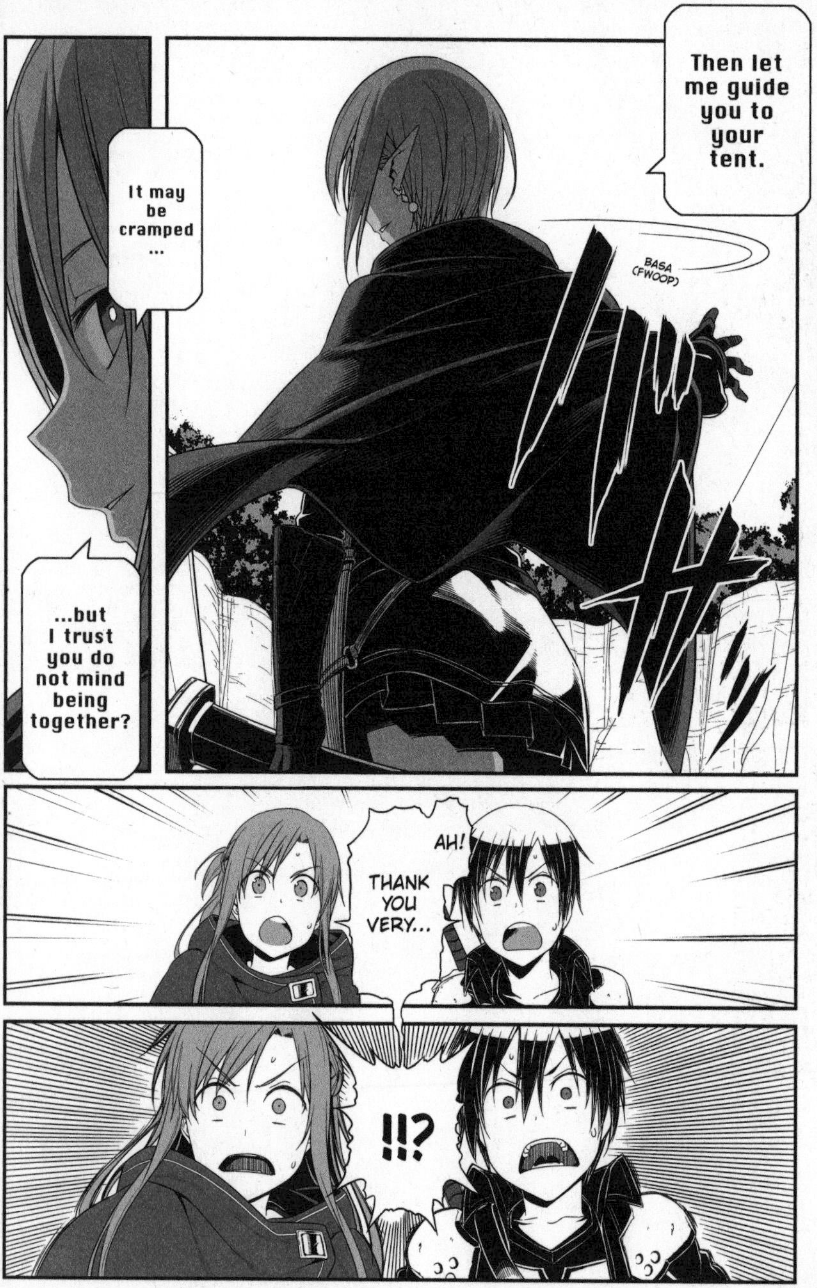
Then let me guide you to your tent.
BASA (FWOOP)
It may be cramped...
...but I trust you do not mind being together?
AH!
THANK YOU VERY...
!!?

#028: The Protector

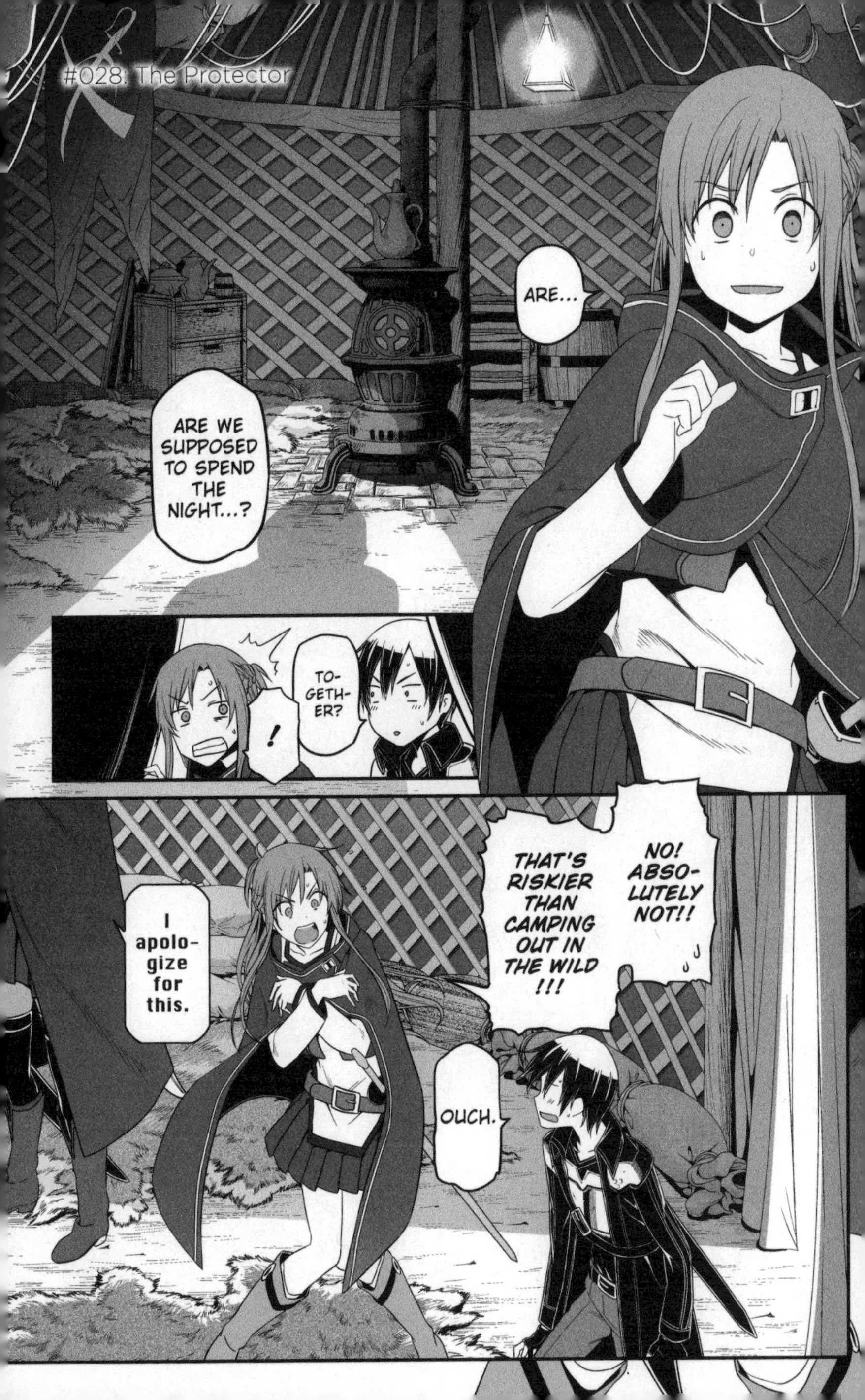
ARE...
ARE WE SUPPOSED TO SPEND THE NIGHT...?
TO-GETH-ER?
!
NO! ABSO-LUTELY NOT!!
THAT'S RISKIER THAN CAMPING OUT IN THE WILD!!!
I apolo-gize for this.
OUCH.

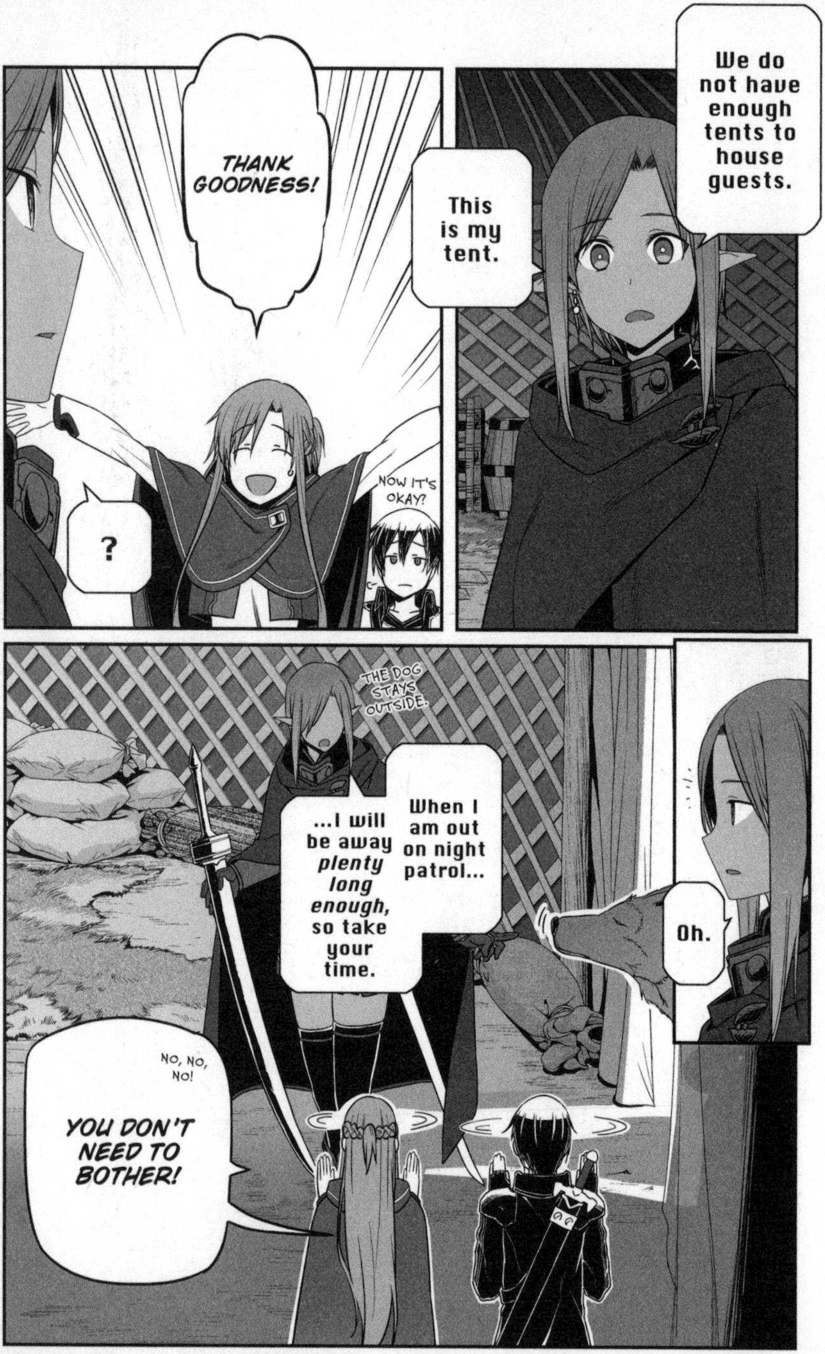
We do not have enough tents to house guests.
This is my tent.
THANK GOODNESS!
NOW IT'S OKAY?
?
Oh.
THE DOG STAYS OUTSIDE.
When I am out on night patrol...
...I will be away plenty long enough, so take your time.
NO, NO, NO!
YOU DON'T NEED TO BOTHER!

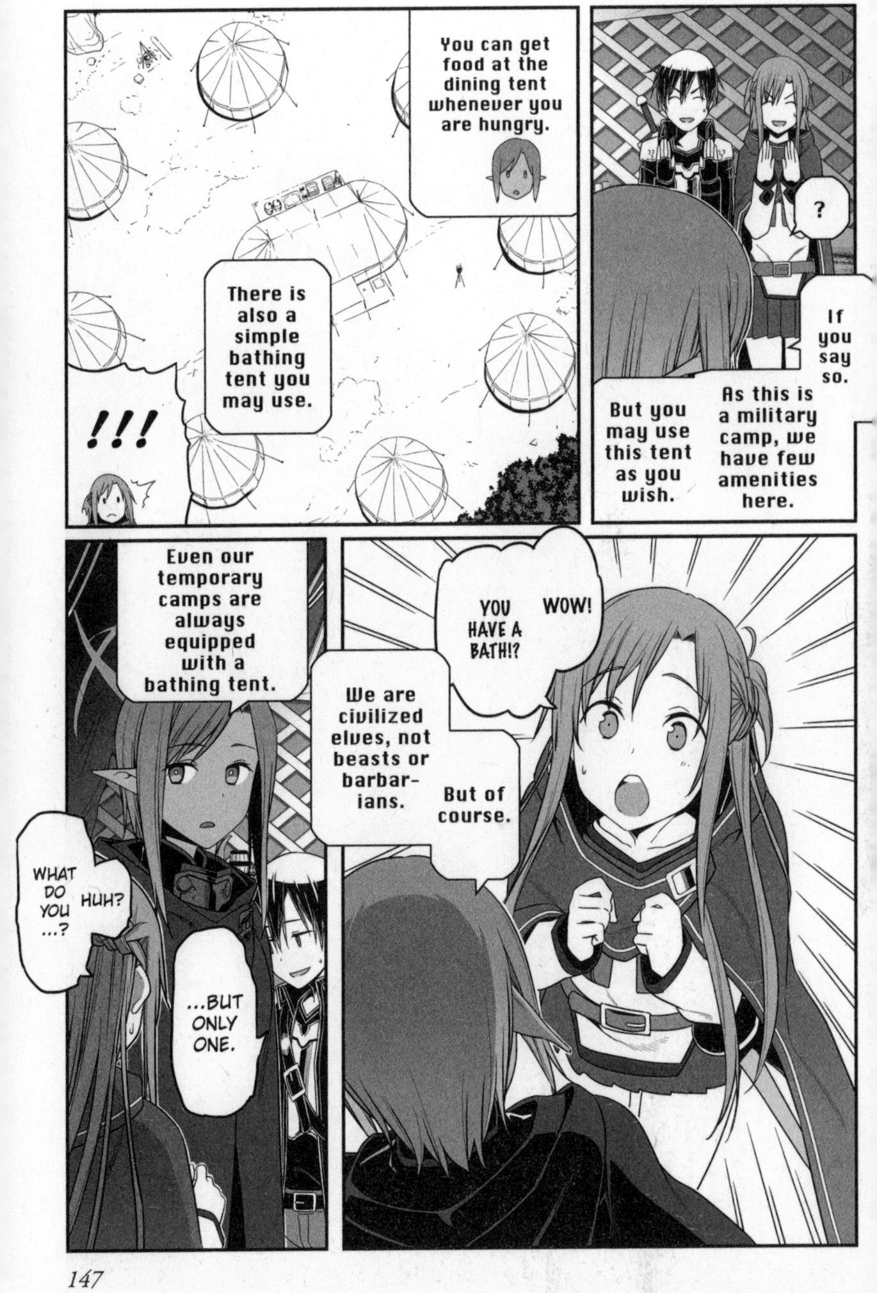
?
If you say so.
As this is a military camp, we have few amenities here.
But you may use this tent as you wish.
You can get food at the dining tent whenever you are hungry.
There is also a simple bathing tent you may use.
!!!
WOW!
YOU HAVE A BATH!?
But of course.
We are civilized elves, not beasts or barbar-ians.
Even our temporary camps are always equipped with a bathing tent.
HUH?
WHAT DO YOU ...?
...BUT ONLY ONE.

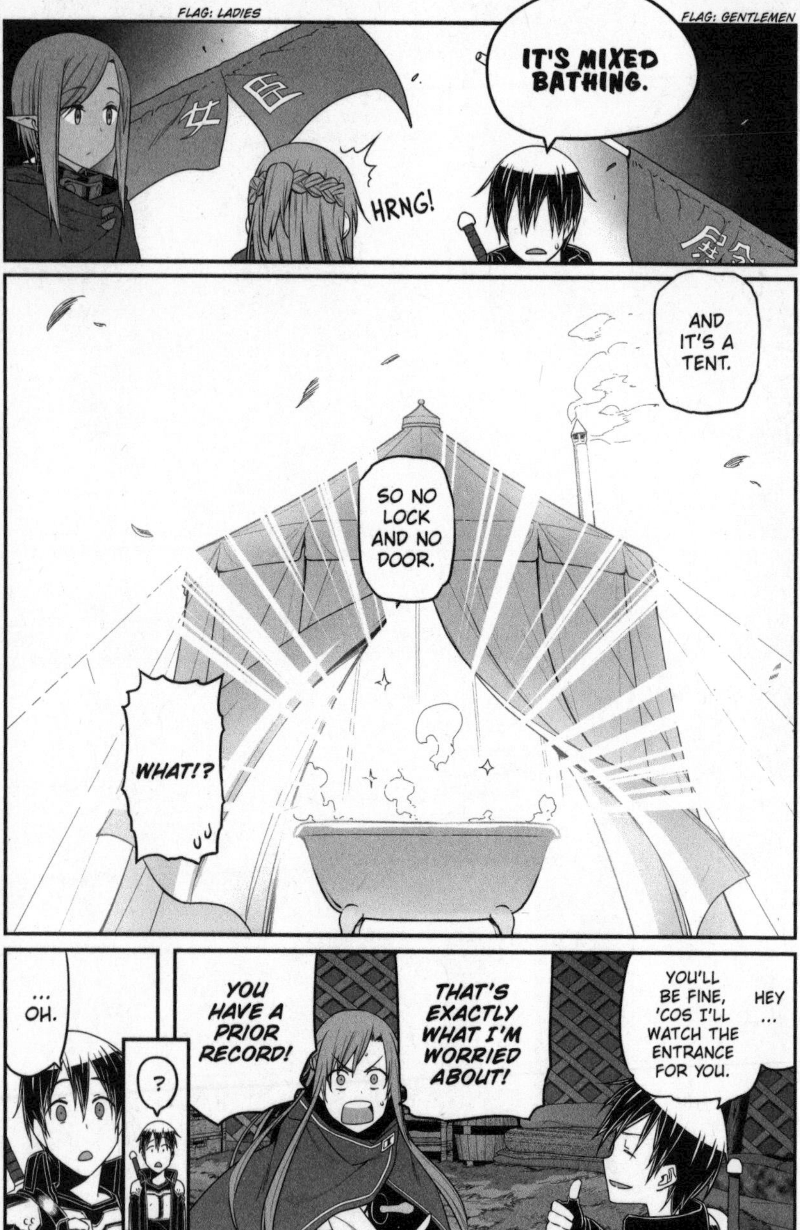
FLAG: GENTLEMEN
FLAG: LADIES
IT'S MIXED BATHING.
HRNG!
AND IT'S A TENT.
SO NO LOCK AND NO DOOR.
WHAT!?
HEY ...
YOU'LL BE FINE, 'COS I'LL WATCH THE ENTRANCE FOR YOU.
THAT'S EXACTLY WHAT I'M WORRIED ABOUT!
YOU HAVE A PRIOR RECORD!
?
... OH.

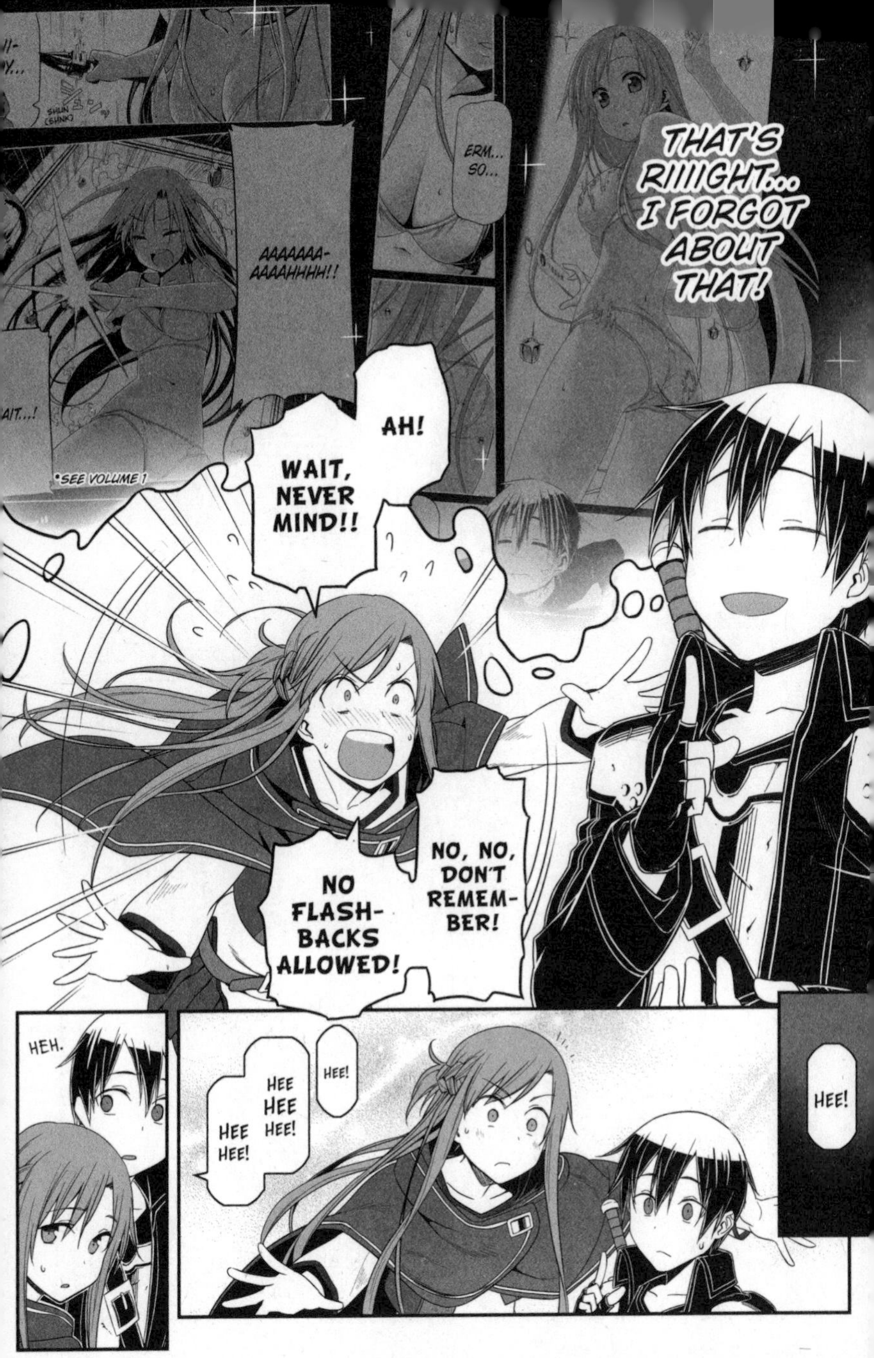
THAT'S RIIIIGHT... I FORGOT ABOUT THAT!
ERM... SO...
SHUN (SHNK)
AAAAAAA-AAAAHHHH!!
AIT...!
*SEE VOLUME 1
AH!
WAIT, NEVER MIND!!
NO, NO, DON'T REMEM-BER!
NO FLASH-BACKS ALLOWED!
HEE!
HEE!
HEE HEE HEE!
HEE HEE!
HEH.

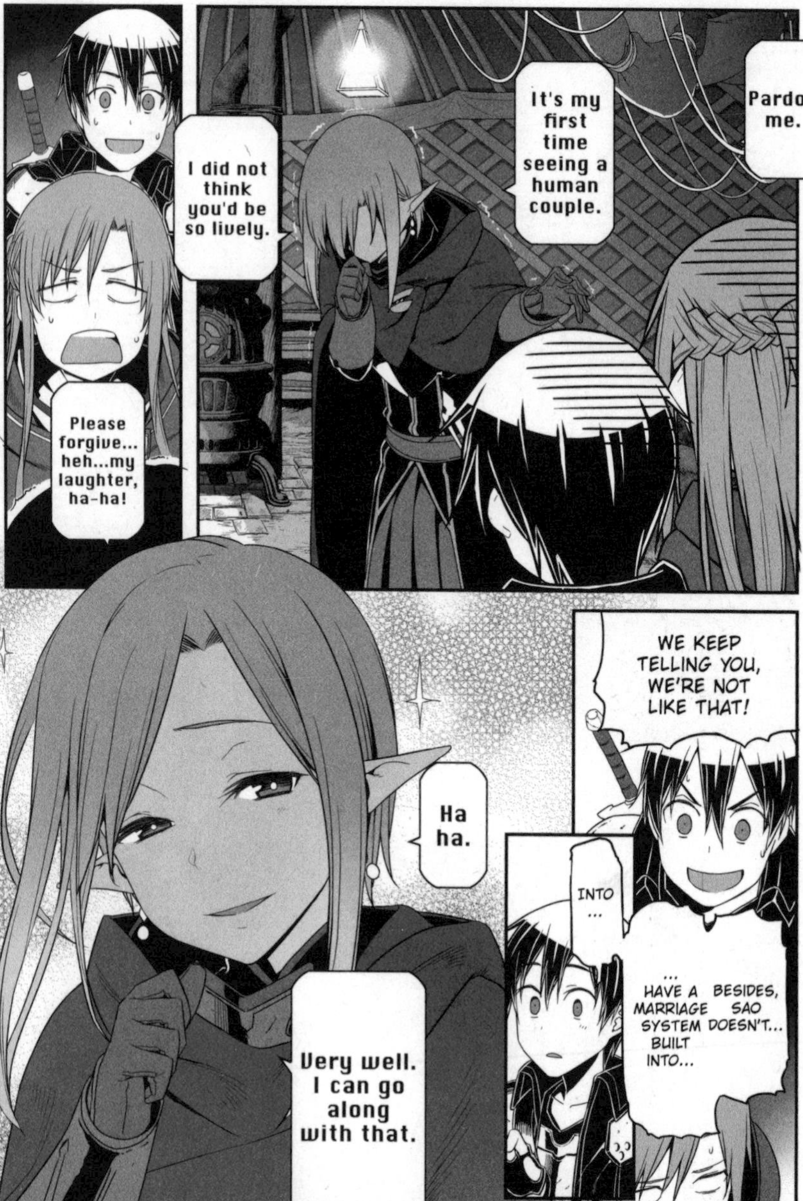
Pardon me.
It's my first time seeing a human couple.
I did not think you'd be so lively.
Please forgive... heh...my laughter, ha-ha!
WE KEEP TELLING YOU, WE'RE NOT LIKE THAT!
BESIDES, SAO DOESN'T...
... HAVE A MARRIAGE SYSTEM BUILT INTO...
INTO...
Ha ha.
Very well. I can go along with that.

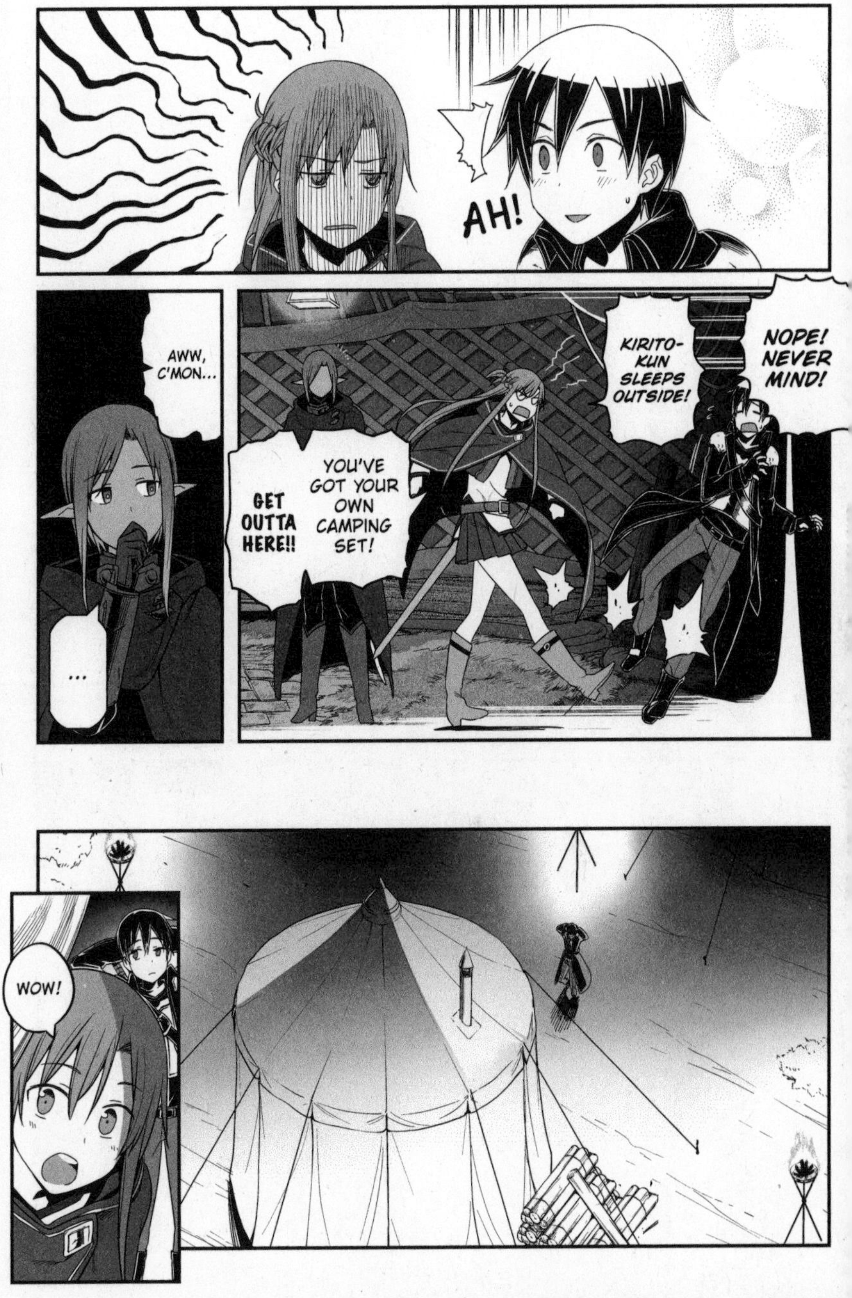
AH!
NOPE! NEVER MIND!
KIRITO-KUN SLEEPS OUTSIDE!
YOU'VE GOT YOUR OWN CAMPING SET!
GET OUTTA HERE!!
AWW, C'MON...
...
WOW!

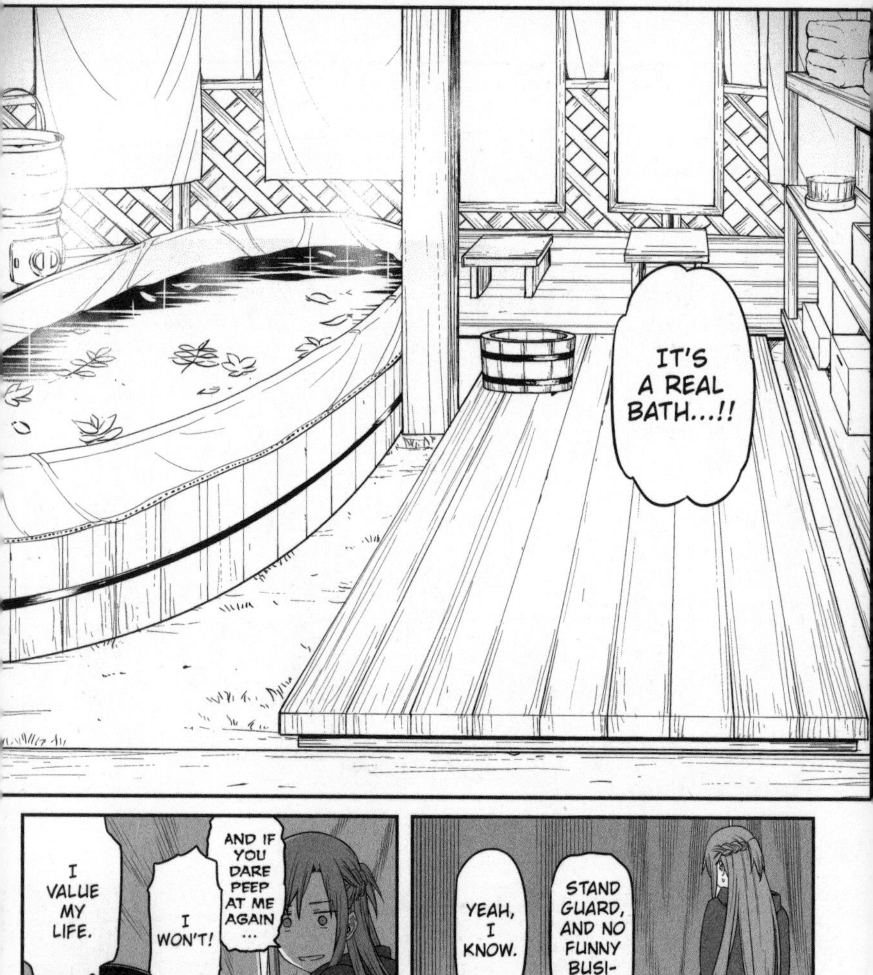
IT'S A REAL BATH...!!

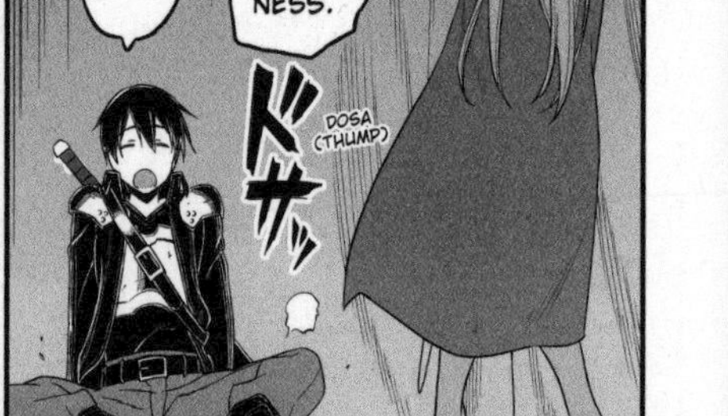
STAND GUARD, AND NO FUNNY BUSI-NESS.
YEAH, I KNOW.
DOSA (THUMP)

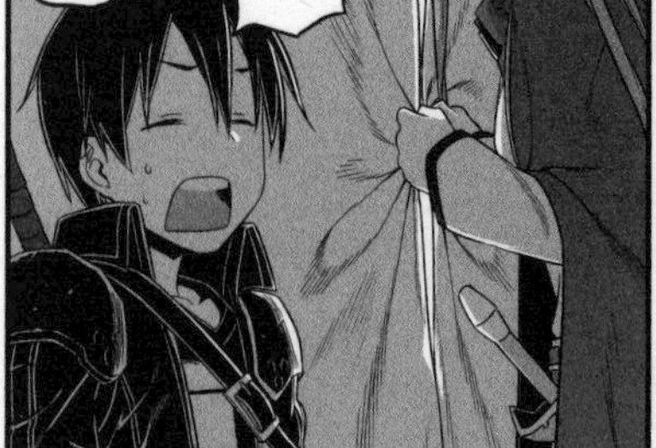
AND IF YOU DARE PEEP AT ME AGAIN ...
I WON'T!
I VALUE MY LIFE.

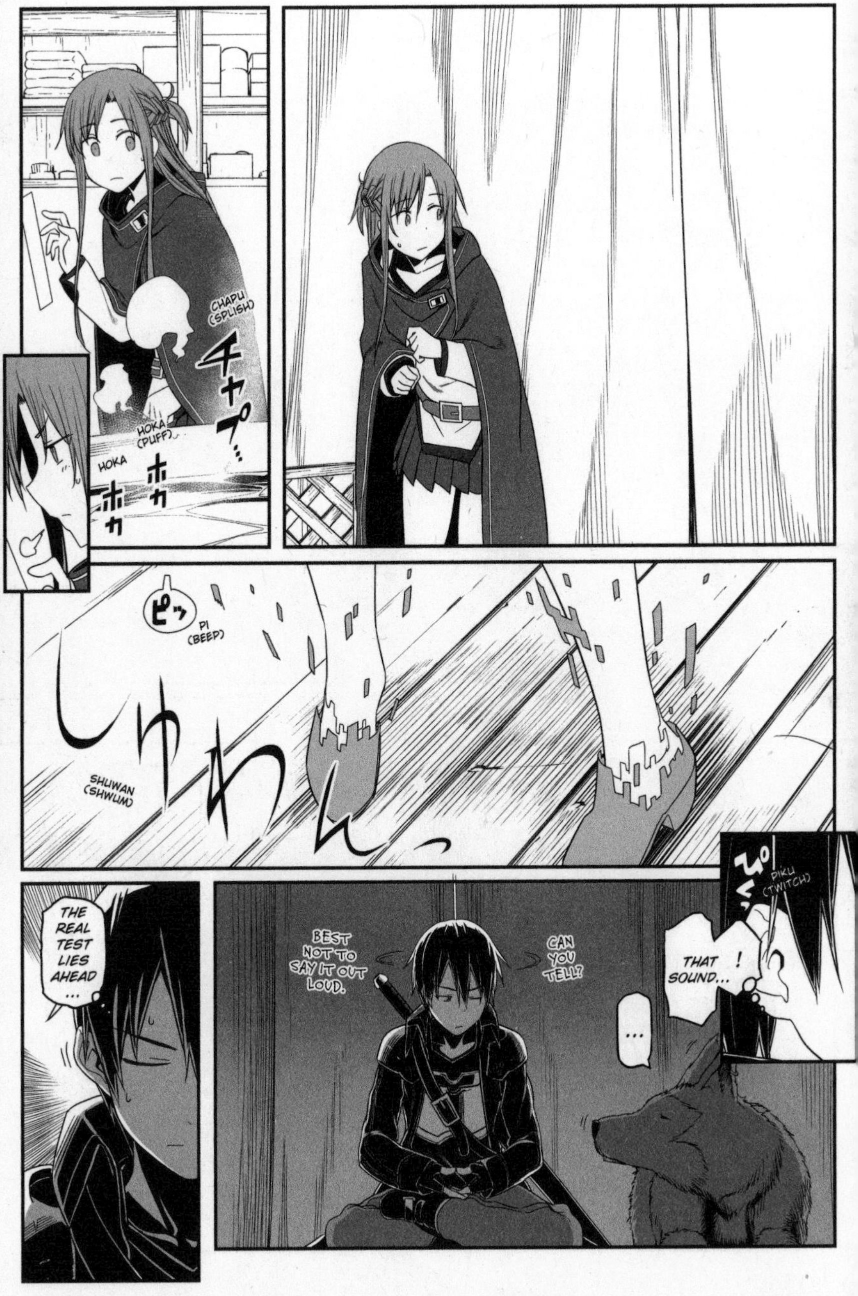
チャプ…
CHAPU (SPLISH)
ホカ
HOKA (PUFF)
ホカ
HOKA
ピッ
PI (BEEP)
しゅわん
SHUWAN (SHWUM)
ぴく
PIKU (TWITCH)
THAT SOUND…!
CAN YOU TELL?
BEST NOT TO SAY IT OUT LOUD.
…
THE REAL TEST LIES AHEAD…

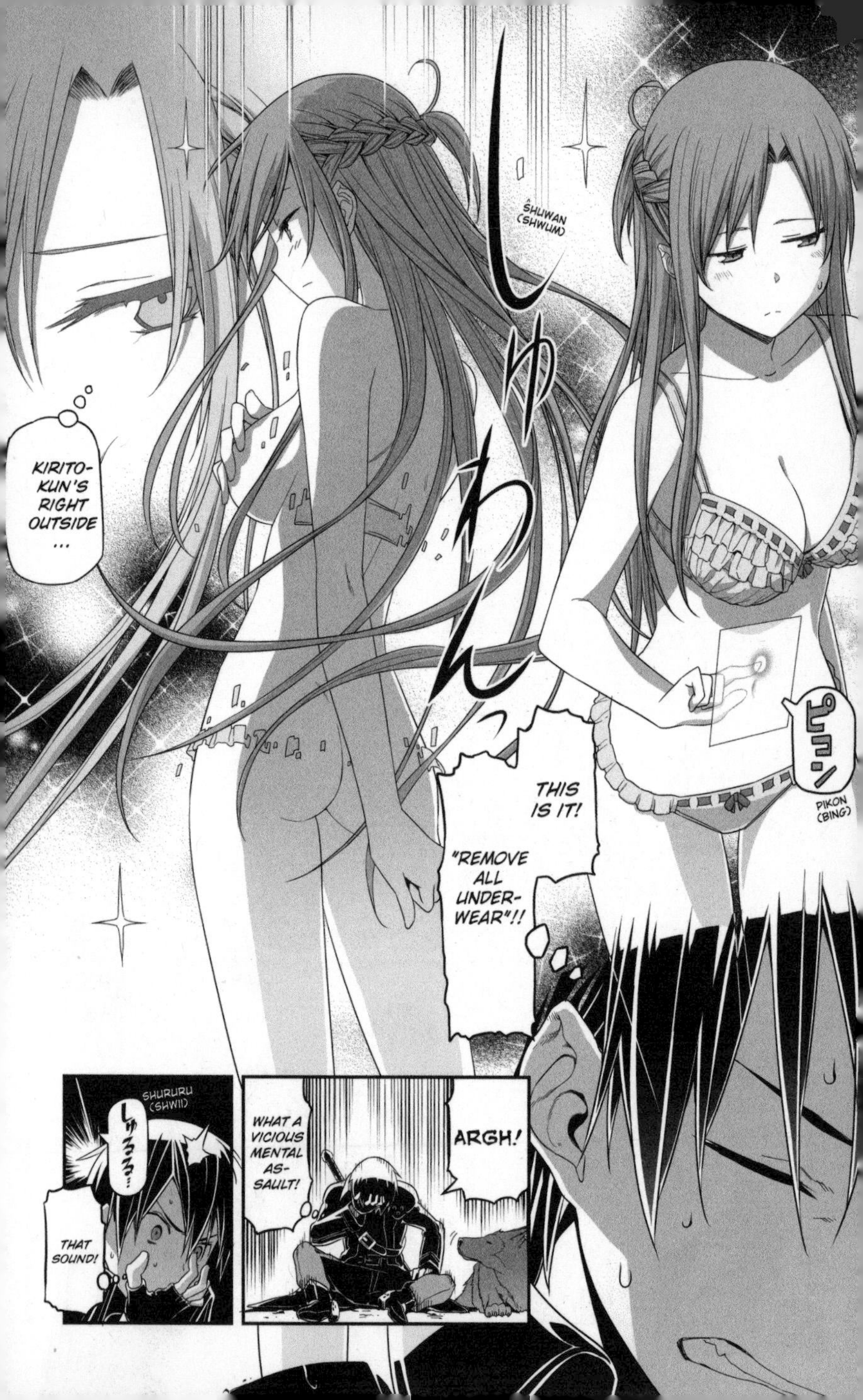

しゅわん
SHUWAN (SHWUM)
KIRITO-KUN'S RIGHT OUTSIDE...
ピコン
PIKON (BING)
THIS IS IT!
"REMOVE ALL UNDERWEAR"!!
ARGH!
WHAT A VICIOUS MENTAL ASSAULT!
しゅるるる…
SHURURU (SHWII)
THAT SOUND!

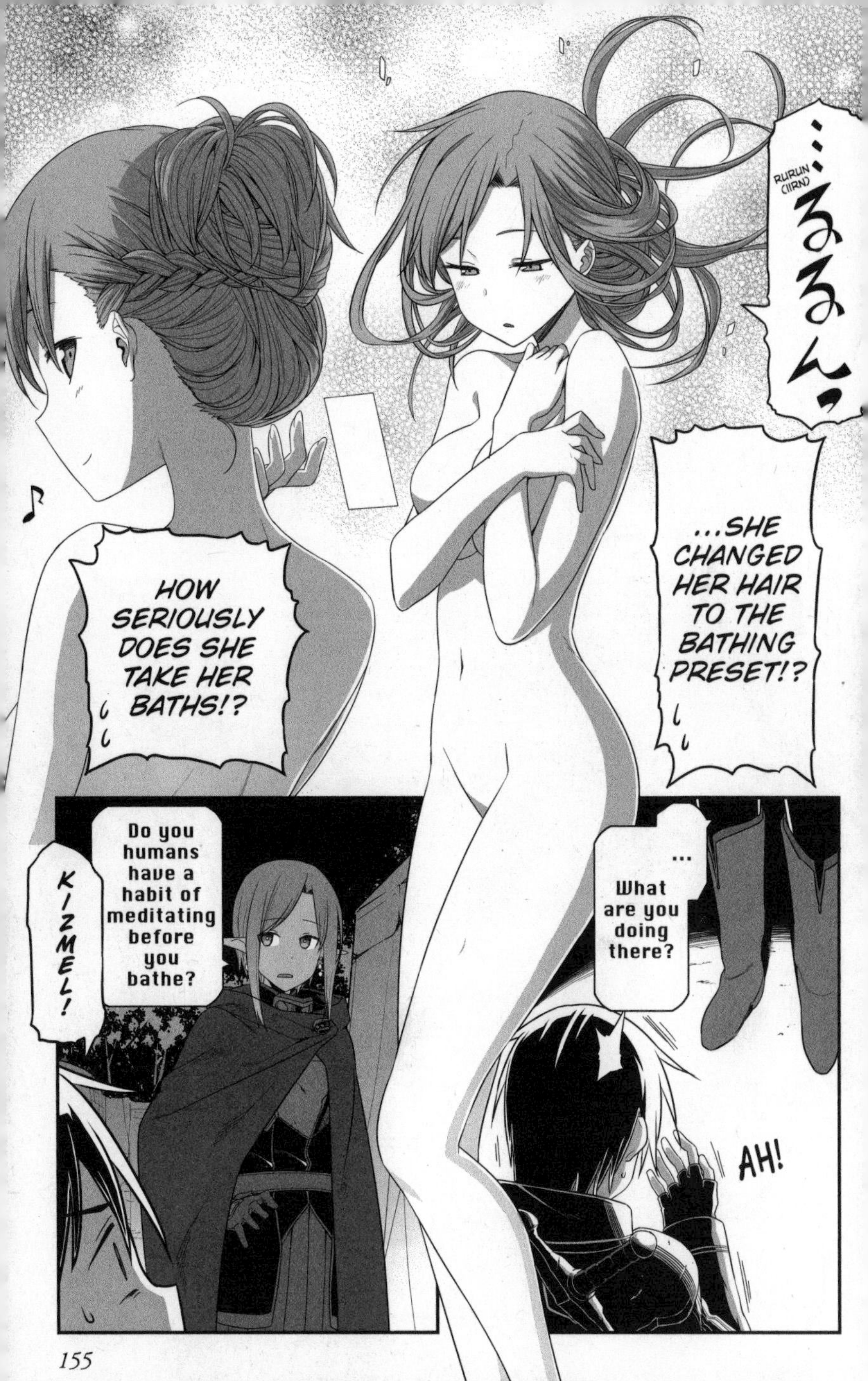

RURUN (IIRN)
るるん
...SHE CHANGED HER HAIR TO THE BATHING PRESET!?
HOW SERIOUSLY DOES SHE TAKE HER BATHS!?
... What are you doing there?
AH!
KIZMEL!
Do you humans have a habit of meditating before you bathe?

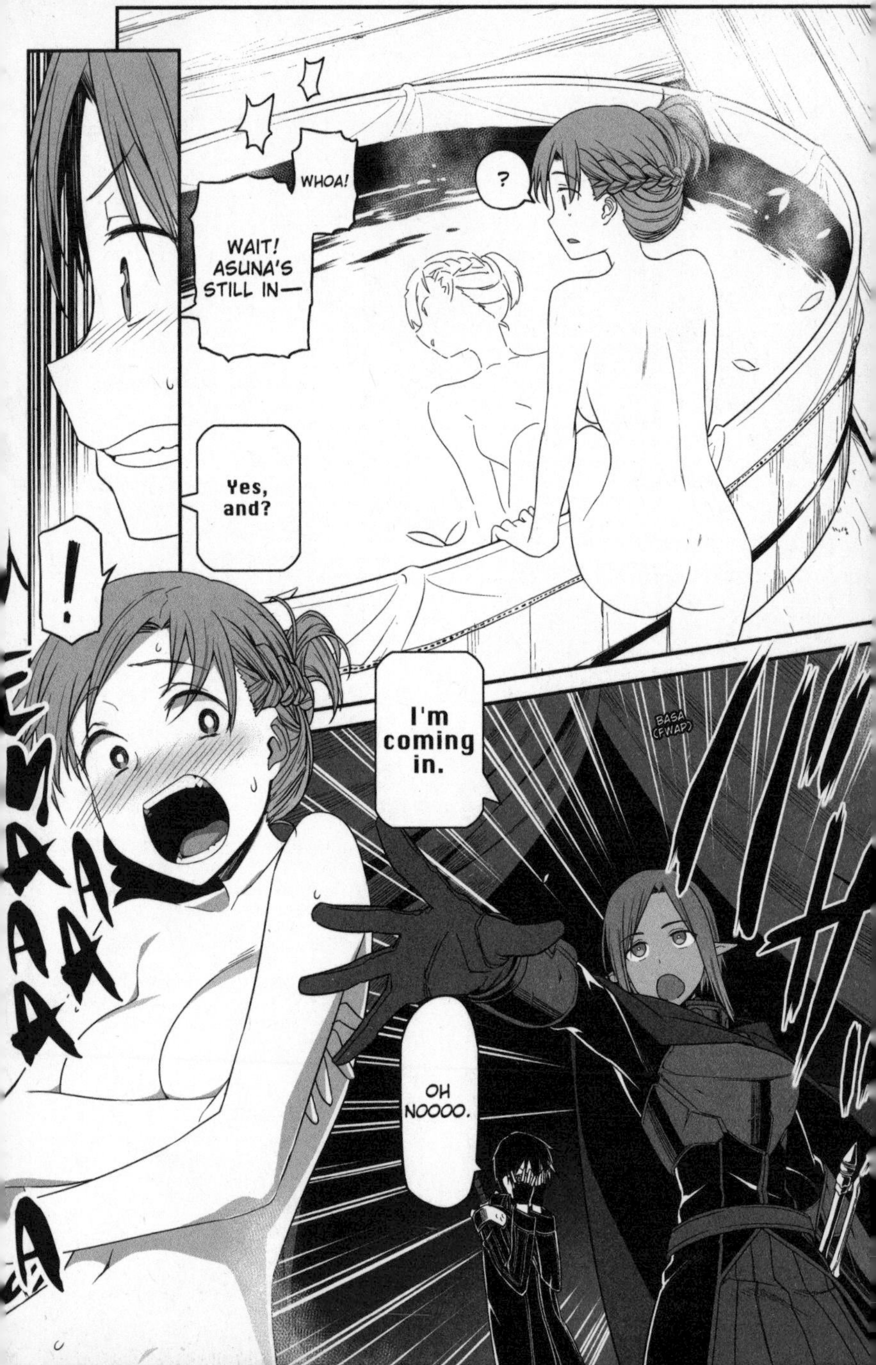
?
WHOA!
WAIT! ASUNA'S STILL IN—
Yes, and?
BASA (FWAP)
I'm coming in.
!
OH NOOOO.

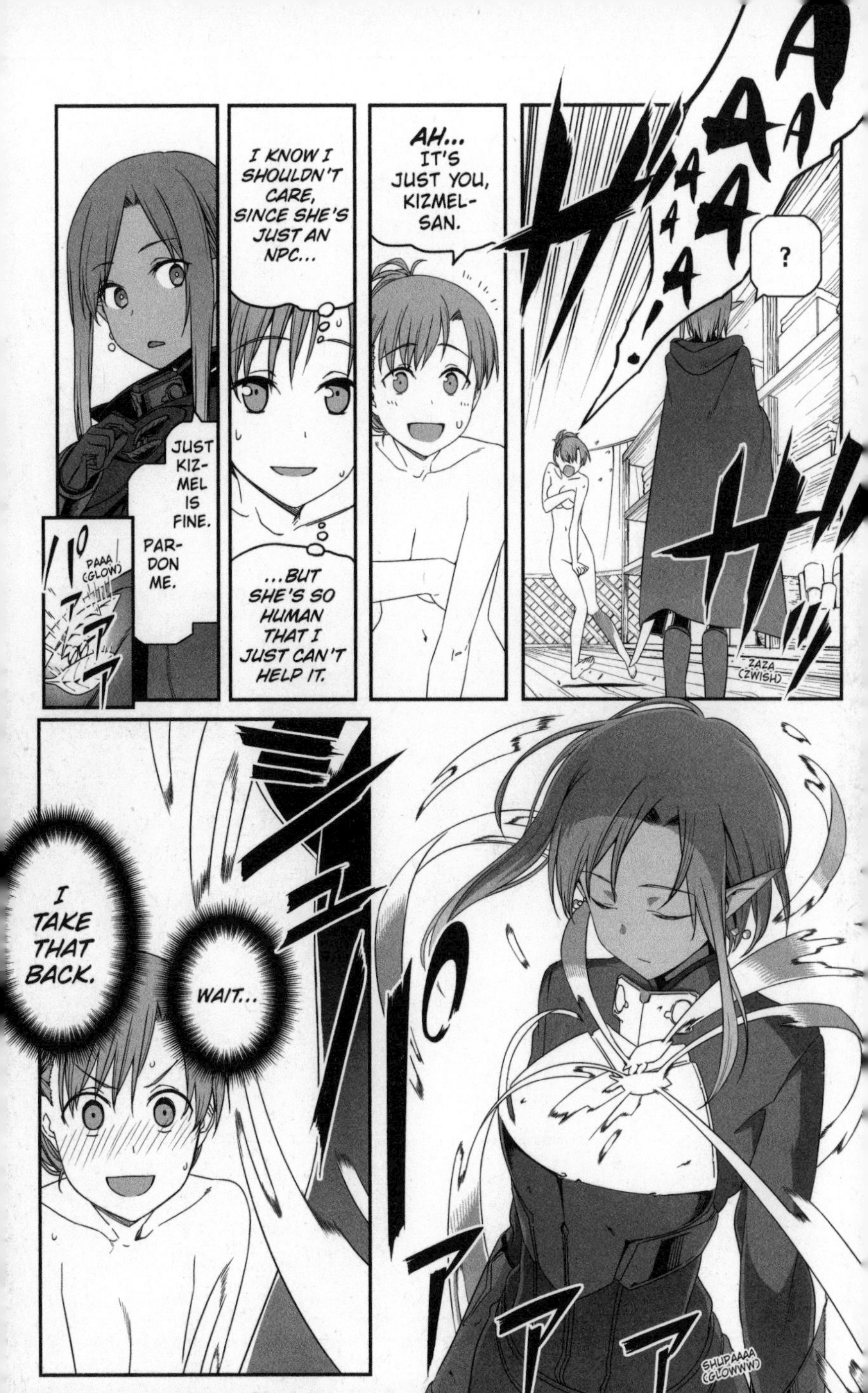
HAAAAAAAAA!
?
HH!!
ZAZA (ZWISH)
AH... IT'S JUST YOU, KIZMEL-SAN.
I KNOW I SHOULDN'T CARE, SINCE SHE'S JUST AN NPC...
...BUT SHE'S SO HUMAN THAT I JUST CAN'T HELP IT.
JUST KIZ-MEL IS FINE.
PAR-DON ME.
PAAA (GLOW)
SHUPAAAA (GLOWWW)
WAIT...
I TAKE THAT BACK.

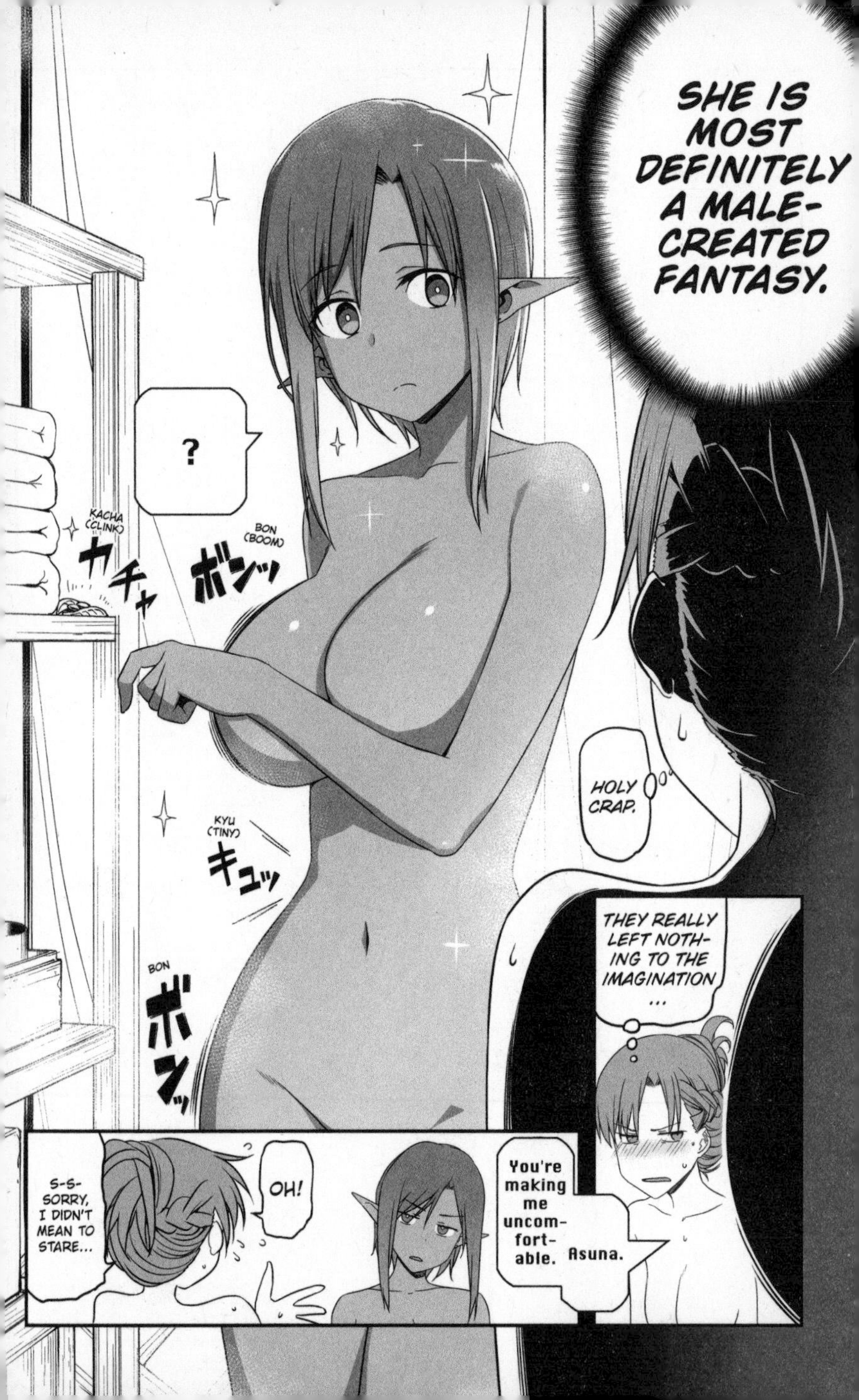
SHE IS MOST DEFINITELY A MALE-CREATED FANTASY.
?
KACHA (CLINK)
カチャ
BON (BOOM)
ボンッ
KYU (TINY)
キュッ
BON
ボンッ
HOLY CRAP.
THEY REALLY LEFT NOTHING TO THE IMAGINATION...
You're making me uncomfortable.
Asuna.
OH!
S-S-SORRY, I DIDN'T MEAN TO STARE...

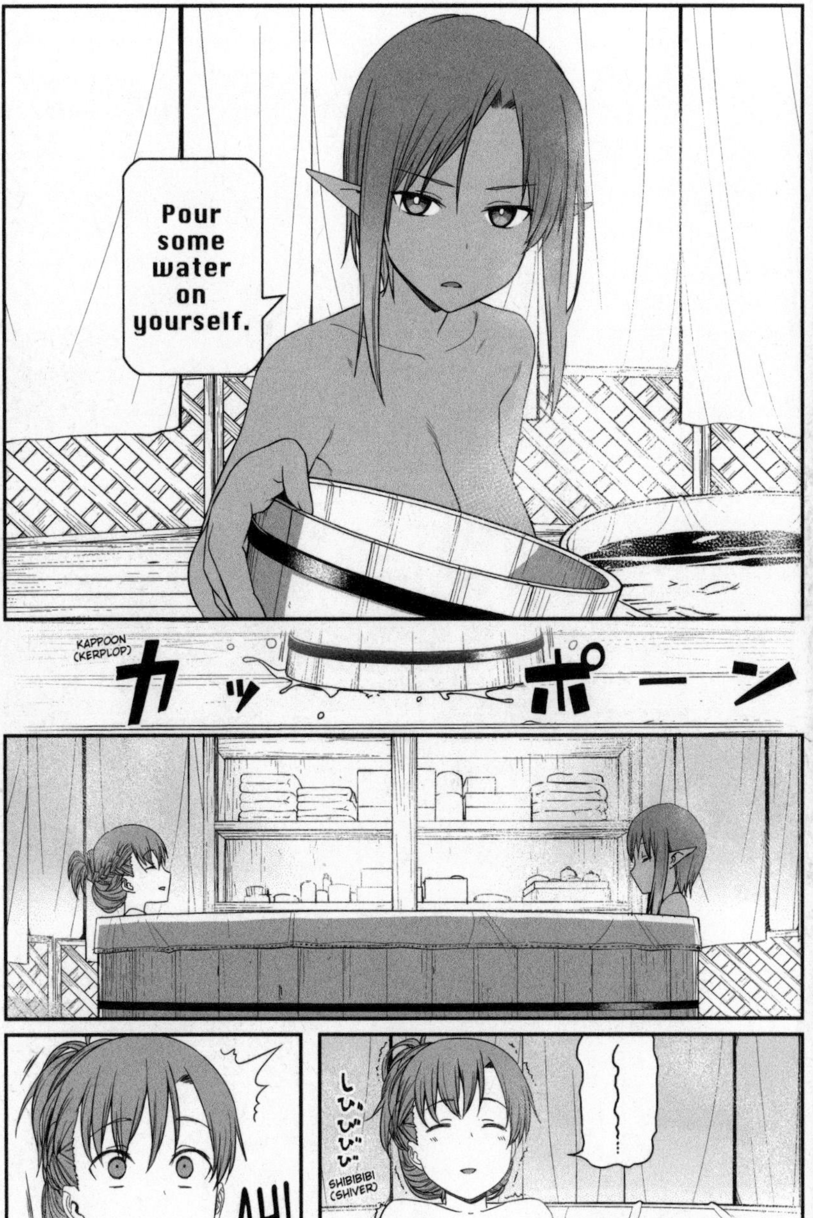
Pour some water on yourself.
KAPPOON (KERPLOP)
カッポーン
しびびび
SHIBIBIBI (SHIVER)
......
AH!

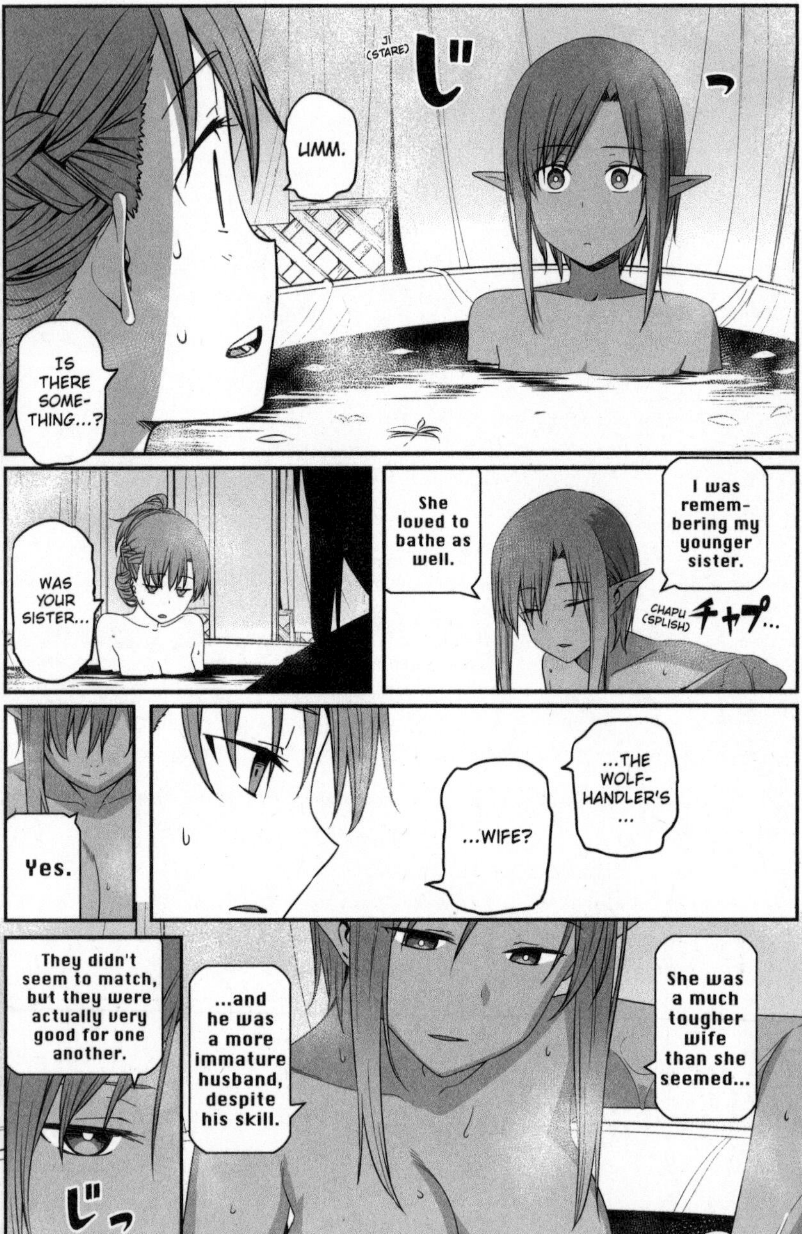
JI (STARE)
じっ
UMM.
IS THERE SOME-THING...?
I was remem-bering my younger sister.
She loved to bathe as well.
CHAPU (SPLISH)
チャプ...
WAS YOUR SISTER...
...THE WOLF-HANDLER'S ...
...WIFE?
Yes.
She was a much tougher wife than she seemed...
...and he was a more immature husband, despite his skill.
They didn't seem to match, but they were actually very good for one another.
じっ
JI

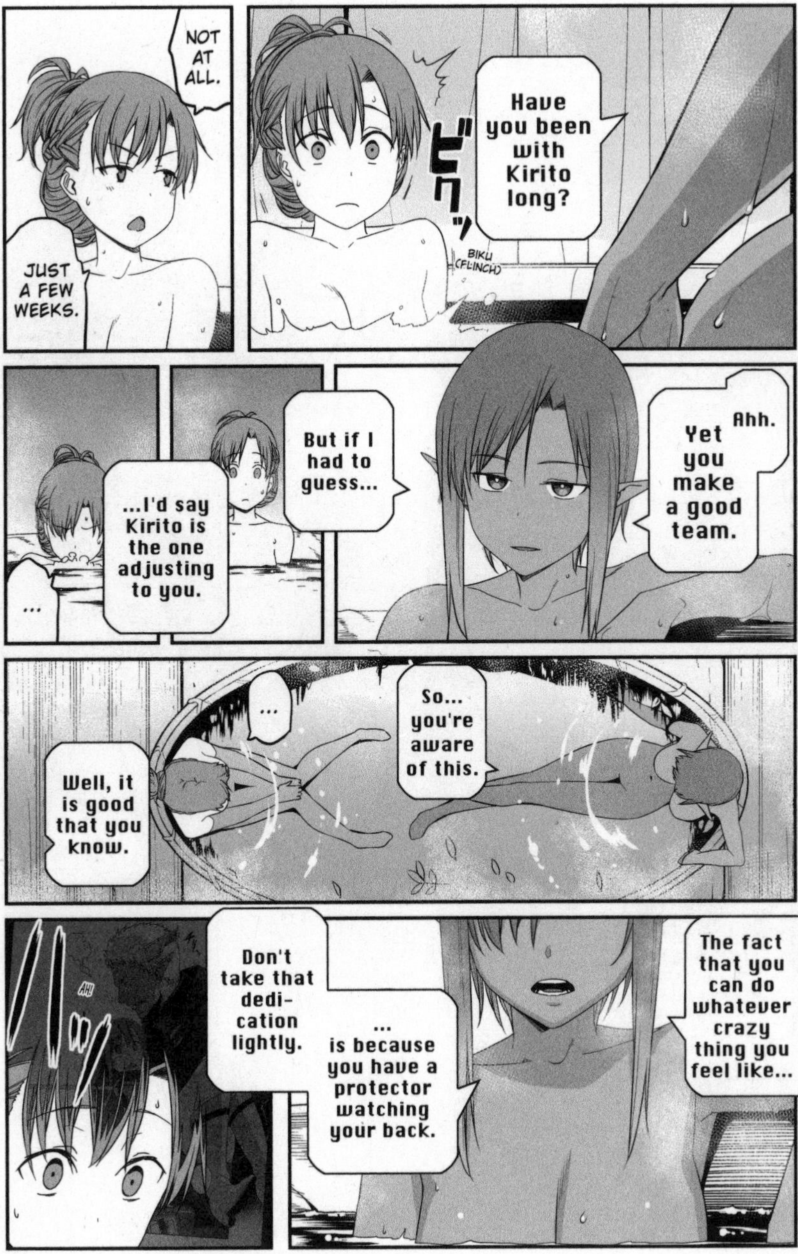
Have you been with Kirito long?
ビクッ
BIKU (FLINCH)
NOT AT ALL.
JUST A FEW WEEKS.
Ahh. Yet you make a good team.
But if I had to guess...
...I'd say Kirito is the one adjusting to you.
...
So... you're aware of this.
...
Well, it is good that you know.
The fact that you can do whatever crazy thing you feel like...
... is because you have a protector watching your back.
Don't take that dedi-cation lightly.
AH!

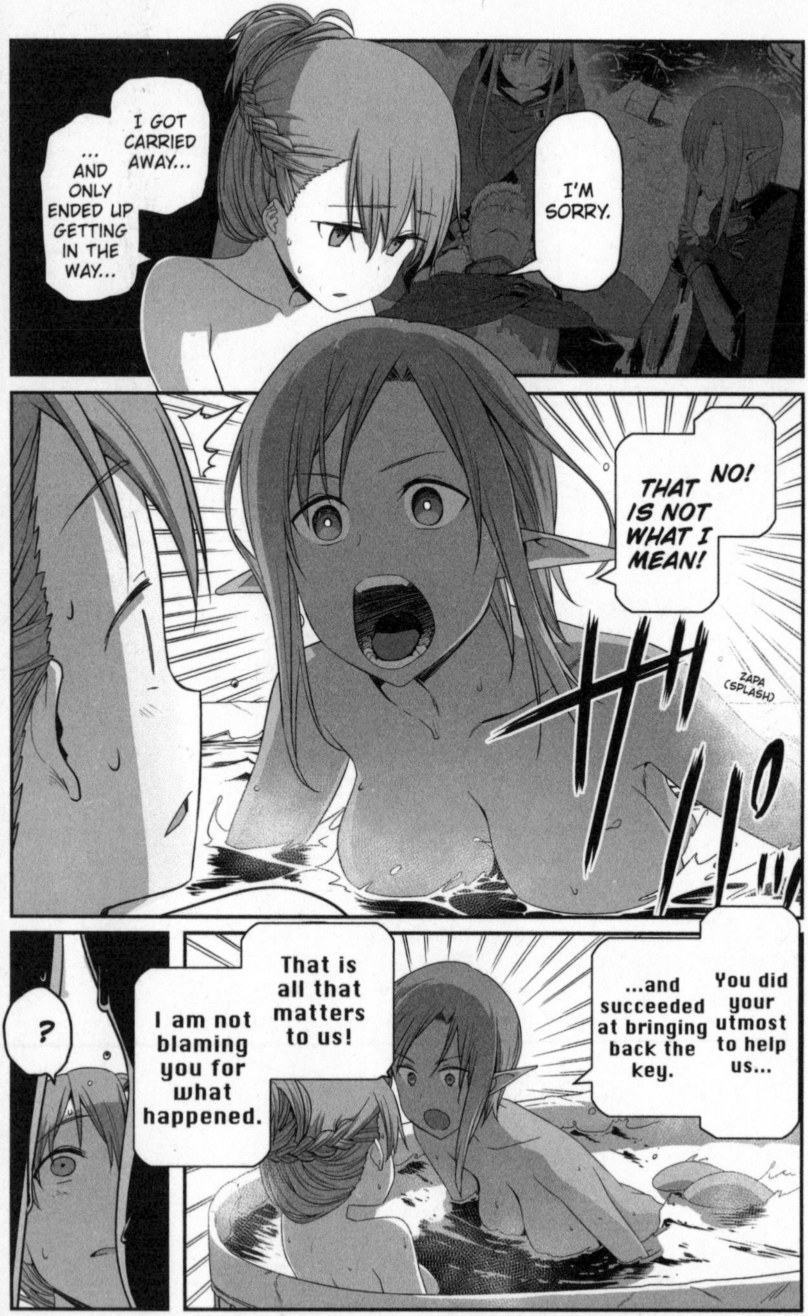
I'M SORRY.
I GOT CARRIED AWAY... ...AND ONLY ENDED UP GETTING IN THE WAY...
NO! THAT IS NOT WHAT I MEAN!
ZAPA (SPLASH)
You did your utmost to help us... ...and succeeded at bringing back the key.
That is all that matters to us!
I am not blaming you for what happened.
?

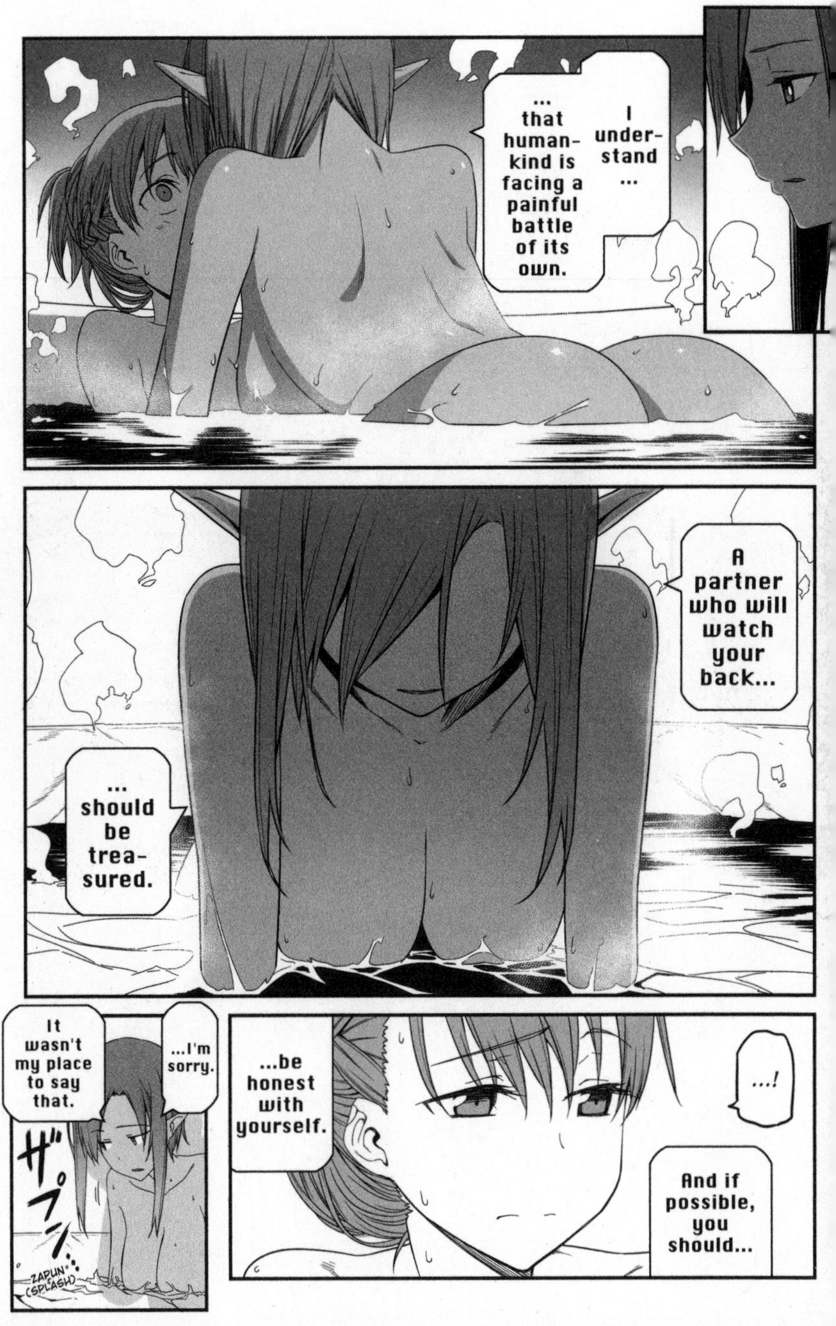
I understand...
...that humankind is facing a painful battle of its own.
A partner who will watch your back...
...should be treasured.
...!
And if possible, you should...
...be honest with yourself.
...I'm sorry.
It wasn't my place to say that.
ZAPUN (SPLASH)

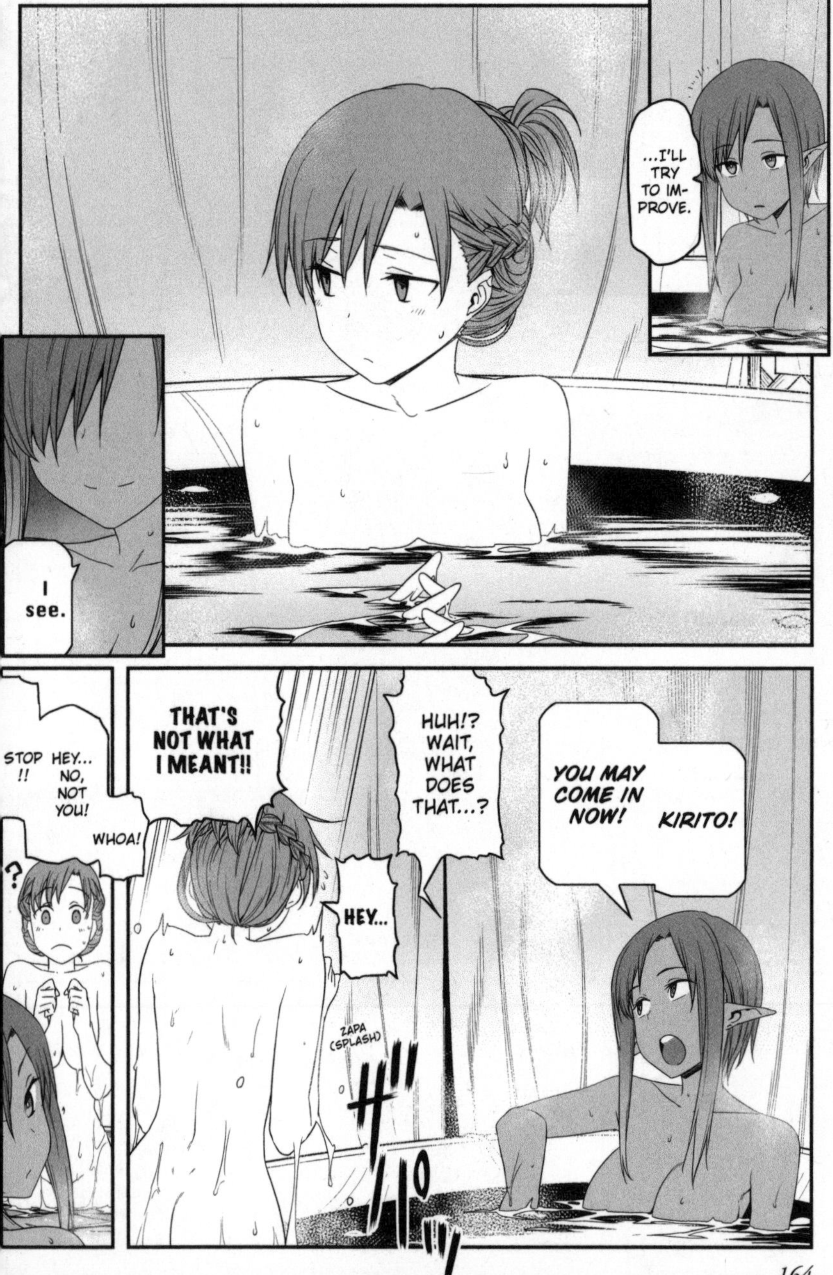
...I'LL TRY TO IMPROVE.
I see.
YOU MAY COME IN NOW! KIRITO!
HUH!? WAIT, WHAT DOES THAT...?
THAT'S NOT WHAT I MEANT!!
HEY...
ZAPA (SPLASH)
HEY... NO, NOT YOU!
STOP!!
WHOA!
?

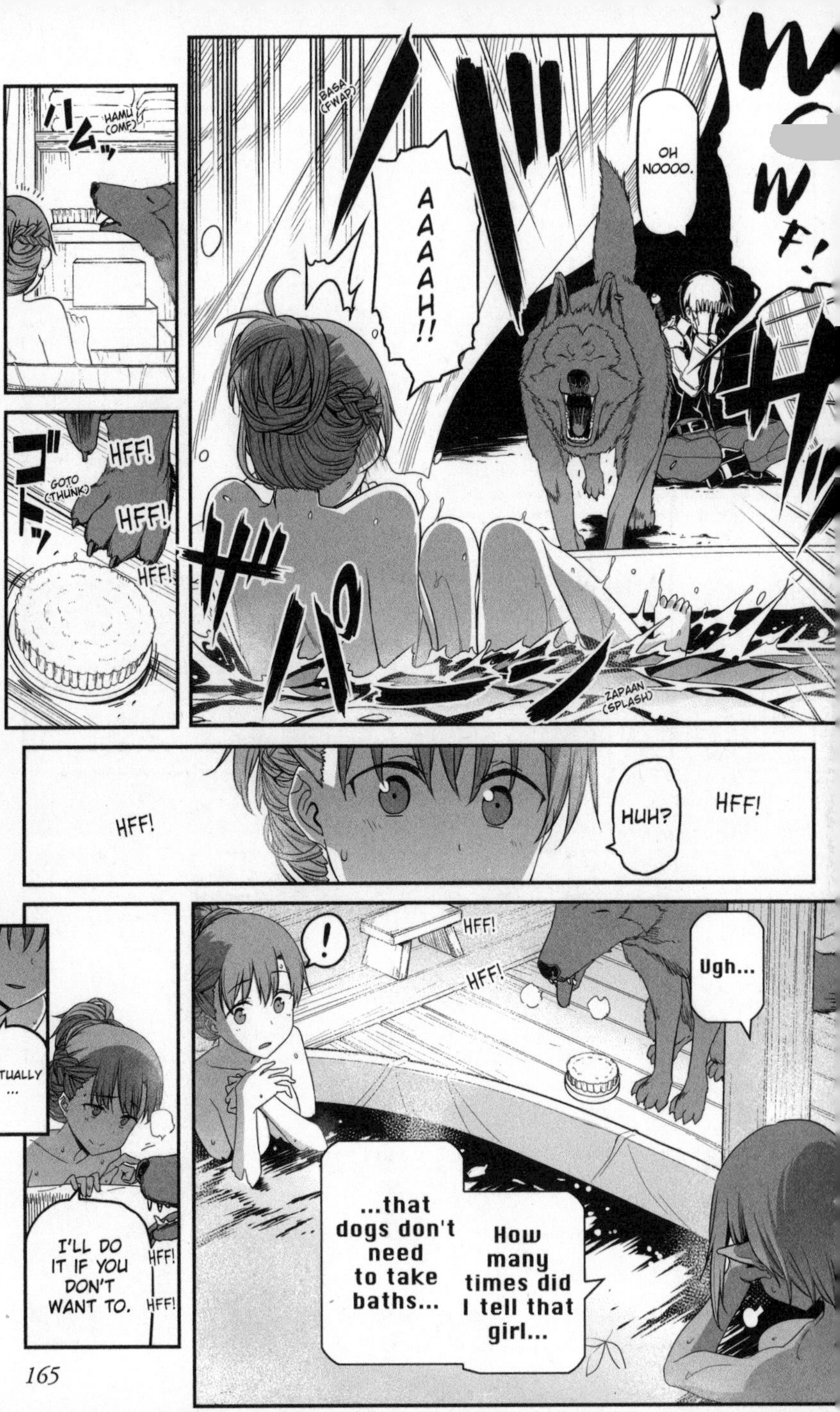

OH NOOOO.
BASA (FWAP)
AAAAAH!!
ZAPAAN (SPLASH)
HAMU (COMF)
HFF!
GOTO (THUNK)
HFF!
HFF!
HFF!
HUH?
HFF!
Ugh...
HFF!
HFF!
!
How many times did I tell that girl...
...that dogs don't need to take baths...
ACTUALLY...
I'LL DO IT IF YOU DON'T WANT TO.
HFF!
HFF!

PLEASE
LET ME!

GUH...

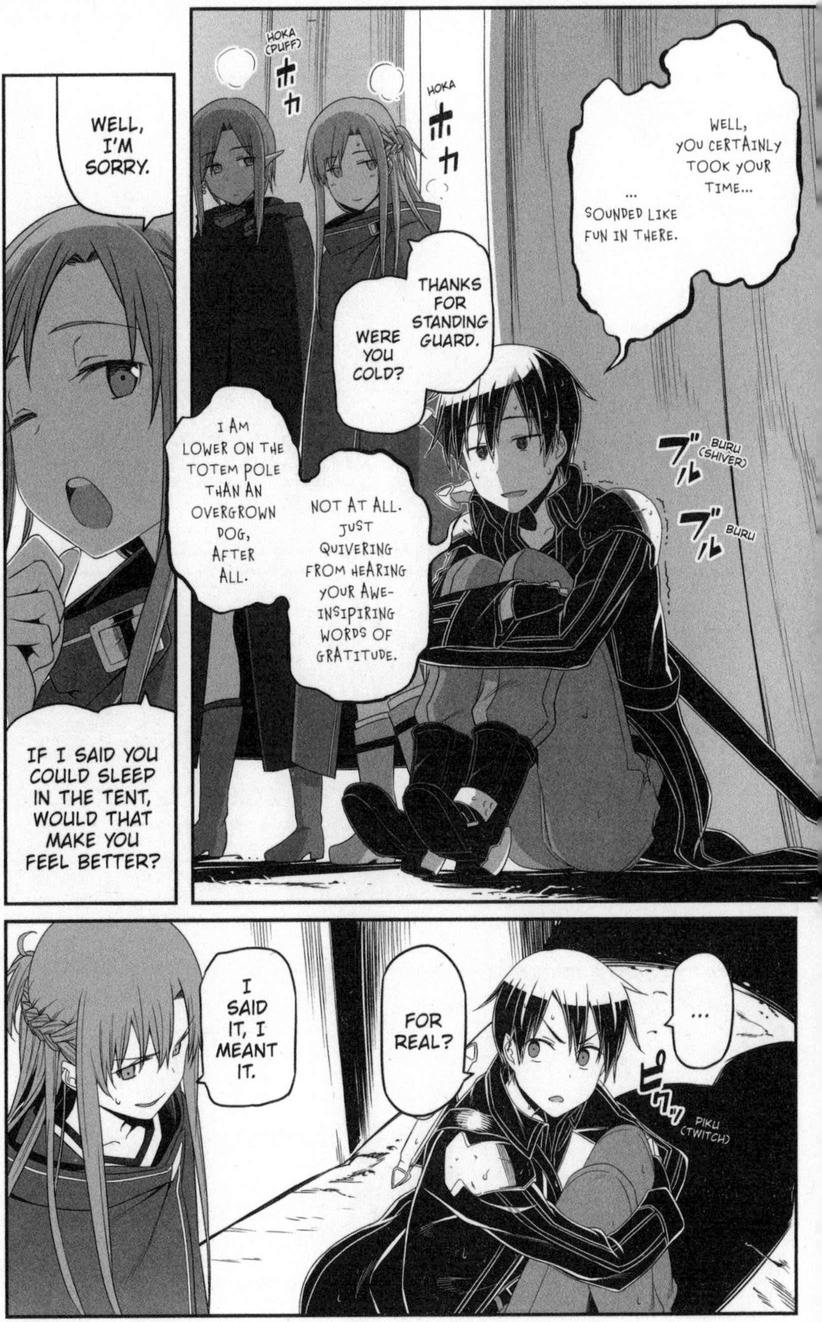

WELL, YOU CERTAINLY TOOK YOUR TIME...
... SOUNDED LIKE FUN IN THERE.
HOKA ホカ
HOKA (PUFF) ホカ
THANKS FOR STANDING GUARD.
WERE YOU COLD?
BURU (SHIVER) ブル
BURU ブル
NOT AT ALL. JUST QUIVERING FROM HEARING YOUR AWE-INSPIRING WORDS OF GRATITUDE.
I AM LOWER ON THE TOTEM POLE THAN AN OVERGROWN DOG, AFTER ALL.
WELL, I'M SORRY.
IF I SAID YOU COULD SLEEP IN THE TENT, WOULD THAT MAKE YOU FEEL BETTER?
...
PIKU (TWITCH) ピクッ
FOR REAL?
I SAID IT, I MEANT IT.

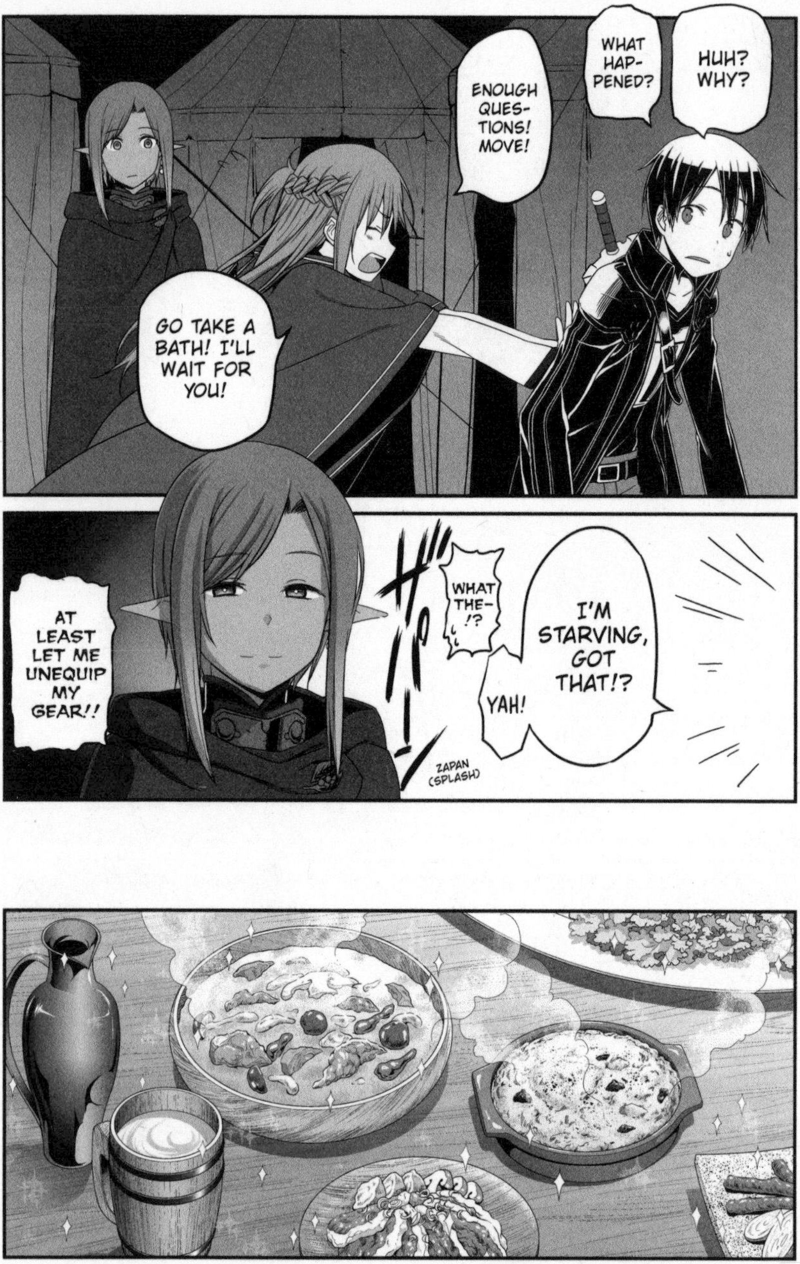
HUH? WHY?
WHAT HAP-PENED?
ENOUGH QUES-TIONS! MOVE!
GO TAKE A BATH! I'LL WAIT FOR YOU!
I'M STARVING, GOT THAT!?
WHAT THE-!?
YAH!
ZAPAN (SPLASH)
AT LEAST LET ME UNEQUIP MY GEAR!!

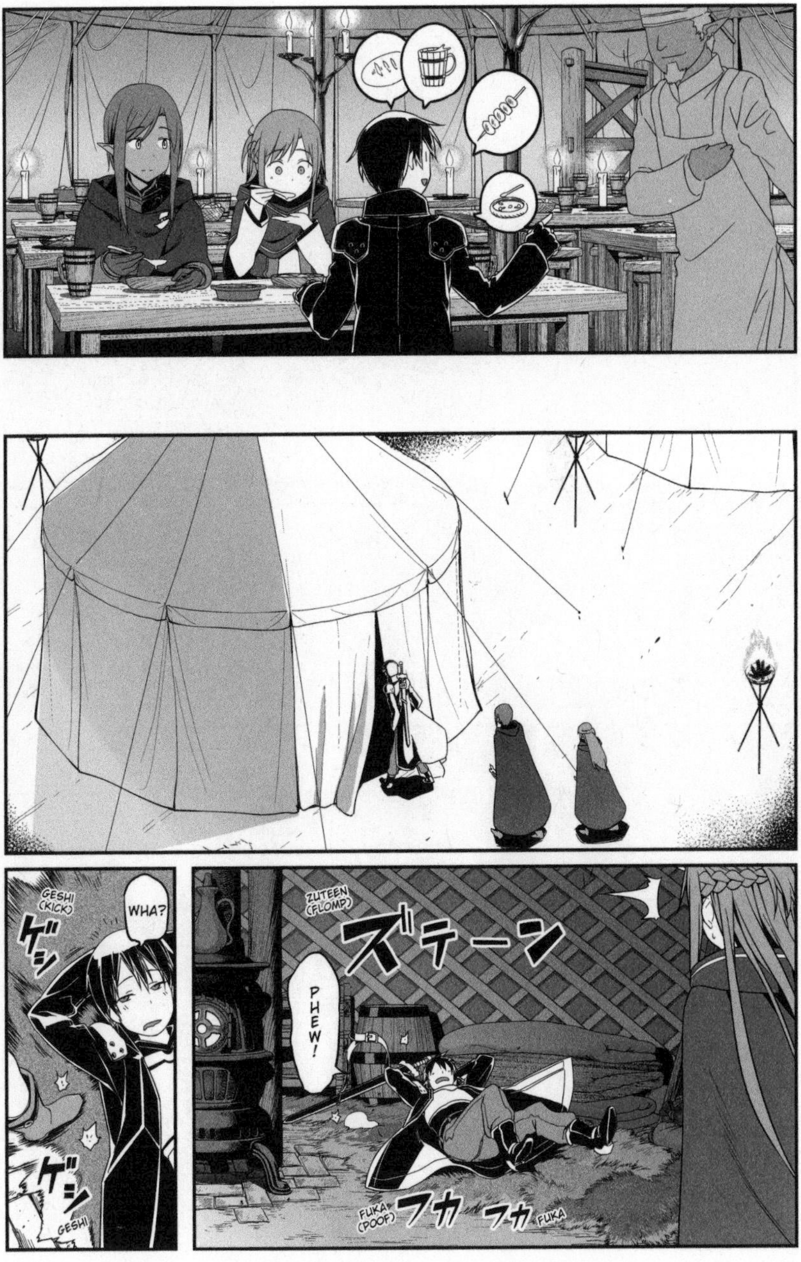
ZUTEEN (FLOMP)
ズテーン
PHEW!
FUKA (POOF) フカ
フカ FUKA
GESHI (KICK)
ゲシ
WHA?
ゲシ
GESHI

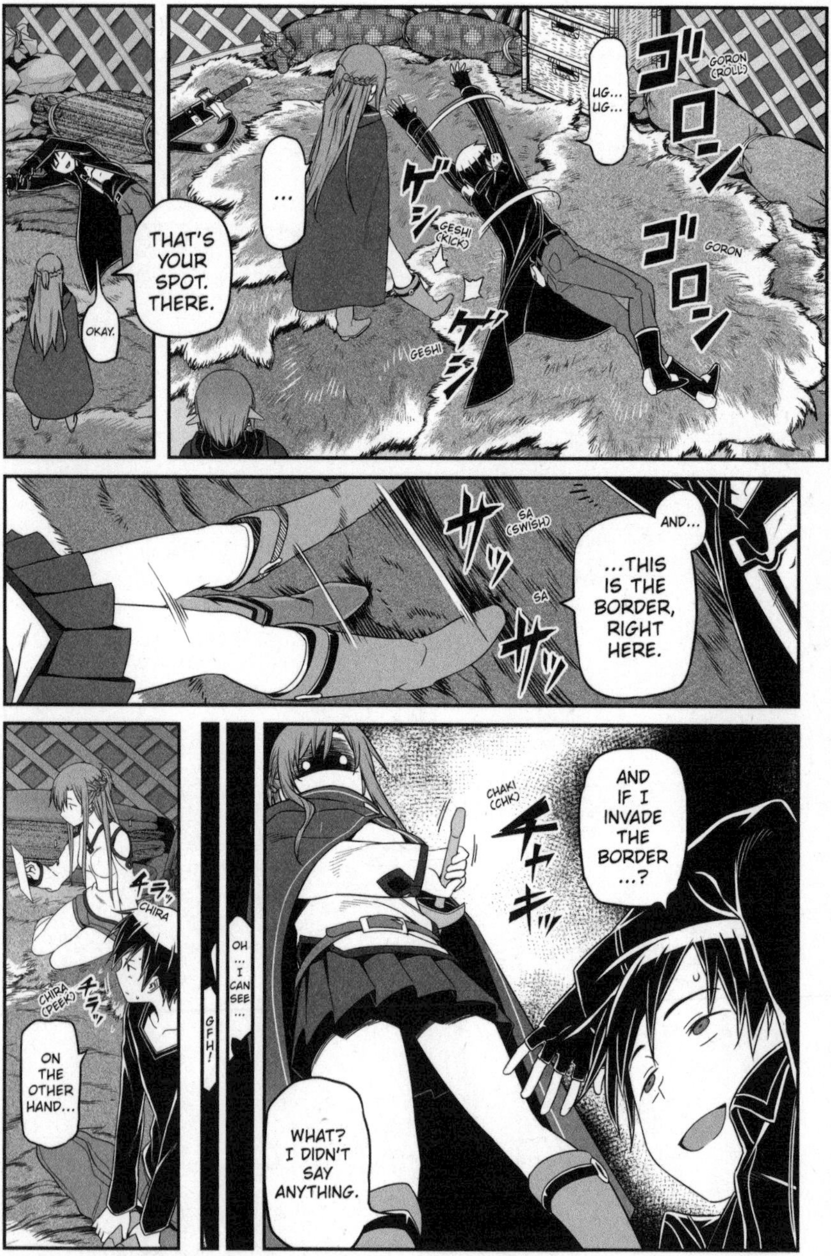

ゴロン
GORON (ROLL)
UG... UG...
ゴロン
GORON
...
ゲシ
GESHI (KICK)
ゲシ
GESHI
THAT'S YOUR SPOT. THERE.
OKAY.
AND...
...THIS IS THE BORDER, RIGHT HERE.
サッ
SA (SWISH)
サッ
SA
AND IF I INVADE THE BORDER...?
チャキッ
CHAKI (CHK)
WHAT? I DIDN'T SAY ANYTHING.
OH... I CAN SEE...
GFH!
チラッ
CHIRA
チラッ
CHIRA (PEEK)
ON THE OTHER HAND...

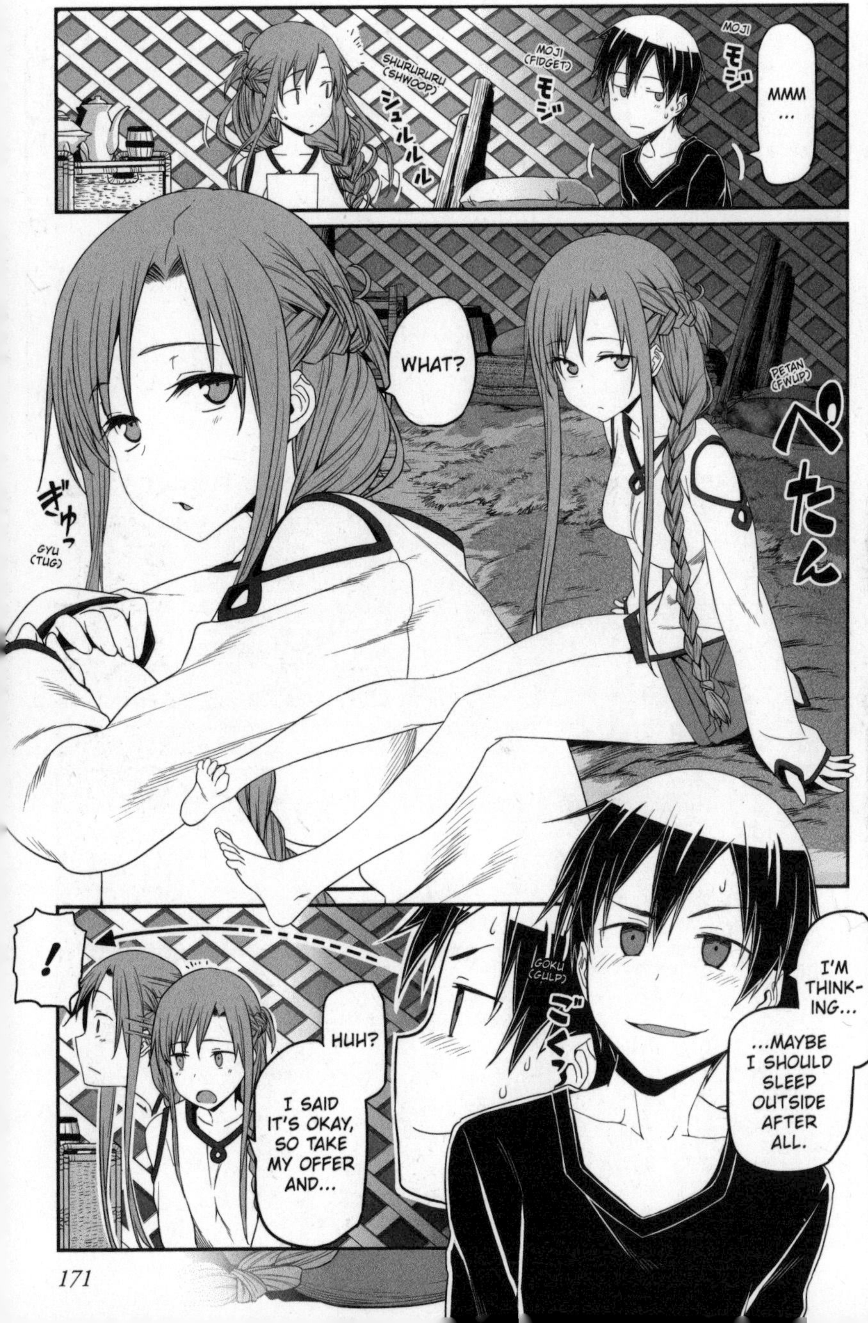
MOJI
モジ
MMM...
MOJI (FIDGET)
モジ
SHURURURU (SHWOOP)
シュルルル
PETAN (FWUP)
ぺたん
WHAT?
ぎゅっ
GYU (TUG)
I'M THINKING...
...MAYBE I SHOULD SLEEP OUTSIDE AFTER ALL.
GOKU (GULP)
ごくっ
HUH?
I SAID IT'S OKAY, SO TAKE MY OFFER AND...
!

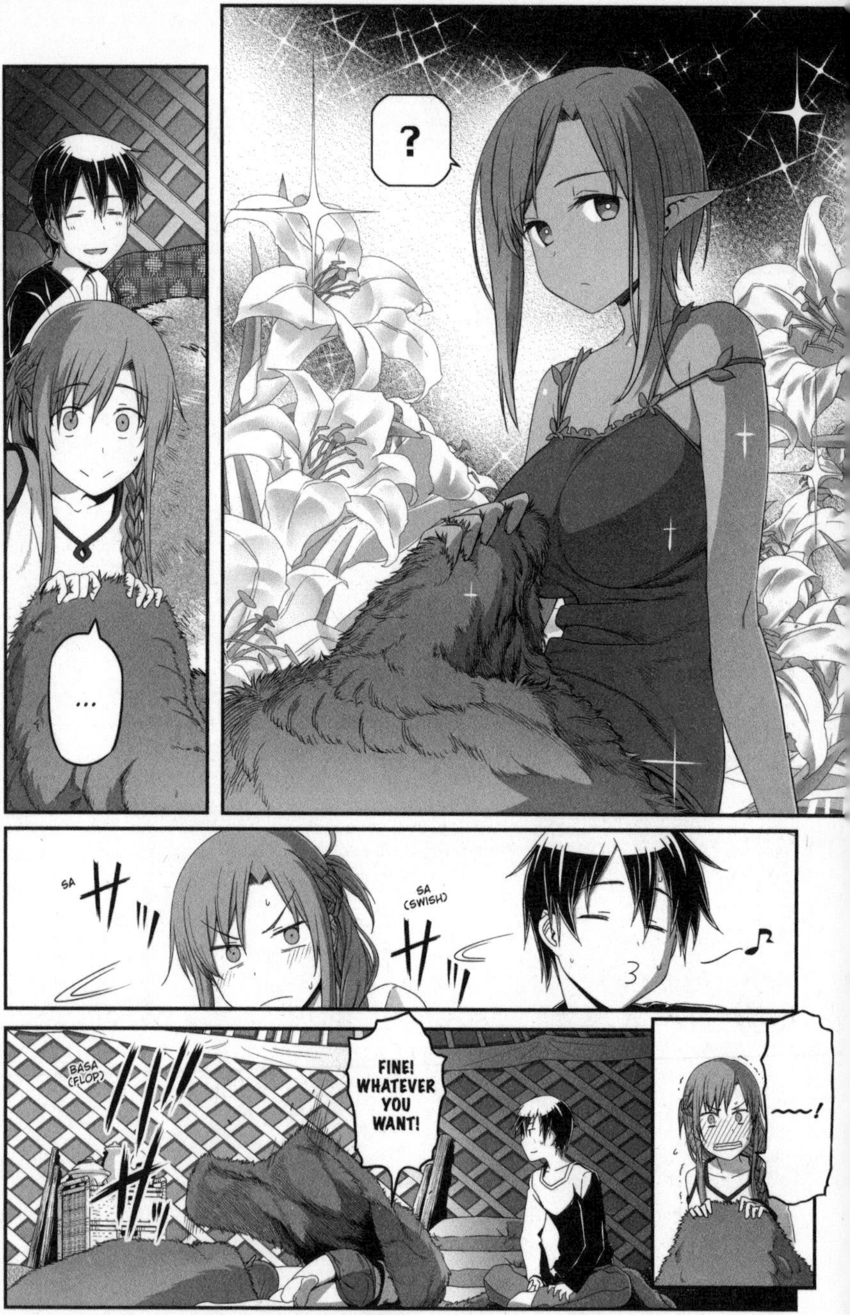
?
...
SA (SWISH)
SA
~~~!
FINE! WHATEVER YOU WANT!
BASA (FLOP)
~~~

#029: Story

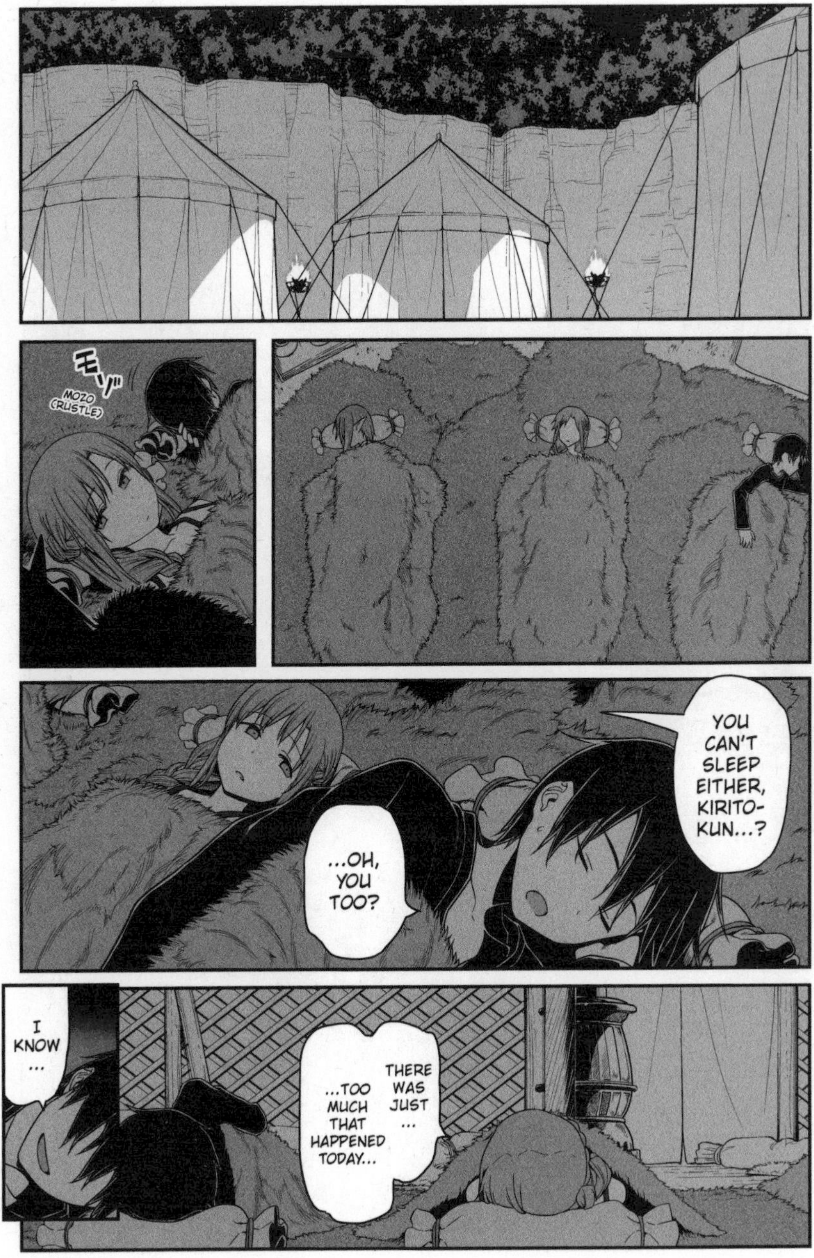
モゾ
MOZO (RUSTLE)
YOU CAN'T SLEEP EITHER, KIRITO-KUN...?
...OH, YOU TOO?
THERE WAS JUST ... ...TOO MUCH THAT HAPPENED TODAY...
I KNOW ...

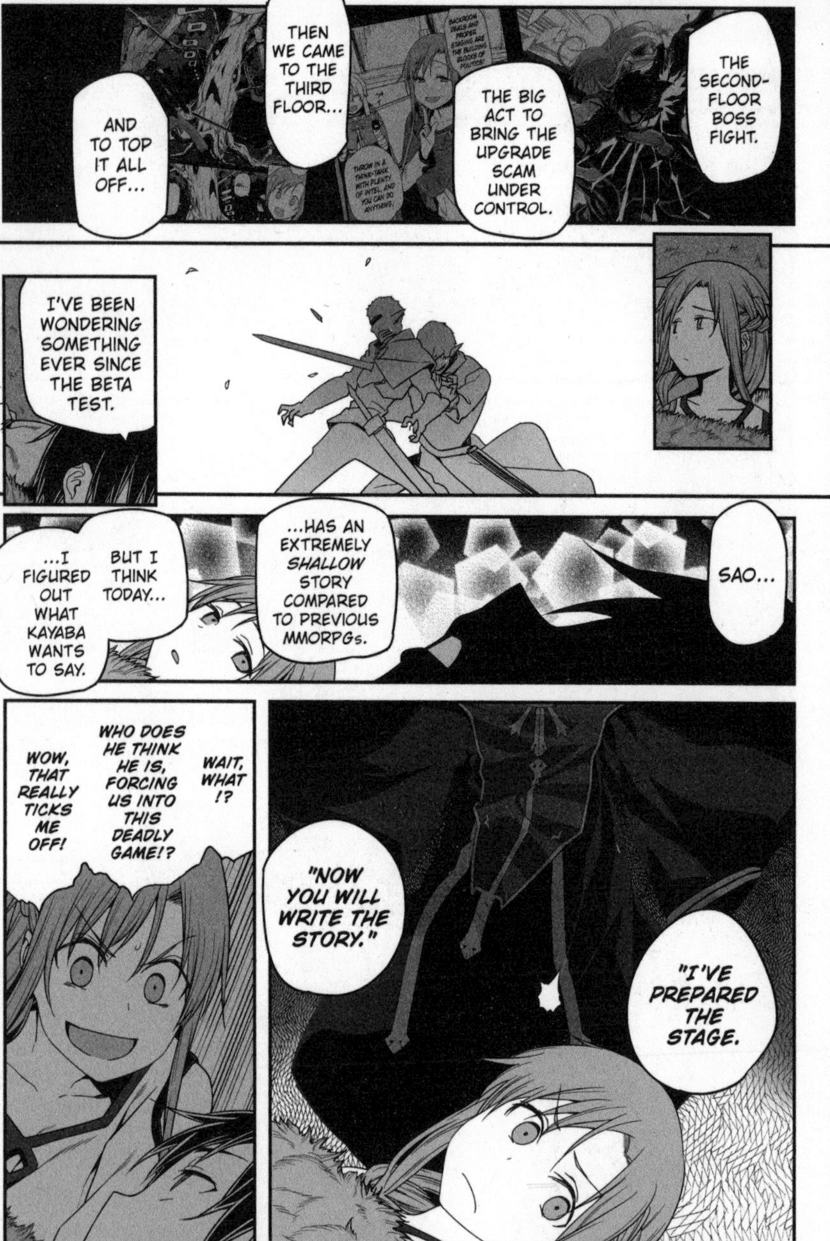
THE SECOND-FLOOR BOSS FIGHT.
THE BIG ACT TO BRING THE UPGRADE SCAM UNDER CONTROL.
BACKROOM DEALS AND PROPER STAGING ARE THE BUILDING BLOCKS OF POLITICS!
THEN WE CAME TO THE THIRD FLOOR...
THROW IN A THINK-TANK WITH PLENTY OF INTEL, AND YOU CAN DO ANYTHING.
AND TO TOP IT ALL OFF...
I'VE BEEN WONDERING SOMETHING EVER SINCE THE BETA TEST.
SAO...
...HAS AN EXTREMELY SHALLOW STORY COMPARED TO PREVIOUS MMORPGs.
BUT I THINK TODAY...
...I FIGURED OUT WHAT KAYABA WANTS TO SAY.
"I'VE PREPARED THE STAGE.
"NOW YOU WILL WRITE THE STORY."
WAIT, WHAT!?
WHO DOES HE THINK HE IS, FORCING US INTO THIS DEADLY GAME!?
WOW, THAT REALLY TICKS ME OFF!

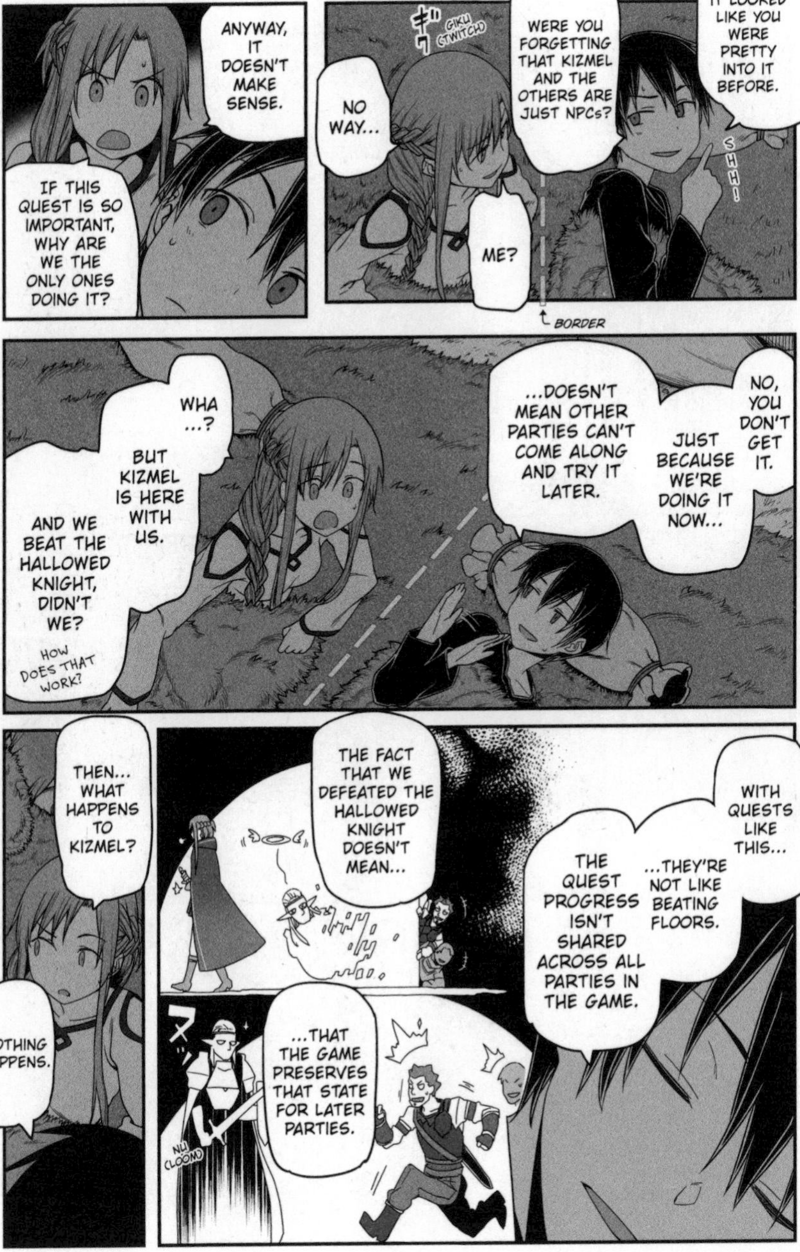
I DUNNO, IT LOOKED LIKE YOU WERE PRETTY INTO IT BEFORE.
SHHH!
WERE YOU FORGETTING THAT KIZMEL AND THE OTHERS ARE JUST NPCs?
GIKU (TWITCH)
NO WAY...
ME?
BORDER
ANYWAY, IT DOESN'T MAKE SENSE.
IF THIS QUEST IS SO IMPORTANT, WHY ARE WE THE ONLY ONES DOING IT?
NO, YOU DON'T GET IT.
JUST BECAUSE WE'RE DOING IT NOW...
...DOESN'T MEAN OTHER PARTIES CAN'T COME ALONG AND TRY IT LATER.
WHA...?
BUT KIZMEL IS HERE WITH US.
AND WE BEAT THE HALLOWED KNIGHT, DIDN'T WE?
HOW DOES THAT WORK?
WITH QUESTS LIKE THIS...
...THEY'RE NOT LIKE BEATING FLOORS.
THE QUEST PROGRESS ISN'T SHARED ACROSS ALL PARTIES IN THE GAME.
THE FACT THAT WE DEFEATED THE HALLOWED KNIGHT DOESN'T MEAN...
...THAT THE GAME PRESERVES THAT STATE FOR LATER PARTIES.
NU (LOOM)
THEN... WHAT HAPPENS TO KIZMEL?
NOTHING HAPPENS.

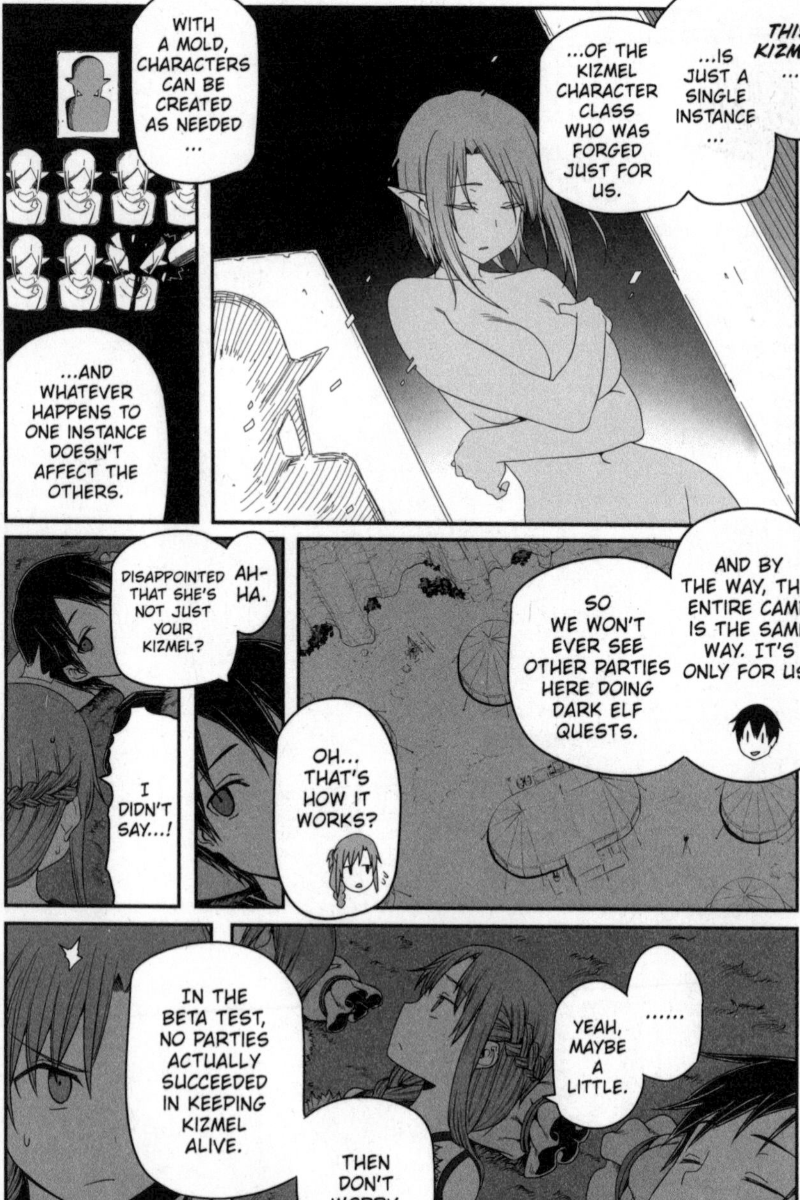
THIS KIZMEL ...
...IS JUST A SINGLE INSTANCE ...
...OF THE KIZMEL CHARACTER CLASS WHO WAS FORGED JUST FOR US.
WITH A MOLD, CHARACTERS CAN BE CREATED AS NEEDED ...
...AND WHATEVER HAPPENS TO ONE INSTANCE DOESN'T AFFECT THE OTHERS.
AND BY THE WAY, THIS ENTIRE CAMP IS THE SAME WAY. IT'S ONLY FOR US.
SO WE WON'T EVER SEE OTHER PARTIES HERE DOING DARK ELF QUESTS.
OH... THAT'S HOW IT WORKS?
AH-HA.
DISAPPOINTED THAT SHE'S NOT JUST YOUR KIZMEL?
I DIDN'T SAY...!
......
YEAH, MAYBE A LITTLE.
IN THE BETA TEST, NO PARTIES ACTUALLY SUCCEEDED IN KEEPING KIZMEL ALIVE.
THEN DON'T WORRY.

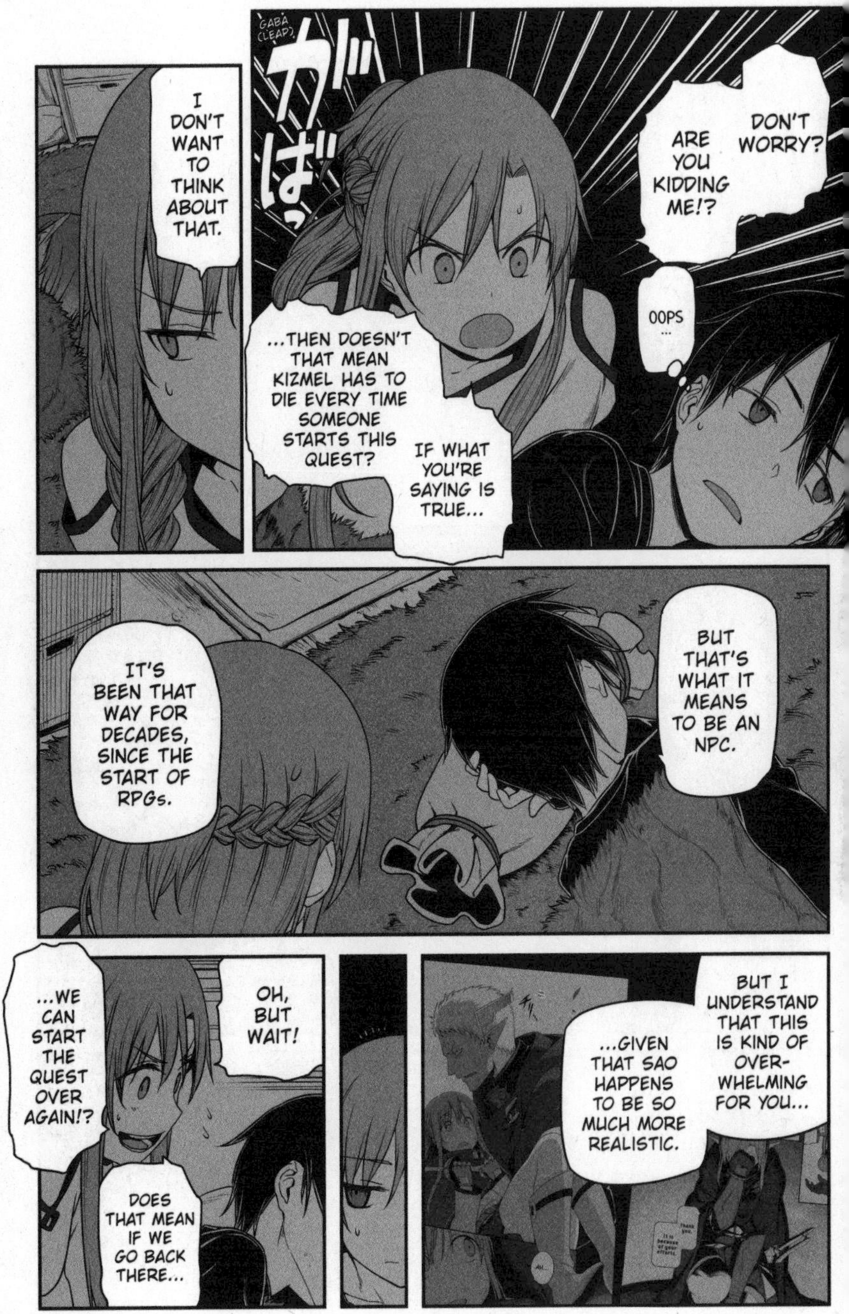
GABA (LEAP)
がばっ
DON'T WORRY?
ARE YOU KIDDING ME!?
OOPS...
IF WHAT YOU'RE SAYING IS TRUE...
...THEN DOESN'T THAT MEAN KIZMEL HAS TO DIE EVERY TIME SOMEONE STARTS THIS QUEST?
I DON'T WANT TO THINK ABOUT THAT.
BUT THAT'S WHAT IT MEANS TO BE AN NPC.
IT'S BEEN THAT WAY FOR DECADES, SINCE THE START OF RPGs.
BUT I UNDERSTAND THAT THIS IS KIND OF OVER-WHELMING FOR YOU...
...GIVEN THAT SAO HAPPENS TO BE SO MUCH MORE REALISTIC.
OH, BUT WAIT!
DOES THAT MEAN IF WE GO BACK THERE...
...WE CAN START THE QUEST OVER AGAIN!?

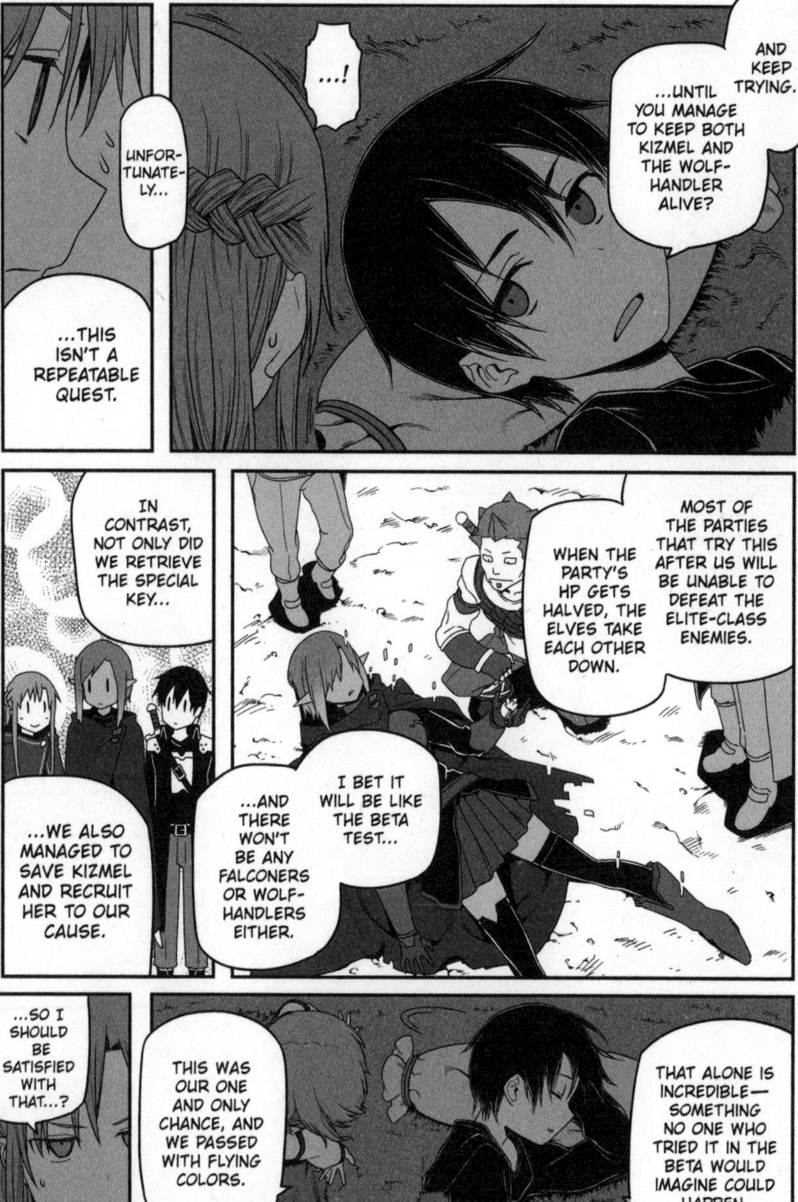
AND KEEP TRYING...
...UNTIL YOU MANAGE TO KEEP BOTH KIZMEL AND THE WOLF-HANDLER ALIVE?
...!
UNFOR-TUNATE-LY...
...THIS ISN'T A REPEATABLE QUEST.
MOST OF THE PARTIES THAT TRY THIS AFTER US WILL BE UNABLE TO DEFEAT THE ELITE-CLASS ENEMIES.
WHEN THE PARTY'S HP GETS HALVED, THE ELVES TAKE EACH OTHER DOWN.
I BET IT WILL BE LIKE THE BETA TEST...
...AND THERE WON'T BE ANY FALCONERS OR WOLF-HANDLERS EITHER.
IN CONTRAST, NOT ONLY DID WE RETRIEVE THE SPECIAL KEY...
...WE ALSO MANAGED TO SAVE KIZMEL AND RECRUIT HER TO OUR CAUSE.
THAT ALONE IS INCREDIBLE—SOMETHING NO ONE WHO TRIED IT IN THE BETA WOULD IMAGINE COULD HAPPEN.
THIS WAS OUR ONE AND ONLY CHANCE, AND WE PASSED WITH FLYING COLORS.
...SO I SHOULD BE SATISFIED WITH THAT...?

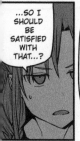

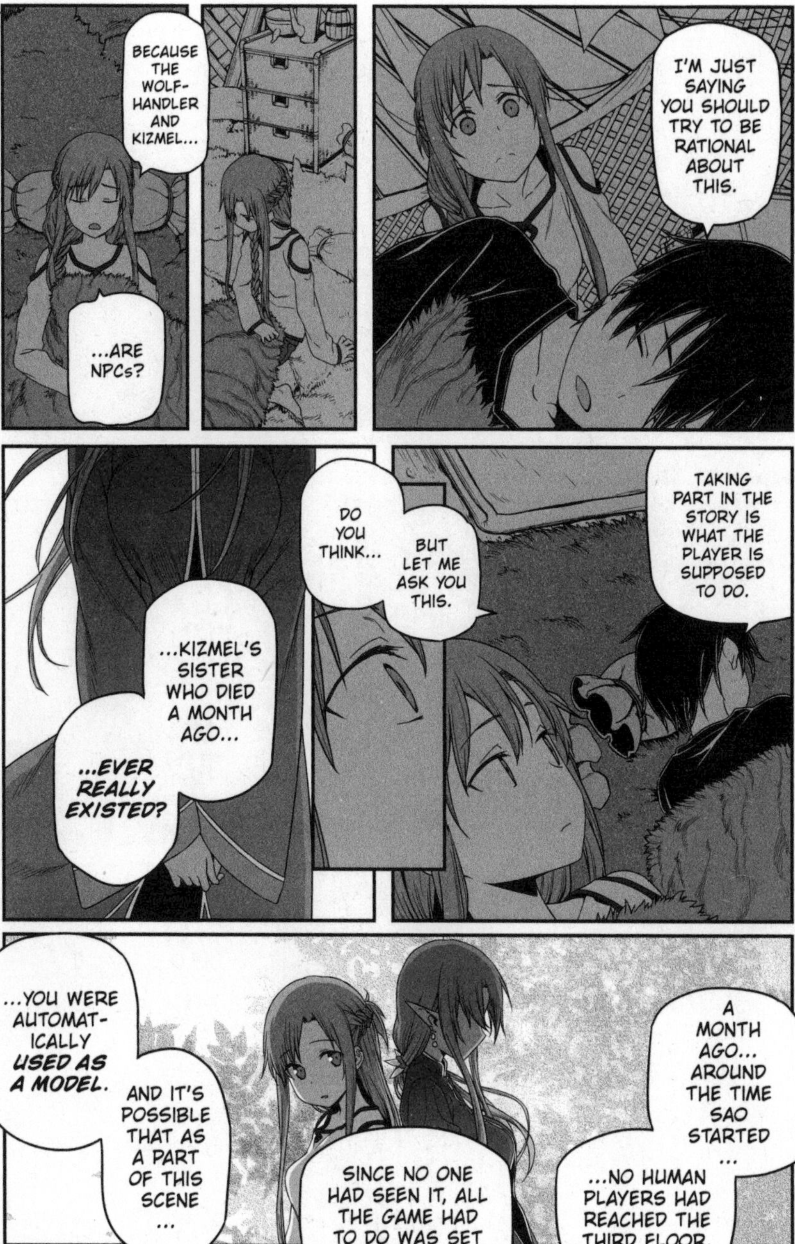
I'M JUST SAYING YOU SHOULD TRY TO BE RATIONAL ABOUT THIS.
BECAUSE THE WOLF-HANDLER AND KIZMEL...
...ARE NPCs?
TAKING PART IN THE STORY IS WHAT THE PLAYER IS SUPPOSED TO DO.
BUT LET ME ASK YOU THIS.
DO YOU THINK...
...KIZMEL'S SISTER WHO DIED A MONTH AGO...
...EVER REALLY EXISTED?
A MONTH AGO... AROUND THE TIME SAO STARTED...
...NO HUMAN PLAYERS HAD REACHED THE THIRD FLOOR.
SINCE NO ONE HAD SEEN IT, ALL THE GAME HAD TO DO WAS SET THE SCENE.
AND IT'S POSSIBLE THAT AS A PART OF THIS SCENE...
...YOU WERE AUTOMATICALLY USED AS A MODEL.

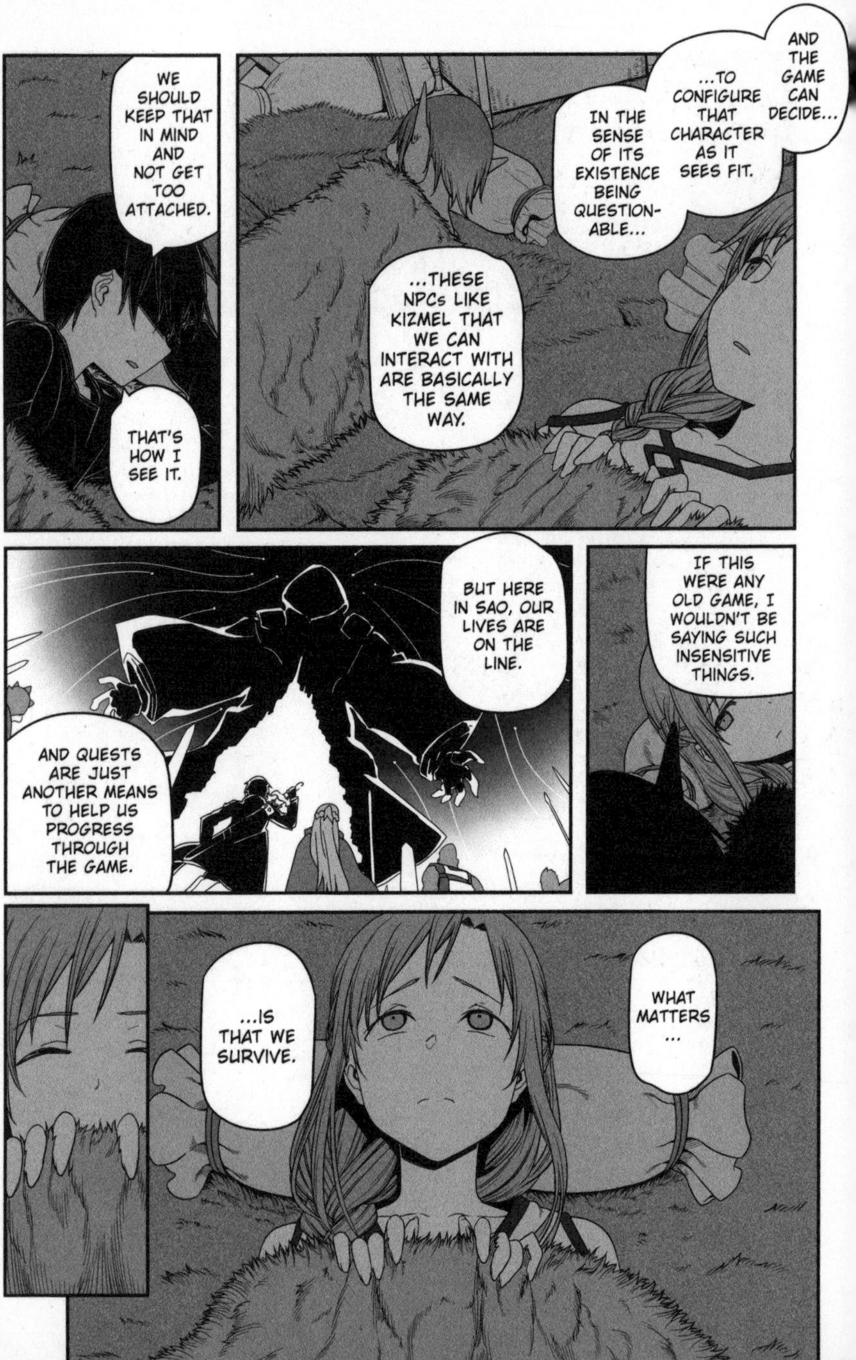
AND THE GAME CAN DECIDE...
...TO CONFIGURE THAT CHARACTER AS IT SEES FIT.
IN THE SENSE OF ITS EXISTENCE BEING QUESTION-ABLE...
...THESE NPCs LIKE KIZMEL THAT WE CAN INTERACT WITH ARE BASICALLY THE SAME WAY.
WE SHOULD KEEP THAT IN MIND AND NOT GET TOO ATTACHED.
THAT'S HOW I SEE IT.
IF THIS WERE ANY OLD GAME, I WOULDN'T BE SAYING SUCH INSENSITIVE THINGS.
BUT HERE IN SAO, OUR LIVES ARE ON THE LINE.
AND QUESTS ARE JUST ANOTHER MEANS TO HELP US PROGRESS THROUGH THE GAME.
WHAT MATTERS ...
...IS THAT WE SURVIVE.

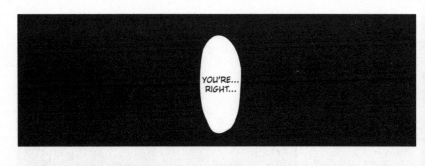

YOU'RE... RIGHT...

ゴソ
ゴソ
GOSO (RUSTLE)

GOSO

...WHA...?

ドクン
ドクン
ドクン
DOKUN (BA-BUMP)

DOKUN

ZZZ...

ドクン
DOKUN (BA-BUMP)

ゴロ〜ん
GORON (ROLL)

WHAT IS IT, ASUNA? JUST GO TO SLE...

ZZZ...

ドキ
DOKI (BA-BUMP)

ZZZ...

ドズゥ

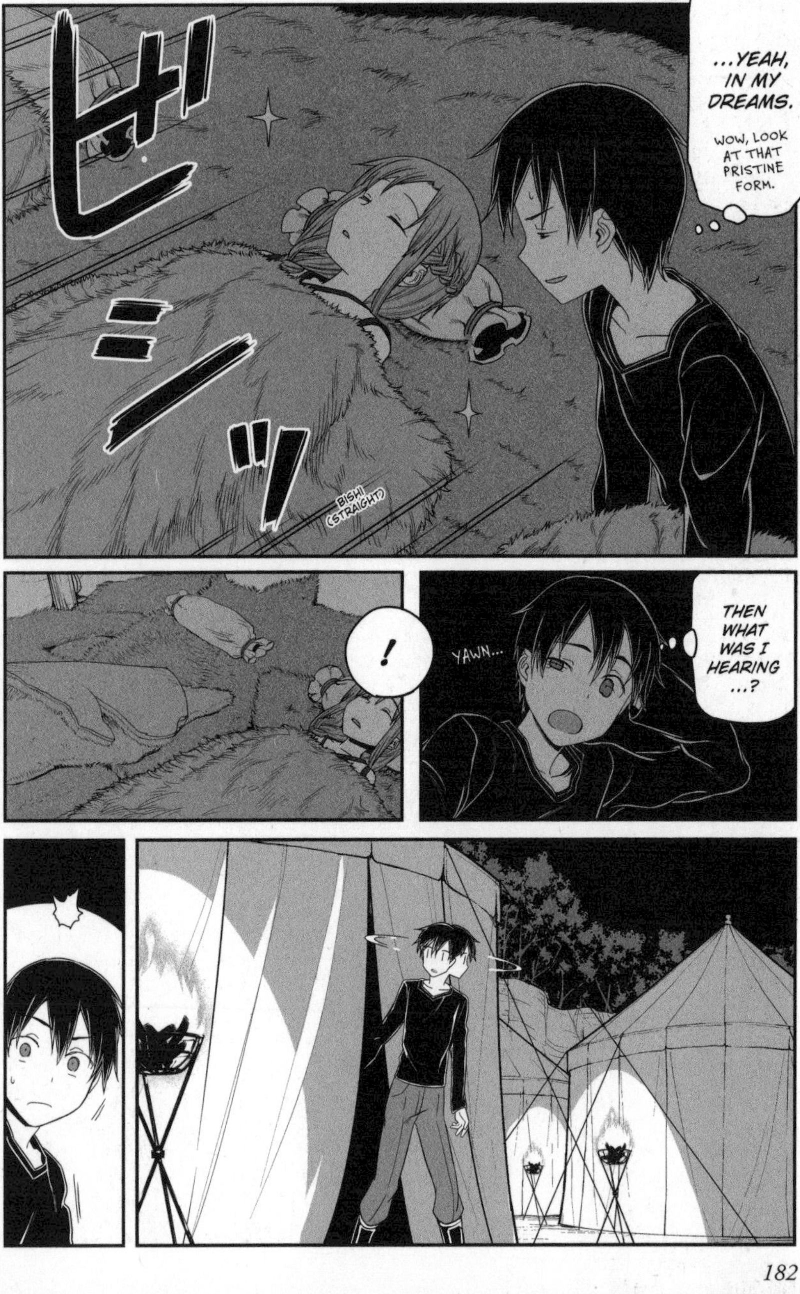
...YEAH, IN MY DREAMS.
WOW, LOOK AT THAT PRISTINE FORM.
ビシーッ
BISHI (STRAIGHT)
THEN WHAT WAS I HEARING ...?
YAWN...
!

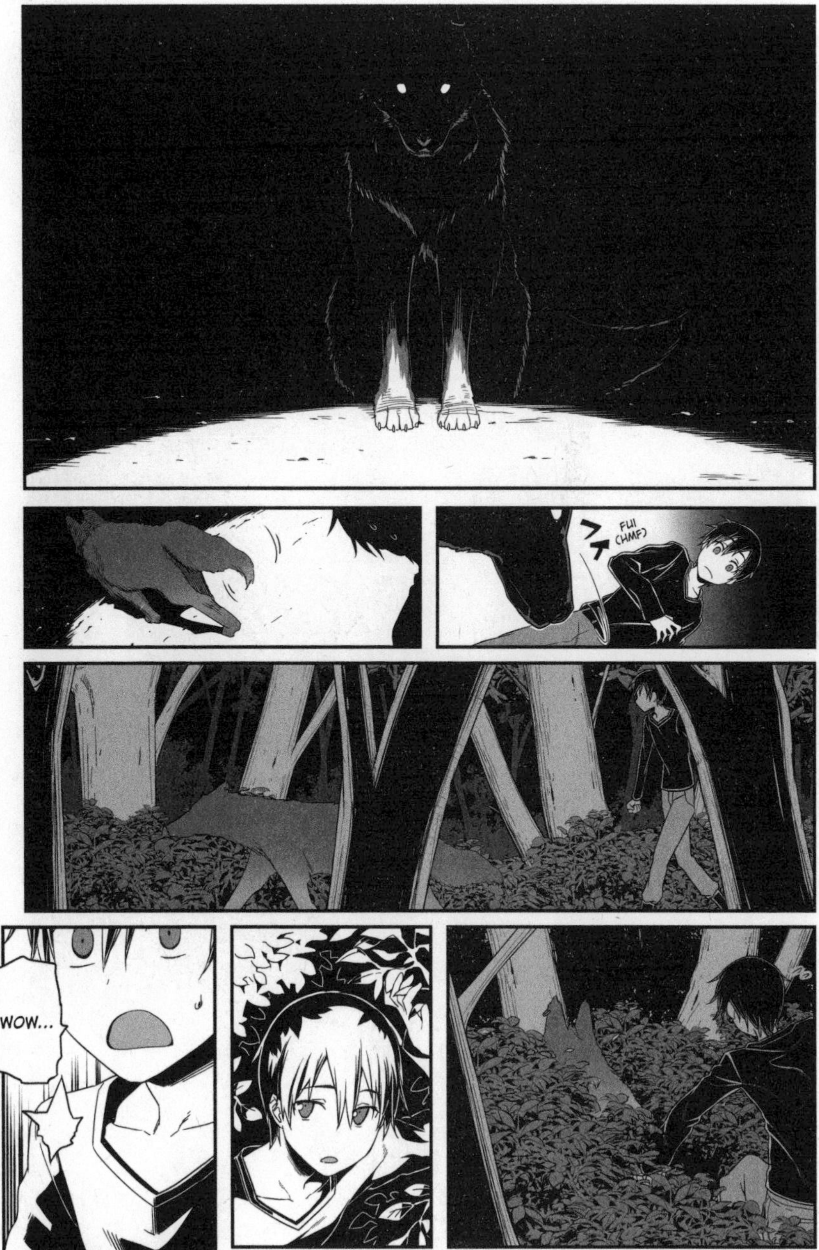
FUI
(HMF)
WOW...

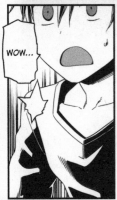

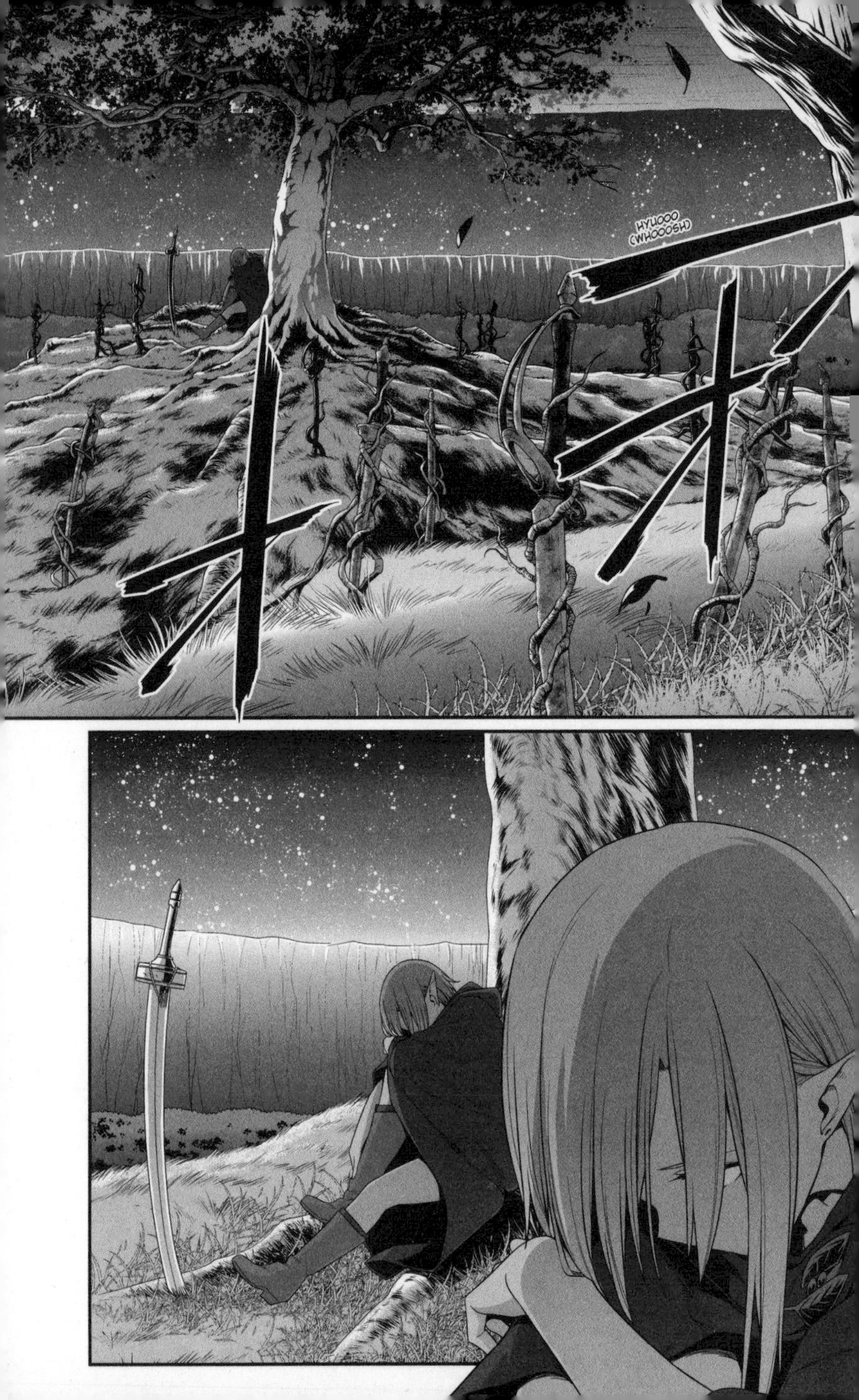
HYUOOO
(WHOOOSH)

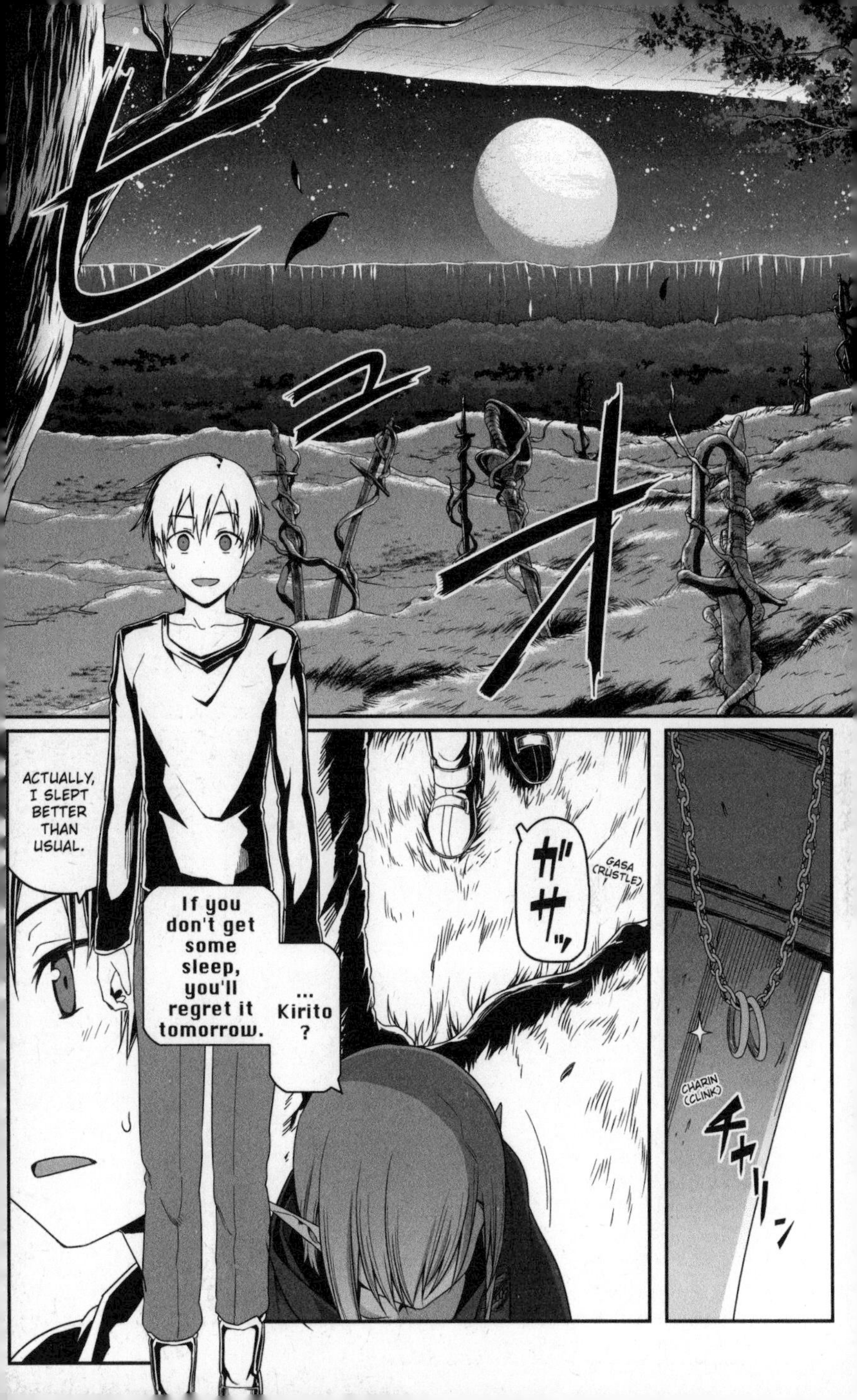
ヒュオ
チャリーン
CHARIN (CLINK)
ガサッ
GASA (RUSTLE)
... Kirito ?
If you don't get some sleep, you'll regret it tomorrow.
ACTUALLY, I SLEPT BETTER THAN USUAL.

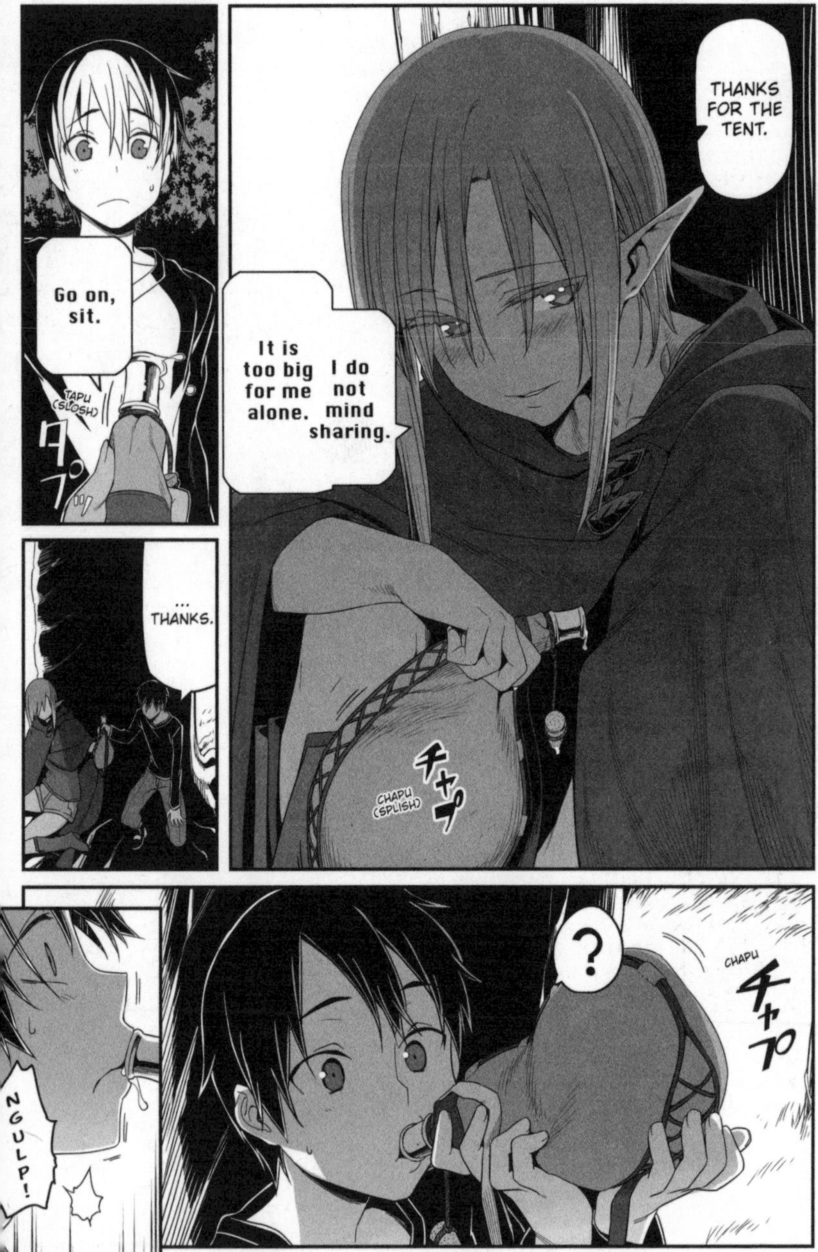
THANKS FOR THE TENT.
It is too big for me alone. I do not mind sharing.
CHAPU (SPLISH)
Go on, sit.
TAPU (SLOSH)
... THANKS.
CHAPU
?
NGULP!

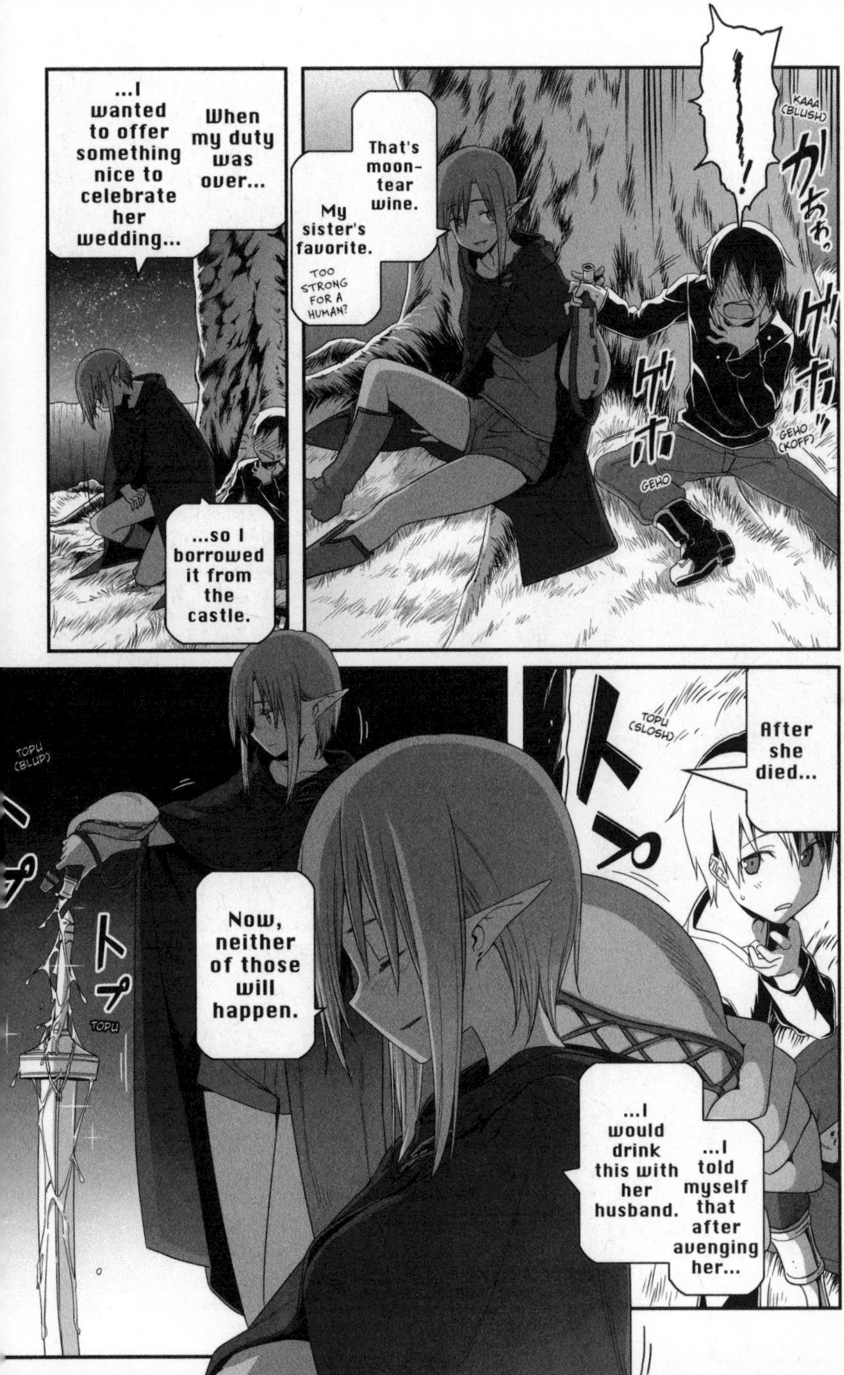
————!
KAAA (BLUSH)
カァァ
That's moon-tear wine.
My sister's favorite.
TOO STRONG FOR A HUMAN?
ゲホッ
GEHO (KOFF)
ゲホ
GEHO
When my duty was over...
...I wanted to offer something nice to celebrate her wedding...
...so I borrowed it from the castle.
TOPU (SLOSH)
トプ
After she died...
...I told myself that after avenging her...
...I would drink this with her husband.
TOPU (BLUP)
Now, neither of those will happen.
トプ
TOPU

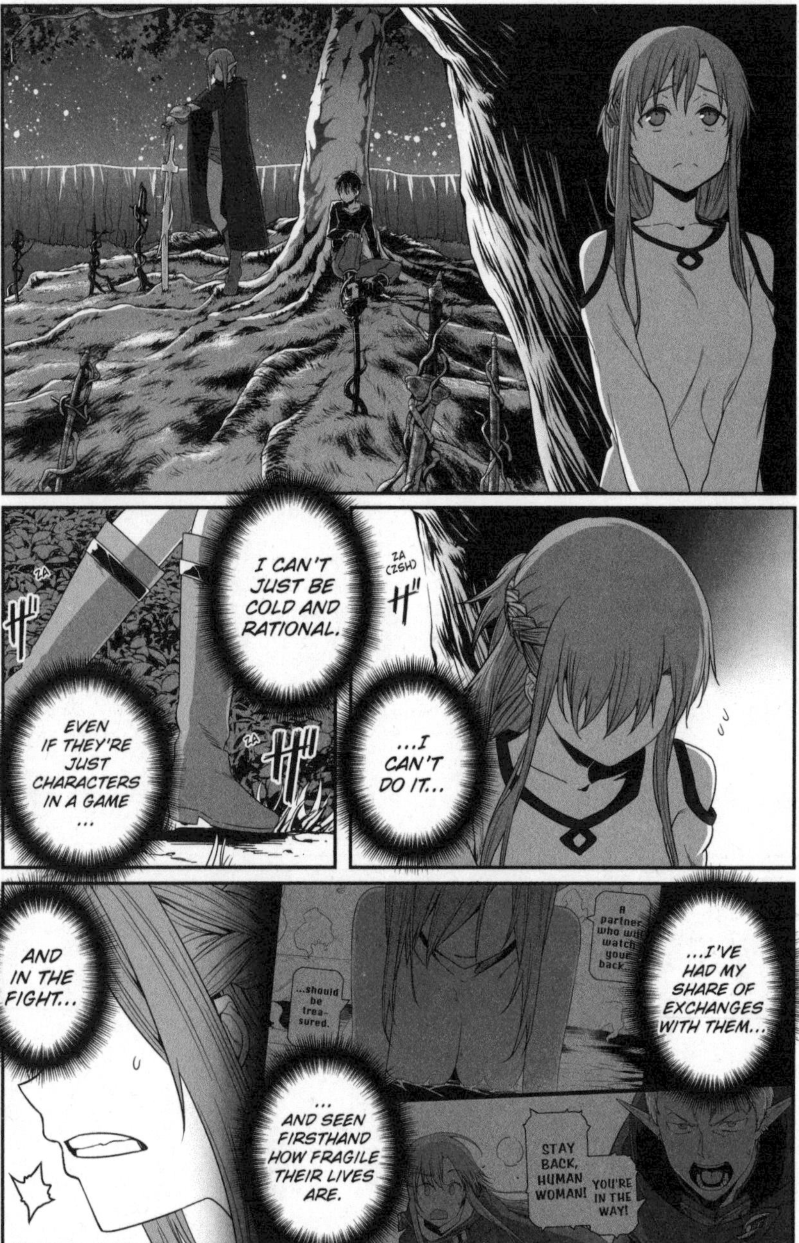
ZA (ZSH)
...I CAN'T DO IT...
I CAN'T JUST BE COLD AND RATIONAL.
ZA
EVEN IF THEY'RE JUST CHARACTERS IN A GAME ...
ZA
...I'VE HAD MY SHARE OF EXCHANGES WITH THEM...
A partner who wil watch you back.
...should be trea-sured.
YOU'RE IN THE WAY!
STAY BACK, HUMAN WOMAN!
... AND SEEN FIRSTHAND HOW FRAGILE THEIR LIVES ARE.
AND IN THE FIGHT...

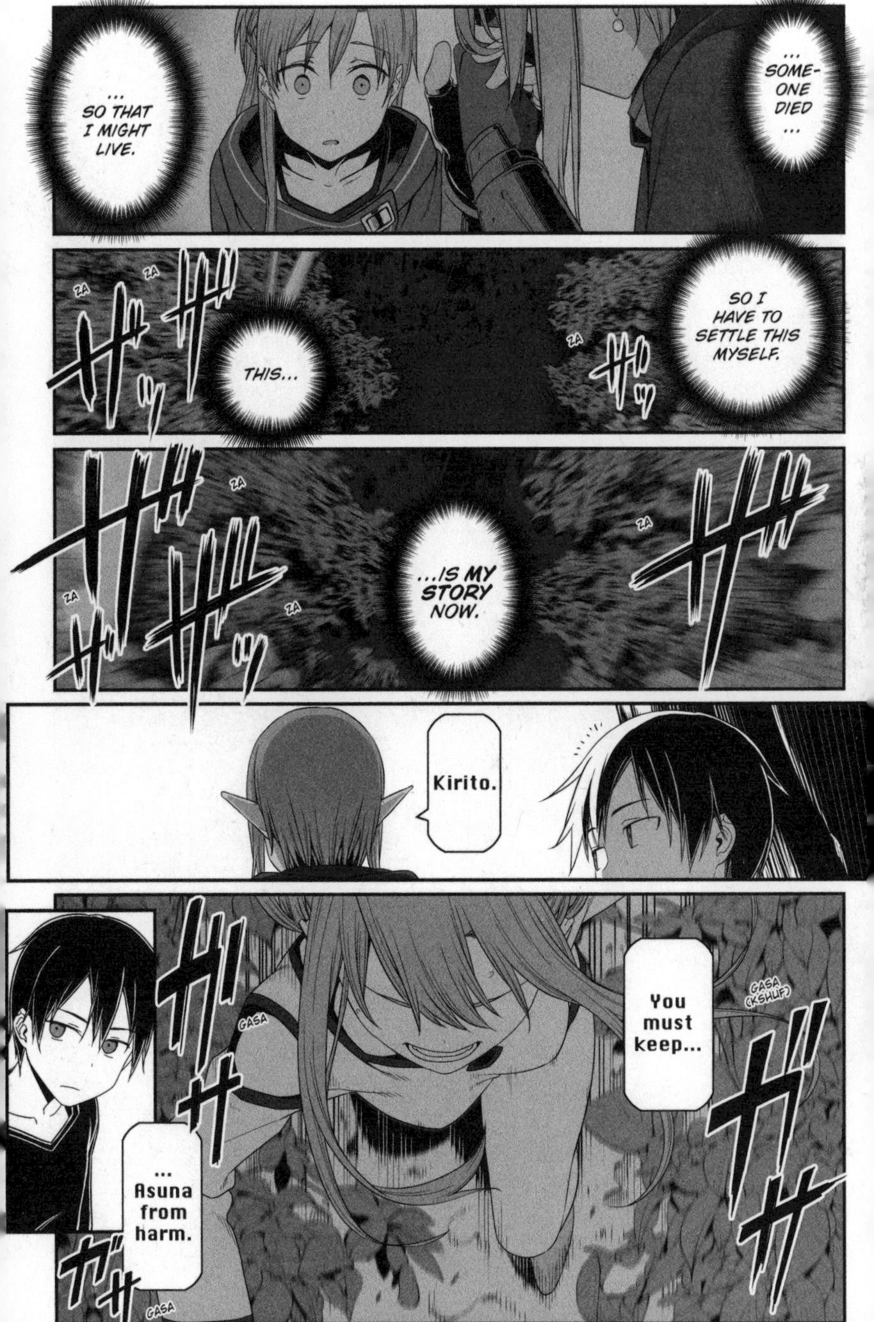
...SOMEONE DIED...
...SO THAT I MIGHT LIVE.
SO I HAVE TO SETTLE THIS MYSELF.
ZA
THIS...
ZA
ZA
ZA
...IS MY STORY NOW.
ZA
ZA
Kirito.
GASA (KSHUF)
You must keep...
GASA
...Asuna from harm.
GASA

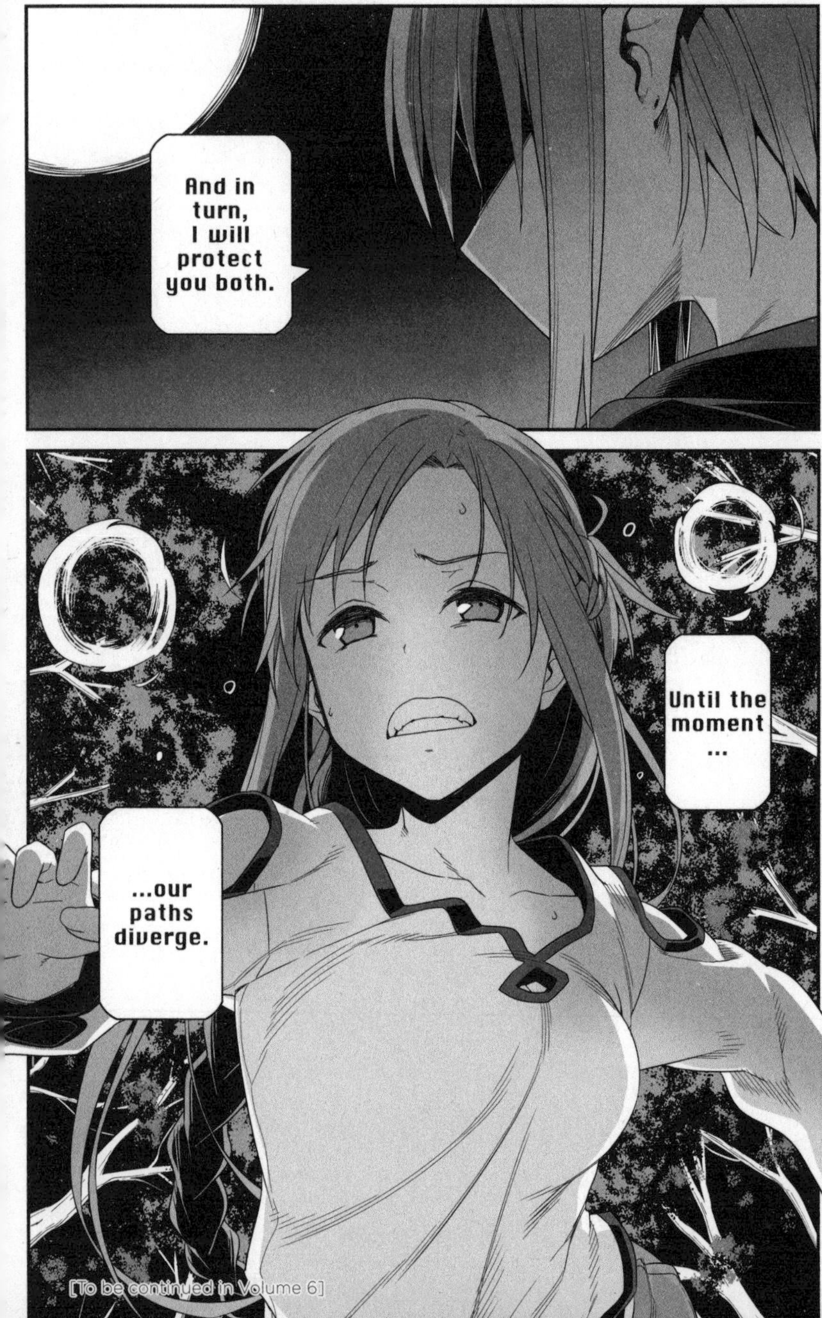
And in turn, I will protect you both.
Until the moment...
...our paths diverge.
[To be continued in Volume 6]

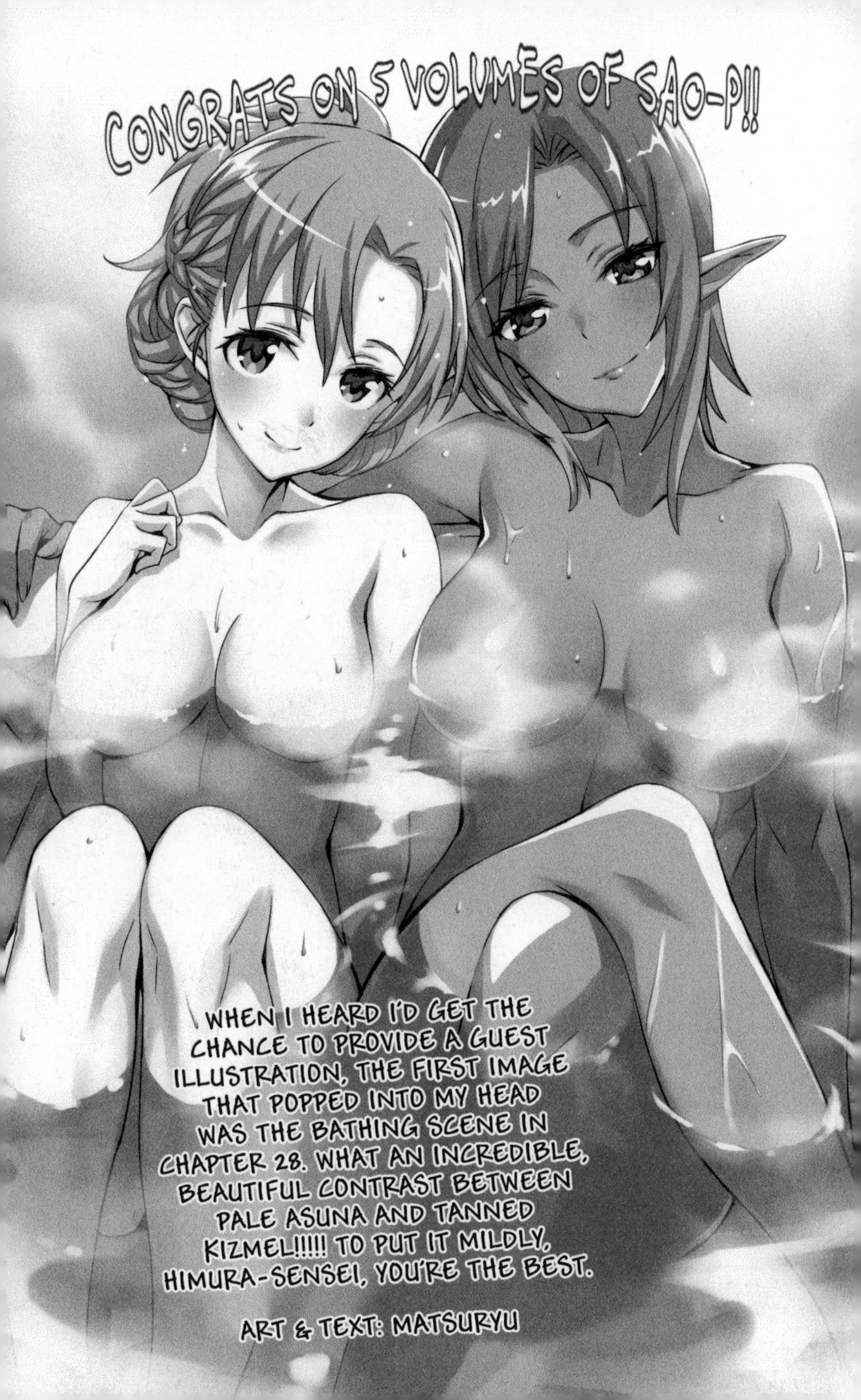
CONGRATS ON 5 VOLUMES OF SAO-P!!
WHEN I HEARD I'D GET THE CHANCE TO PROVIDE A GUEST ILLUSTRATION, THE FIRST IMAGE THAT POPPED INTO MY HEAD WAS THE BATHING SCENE IN CHAPTER 28. WHAT AN INCREDIBLE, BEAUTIFUL CONTRAST BETWEEN PALE ASUNA AND TANNED KIZMEL!!!!! TO PUT IT MILDLY, HIMURA-SENSEI, YOU'RE THE BEST.
ART & TEXT: MATSURYU

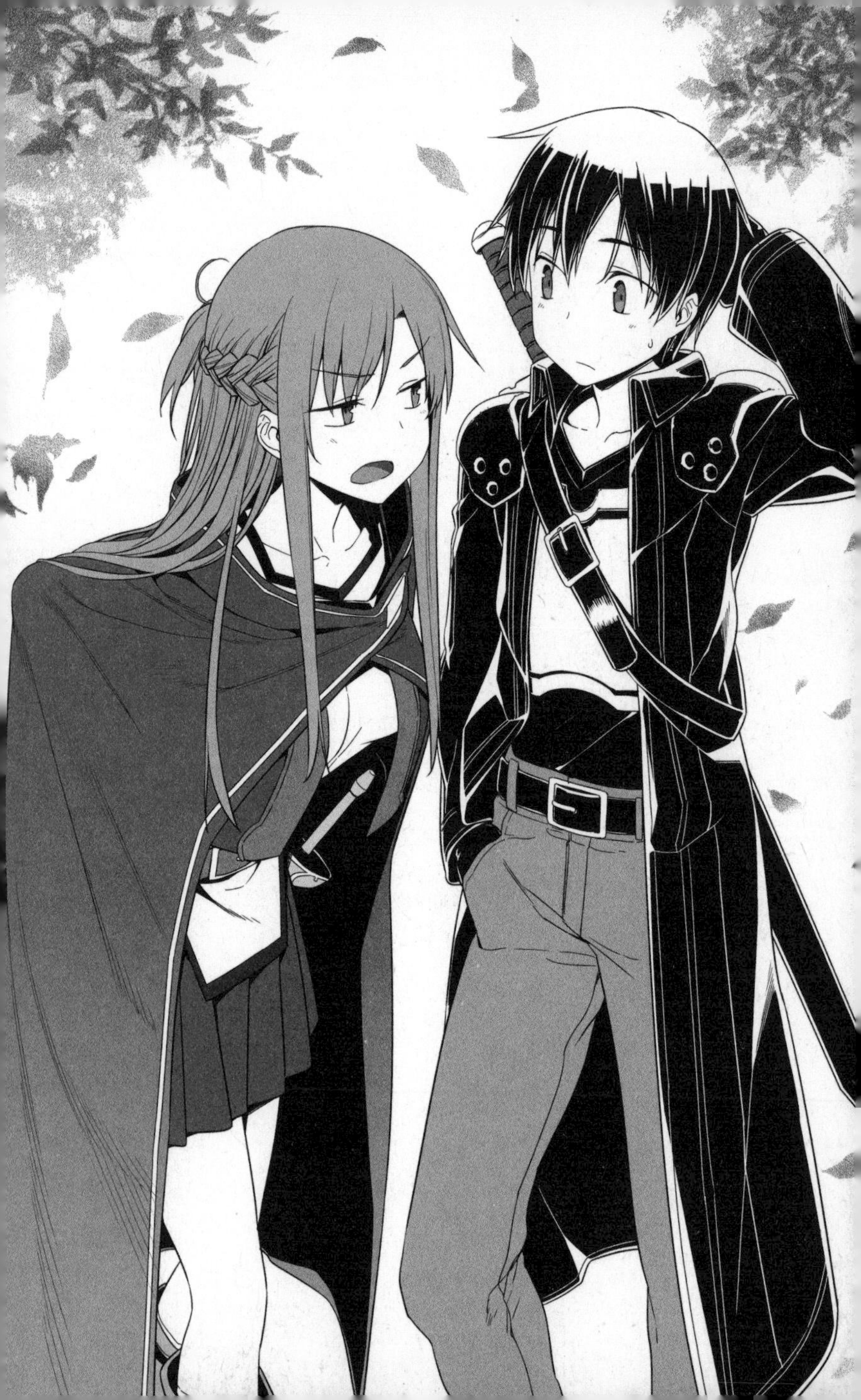

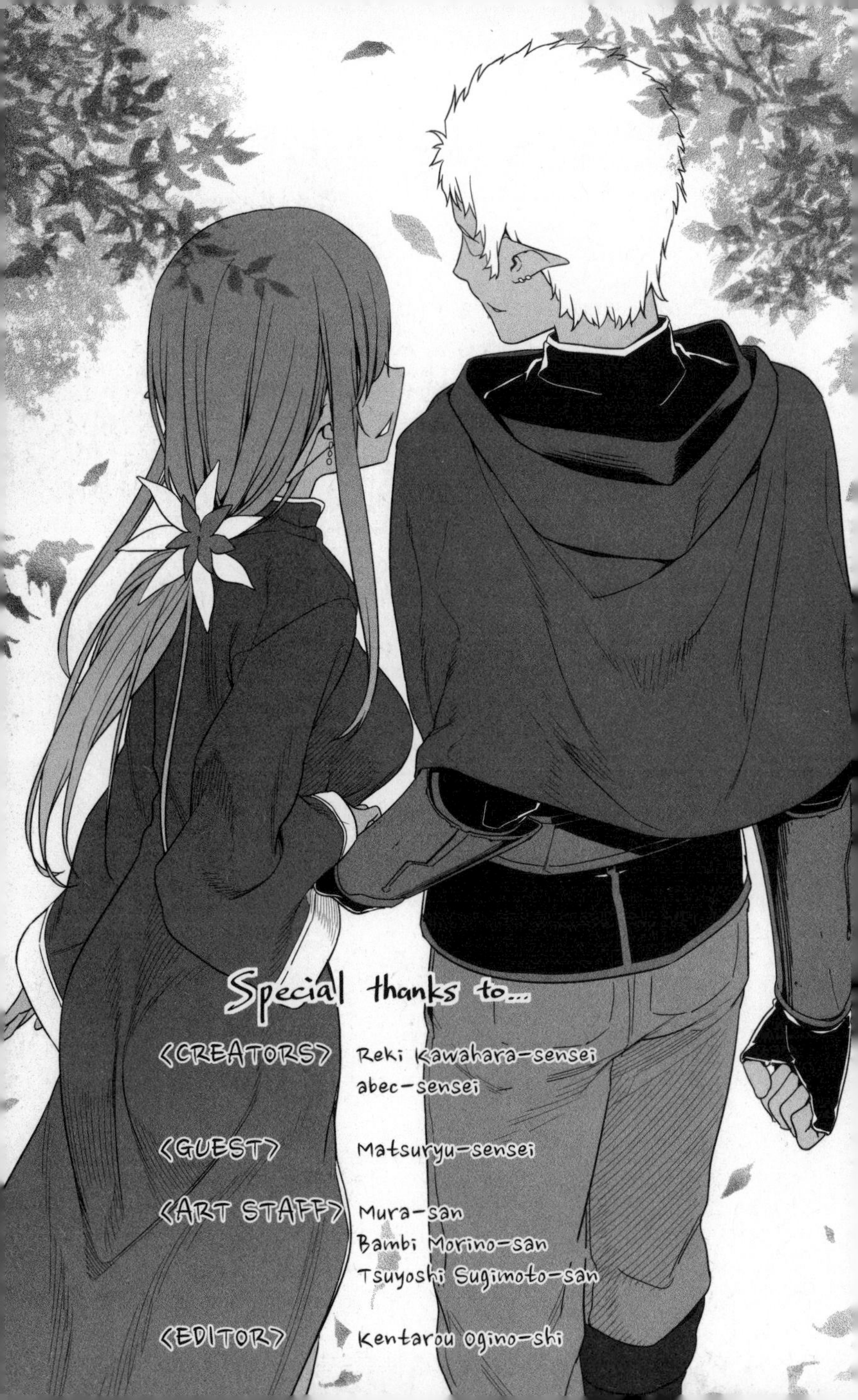
Special thanks to...
<CREATORS> Reki Kawahara-sensei
abec-sensei
<GUEST> Matsuryu-sensei
<ART STAFF> Mura-san
Bambi Morino-san
Tsuyoshi Sugimoto-san
<EDITOR> Kentarou Ogino-shi

SWORD ART ONLINE: PROGRESSIVE 5

ART: KISEKI HIMURA
ORIGINAL STORY: REKI KAWAHARA
CHARACTER DESIGN: abec

Translation: Stephen Paul
Lettering: Brndn Blakeslee & Katie Blakeslee

SWORD ART ONLINE: PROGRESSIVE
© REKI KAWAHARA/KISEKI HIMURA 2016
All rights reserved.
Edited by ASCII MEDIA WORKS
First published in Japan in 2016 by KADOKAWA CORPORATION,Tokyo.
English translation rights arranged with KADOKAWA CORPORATION,Tokyo, through Tuttle-Mori Agency, Inc., Tokyo.

English translation © 2017 by Yen Press, LLC.

Yen Press
1290 Avenue of the Americas
New York, NY 10104

Visit us at yenpress.com
facebook.com/yenpress
twitter.com/yenpress
yenpress.tumblr.com
instagram.com/yenpress

First Yen Press Edition: March 2017

Yen Press is an imprint of Yen Press, LLC.
The Yen Press name and logo are trademarks of Yen Press, LLC.

Library of Congress Control Number: 2015956857

ISBNs: 978-0-316-46926-5 (paperback)
       978-0-316-44038-7 (ebook)

10 9 8 7 6 5 4 3 2 1

BVG

Printed in the United States of America